Readers love *A*
by K.C.

"If you want magic, light, all good things, and a love between three men that is foretold in dreams, you really can't go wrong with *A Bond of Three*."
—Joyfully Jay

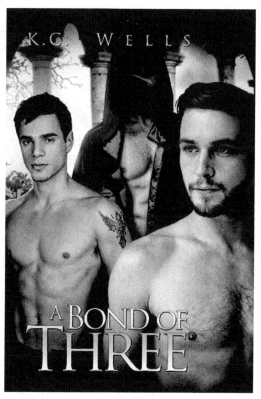

"It was sweet, the angst was low and it was everything I look for in a read. I enjoyed it from the first page all the way till the last."
—It's About The Book

"The display of compassion in each man is heartwarming; the intimacy scenes are superb."
—Literary Nymphs Reviews

"This is high fantasy at its best. I loved this book!"
—Love Bytes

By K.C. WELLS

Debt
First
Love Lessons Learned
Waiting For You

COLLARS & CUFFS
An Unlocked Heart
Trusting Thomas
With Parker Williams: Someone to Keep Me
A Dance with Domination
With Parker Williams: Damian's Discipline
Make Me Soar
With Parker Williams: Dom of Ages
With Parker Williams: Endings and Beginnings

DREAMSPUN DESIRES
#15 – The Senator's Secret

LEARNING TO LOVE
Michael & Sean
Evan & Daniel
Josh & Chris
Final Exam

SENSUAL BONDS
A Bond of Three
A Bond of Truth

Published by DREAMSPINNER PRESS
www.dreamspinnerpress.com

A BOND OF TRUTH

K.C. WELLS

Published by
DREAMSPINNER PRESS

5032 Capital Circle SW, Suite 2, PMB# 279, Tallahassee, FL 32305-7886 USA
www.dreamspinnerpress.com

ISBN: 978-1-63533-133-2
Digital ISBN: 978-1-63533-134-9
Library of Congress Control Number: 2016917069
Published December 2016
v. 1.0

Printed in the United States of America
∞
This paper meets the requirements of
ANSI/NISO Z39.48-1992 (Permanence of Paper).

As usual, thank you to my wonderful team of betas:
Jason, Bev, Debra, Helena, Mardee and Lara.
Jason, my star. You rock.
A special thank you to Tricia Kristufek,
who insisted I *had* to write this book—
and then went to tell my publisher the same thing.

CHAPTER
ONE

DAINON PACED up and down the stone-flagged hallway that led to the royal chamber, his mind in turmoil. When the king's messenger had arrived at the barracks, demanding his presence immediately, Dainon had been at a loss. He'd wondered briefly if it was a mistake before leaving his chores and hastening to the palace.

Why should the King wish to see me? Dainon was no one special, merely a warrior in the Kandoran army. Waiting in the quiet hallway only served to exacerbate his nerves.

Behind him, the vast, aged, wooden door to the royal chamber creaked open. "His Majesty will see you now, Dainon."

He gave a brief nod to Sefarr, chief adviser to the king, and strode into the chamber, his gait firm, back straight, chin lifted high, his momentary knots of unease pushed aside, replaced by the demands of duty. The doors creaked shut behind him.

King Rohar stood by the window at the end of the long throne room, gazing out, his brow furrowed. He turned his head briefly at Dainon's approach and gave him a single nod of recognition before gesturing to a chair placed before the throne.

For a moment Dainon faltered. *Since when does a warrior sit in the presence of the king?*

Then he noticed they were the only two in the room. No advisers, no warriors. Dainon's unease returned, his stomach churning. He fought back his shiver at the unusual nature of the meeting.

The king apparently caught his apprehension. He turned to regard Dainon, his young face prematurely lined, his formerly bright eyes dulled. "Yes, Dainon, sit. I would speak with you."

Dainon did as instructed, his back still straight.

The king walked slowly across to the throne and sat, his movements heavy with weariness. He pulled his robes around him and clasped his hands in his lap before meeting Dainon's gaze. "Doubtless you are wondering why I sent for you."

"Yes, Sire." Dainon had served as a warrior since his eighteenth year, but he had no status within the army, save for acting as a trainer for the new recruits.

King Rohar's deep blue eyes did not break contact with his. "I need your help," he said simply.

Dainon pushed out his chest and lifted his chin higher. "Tell me what you require, Your Majesty." His voice came out strong.

The king regarded him in silence before nodding. "Yes, you are the one for this mission." It was almost as if he was saying the words aloud to convince himself.

Dainon's mind seized on the one word that carried such import: *mission*. "What would you have me do, Sire?" *Why would he choose me?*

"You have dwelt in Kandor all your life. You have lived, as I have, through the darkest point in its history, so I will speak plainly. It would not surprise you if I were to say the kingdom is in dire straits."

The king's utterance was no surprise at all. The epidemic that had laid waste to a third of Kandor's inhabitants had left the kingdom struggling, even sixteen years later. Dainon's chest tightened as grief stabbed at his heart with its habitual barbs, but he breathed deeply and focused on his king.

"A sad but accurate statement, Sire."

The king nodded slowly. "Since I became King, it has been my desire to see Kandor thrive once more. With this purpose in mind, I wish you to go to Teruna."

Dainon stiffened at the unexpected request. "Teruna, Sire?" That kingdom lay three days' travel to the east of Kandor, and the two lands had once been in conflict. Dainon had never seen Teruna, but like many Kandorans, he had heard the tales brought by those who had.

King Rohar's gaze grew more intent. "Surely you have heard the rumors? The stories that abound of how Teruna is flourishing, its *Seruani* emerging in great numbers and with more powers and gifts than ever before?"

"I have heard the tales, yes." Everyone had. It seemed each day brought more news of the neighboring kingdom, though how much was fact was unknown. Dainon had wondered on several occasions whether the tall stories were apocryphal.

"This, then, is your mission. You are to travel to Teruna and learn the truth. If all we hear is true, then perhaps our neighbors might be in a position to grant us aid."

"Your Majesty...." Dainon hesitated, unsure of how to phrase his question in such a way so as not to overstep the mark.

The king smiled, his expression lightening. "Speak, Dainon. I chose you because of all my warriors, I trust you. I have watched you, how you act with integrity and honor. The captain of the royal guard speaks highly of you. He says your instincts are good." He paused, his expression growing more serious. "I have need of those instincts, so feel free to say what is on your heart."

"Sire, why not visit King Tanish? Surely you would be able to judge for yourself." It seemed strange to send a warrior. *Surely so important a mission calls for a diplomatic visit.*

King Rohar pushed out a heavy sigh. "There is too much history between our two kingdoms. Let us not forget my uncle would have forged ahead with his plans to overthrow Teruna had he not been taken from us in the first wave of the plague. And it may be that the Terunans cannot help us. Given all that I have said, I admit it may be unrealistic to assume they would even countenance such a thing. Therefore, I need you to go there ahead of me."

"Am I to be a spy, then?" The thought did not sit well with Dainon, and his unease must have been palpable.

King Rohar shook his head, his expression grave. "No, nothing so clandestine. Visit the kingdom, find out what you can, but do not hide your origins if people should ask. They do not need to know that I have sent you, however. When you return to me with your report, I shall decide what steps need to be taken, if any."

"If half of what we hear is true, surely Teruna will help Kandor. They are a peaceable people by all accounts." Dainon had heard nothing to make him think Teruna would react aggressively. King Tanish was close to his own age, if what he'd heard was true, and it was said that he was a wise ruler.

There were other stories shared about Teruna's king, however, that were far more... fantastical.

King Rohar's deep voice pulled Dainon from his recollections.

"They are also a people whose former ruler once led them into battle when Kandor threatened them in the past. They may be peaceful now, but I doubt old hostilities could have been forgiven and forgotten so soon." The king pierced Dainon with a direct glance. "Do you accept this mission?"

Dainon rose to his feet and stood at attention. "I do, Your Majesty. I will serve you faithfully in all things." He knelt on the cold stone, his head bowed, pride swelling within him that the king should have chosen him. "When would you have me leave, Sire? And how long must I spend in Teruna?"

"You shall leave immediately," the king informed him. "As for how long, I leave that in your capable hands. When you judge that you have enough information to help inform my decision, then you may return." King Rohar rose from his throne and crossed the floor to lay his hand on Dainon's head. "I send you out with my blessing. Learn all you can and then return to us, my faithful warrior. Return to your home."

Dainon swallowed, his throat tight. He had lost his home sixteen years ago.

When the king stepped back, Dainon rose to his feet and dipped his chin toward his chest. "Your Majesty." He left the chamber, head still held high. When the doors closed behind him once more, he relaxed. He walked along the hallway, nodding in passing to the royal warriors who guarded the palace. Not that Kandor had need of such a thing. Those days were past, the army merely a tradition to be upheld and maintained. Kandor had nothing to fear from invaders.

It had already lost its most precious possessions.

He walked over to the balcony that overlooked the city, his mind not seeing the day-to-day bustle of Kandor's inhabitants going about their lives. Instead he saw the funeral processions of years ago, so many of them, winding their way in silence toward the hills where Kandor interned its dead. Sixteen years had passed, and yet Dainon remembered with startling, painful clarity that day when he'd followed the slow progress of the carriage that had borne his Tarisa, his beautiful Merron, to their final resting place.

Will the ache ever truly fade?

Dainon thought not. How could one ever get over the loss of a soul mate?

HIS SADDLE bags were packed, his sword in its sheath, and his supplies for the journey laid across his mare Tarrea's broad back. Dainon had no way of knowing how long he would be away from Kandor, but years of training had enabled him to pack the essentials. The skills he had acquired as a new recruit, however, were fast becoming a thing of the past. There remained but a few warriors who had survived the plague. Dainon knew all too well how they were regarded by the younger members of the Kandoran army, who had never known battle and were dismissive of Dainon's rigorous training methods.

He was not deaf to their grumblings. Their duties consisted of guarding the royal palace, maintaining order within the city walls, and patrolling Kandor's borders. Since no threat to the kingdom's safety existed, and skirmishes were virtually nonexistent, nothing taxed their skills or provided them with the excitement they'd craved upon choosing a life in the military. Certainly nothing like the life Dainon had known when he'd become a young warrior. He could recall being in his early twenties, the air alive with the anticipation of war when King Ceros had taken the throne, determined to vanquish any and all who stood in his way.

Dainon pushed away his memories. Such reflection could wait.

He had a mission.

"Ready to begin an adventure, girl?" he murmured, stroking Tarrea's mane. She whinnied and pressed her nose against his chest. Tarrea had been his quiet joy since the days when he'd broken her in. Dainon made sure she was treated with the utmost care, ridden lightly and only by him. Not that she was a girl anymore.

He stroked down her neck, his touch gentle. "You're getting to be an old lady, aren't you?" He knew the span of a horse's life. Tarrea would not be his for much longer, and the thought made his heart quake. She had been in the army as long as he had. There was always a tightening around his heart when he remembered Tarisa bringing their little boy to the barracks' stables. Merron had been three the first time he'd laid a tentative hand on Tarrea's flanks, and she had been so gentle and still around him.

Dainon fought the painful memory, pushing it down hard. The years might have passed since he'd lost his beautiful Merron, but time had not diminished the ability of that memory to pierce him with its sharpness. Besides, he knew the memories would return to haunt his thoughts in the middle of the night when he'd awaken alone in his bed.

Nights were always the worst.

He stroked Tarrea's warm nose and gazed into liquid brown eyes. "Time to go, my beauty."

In the early morning light and with no fanfare, Dainon left the barracks that had been his home since Tarisa and Merron were taken from him. He had not lived in the years that had passed since then, merely existed. Nothing had filled the hole left by Tarisa's death; he had never once imagined that something could. When the epidemic had passed, there had been those who suggested it was his duty to take a new wife while he was still in his late twenties, to aid Kandor in its efforts to repopulate. He had chosen not to do so, however, preferring instead to bury himself in his military obligations. As a member of the old guard, Dainon had taken it upon himself to train the new recruits, but the heart of the army had died along with the thousands of Kandorans claimed by the fever.

Dainon kept the pace steady, determined not to tire Tarrea beyond what he felt she could endure. By the end of the afternoon, he had left the city behind him and was riding toward the mountains. The day was a perfect blend of warm temperature, subtle breezes, the call of birds high in the sky above him, and a clear path to follow. When he came closer to the mountain pass through which he had to travel to reach the farthest borders of Kandor, he stopped for the night. After ensuring Tarrea was comfortable, he threw a blanket on the ground and lay on his back, gazing up into the starry heavens. Beside him a small fire crackled, its noise a welcome, almost cozy intrusion.

His mission intrigued him. The stories concerning Teruna had begun to circulate a few years before the plague had struck. Tall tales that spoke of magical, mystical happenings that could not possibly be true. But as the years had passed, more tales found their way to Kandor. Dainon was proud to have been chosen, but the opportunity to finally learn the truth was an even greater incentive. A far more subtle one was the chance to break free of the cycle in which he found himself ensnared. His grief was always present, a thick cloak through which little penetrated, but for the first time since their deaths, Dainon ached to feel the warmth of the sun on his skin, to bare his body to the elements.

Can it be that I am ready to cast off grief? His memories of Tarisa and Merron were both comforting and torturous. He clung to them, his greatest fear that in putting them aside, he would somehow lose his precious recollections, that their faces would grow dim in his head. *I cannot lose her. She was my life, my soul. There will never be another like her.*

He closed his eyes to the brilliance above his head and sank into a dreamless sleep.

Morning brought peace, albeit accompanied by a stiffness in his limbs. Dainon fed Tarrea and ate some of the fruit he'd brought. Once they were back on the path, the mountain range rose up before him, gray and forbidding, its peaks topped with snow, glowing pink in the light of the rising sun. The pass was wide enough for a carriage to travel through easily. It was a route Dainon knew well, having spent many a tour of duty patrolling between the city and the border. He trotted through the familiar pass, its dark granite walls climbing steeply, the air cool where little sunlight penetrated. When he emerged into the warmth once more, the full rays of the sun falling over the land before him, Dainon's heart quaked. For the first time in his life, he was about to leave the only place he'd ever known, the land where he'd been born. He was bound for a kingdom where, if the tales were to be believed, magic existed.

Once upon a time, Dainon had believed in magic. Had he not felt that buzz of... *something* when he'd first touched Tarisa's hand? Some innate sense that had told him she was the missing piece of his life, the other half of his soul? But losing her had robbed him of his beliefs.

He was forty-four. He was too old to believe in magic.

DAINON'S PROGRESS was slow, but he was in no hurry. He traveled by day, pausing to rest and eat, and at night he slept on the ground, a small fire burning beside him, a rough blanket beneath him, and the stars sprinkled across the black night sky, too numerous to count. When he reached a river, he bathed in its cold waters and refilled his water bags. Five days of travel past Kandor's boundaries brought Dainon to the sea, and the ocean took his breath away.

He'd come over the crest of a hill and there it was before him, spread out as far as the eye could see. The size of it, the vast expanse of sky across the horizon, the way its hue was reflected in the rolling waves, an ever-changing, constantly moving carpet of color and light.... Dainon had read of such things, but his first encounter with the sea left him in awe. The lakes where men fished in Kandor were tiny in comparison, and although Dainon had learned to swim in their waters, he yearned to dive beneath these huge, tumbling waves and feel them lift him up, support him. He wanted to sink below the surface and discover the mysteries hidden in its depths.

Dainon leaned over and patted Tarrea's neck. "Shall we ride along the shore, girl? Kick up some sand?" She had earned a rest, as they'd been traveling since daybreak at a steady pace. He descended the hillside at a slow trot and followed the crooked path down through a rocky outcrop to the beach, its outer edges mainly shingle but giving way to white sand where the waves crashed in, all froth and lace. They trotted along the shoreline, the sound of the incoming tide loud after the quiet of his journey.

What brought him to a halt was the view of a saddled black horse tethered to a rock roughly half Dainon's height. Five days without a single person crossing his path and his ears yearned for another's voice, but there was no one in sight. Dainon scanned the beach, searching for some sign. He came to a stop and climbed down from Tarrea's back before reaching for the food bag to hang over her ears. "Have a rest, girl." He tethered her reins securely around another craggy boulder and left her to eat.

Dainon walked over the soft sand that firmed where the tide had washed over it. The air was salty and fresh, coming off the sea in cool wafts that made his skin tingle and revived his senses. He longed to take off his sandals and dip his hot feet into the cool water. Then he remembered that time was his own. He could do whatever he wanted.

He perched on a rock and removed the heavy leather sandals, dropping them to the ground. The breeze over his heated flesh was very pleasant. Dainon stood on the cool, damp sand and let out a sigh of contentment.

"It feels good, does it not?"

He jerked up his head and stared at the figure emerging from the waves. The young man was tall and lean, with bronze skin and toned muscles. He was perhaps in his early twenties, with light brown hair and blue eyes, the hint of a scruffy beard along his jaw, and the merest hint of hair on his chest. Water dripped off him, what remained beading on his glowing tanned skin.

Dainon caught his breath, shaken by his body's reaction to the nude figure. Dainon had grown up in the company of warriors and was accustomed to nudity, but for some reason, the sight of all that toned olive flesh disconcerted him. The young man's torso rippled with muscle, with a clearly defined vee where it dipped to his groin. His hips were slim, leading to toned thighs, and his penis, long even when flaccid, was the same warm color as his skin. It spoke of time spent nude in the sun, and the thought sent a shiver sliding down Dainon's spine, though he had no idea why. He brushed aside his unaccustomed discomfort and rose. "After a long journey, it feels wonderful."

The young man came to a halt before him, apparently unperturbed about being naked in his presence. "Have you traveled far?" he asked in a clear, rich voice.

"About five days on horseback," Dainon replied.

The young man's eyes lit up. "Where have you journeyed from?"

Mindful of his king's instructions, Dainon replied truthfully. "From Kandor."

Cool blue eyes regarded him with interest, but then the stranger tilted his head. "You appear weary. May I offer you some hospitality? My home is not far from here, and I can promise you plentiful food and a comfortable bed for the night." Before Dainon could reply, he plowed on. "Please, do not refuse me. It would be no trouble, and I have been brought up to show kindness to strangers. Indeed, if my fathers knew I had not made such an offer, they would be ashamed of me."

Fathers?

Perhaps Dainon was more tired than he had realized. And he couldn't deny the idea of sleeping in a bed was extremely appealing. It had been many years since he'd spent more than one night on the hard ground, and he yearned for the softness of a mattress.

"Your offer is a welcome one," he admitted, "and I would be a fool to turn you down."

The young man's face lit up, his eyes bright. "Excellent! Then perhaps I should introduce myself. I am Arrio, and I dwell in the city of Teruna. My home is only an hour or so from here. Shall we ride together?" He glanced down at his body. "Although I should probably dress first." His mischievous smile was a delight.

Dainon extended his hand. "I am Dainon of Kandor."

Slim, cool fingers wrapped around Dainon's. Seconds later, the jolt that shot up his spine, lighting every nerve ending, froze him into stillness.

By all that is holy.

Dainon stared at their conjoined hands, his brain struggling to process what his body was telling him. Only once before had he experienced such a phenomenon, and in such different circumstances that he was left shaken to the core.

"What...?" He sought the words, but they remained tantalizingly out of reach.

"Is something wrong?" Arrio's brow furrowed. "You are pale, almost as if you are on the verge of collapse." He put his arm around Dainon and eased him into a sitting position on a nearby boulder. When he broke contact to move to his horse and grab the cream robe that lay across the stallion's back, the sensations ceased abruptly.

Dainon found his voice. "Who... who are you?" It was on the tip of his tongue to ask *what* the young man was. Surely there was something... magical about him, some unearthly force that clung to him in an attempt to unseat Dainon's reason. It would be the only explanation for what he had experienced.

I have felt such... power before. And the memory of it was as sharp as if it had been yesterday.

When I first felt the touch of my Tarisa's hand in mine, and knew her for what she was—my soul mate.

The question appeared in the forefront of his mind before he could stop it. *Then who are you, Arrio, that you should have such an effect on me?*

CHAPTER
TWO

DAINON KEPT Tarrea's pace matched to that of Arrio's stallion as they rode through rolling hills and fields, alongside a river that wound its way through the green, its crystal-clear waters sparkling in the sunlight. The sound of water trickling over rocks, added to the bursts of birdsong from the trees that lined their route, all conspired to engender in Dainon a feeling of peace. That momentary jolt had passed, already slipping from his memory. He could not explain it, but he had no desire to repeat the experience, preferring to keep his hands to himself.

"Are we within Teruna's borders?" he asked, having seen no patrols, nor anything that marked out the beginning of the kingdom's boundaries.

Beside him, Arrio nodded, sitting upright on his horse. There was a grace to him that gave an impression of familiarity with his mount. "Is Kandor like this?" Arrio asked, gesturing to the landscape.

"To the south, yes," Dainon responded, "but to the east are many mountains. Teruna's terrain appears to be more hospitable. And we have no ocean, of course." He sighed. "I must confess, I loved it—its size, its sheer majesty." To speak of his home eased the disquiet in him. He could not account for the way he was feeling around Arrio. He knew nothing about him, and yet he felt comfortable in Arrio's presence, as though they had known each other many years instead of minutes.

"What is your occupation?" Arrio asked.

It was a question Dainon had already anticipated. "I am a farmer. I have livestock that I breed for wool and meat." He hated the fact that he had to lie to the first Kandoran he had met, but his mission required some degree of secrecy. Whether his lie would be readily accepted remained to be seen.

Arrio brought his horse to a stop and observed Dainon in silence for a moment, his eyebrows raised. "Forgive me for commenting, but your livestock must require much handling, judging by your size." When Dainon regarded him in surprise, Arrio's face flushed. "You are a large man, Dainon. Your physique implies your work is strenuous. I have grown up around warriors with fewer muscles than you possess." His lips bore the faintest trace of amusement.

Dainon was unsure whether it was his poor skill at lying or simply his muscles that had betrayed him, but it was clear Arrio had not accepted his story. He was not about to make matters worse by reinforcing the lie. Instead he focused on Arrio's words. "You are a warrior, then?" It did not seem likely, given Arrio's youthful appearance, but Dainon had no idea at what age Terunan warriors commenced their training.

Arrio chuckled. "No, although I have trained with them. Papa insisted on it." He sighed. "Not that he wants me to be a warrior, but he believes it is good for my physical well-being, as well as my agility."

"Is it not your choice? If you wish to be a warrior, can you not decide for yourself?"

Arrio's smile grew rueful. "Alas, no. My destiny is not mine to choose."

Dainon did not want to pursue the topic for fear of appearing too inquisitive. He peered into the distance. "Where do you live?"

"In the center of the city," Arrio said. "We are not that far now. Soon you will be able to see the white stone walls that surround it." He shook his head. "Once, the people of Teruna were able to dwell completely within the city boundaries, but the walls can no longer contain the population."

The irony of the situation was not lost on Dainon. "Then why not build out? Expand the city?"

Arrio sighed. "We cannot keep pace with the demand for more homes. As fast as new settlements are established, they are filled. We are having to contend not only with an increasing birth rate, but also with a lower mortality rate. Our healers are clearly too good: our people are living longer, and in better health than ever before. Teruna flourishes."

His words confirmed some of the stories brought to Kandor by merchants, who told of Teruna's population explosion. Dainon gazed with interest at Arrio. "You appear knowledgeable about such matters." It had crossed his mind briefly that Arrio was an official of some kind, but he'd dismissed it almost as quickly. Arrio could not be more than twenty-two, surely too young for a person in such a responsible role.

Arrio shrugged. "It is fitting that I should be aware of all that takes place in the kingdom." Before Dainon could question this statement,

Arrio pointed ahead. "See? The city walls." He drew himself up tall in his saddle and smiled. "Welcome to Teruna, Dainon." He lifted his stallion's reins and picked up the pace a little, and Dainon matched his speed.

The city was built on a hill, encircled by white walls that sparkled with quartz. The buildings that lay within the walls were constructed of the same stone. At the top of the hill, Dainon spied what had to be the royal palace. Even at this distance, the air buzzed with noise, giving an impression of vibrancy and activity.

As they approached the city, he got his first glimpse of Terunan militia when two soldiers with spears pulled open the heavy wooden gates below an arch of stone. When they caught sight of Arrio, they straightened instantly.

"Your Highness." They stepped aside to let him pass through, their heads held high. Their gazes fell upon Dainon, and rather than the suspicion he would have faced in his own kingdom, he was merely aware of their interest.

Then the full import of their greeting struck him. *Your Highness.* His mind began to piece together fragments from remembered tales. Perhaps Arrio's reference to his fathers was not an error, not a mishearing on Dainon's part.

He brought Tarrea to a halt when they were within the walls, and faced Arrio. "Excuse my ignorance, but exactly with whom am I riding?" Around them were people of all shapes and sizes, going about their lives, but there was no mistaking their reaction when they saw Arrio. Most greeted him with a smile or a friendly nod, but all of them bowed.

Arrio smiled. "I am still Arrio. And it is not ignorance on your part. You are a stranger here." He tilted his head to one side. "Does it matter to you that I am also Prince Arrio? Would it change how you see me?" His frank gaze was unsettling, stirring something in Dainon's belly.

"No," Dainon admitted truthfully. "King Tanish is your father?" Arrio nodded, and Dainon's heartbeat raced. "I have a question. You made mention of how your fathers had brought you up. Many years ago there was a tale of how King Tanish joined himself in marriage to two men. It was true, then?"

Arrio's smile lit up his face. "The king is my *papa*. Prince Sorran is my *papa-turo*, my teacher in all things. There is also *Papi*." His smile widened. "Although to my people he is Prince Feyar, a *Seruan* possessed of great skill."

"I have heard tales of the *Seruani*," Dainon acknowledged. "Indeed, all Kandor hears such talk. I have long wondered how much of what the traveling merchants speak is true."

"And what do those merchants say?" Arrio asked softly, reaching down to stroke his stallion's mane.

Dainon took a deep breath. "They speak of a people who possess rare gifts and abilities. Those who can see into the future, see what will come to pass. Those who heal with their touch. Those who bring peace where there is conflict. People who are as one with the land, the elements." He paused. "And they spoke of a baby, found with its dying mother. A baby who was brought up by the king and his consorts to be a prince, and heir to the throne." He stared at Arrio. "They spoke of you?"

Arrio gave a single nod, his blue eyes focused on Dainon's. "I am told my mother died days after they came upon me in the ruins of a temple. You and I passed the spot on our way here. Since then I have been their son."

Dainon's breathing quickened. *If this much is true, then what of the rest of the fantastic tales? Is there truly magic within the walls of Teruna?* Something deep inside him hungered to know.

Arrio laid a hand lightly on his shoulder. "So now that you know my home is the royal palace, will you still stay? You will be most welcome, Dainon." His gaze was earnest, watchful, his posture stiff.

Dainon could not believe his fortune. His king sought information, and here *he* was, about to meet the ruler of Teruna. And all because he had come across Arrio on that beach, walking out of the sea, tall and regal, so beautiful.

Beautiful? It was not a word Dainon had applied to another man in his life, but for some reason, it seemed… right. There was a beauty to Arrio, evident in his face, the lines of his body, and the way he carried himself.

"If the invitation still stands, then yes, I will stay with you."

Arrio relaxed. "Then follow me to the palace. I will make sure your mare is given the best of care, and you shall meet my fathers."

The fact that he had thought of Tarrea's comfort sat well with Dainon. "Thank you. She is in need of rest after her journey. And I should like to meet the king and his consorts."

Arrio's genuine delight in his response warmed him.

Dainon picked up the reins and guided Tarrea through the streets, following Arrio. Along the route he was conscious of the manner in which the populace greeted Arrio. It was plain the Terunans loved their prince. The people called out greetings and blessings upon him, and Arrio thanked them with a bow of his head.

The way grew steep, and Dainon looked up to the top of the city where the white stone palace stood, its walls gleaming in the sunlight. From its ramparts hung banners in bright colors, so vivid against the quartz-like stone. But what struck him most was the sheer number of people who filled the streets. *So many of them.* There was an atmosphere in the city unlike anything he had encountered in Kandor. Dainon observed the smiling faces around him, heard the laughter, the lively chatter, and let it all sink in. It came to him suddenly: Teruna and Kandor were as the light and the dark—one kingdom filled with a joy that no longer existed in the other.

A desire welled up from deep inside Dainon, making his heart ache. *I want to see Kandor filled once more with such light.* He would find out all he could for his king, but *this* was now his mission—to help his land heal itself.

Arrio led them up to a stone archway, their passage blocked by wooden gates that swung open as they approached. Once through, Dainon found himself in a familiar setting. The smell of horses and straw filled his nostrils. Across one wall were several stalls, with grooms bustling in and out of them, feeding, cleaning, everyone busy.

A groom approached them and bowed to Arrio, who gave him instructions to take care of Tarrea. Dainon climbed down and removed his saddle bags and sword before patting her on the back.

"She will be comfortable here," Arrio told him. "Timur will see to that."

Before Dainon could inquire further, a man strode across the stable grounds, dressed in a leather tunic. He greeted Arrio warmly with a brief hug. "I know where you've been," he said with a grin. "I can smell the salt in your hair." He appeared to be close to Dainon's age, his arms and neck thick with muscle. His lack of formality with the prince surprised Dainon.

Arrio laughed. "It was too good a day to miss the chance of a swim. But I was not there alone." He gestured toward Dainon. "We have a guest."

Dainon couldn't help but compare Arrio to King Ceros, the former ruler of Kandor. Dainon recalled Ceros's manner before he'd ascended the throne. Ceros had been imperious, cold, devious—not likable traits in a ruler, and unfortunately he had worsened once he held power. Though Dainon would never have dared to say as much aloud, it had been a relief when the king had met an untimely end.

But Arrio? The prince had no airs about him, and his people appeared to love him dearly. His easygoing manner with Timur was not what Dainon had expected of a royal prince.

"Dainon, this muscled bear is Timur, the head of the royal stables," Arrio said with a grin. "He and my *papa* were boys together, and he and his husband, Erinor, are as close to my fathers as any brothers could be."

Husband. Dainon had so many questions, but this was not the time. He nodded to Timur in greeting.

"This is Dainon, a visitor from Kandor," Arrio told Timur as he handed his reins to a stable boy.

Timur cocked his head. "That black mare yours?"

"Yes, my Tarrea."

Timur smiled, his eyes warm. "Do not worry. We will treat her with the care she deserves." He glanced at Arrio, his eyebrows lifted. "Sorran was looking for you earlier. Did you not tell him where you were going—again?" He grinned. "You are *so* like your *papa*."

Arrio bit his lip. "I may have forgotten to mention that I was going for a ride after my workout with the guards." His gaze met Dainon's. "My fathers like to know where I am, and—"

"And he likes to sneak out of the palace," Timur added with a chuckle. "Just like his fathers when they were his age."

Dainon wanted to laugh at the expression on Arrio's face. "Are you in trouble, Your Highness?" In that moment he seemed younger.

"Probably," Arrio muttered. He gave a nod in Timur's direction. "Greet Erinor for me?"

"I will. Now go find your fathers and put their minds at rest." He patted Arrio on the back. "Not that you won't do the same thing again." Laughing, he strode toward the stalls.

Arrio glanced at Dainon. "I will take you through the garden into the palace." He led Dainon out of the stables and through a quiet courtyard. As they passed through a doorway, Dainon caught the sound of trickling water. A fountain bubbled in the center of the garden, surrounded by flower beds and trees, from whose branches came the sound of birds chirruping away happily. A sense of peace pervaded the air.

"What a tranquil place," Dainon murmured.

Arrio smiled. "My *papa-turo* loves to meditate here. And I often find my fathers sitting here in the evening."

"May I ask a question?"

Arrio paused at another doorway and turned to face him. "Of course."

"Do others in Teruna have marriages like that of your fathers?"

Arrio regarded him steadily. "In what sense?"

"A marriage of three, for instance. Or between two men or two women."

Arrio smiled. "All people are free to marry whomever they love. And yes, marriage between three partners does exist, though there are not many." He peered intently at Dainon. "Why do you ask? Is it not similar in Kandor?"

Dainon shook his head. "In recent years, marriage has had but one main purpose—procreation. To that end, relationships between two men or two women are frowned upon."

Arrio became still. "'Frowned upon'? Are those who engage in such relationships punished?"

Dainon sighed. He had no desire to reveal Kandor's tragic past. "As far as the kingdom is concerned, such relationships do not exist," he said, choosing his words carefully.

Arrio's eyes sparkled. "Ah. Then they exist in secret." Dainon caught his breath and Arrio nodded. "I see the truth of this in your face."

Dainon fell silent. He knew of one fellow warrior who hid his male lover's existence from all but a few whom he trusted. No one truly believed there would be repercussions if they were found out—there had been enough suffering in Kandor without adding to it—but no one was prepared to put their incredulity to the test.

"Are you in such a relationship?" Arrio asked him suddenly.

Dainon stared at him. "No. I... I was married once, but...." He swallowed past the lump in his throat, the words there on his tongue, bitter to the taste. "My wife was taken from me years ago."

Arrio bowed his head. "Forgive me. I was wrong to question you in such a way. You are a guest here."

When he lifted his chin, Dainon was astonished to see Arrio's eyes glistening.

"And I have caused you pain."

Dainon wanted to reassure him that the fault was not Arrio's but his own. He had not expected to find the prince so sensitive to the emotions of others. "Your Highness, my pain is not of your making. This is an old wound, one that should have healed long ago."

Before he could speak further, the heavy wooden door before them swung open.

Arrio led him into the cool interior. "Where is his Majesty?" he asked the young man who held the door for them.

"In the royal audience chamber, Your Highness, with Prince Sorran and Prince Feyar."

Arrio thanked him. "Please have a room prepared for my guest."

The young man bowed, his gaze flickering in Dainon's direction as he straightened, before leaving them.

Arrio turned to Dainon, gesturing to a long, stone-flagged hallway. "I shall present you to my fathers immediately."

Dainon's heartbeat raced. He thought it unlikely that the king of Teruna would be as easygoing as his son. And the prospect of meeting a *Seruan* filled him with trepidation.

Will they see through me?

He followed Arrio along the hallway. As they approached the huge ancient door, Dainon summoned up his courage, mentally preparing himself for the questions that were certain to come.

CHAPTER
THREE

DAINON HARDLY took in the room. His attention was focused on the three men at the far end, the only figures present. The king was recognizable by the thin circlet of gold set on top of his head, but that was all he wore in the way of insignia. His dark blue robe was simple, but what made Dainon unable to look away was his dark brown hair, peppered with a few gray strands here and there. It rippled in long waves over his shoulders and down his back, a striking feature. He was standing by a throne, one of three that dominated the far end of the chamber, his being the largest. Warm brown eyes regarded Dainon as he approached, walking behind Arrio.

"We are accustomed to you returning from the beach with a bag full of pretty shells, interesting rocks, and maybe a fish or two." King Tanish arched his eyebrows. "You appear to have caught something a little different this time, son." A hint of a smile played around his lips.

The man standing beside him laughed. "I do not think Arrio possesses a line strong enough to hook such a catch." He appeared shorter than the king, with eyes so dark, they were almost black, and black hair that curled on his forehead and over the tips of his ears. His skin tone was a warm olive, complemented by his deep cream robe.

Their banter helped to ease Dainon's nerves a little. He came to a stop at Arrio's side and knelt on the stone floor, head bowed. "Your Majesty, Your Highnesses." He spoke in a low voice, his gaze trained on the space between him and the throne.

"Rise, friend," the king said quietly. When Dainon lifted his head, King Tanish smiled. "If my son brought you here, he trusts you, and I trust Arrio's instincts." He glanced at the man beside him. "He has a good teacher."

Dainon rose and stood with his hands at his sides.

"Good? My *papa-turo* is the best!" Arrio lurched forward and hugged the olive-skinned man, who laughed and returned his hug. It was such an unexpectedly candid moment, the loving embrace as natural as breathing. When Arrio released him, he stepped back and gestured toward Dainon. "This is Dainon, who comes to us from Kandor. I have offered him a bed for the night." He smiled at Dainon. "Although I hope you will stay longer."

"When you have finished acting in so impulsive a manner," the third man murmured, "perhaps it might be an idea to introduce us?" Dainon heard an undercurrent of laughter in his voice.

Arrio flushed. "My apologies, *Papi*. Dainon, may I present my fathers, King Tanish, Prince Sorran, and this is Prince Feyar."

Dainon bowed his head to each of the men. "You are to be congratulated, Sires. You have raised a wonderful young man." His words were not mere flattery. There was something attractive about Arrio, more than his looks or his demeanor. Dainon was at a loss to understand why Arrio affected him so. *Is it that Merron might have been Arrio's age now, had he lived?* It was as good an explanation as any, although Dainon did not feel paternal toward him.

"Welcome, Dainon." The king's voice was rich and deep. "We would be delighted to have you remain with us for as long as you feel happy to do so."

"Your Majesty is most kind," Dainon said with another bow.

"Then I shall go and see that all is ready for you," Arrio said with a smile. "I am sure my fathers will take good care of you." He patted Dainon on the arm and left the chamber.

"I need to speak with Arrio," Prince Sorran said, "so I will leave you with my husbands." His dark eyes focused on Dainon. "You are most welcome here." He followed Arrio from the chamber.

Dainon's stomach roiled. *Alone with the King—and a* Seruan. His skin tingled as the two men regarded him steadily. *They see me.* Never had Dainon felt so… naked, so vulnerable. He bowed his head to hide his burning face.

"Dainon, what is your profession?" Prince Feyar asked. His black beard was gray at his chin.

"I am a farmer, Your Highness." His heart pounded and he fought to maintain his composure, but the silence that followed set his nerves on edge. He lifted his head to find the king regarding him with mild amusement. It was only then that it struck him.

No wonder he appears incredulous. I doubt a farmer would be so comfortable with royal protocol.

"I may not have my husband's gifts," King Tanish admitted, "but even I know that to be a lie. The way you carry yourself, your manner of speaking, the way you entered this chamber—all these things betray you, Dainon. Perhaps this time you will tell us the truth. I know a warrior when I see one. Have I not trained with them, ridden with them?" His smile faded and his voice grew firmer. "Unless you feel it is acceptable to reward our hospitality with falsehoods?"

By the heavens. He had not expected to be found out so quickly, and faced with the king's calm but firm demeanor, Dainon realized he could not hide any longer. There was a compulsion to be honest with King Tanish.

"What you say is true, Your Majesty. I am a warrior in the Kandoran army." He held his head high, meeting the king's gaze. He glanced toward Prince Feyar, who was watching him, his blue eyes bright.

Feyar nodded, his gaze watchful. "Be at peace, Dainon. I sense no threat from you, but you hide something from us. Now is the time for honesty."

Dainon dropped to his knees, his head bowed. "Forgive me, I meant no offense. I am simply following orders."

"Whose orders?" the king demanded.

Dainon raised his chin to look the king in the eye. "King Rohar of Kandor." His heart was still racing, his breathing rapid. He waited for the anger he felt sure was about to descend on him, but instead the two men merely nodded.

King Tanish walked slowly over to where Dainon knelt. He smiled at him and glanced at his husband. "There are times when I wish I had Sorran's eyes. To be able to see what he sees…."

Prince Feyar's expression softened. "You see enough, my *corishan*." The unguarded moment brought a lump to Dainon's throat. Feyar looked down at Dainon. "We have heard many sad tales of what has befallen Kandor these last years. Do the merchants speak truly?"

Dainon sought the words to respond, his throat tight.

The king placed his hand upon Dainon's shoulder. "Rise, friend. You have nothing to fear here, as long as you are honest with us." He crossed the floor to sit upon his throne, his thoughtful gaze trained on Dainon. Feyar sat at his side.

Dainon rose to his feet, his breathing under control. "What have you been told of Kandor?" It made sense that the merchants who passed through the two kingdoms would speak of what they saw. *Why would I think Kandor's suffering is unknown to them?*

"That a plague had swept through the land, and many thousands had died," Feyar said quietly.

Dainon nodded, his heart heavy. "This is true."

Feyar regarded him keenly. "You wear your loss like a garment. I see the pain that lingers still. You have our sympathies." He bowed his head.

"Why are you here?" the king asked, his gaze trained on Dainon.

He took a deep breath. "My mission was to learn all that I could about Teruna and then report back to my king. He seeks your help, if it is indeed possible to provide any. When the plague was at its worst, half the kingdom was infected."

Feyar paled. "So many?"

Dainon nodded. "But not all those infected died. The plague took a third of the population, but those who survived were left with an irreversible legacy: they were sterile. So the half that had remained clear of the epidemic were the only ones capable of bearing children. Not that many were left of child-bearing age—the young were the first to die. The elderly followed them." When Tarisa had fallen to the plague, Merron swiftly after her, Dainon had prayed to be taken also. In the days and weeks that had followed, he had wondered over and over why he should have been spared when so many of his generation were not.

"I do not see how we can help you," the king observed, his expression grave.

"It is not simply a matter of increasing the population, Your Majesty. Kandor lost many of its most skilled artisans, those who passed their skills on to the next generations. Gone are our master builders, our craftsmen, our teachers…." Dainon let his gaze drop, the weight of Kandor's losses heavy on his heart.

"Dainon?"

He raised his head to regard Prince Feyar. "Your Highness?" To Dainon's surprise, Feyar's dark eyes glistened with tears.

"Your words paint a picture of sadness, but more than that, I feel your sorrow here." Feyar pressed a hand over his heart.

King Tanish nodded. "I feel the same. I ask that you leave this in our hands, to be discussed with our advisers and ministers." His gaze grew more intense. "It would appear you have achieved your goal much sooner than you anticipated. I am certain you had no idea this day would bring you to us. That being the case, must you return to Kandor sooner than expected?"

The king had a point. Dainon's covert mission was definitely in the open. "King Rohar gave no specific time frame for my return," he replied truthfully. The notion of relaxing in the beautiful city was an alluring one. Even the light was different in Teruna, and he ached to see and learn more about the kingdom.

"Then stay with us as our guest for a while," Feyar said. "Spend time in the city, go where you will. Put your mission from your mind—it is now in our hands."

Dainon smiled broadly, his heart light. "Thank you. I would be delighted to accept such a generous offer." He was suddenly aware of his aching limbs. Apparently the journey had taken more out of him than he had thought.

"Perhaps you might like to rest before we dine this evening?" Feyar suggested.

Dainon smiled. "Is my fatigue so obvious?"

King Tanish's expression was kind. "My husband often sees what others may miss. Rest, Dainon. Bathe. Refresh your body and mind. This evening you shall dine with us."

Dainon bowed his head in acknowledgment of the king's words. "Then I shall take my leave of you."

Feyar rose to his feet. "Come with me, and I shall instruct a servant to take you to your room. By now all should be ready for you."

Dainon bowed once more to the two men and followed Feyar to the chamber door, his head in a spin. *This was something I did not foresee.* Good fortune seemed to be on his side, although that one moment of... strangeness had not left him entirely.

It was nothing. A consequence of my long journey, nothing more.

Even as the thought flitted through his consciousness, the image in his head was Arrio, tall, regal, and....

There was that word again. Try as he might, Dainon could not shake it loose from his mind.

Beautiful.

ARRIO CAST a final glance around the room, pleased with what he saw. The windows were open, and the cool evening breeze wafting through them brought with it the scents from the garden below. "Dainon should be comfortable here." As the words left him, he grew aware of the silence in the room. He turned to find Sorran staring at him, his lips twisted in obvious amusement. "What is it? What amuses you?"

Sorran arched his eyebrows. "I am waiting for you to reveal what is going on in that head of yours."

Arrio stilled. "I do not understand." *Then why does my heart beat so fast?* As skilled as his *papa-turo* was, he could not possibly divine the cause of Arrio's present state. *Can he?* Arrio had been so careful to conceal his inner turbulence—maintaining a composure he did not feel during the ride from the beach had exhausted him.

Sorran grinned. "Do not think to hide from me, my son. I know you." He tilted his head. "So tell me: what is it about our guest that sets your pulse racing?"

By the Maker. There had been so many times as a child that Arrio had wished for a cloak capable of hiding his thoughts from one or more of his fathers. "Is there *nothing* I can hide?"

Sorran laughed, the sound clear and musical. "Nothing."

Arrio let out a sigh. "I like him."

"He seems a pleasant man. Easy to like." Sorran's lips were still twitching.

Arrio could not keep the groan within him. "Stop."

Sorran's peal of laughter rang out. He clasped Arrio to him in a brief hug. "Surely I have not embarrassed you? This cannot be Arrio, the same young man who declared candidly on his sixteenth birthday that women were of no interest to him, as only men made him hard?"

"Must you recall *everything* I have ever said?" Arrio's face was hot. He was twenty-one, and yet there were times when he felt himself to be such a child.

Sorran became still. "I am sorry. I should not tease. Stirrings of desire are heady, and although you know where your tastes lie, I feel this is the first occasion when you are truly aware of your body's reaction to another man. Do I read you correctly?"

All Arrio could do was nod. It had taken all his effort to remain calm when he had walked out of the sea and found the handsome man standing by his stallion. He could not decide what it was that made Dainon so attractive. Arrio had always admired the physique of the warriors with whom he trained, so it was no surprise that Dainon's muscles caught his attention. Dainon's brown eyes were kind, yet they held another quality that drew Arrio to him: a knowledge of sorrow. Arrio did not possess his *papa-turo*'s skill to be able to read the emotions of those about him, but Dainon's pain had somehow reached out to him with subtle, gentle fingers that crept around Arrio's heart.

"There is something about him," Arrio admitted in a low voice. "Something more than the sum of his looks, his manner, his voice, his gait.... He stirs something in me." *My interest, my emotions, my desires....*

And something else. Each time Arrio looked at Dainon, he was aware of a memory, almost lost, a fragment of a dream from long ago.

Did I dream of you?

Sorran gazed into his eyes. "This stirring you speak of... this should be a good thing, and yet I sense you are not at peace. What troubles you about this attraction?"

Arrio crossed the floor to the open window and stared out at the landscape beyond, seeking a balm to calm the conflict within him. He knew without turning that Sorran had followed him. Arrio placed his hands on the cool stone ledge and breathed deeply. "It does not matter that I find him attractive. He had a wife."

There was a pause. "And this signifies what, exactly?"

Arrio faced Sorran. "That he likes women? He prefers them to men? He told me that relationships between men are frowned upon in Kandor."

Sorran smiled. "That does not mean such relationships are nonexistent."

That gave him pause as he recalled Dainon's hesitation when Arrio had made such a suggestion. "That may be the case. But what if he is not attracted to men? What if I reveal how I feel and he—"

Sorran placed a hand on his back, the touch light. "And already you speak of feelings. I think you need to stop for a moment and assess *how* he makes you feel."

"But that is what troubles me," Arrio said with a groan. "Is it lust? Attraction? More? When I first saw him, then yes, I knew what it was to want someone, because by the Maker, I wanted him, as I have never wanted another." He shivered at the memory, the reaction he had pushed aside so fast, lest Dainon recognize it for what it was—desire.

Sorran's eyes gleamed. "And did Dainon know you wanted him?"

Arrio scrunched his brows together. "I fought hard not to let him see. How could he know that?"

"I am assuming there would be evidence," Sorran said with a smirk. "Had you not been swimming? Surely he would have seen... something?" His lips twitched.

"The water was cold!" Arrio growled. The sight of Sorran clearly trying hard not to laugh was enough to ease his nerves. "This amuses you?" Arrio affected an outraged tone, although he knew it would not fool Sorran for an instant.

His father's smile warmed him. "Arrio, there are times when your maturity makes me both proud and amazed, but in this moment, I am reminded that you are still so young. You are fretting about matters beyond your control. I feel your uncertainty, your impetuosity, your attempts to make sense of your situation by using logic. Feelings do not have to have a basis in logic."

"I did not know there were so many different levels to my emotions, so much depth to my feelings. I have no experience of this. I do not know what to do, *Papa-turo*." Arrio's gut clenched.

"Then do nothing," Sorran replied simply, rubbing Arrio's back. "I know you feel you must do something, but bide your time. Get to know him." Arrio let out a sigh, and Sorran cupped his cheek. "Listen to me. Two paths lie before you. One is where you let your emotions lead you. The other is where you act logically. Granted, following either path may lead to disappointment, but if that is so, then you will have to deal with it. This is part of life."

"This is hard."

Sorran released him and stepped back. "I know, but you will find your way. Always remember you can talk to us about anything." He tilted his head once more. "As for Dainon, he is an interesting man. Spend time with him while he remains with us. Be a friend to him. Show him Teruna."

"I can do that," Arrio agreed. He stiffened as the door swung open and Dainon entered, coming to a halt when he saw Arrio and Sorran. Arrio forced himself to breathe evenly and addressed Dainon. "I trust the room will be to your liking. I shall take my leave of you and let you rest."

Dainon bowed his head. "You have been most kind."

Sorran guided Arrio toward the door. "We shall both take our leave, and I will send a servant to bring you to dine with us. Please, refresh yourself. Ask if you require anything."

Before Arrio could say another word, Sorran led him from the room. Once they were in the corridor, the door closed behind them, Sorran turned to Arrio.

"Dainon is not the only one who needs to rest." Arrio opened his mouth to protest, but Sorran shook his head. "You worked out with the royal guard this morning. You swam for how long this afternoon? And this was before you put yourself under emotional strain in an effort to hide your feelings. Do not argue with me." His smile belied his stern words. "This evening I shall rely on you to help entertain our guest."

That stopped Arrio. It would be a matter of royal duty. "Of course. I shall do my utmost to make you all proud of me."

Sorran's smile lit up his eyes. "I have no doubt of that." He patted Arrio's arm and walked away along the corridor.

Arrio gave the door before him one last glance before leaving it to go to his room.

I may learn more about Dainon during dinner. The prospect was intriguing—as intriguing as the man himself.

CHAPTER
FOUR

DAINON AWOKE after a surprisingly deep sleep to find his room in semidarkness, the gloom pierced by candlelight. He had no idea what had awoken him. Then he spied a large jug on the nearby table that had not been present before he had slept.

Someone has been here. The room, however, was empty, save for Dainon.

He rose up from the bed, where he had lain naked on top of a layer of fur, and glanced around the room. Something else was new: across the foot of the bed lay a dark blue robe. He picked it up, stroking its soft fabric. He had neglected to bring his saddlebags, having left them in the stables, but another glance found them at the foot of the bed.

My hosts are taking care of me. Dainon could not believe his good fortune.

He walked to the open window and out onto a balcony. The sky was a breathtaking collision of colors, bronze and gold at the horizon where the sun had already sunk from view, fading into dark blue where the night sky seeped lower. A warm breeze, redolent with a strange, heady perfume, stirred his hair and caressed his face and chest. The air carried with it a sound Dainon knew all too well: it recalled to him the barracks bathhouse where the warriors bathed when their duty was done. Low noises that spoke of sexual pleasure reached his ears.

He stared out at the palace, unable to see the perpetrators, but his blood heated at the soft cries and whimpers that crept out of the darkness. When the sound grew louder, he gazed ahead to where a warm light glowed in a window, filtered by a shimmering curtain. *There.* And now it was clearly one person, not two, and definitely male.

Dainon stood transfixed, unable to refrain from listening, his own length hardening as he was caught up in the other man's ecstasy. He pictured a man on his back, hand wrapped around his cock, hips thrusting up as he neared his climax. Without thinking, Dainon grasped his own thick shaft and pumped slowly, closing his eyes to focus on the sensual background noises.

"Oh. *Oh.*" A deep groan of pleasure rumbled out from the room facing his, and Dainon knew the unseen man had succumbed to orgasm. It was too much to bear. He slid his hand faster, squeezing as he neared the wide head, and there he was, spurting his seed onto the stone-flagged surface of the balcony, his body trembling. He leaned on the balcony wall for support, his legs shaking. He could not remember the last time the act had brought him so much satisfaction.

Dainon straightened as the curtain facing him was drawn aside and a figure emerged slowly into the night air. He caught his breath at the sight of Arrio, naked, his chest glistening with a shimmer of sweat. A gasp slipped from Dainon's lips.

Look at him.

Arrio jerked his head up and stared in Dainon's direction, eyes wide. Their gazes locked. When Arrio smiled, holding himself straight and tall, something unfurled in Dainon's belly, some deep, primal sensation he could not name. A shiver skated down his spine. Arrio appeared to be breathing heavily, his chest rising and falling, his gaze still focused on Dainon as he swiped a hand down from his neck to his belly, taking his time. When it slid lower to where the balcony's edge obscured Dainon's view, he caught his breath at the sight of Arrio's arm moving slowly, making it obvious what the prince was doing. What was more of a shock to Dainon was that he *wanted* to see.

What is he doing to me? The hairs on Dainon's arms rose, and another shiver tickled up and down his spine. He could not tear his gaze away from Arrio, who watched him with parted lips, his hand clearly still moving slowly, unseen. The thought of that sensual act made Dainon's balls tingle and tighten.

"Dainon."

His name floated across the distance between them, no more than a whisper. The sound echoed inside Dainon's head, filling him with one desire.

By the heavens, I want to touch him.

No sooner had the thought flitted through Dainon's mind than he clenched his hands by his sides, as if to drive the desire from him. His pulse raced and his belly quivered. Arrio contemplated him with a keen glance, his body at rest, and still Dainon could not look away.

Are you bewitching me? Arrio's smile could certainly make any man's pulse quicken. On the heels of that thought came another. *And it is men who make Arrio's blood heat.*

Dainon's head was spinning. *How can I know that?* But he did. The knowledge was there, clear and sharp.

A knock on his door gave Dainon a jolt of surprise.

"His Majesty requests the pleasure of your company in thirty minutes in his audience chamber," a clear voice called out from beyond the door.

His heart rate quickening, Dainon took a steadying breath. "I shall be there. Thank you." He waited for a moment before returning his attention to the balcony, but Arrio was gone. The light from his room had been extinguished, and all Dainon perceived was the glow of illumination from elsewhere in the palace.

He stepped away from the balcony and went to pour water from the jug into the bowl beside it, his mind turning over and over the last few moments. He washed away what dust remained from the journey before slipping on the dark blue robe. He fastened it at the waist, liking the feel of the fabric against his skin. Dainon was accustomed to the short, coarse tunics he wore under his leather and breastplate, and even though he'd left his armor behind, he'd brought nothing with him as elegant as the fine robe.

One last look in the long, silvered mirror, and he was ready. The thought of dining with the king and his consorts provided him with a sliver of apprehension, but what set his heart pounding was the prospect of sitting at the table with Arrio, the memory of what had passed a shared secret between them.

How can I look him in the eye after this?

"TELL ME of Kandor," Arrio demanded, reaching for a piece of fruit from the platter in the center of the table. "Have you lived there all your life?"

"I have, Your Highness."

"Dainon, please. Call me Arrio?" The young prince regarded him earnestly.

Dainon gazed into deep blue eyes. "Very well—Arrio." The lack of formality made him a little uncomfortable, especially after sharing a moment of—*What can I call it? Intimacy?* In his mind, suddenly, was a vision of Arrio, naked and sated, those same eyes locked on Dainon, those soft-looking lips whispering his name. The memory sent heat racing through him, surging into his groin, pulsing through his shaft. The robe Arrio wore did little to help. A belt secured it at his waist, but above, it was open, revealing a bronzed chest, the nipples hidden by the edges of the garment. Dainon recalled those dark disks of pebbled flesh, the nubs standing proud.

Was he close enough for me to recall such details? Or is this merely my imagination, playing tricks on me? He could still see Arrio standing on that balcony, his arm moving slowly, his hand unseen....

With an inward groan, Dainon forced the images from his head and took a sip from his glass. "This wine is delicious. I have never before tasted anything like it." It was sweet, with a fragrance so heady, he imagined one could become intoxicated simply by inhaling it.

Sorran smiled. "This is Merrova, from my birthplace, Vancor, and it is more of a liquor than a wine."

Feyar chuckled. "What my husband does not tell you is that you will sleep well tonight. Merrova always sends me to sleep. So if you did not rest enough before, you will certainly do so after."

"What are your first impressions of Teruna?" King Tanish asked. "How does it compare with Kandor?"

"Kandor and Teruna are very different," he said with an effort. "At least from what I have seen of Teruna so far." And what he had seen, he liked very much.

"Then I have an idea," Sorran announced, his eyes gleaming. "My husbands have shared your mission here with me, and—"

"Mission? What mission?" Arrio interjected, his eyes wide.

Dainon's heart plummeted. "I am a warrior of the Kandoran army, here at the behest of King Rohar."

Arrio stared at him. "And yet you did not share this with me."

"Dainon's mission was to gather information," King Tanish said quietly, his gaze focused on Arrio. "If you were on such a mission, would you reveal it to the first person you happened to come across? Knowing nothing about them?"

Arrio blinked. "I—"

"Did you introduce yourself as a prince of Teruna when you first met Dainon?" Sorran asked, a gleam in his eyes. "Or did he find this out when you arrived in the city?"

Arrio's face flushed. "I think you already know the answer to that question."

"Dainon has been honest with us," King Tanish said in a firm tone. "It is right that he shared with us, as we are the only ones in a position to help him. I am sure that he will share with you also." His eyes twinkled. "Even if it is no business of yours."

Dainon felt for Arrio. "I am sorry, Arrio, that I was not truthful with you."

Arrio gave him a sheepish smile. "My *papa* speaks rightly. Your mission is clearly important, if it is your king who sends you. And yes, it is none of my business."

Sorran cleared his throat. "If I might continue with what I was saying?" Arrio bit his lip and Sorran chuckled. "Thank you." He turned to Dainon. "With regards to your secret mission," he stressed, with a sideways glance to Arrio, "I agree that for the moment it is out of your hands. Why not spend a few days with us, discovering Teruna? I am sure King Rohar would wish to know more about our land, and what better way to know us than by seeing it for yourself?"

The notion was a tempting one. "Perhaps," Dainon murmured with more reticence than he felt.

"And Arrio will be your guide," Sorran pronounced with a broad smile.

Across the table, Arrio snapped his head up and stared at Sorran, eyes wide. "I will?"

Sorran nodded. "Who better to show our guest all that Teruna has to offer than its prince who has spent his days discovering its treasures for himself?"

"I think this is a wonderful idea." King Tanish beamed. "With Arrio beside you, all who meet you will be keen to extend the hand of friendship. You may ask any questions of our citizens—they will be truthful with you."

"But…." The thought of spending days with the prince at his side was both a delight and a torment. His physical reaction to Arrio perplexed Dainon greatly. "Surely I would be taking Arrio away from his duties."

Feyar snorted. "Duties?" He smirked.

King Tanish arched his eyebrows. "Be kind, my husband," he admonished, before gazing at Dainon. "Arrio divides his time between training with the royal guard and exploring the kingdom. We feel it is important that he sees everything that goes on in Teruna. He can learn more about his future realm that way than by reading about it." He peered at Arrio, his head tilted to one side. "Especially as he hates spending time at his studies when he could be outside, experiencing life here for himself." His lips twitched, and Dainon had the impression that King Tanish was suppressing a grin.

Arrio laughed. "My *papa* knows me too well." He glanced at Dainon through long, dark lashes. "I should be happy to show you our kingdom, if you wish it."

Dainon's heart hammered. "How can I refuse such a kind offer?"

Arrio's face lit up. "Excellent. And while we are together, you must tell me more of Kandor."

"That seems like a fair exchange," Feyar said, helping himself to more of the sweet liquor. "For if it comes to pass that Teruna gives aid to Kandor, this will forge links between our two kingdoms. It will be good for Arrio to know more."

Hearing Feyar couch the situation in political terms settled Dainon's initial apprehension. *This feels right.* Better to think of Arrio as a diplomat, the future king of Teruna who would probably forge alliances with Kandor, than as the young man who, for some inconceivable reason, stirred Dainon's senses. *I cannot think of him in that way.* He could not fathom why Arrio affected him so strongly. Dainon spent his days in the company of men, and yet never had one pierced his consciousness in such a manner.

There are truly forces at work in Teruna. It was the only explanation for everything that had befallen him since that first inexplicable moment when his hand had touched Arrio's.

Dainon took a long drink from his glass, the liquor warming him and spreading a soporific feeling throughout his body. It was a pleasant sensation, creating in him a longing for his comfortable bed, to lie beneath soft sheets and furs.

"I think perhaps our guest is more tired than he had previously thought."

King Tanish's words pierced the soft fog that clouded his mind. Dainon straightened in his chair. "Your Majesty is perceptive. If I may take my leave of you?"

The king nodded. "Of course. Tomorrow you will need to be refreshed."

"Especially if we start the day with a morning swim," Arrio added with a mischievous grin. "There is nothing like diving beneath the waves and battling the tide to stir the blood and awaken the senses." He gave Dainon a sideways glance. "Unless you feel that would be too… vigorous for you." Arrio bit his lip, unveiled amusement dancing in his eyes.

Dainon knew a challenge when he heard one.

"That sounds an excellent way to begin the day," he replied, matching Arrio's grin. *Wait until tomorrow, Your Highness.* A good night's sleep and Dainon would be more than a match for the pup. At least, he fervently hoped that would be the case. He rose to his feet. "Then I shall bid you all a peaceful night." He bowed his head before stepping away from the table.

The king and the two princes acknowledged him with a bow of their heads.

Arrio was on his feet. "Wait, Dainon. I shall walk with you to your chamber."

Dainon's momentary confidence gave a stutter. "Very well." He waited until Arrio was at his side and then followed him from the room. They walked in silence through the cool hallways, their footfalls echoing against the stone walls. Dainon was relieved at the lack of conversation. Tension filled him at the thought that Arrio might mention their earlier… moment. Dainon was not embarrassed to have heard the prince in the act of pleasuring himself—years spent dwelling in barracks had long since rendered him immune to such discomfiture. What plagued him still was the way Arrio had looked at him, the way Dainon's body had reacted to that heated glance.

What is it about you, Arrio, that plunges me into such confusion?

When they reached his bedchamber, Arrio paused at the threshold. "I am glad you are staying with us," he said in a low voice. "And I look forward to hearing more of your mission, and to being your guide." The light from the candle burning in its holder next to the door caught in his eyes. Arrio held out his hand. "Sleep well, Dainon. I wish you the sweetest of dreams."

Dainon hesitated before clasping Arrio's hand in his. "Thank you, and the same to you."

Arrio's lips parted, and Dainon wondered what was to come. But after a second or two of silence, the prince bowed his head. "Good night."

His grin returned. "And tomorrow we swim." He withdrew his hand and walked off along the corridor.

Dainon watched his retreating figure, the bronze robe clinging to his slim body.

Will you be in my dreams?

The prospect was both alluring and frightening. Dainon prided himself on always being in control. He was a level-headed man with a good grip on reality and the ability to see both sides of an argument. Among his fellow warriors, he was a mediator, one who brought the calm light of reason to many a hostile situation.

Except in Arrio's presence he felt anything but calm. Arrio had upset the balance, destroyed it with little more than a beautiful body, a charming demeanor, and good humor. He created in Dainon a yearning he had never known, an ache that filled him, a longing for....

For what?

For the life of him, Dainon did not know.

TANISH SETTLED between his husbands with a sigh of contentment. Sorran was in his arms, Tanish's face buried in the curve of his neck, and Feyar's body curved around his, Feyar's breath stirring Tanish's hair, which was twisted into a long silken rope as it always was while he slept. He listened to the sound of their combined breaths, and inhaled the peace that filled their chamber.

Night was his favorite time, when the world was beyond their door and all that existed was *this*, three bodies wrapped around each other, a time for love and passion and desire. Twenty years of marriage and he still longed for those moments when the three of them made love.

Then he remembered.

"Tell me, *dorishan*," he said softly, kissing Sorran's shoulder and eliciting a sigh. "Why did you suggest that Arrio act as Dainon's guide?"

"I thought it a good idea," Sorran replied after a moment, rocking his body against Tanish.

The sensation was so sensual, so full of import for the night to come, that it robbed Tanish briefly of his purpose. *Which was undoubtedly Sorran's intention.* "Oh, so did I," Tanish assured him, "but I am certain you were not thinking of Arrio showing Dainon all of Teruna's undiscovered corners when you made the offer. I know you."

He stroked Sorran's chest, noting the way Sorran trembled when Tanish brushed his fingertips over Sorran's nipples, the soft moan that escaped Sorran's lips.

"I love that sound," Feyar murmured. "Nights that begin with our *dorishan* moaning thus usually end with him crying out our names."

Tanish knew he was right—his cock was already filling at the prospect of burying himself in Sorran's tight body—but he could wait. Sorran was hiding something. After more than twenty years of marriage, Tanish knew the signs.

Sorran pushed back against Tanish's stiffening shaft. "Later," he said, a plaintive edge to his voice that told Tanish his husband *wanted*.

"Now," he responded firmly, holding himself still, though his body ached to take Sorran. "What is it that you have not told us?"

Sorran pushed out a sigh. "Arrio likes Dainon. Or perhaps I should clarify that statement. Arrio *wants* Dainon."

"Oh." Tanish fell silent. He'd always known—they all had—that Arrio preferred men: their son had hidden nothing. But this was the first time he'd voiced interest in a particular man.

Our boy is truly growing up.

"And how do you feel about this?" Feyar asked Sorran. "What do you feel when you look on Dainon?"

"My senses tell me this is… right. I have counseled Arrio to get to know him. I thought this a good way for him to do so."

"I see." Tanish had to smile at the thought of Sorran playing matchmaker.

"I would feel happier about this situation if Arrio had had some experience of being with a man. He has never been with anyone," Feyar murmured. "I did ask him if he wanted some instruction from a *Seruan* when he first announced his preferences, but he refused. He has never said why."

Tanish remembered. "Arrio has always known his own mind. We have to trust his senses."

"Let us not forget," Sorran added, "he is *Seruan*. We do not know if he has revealed all that his gifts tell him, but we must trust those gifts." Another sigh slipped from his lips. "I often wonder at his parentage, especially since his gifts began to emerge."

Tanish held Sorran tightly. "Peace, *corishan*. All that matters now is that he is our son. We have brought him up as best we could. You have helped him to accept and develop his senses."

"And those senses are in conflict," Sorran said. "He is struggling to understand what is happening to him."

Feyar laughed softly. "That has nothing to do with his gifts and *everything* to do with the fact that he is young, *terushan*. Do you not recall how you felt at his age? The first stirrings of desire? The urgency of it all?"

"I think Sorran needs a reminder," Tanish concluded, grabbing his husband and rolling him until Sorran lay between them, Feyar moving to allow Sorran room. Tanish leaned over and kissed him on the mouth, Sorran feeding a sigh between his lips. Tanish drew back. "Put Arrio from your mind for now, my love." He pressed his body to Sorran's side, letting him feel the rigid heat of his length. "This is *our* time for urgent desire."

"And do you? Desire me urgently?" Sorran's voice was suddenly husky.

Feyar rolled on top of him with a growl. "Always."

Three mouths met in a lingering kiss that held the promise of a long night.

CHAPTER
FIVE

THE SEA was so cold, it made Dainon's naked flesh sing, but that did not detract from the feeling of sheer joy that filled him as he dived deep into the clear water. The early morning sunlight filtered down through the waves, and when he kicked for the surface, he burst through into the warmth above with a cry of happiness.

A few feet away, Arrio floated on his back, hands gently sculling, his face upturned toward the sun, eyes closed.

It had been years since Dainon had felt so... alive. Vibrant. Energized.

He had slept well, awaking to a chorus of birds in the garden below his balcony, all singing their hearts out to welcome the new day. Dainon had reached for his saddle bag, withdrawn a tunic, and dressed, eager to greet the dawn.

That liquor was as potent as Feyar claimed. Yet he knew it was more than the alcohol. The prospect of a day of discovery, seeing all that Teruna had to offer, sent a thrill of anticipation coursing through him.

He told himself it had nothing to do with the company he would be keeping. He knew it to be a lie as soon as the thought occurred to him, but he pushed the realization aside.

He glanced at Arrio. "I thought you came here to swim?" To Dainon's mind, Arrio seemed relaxed, without a care in the world.

Arrio turned gently in the water and swam toward Dainon with a leisurely stroke, his head dipping below the waves as he pulled back with his arms. He shook back the wet hair from his eyes and grinned, treading water. "If you want to race to the shore, I might be persuaded."

"A race?" Dainon matched Arrio's grin. "What is the prize?"

"That is for the winner to decide." His eyes gleamed mischievously. "Will you accept such a challenge?"

Dainon's heart raced, blood pumping through his veins, energy pulsing through him. "I accept."

Arrio swam until he was at Dainon's side. "On the count of three…."

Dainon readied himself, muscles tensed. At "three" he launched his body into the waves, swimming against the tide, and struck out for the shore. He cupped his hands and pulled at the water, propelling himself forward, legs kicking strongly, focusing on the beach and not his opponent. Halfway there, however, he was aware that Arrio had pulled ahead, and he redoubled his efforts. But when he scrambled out of the water, Arrio had beaten him and had already collapsed onto the damp sand, his chest heaving.

Dainon dropped onto his back beside him, gasping. "Oh, the… advantages of… youth."

Arrio found enough breath to laugh. "So it is… because I am younger… and not because I… am the stronger swimmer?"

Dainon waited until he was no longer sucking in great gulps of air before responding. "You are at least twenty years younger than I," he said with a smile. The exercise had proved exhilarating, and his whole body was warm from it.

"But I am still the winner." Arrio rolled onto his right side, the sand clinging to his nude body. Dainon tried not to let his gaze wander over the lean figure next to him, but it was an impossible task. Arrio's bronzed skin sparkled with golden sand, and on his left shoulder was a birthmark in the shape of a heart, the skin red there. But what claimed Dainon's attention was Arrio's taut belly, Arrio's toned thighs, and… Arrio's cock, which thickened before his eyes.

By the heavens, he is aroused. With a jolt of dismay, Dainon realized his own shaft lengthened and grew hard, as if in reaction to the invisible yet potent waves of desire that poured off Arrio and rippled through the air toward Dainon.

"You are," he admitted, his voice cracking. Inside he was a seething mass of tension. *And what will you claim as your prize, Prince Arrio?*

Slowly Arrio rose from the sand and crawled over to where Dainon lay. He stared down at Dainon, eyes bright, cheeks pink. "Then as the winner, I demand…." He paused, his face inches from Dainon's, lips parted, his skin glowing in the light that reflected off the golden sand.

When nothing more came forth from Arrio's mouth, Dainon let out a low noise of discomfort. "What?" he whispered. Time seemed to have frozen, the moment poised on a knife edge as though all creation awaited Arrio's response. Dainon held his breath, his stomach churning.

Arrio smiled. "A kiss."

Dainon stiffened, the words ready to tumble from his lips to tell his young companion to claim some other trophy, that Dainon had different... appetites, but what came out shocked him to his core. "Then take your prize, Your Highness."

Arrio caught his breath, and slowly, so slowly, he pressed his lips to Dainon's, his mouth closed, eyes open wide, inhaling deeply through his nostrils as though he were breathing Dainon in.

Dainon closed his eyes and accepted the chaste kiss, holding himself still, lost in disbelief that he had allowed this. No revulsion arose in him. On the contrary, Arrio's lips were soft and warm, his fragrant sun-heated skin stirring Dainon's senses.

It was another shock for Dainon to realize he was enjoying the kiss.

When Arrio's tongue parted Dainon's lips, he froze for a moment and then opened with a low moan, unable to deny him entry. Eyes still tight shut, he slid his tongue deep between Arrio's lips, his heart leaping at the groan of pleasure that rolled out of Arrio. Dainon was drowning in that kiss, lost in its sensuality, the heat of it, the... rightness of it. *How long have I remained unkissed? Not since I had Tarisa in my arms, that last time we made love.*

Dainon's mouth was suddenly filled with the taste of ashes.

He opened his eyes and pushed at Arrio, sending him toppling to the sand. Dainon scrambled to his feet and stared at Arrio, aghast.

Arrio knelt up on the sand, the pain in those deep blue eyes all too visible. "Forgive me," he begged. "I acted unwisely and I have wronged you." Arrio was trembling.

Dainon let out a sigh. "No, Arrio. There is nothing to forgive."

Arrio shook his head. "You recoiled from me. I have offended you," he insisted.

"I should not have reacted so harshly. It was simply that your kiss triggered a... memory."

Arrio's eyes widened. "A painful one, judging by your reaction." He bowed his head. "I am sorry."

When Dainon saw tears sparkle on Arrio's cheeks, his chest constricted. *For a second time, I have caused him to shed tears.* He lurched forward and pulled Arrio into his arms, holding him against his damp chest. "The fault is not yours," he whispered. *And until my recollection, I was enjoying your kiss.* The realization hit him hard, but he could not deny it.

Then it happened again, shock rippling through him, the same jolt he had felt the first time he had touched Arrio. Dainon's skin tingled and his balls tightened, his sac drawing up to his body. His shaft throbbed with a life of its own.

Arrio's body shook, tremors jolting him, and Dainon was pulled back into the moment. He released Arrio and sat on the sand. In that instant, the sensations ceased and he was left shaking.

Arrio sat facing him, wearing an expression of concern.

Dainon was not about to share the… phenomenon. *How can I explain something I do not understand?* One glance at Arrio's face was enough to decide him to speak further. *He deserves to know of my past, if only to put his mind at ease.*

"I told you that my wife was taken from me." Dainon's throat seized and he swallowed hard.

"Yes." Arrio watched him, wiping the moisture from his cheeks with his hand.

"A plague swept through Kandor. It claimed my wife, Tarisa, and our little son, Merron." Dainon paused, unsure of how to continue. "Since her death sixteen years ago, there has been no one else. The last time I shared a kiss was… when we made love before she became ill." *But that was not the last time I kissed her.* Ice slid down his spine as Dainon recalled pressing his lips to hers before wrapping her in her burial robes. He quashed his grief and drew in a deep breath. "Your kiss simply stirred my memory."

"Then I am sorry to have caused you such pain. I was too bold. I should not have acted so… wantonly." Arrio bowed his head once more.

Dainon could not let him continue thus. He lifted Arrio's chin with his fingers. "You did nothing wrong," he insisted, gazing into his eyes. The urge to be truthful swelled within his chest. "There was nothing wanton about your desire to kiss me. You are young, Arrio, and the young are often impulsive. I was the same, believe me. You simply acted according to your body's urges. And there were two of us caught up in that kiss. You may have initiated it, but I reciprocated. I kissed you back." Though why he had done so, Dainon had no idea. He could only remember that it had felt right.

"Then… all is well between us?" Arrio locked gazes with him, anxiety etched on his face.

Dainon cursed himself for causing Arrio pain and worry. He nodded. "All is well." As if to convince Arrio of the truth of his statement, Dainon leaned forward and kissed him on the mouth, no more than a gentle brushing of lips.

Why did I do that? The action had seemed as natural as breathing.

Arrio sighed against his mouth, and the tension seemed to melt from his body. He sat on his haunches. "I am glad," he said quietly. "I like you, Dainon. I would like to be your friend."

For a moment Dainon was tempted to respond that Arrio's kiss had not been that of a friend, but he held back. *Did not my own reaction share some of his... passion?* "That is my wish, also."

Arrio tilted his head to one side. "You kissed me back," he said, echoing Dainon's words. When Dainon nodded, Arrio smiled. "You have caused me to wonder. Have... have you kissed a man before today?"

A shiver trickled down Dainon's spine. "No. You are the first." *And why I should have kissed you the way I did is still a mystery.* It seemed that Arrio created confusion in Dainon's breast at every turn.

Arrio's face flushed. "You were my first, also."

Dainon stared at him. "Truly?"

Arrio nodded slowly. "I have always known I like men," he said honestly, "but I have never acted on my desires. There was no one who stirred my senses. Until yesterday." He bowed his head, but then regarded Dainon from beneath long lashes. "It shames me to admit it, but from the moment I first saw you, I... I wanted you." He bit his lip. "Perhaps I should have kept my desires to myself." Arrio focused on the ground.

Dainon caught the bitter edge in Arrio's voice and hastened to reassure him. "Listen to me, Arrio. There is nothing wrong with wanting someone. Nothing at all. And if I had not wanted to be kissed, I assure you, the situation would have ended very differently." When Arrio snapped his head up, Dainon gave him a grim smile. "You were very perceptive. I *am* a warrior. You cross a warrior at your own peril."

Arrio chuckled. Then his eyes widened. "You... wanted me to kiss you?"

Dainon's heartbeat quickened. "I did." He could not lie. He waited, stomach tight, for Arrio to respond, but he remained silent. Relief surged through him. "Perhaps we should return to the palace."

"Perhaps we should wash off the sand first," Arrio suggested. "Unless you want to ride back like this?"

Dainon winced. Sand had a habit of infiltrating the most awkward places. "Let us wash."

Arrio stood and walked to the water's edge, and Dainon watched as he bathed.

For a man who has never desired men, I seem to enjoy gazing at Arrio when he is naked. The realization sent heat spreading throughout his body, and with it came the recollection of Arrio's kiss. *What would have happened if I had not broken away?*

Dainon did not want to consider that.

Arrio turned and beckoned. "Are you going to stand there, or are you going to join me?"

Dainon sighed before walking over to him.

Heavens help me, but I want to kiss him again.

ARRIO SAT on the stone bench in the garden under the shade of the *Dorindar* tree, its fragrant leaves hanging low, stirred by the warm evening breeze. The air was filled with birdsong and the trickling of the fountain, and normally the sound of the water splashing would have filled Arrio with quiet joy. That evening, however, Arrio's mind was preoccupied.

Dainon was with Timur in the stables, grooming his mare. Arrio had observed him there, as he took care of Tarrea. It was obvious how much love and affection he had for his mount, and watching him pet the horse and talk to her warmed Arrio's heart. *He is a good man.* Good enough that he'd reacted graciously when Arrio had acted so rashly. *Why did I kiss him?* A groan forced its way out of Arrio when he recalled the expression on Dainon's face as he sprang to his feet and pushed Arrio from him.

"I knew something was wrong."

Arrio spun around at the sound of his *papi*'s voice. Feyar was standing by the fountain, Sorran at his side, and both men were frowning.

Arrio shook his head. "It is nothing. Be at peace, my fathers." He rose, his heart pounding.

Sorran held up a hand. "Not so fast. We are here because both of us have been concerned about you ever since you returned to the palace this morning. When you returned from your ride this afternoon and your mood had not changed, our anxiety increased. It is obvious something happened, so do not deny it. We know you too well.

Arrio slumped on the bench and covered his face with his hands. "I brought shame upon myself and you." He felt the comforting weight of Sorran's hand on his shoulder, and Feyar's on his back.

"Let us decide if that is true," Sorran said quietly. "Tell us what lies on your heart."

Arrio sat up and sighed in resignation. He reached up, plucked a bronze leaf from a low-hanging branch, and rubbed it between his fingers. The familiar citrus scent invaded his nostrils, bringing him calm.

"Clever boy." Feyar rubbed his back. "It took me years to discover the healing properties of the *dorindar*. This is why I come here when there is discord."

Arrio let out a low chuckle in spite of his previous agitation. "Discord would dare to find its way into the palace?"

Sorran laughed. "My husbands and I may rule in Teruna, but we are married men, after all. All marriages encounter a little discord now and again." He cupped Arrio's cheek and gazed at him with love. "And what has brought discord into *your* life?"

Arrio breathed in more of the sweet fragrance that surrounded them, and told them of his actions on the beach. They listened without comment until he was finished.

Feyar sighed. "It seems to me your only crime is being young and inexperienced, my son."

"I agree," Sorran added. "And when I saw Dainon, he did not appear to be upset by your action. Perhaps this is not as shameful as you feel it to be."

"I agree that Dainon reacted unexpectedly. During the hours we spent riding through the countryside this afternoon, he did not once allude to the incident, and appeared at ease with me," Arrio admitted. "But he has created such confusion in me."

"In what way?" Feyar asked.

"He had a wife, there has been no one in his life since her death, he has never kissed another man—all these things I understand—but...." Arrio closed his eyes, recalling that heart-stopping moment when Dainon's tongue slid between his lips, his unguarded manner as he returned the kiss, the soft moan that spoke of sensual pleasure. "By the Maker, the way he kissed me...." *Did I imagine the hint of heat in that embrace?*

"Arrio, look at me."

Slowly Arrio opened his eyes and regarded his *papi*. Feyar's dark eyes were focused on him.

"You kissed him. He returned it. Leave it there."

Arrio's chest tightened. "And what if I do not want to leave it there?" he whispered. "What if my senses tell me there is… more?" One simple kiss, and yet it had awakened in him such a yearning, as if his body had lain dormant, only to spark into life with the touch of Dainon's lips to his.

"You have set Dainon on a new path. It is now up to him to decide if he wishes to proceed," Sorran said simply. "You have opened his eyes to new possibilities, that much is certain, but you *cannot* force him to seek more. I trust your senses, but Feyar is right. You are young. I know how impatient the young can be, but this is something you must learn." He smiled. "I was the same at your age, believe me."

Arrio stared at him. "You are telling me to let Dainon set the pace?" When both Sorran and Feyar nodded, Arrio lurched to his feet, hands clenched at his sides. "But what if he does nothing? What if he decides this is not a path he wishes to follow?" His heart sank. "Since this morning, I have exerted so much effort to act normally around him, to put him at his ease. But inside I ache. I watch him, my heart hammering in my breast to know if he wants me too." Everything was happening so swiftly, plunging him into a world of tortuous emotions.

Feyar sprang to his feet and put his arms around Arrio, drawing him into a tight embrace. Arrio sagged into it, his head on Feyar's shoulder.

"I know, I know," Feyar whispered. "It hurts. You want him, my son. Your body and mind tell you there could be something between you, and patience is not one of your virtues. But you must be strong."

Arrio straightened and looked *Papi* in the eye. "I do not know if I am capable of such strength."

Feyar kissed his forehead. "You are more capable than you realize."

Sorran stood, joined them, and put his arm around Arrio. "Yes, you are. And whatever befalls you, your fathers will be at your side to support and love you."

Arrio smiled and kissed them both. "I love you so much." He hugged them and then released them. Arrio held his head high. "Perhaps I should see to our guest."

"And there is our Arrio," Feyar said, returning his smile. "You make us proud."

Arrio walked with them toward the door that led into the palace, affecting a calm demeanor that he certainly did not feel.

All of this emotion, unleashed by a kiss.

It was only then that another thought occurred to him.

And if there is more… can I survive it?

CHAPTER
SIX

KEI STARED at his father, his heart like a stone. "I am not ready," he whispered.

King Beron crossed the chamber and grasped him by the shoulders, looking into his eyes. He smiled. "I did not say you are to take the throne of Vancor today, my son. But it is time to prepare yourself, at least mentally."

Kei swallowed. "But you have years left to reign as king, father."

King Beron's expression grew more sober. "My sweet boy. Our healers are good, but even they cannot fight the passage of time. My body is wearing out, and there is naught they can do to stop it. You must accept the situation. The day is coming when you shall be king of Vancor." He released Kei and returned to his chair at the table, strewn with scrolls. The king sat gingerly, weariness cloaking his movements.

He seems so tired. Kei gazed at him, taking in his long gray hair, his lined face. In that moment Kei knew his father was right. He had known his father spoke truly as soon as he had felt his hands on Kei's shoulders. Kei had to prepare himself for what was coming. It was inevitable.

There were times when the gift of Truthspeak was a burden.

Then sorrow gave way to a wave of anger he could not hold back.

"How can I be king?" Kei protested. "I know so little of life beyond the palace walls."

His father scowled but said nothing. Kei knew his argument was a valid one. He was twenty years old and yet he had no experience of the world.

At least my brother got to see what lies beyond our kingdom. He is the lucky one.

Kei loved it when Sorran came on a visit. Two or three times a year, he made the trip from Teruna with one or both of his husbands, and Kei looked forward to their visits with such longing. He listened to their tales of Teruna with rapt attention, but always with a pang of jealousy, for which he berated himself constantly. Kei loved seeing the three men together, their love for each other evident in their expressions, words, and actions. He had never met his nephew, Arrio, although Sorran spoke often of their son. On more than one occasion, Kei had begged his parents to let him visit Teruna, but each time his mother had refused instantly and he could not sway her.

But perhaps this changes things. Perhaps my father may succeed where I have failed.

It was worth a try.

Kei walked to his father's chair and knelt beside it. "Father, I have an idea."

The king turned his head slowly, focusing on Kei. His lips twitched. "I have come to dread your ideas." His eyes regained a little of their brightness.

Kei rejoiced inwardly to see his father's change of mood. "What do you mean?" he replied with a grin.

King Beron snorted. "Let me think. There was the time you decided to saddle a *rastor*."

"That was a good idea!" Kei retorted. "And it would have worked if you had not taken away my saddle."

"Kei," his father said patiently, "one does not saddle a six-foot-tall bird with a three-foot beak and a thirty-foot wingspan in an attempt to fly. If we were meant to fly, the Maker would furnish us with wings too. But apart from that, a *rastor* could break your arm with one snap of that beak. You were lucky that one of the guards saw you and brought it to my attention."

"But I'd *trained* it," Kei whined. "Do you know how long it took me to get that bird to trust me? How much fish I had to feed it?" Months of preparation, lost when the palace guards had circled Kei's new friend and forced it into the air. Kei had never seen it again.

The king laughed. "I have no doubt of that. At least it explained why fish continued to disappear from the palace kitchens." He folded his arms across his chest. "Then there was the time you decided to take a *coutar* as a pet, without telling anyone."

"It was to be a surprise." Kei pouted. He did not understand why his parents and the royal advisers had reacted with such panic when they'd discovered the animal in the walled garden below Kei's window.

"Kei, a *coutar* may have seemed appealing, with all that fur and those huge eyes, but it was five times your size, with claws and teeth. And you were seven years old at the time."

He sighed. *No one* understood, with the exception of Sorran, although he had joined in the public display of horror at Kei's actions. In the privacy of Kei's chamber, however, he had roared with laughter. Sorran knew: no animal would harm Kei.

"So you will forgive me," his father continued, "if I greet the prospect of another of your ideas with apprehension." He chuckled. "I am ready. Tell me the worst."

Kei sat up on the chair beside his father. "I want to visit Sorran." When his father's eyes widened, Kei pressed on hurriedly. "I will not become King without seeing something of the world beyond Vancor. Beyond this palace, if I speak truthfully." He had never set foot outside the palace grounds. Attracting the *rastor* in the first place had been nothing short of a miracle.

I am supposed to go to Teruna. That was knowledge not to be shared with his father. King Beron would not understand.

The king scowled, but then his features relaxed. "You are right. And I have let this situation continue for long enough."

"What situation?"

Both Kei and his father stiffened at the sound of Queen Vasha's voice as she entered the chamber.

Kei rose to his feet and bowed his head as always. "Mother."

"I came to find you, Kei. You were not in your room." She looked from him to his father. "And I repeat: what situation?"

King Beron turned to regard his wife. "Kei and I have been discussing his future. He is going on a visit to Teruna." He set his jaw.

Kei gaped at his father in shock, too startled to utter a word. His heart soared.

Queen Vasha stiffened. "No, he is not," she said through gritted teeth.

Kei's momentary joy seeped from him. *I should know better than to hope.* Then he glanced at his father and froze. King Beron's face was grim, his eyes cool.

All the hairs on Kei's arms stood on end when Queen Vasha gasped and pressed her hands over her heart.

Slowly his father rose to his feet. "I have let you have your way for far too long." His expression softened. "I understand, my love, truly. Kei is the child you thought you would never carry, and as such you have protected and watched over him since the day he was born. You have coddled him, swaddled him, and prevented him from taking a single risk. Yet despite your efforts, our son has prevailed, sometimes spectacularly so. He is of an age now where we have to think of the future, which for him is to rule this kingdom."

"What has that to do with Kei visiting Teruna?" she responded. "He sees his brother when they visit us."

"That is not the point and you know it. Do not think to prevaricate with me."

Kei saw for the first time that his parents were as stubborn as each other.

"Kei is going to visit Teruna. He needs new experiences if he is to mature as an adult." When she opened her mouth to respond, his father lifted his hand. "I know he is gifted. It may be that his gifts rival Sorran's, but that does not mean he is mature. He meets no one except those who dwell within the palace grounds. It is time for him to undertake this journey."

Queen Vasha stared at him in silence, her lip quivering. "You mean this," she said at last. The king nodded, and she sighed. "I know you speak the truth. It shall be as you say. I will organize the carriages and a royal entourage. He can leave in a day or—"

"No."

Kei swiveled to gape anew at his father.

His mother did the same. "What do you mean, no?" she demanded.

"Kei will travel on horseback—alone."

Kei could not believe the path his life had just taken. "Oh yes," he whispered.

"Alone?" His mother glared at her husband. "He is a royal prince, who—"

"Who is unknown beyond the boundaries of Vancor," the king concluded. "None shall harm him. He may travel in safety—taking precautions, of course," he added with a firm stare to Kei, who bobbed his head immediately. "Think of the surprise when he arrives at the palace. No, it is time. Kei needs to do this." He smiled at Kei. "I hear no arguments from you."

Kei grinned. "Nor will you. This... this is wonderful, father. Thank you. I never hoped to be allowed to do this."

"And that is the problem. For a prince to think thus is unacceptable. So, travel to Teruna. Spend time with your brother. Live a little." His eyes gleamed. "Though maybe not as much as your brother did, his first journey out of Vancor."

"Why—what did he do?"

His mother huffed. "He met and fell in love with two men."

"And set in motion events that led to Kei's birth." The king regarded her keenly. "For which we will be forever grateful."

His mother sighed. "You speak the truth. I cannot deny this." She held out her arms to Kei, who walked into them. She enfolded him in a tight embrace. "Your father is right. You must do this. I ask only that you take care and return to me safely." She kissed his forehead.

"I shall," he promised. His head was spinning with the prospect.

So much awaits me on this journey. He closed his eyes and drank in her familiar scent, trying not to think about those things he had kept hidden from his parents. He had dreamed long ago of what was to pass, but as the years had gone by and he saw nothing but the palace grounds, he had begun to think his dreams false. In the space of one hour, however, everything had changed. Not that he would share that.

They do not need to know everything.

They certainly did not need to know that Kei's destiny awaited him in Teruna. Something pulled him there—what exactly, he did not know—and he could not wait to discover what lay ahead for him. He had seen signs in his dreams, although they had made little sense.

All I can recall is a pair of deep blue eyes, and a bear wearing a sword.

Then he pushed the images from his mind.

It shall all become clear when I reach Teruna. Have I not seen the truth of it?

KEI PLACED more wood on the fire and then lay down on his rough blanket, gazing up at the heavens. His first night of freedom, and he doubted the air had ever tasted so sweet. Above him stretched out the vast velvet canopy strewn with stars. Kei stared in wonder at their number.

How many times have I looked up at the night sky, and yet I have never noticed such magnificence? He was humbled, in awe of the grandeur surrounding him. His senses were heightened: each scent, each sound, each view awakened in him a renewed appreciation for this new world.

He was alone in open country; it had been hours since he'd glimpsed anyone, and they had been at a distance. His horse had eaten and was tethered to a tree, a blanket slung across her back. Kei had dined on bread and fruit, and had been delighted to find a flask of Merrova tucked into his saddle bag, doubtless meant as a surprise and probably left there by his father. Sated and warmed by the wine, he was enjoying the night in all its glory. The breeze stirring the flaps of his tent was soft, carrying with it sweet and spicy aromas unknown to Kei but there to be discovered. He could hear the river beside which he'd camped, the trickling of water spilling over rocks and boulders. Bathing in it had been yet another experience to heighten his appreciation of his newfound freedom.

A pang of guilt stabbed him as he recalled his farewell to his parents. There was so much he had kept hidden from them, but that had been Sorran's counsel since they had first discussed Kei's dreams.

Mother would only have worried.

Kei closed his eyes, as if that would banish the regrets that pierced his conscience, but he knew it was to no avail. He had been afflicted with such feelings since he was a boy.

He had been less than eight years old when he'd taken Sorran aside during one of his visits, demanding they talk. Kei had been confused and frightened by recent events, but some sense deep within him bade him not to share his revelations with his parents. Once Sorran had heard him speak, he had agreed: there were some things parents did *not* need to know. Especially the fact that their little boy had but to lay a hand on a person to know if they were telling the truth.

It had not been long before Kei realized that Truthspeak was a two-edged sword. Once he had accepted the nature of this gift—that nothing could be hidden from him—he had been relieved. This was truly a gift, to always know when others lied to him.

Only when he ventured into the palace harem for the first time had the full import of his gift dawned on him.

Kei had been sixteen. That first sight of a male nude body had been enough to make him aware of a predilection for men, and he had been eager to learn more. He had chosen a young man not much older than himself, with a firm body and a beautiful face, and a night of sexual pleasure and sensual discovery beckoned. The colors that surrounded his chosen bedmate spoke of desire and passion. But one touch of his tutor's hand had shattered Kei's illusions. There was *nothing* his companion could hide from him. His feelings, thoughts, emotions, fears, hopes—*all* were bare to Kei's gift and there was no escape. In that moment, the coming night no longer held the promise of ecstasy, but the realization that intimacy would bring with it only discomfiture, frustration, and pain. To know someone thus was to share everything about them, every aspect of them both hidden and seen, and Kei did not think he could bear that.

In that instant, he saw his future mapped out before him, and it was a lonely path.

There had been occasions during the last four years when he had succumbed to his desires and visited the harem, but each time had ended in the same manner: his fears had overtaken him and Kei had fled. In the still of the night, when his body ached with desire, Kei pushed down hard on such urges, telling himself that his hand was enough to satisfy them. He forced from his mind the scenes from the harem, where he'd watched the sensual couplings of two men, watched bodies slick with sweat and seed, heard their low cries as one spilled inside the other....

It did not matter that Kei ached to be taken thus, to be pinned beneath someone who entered him, filling him completely. It did not matter that he yearned for the touch of another's hand on his body, caressing him, loving him.

Such things were not for Kei. Whatever destiny awaited him in Teruna, he was certain that love, passion, and sexual fulfillment were not part of it.

He fell asleep under the stars, his cheeks streaked with tears.

Chapter
Seven

Dainon got down from the horse and patted the stallion's rump. "You were right. He's a beautiful horse, and so swift." He tethered the horse to a column of stone and observed his surroundings halfheartedly. His mind was on Tarrea. Dainon had spent the night in her stall, after Timur had sent a message that she was unwell. He'd lain awake most of the night, rubbing her down to alleviate the night sweats and making sure she drank plenty of water. Timur was unsure what ailed her, which had only served to exacerbate Dainon's anxiety.

"He should be," Arrio said with a faint smile. "His mother was Nerita, my *papa*'s horse, and there were few that could outrun her in her day." He regarded Dainon keenly. "I know where your thoughts lie, but worrying can do nothing for her." He looped his horse's reins around the same column and secured them.

Dainon expelled his tension with a sigh. "You are right, of course. And thank you for staying with me for so long. You should have been in your comfortable bed, rather than sitting on bales of straw in a stable." More than that, Arrio had listened while Dainon had talked, sharing his memories of Tarisa and Merron. Doing so had proved cathartic. For the first time in many years, Dainon had been able to speak without suffering the habitual paroxysms of grief that so often had laid waste to him.

"I could not let you sit all night, your mind in turmoil." Arrio patted his back. "And if my presence was some small comfort to you, then I am glad of it." He removed his cloak and laid it across his stallion's back.

Comfort. If he but knew….

It was his fourth day in Teruna, and Dainon was no nearer to understanding why Arrio affected him so. Each time they were together, his emotions were conflicted. Something deep within Dainon stirred as though trying to awaken, some primal force waiting to be unleashed.

I fear such an unleashing and yet... I yearn for it.

Dainon shook the thought from his mind and concentrated on their surroundings. "What is this place?" They stood in the middle of what appeared to be ruins. A few columns of stone remained upright, but the rest had fallen, cracking the flags with their weight. Ivy and other creeping plants had crawled over nearly every surface, but he could see one area where the growth had been cleared away. Trees had sprung up, their branches providing a dense canopy over part of the ruins, preventing any penetration of light. An almost sweet aroma permeated the air, a heady fragrance that suffused him with a feeling of....

Dainon stilled, trying to pin down what he was feeling. Then it came to him.

Power. The ruins, the air, the foliage—everything seemed to pulse with power, something that reached out to him, tugged him, beckoned him....

Arrio's hand on his arm shocked him back into the present. "Dainon?"

He breathed deeply. "Forgive me, but there is something about this place." He shivered.

Arrio regarded him steadily. "You feel it?" When Dainon nodded, he heaved a sigh and glanced around him. "This is the ruined temple I spoke of the day we met. This is where my fathers came upon me."

"Here?"

"My *papa-turo* says he heard my cries and brought the others here. My mother lay dying with me in her arms."

Dainon stared at him. "But... supposing no one had heard you. You would have perished."

Arrio smiled. "From what *Papi* says, they were meant to find me." He pulled down his robe to bare his left shoulder, revealing his birthmark. "You see this? *Papa-turo* bears the same mark, only his was drawn onto his skin as a result of one of his dreams." He pulled up the robe to cover himself.

"Dreams?" Dainon repeated. He had heard tales of *Seruani* who experienced prophetic dreams. "Is Prince Sorran *Seruan* also?"

"He has dreams where he sees things that will come to pass. It has always been so. He has other gifts also." Arrio tilted his head to one side. "Do you want to hear more of this?"

"I do." Dainon was barely able to keep his enthusiasm in check.

Arrio gestured toward the trees where the ground underneath was thick with moss and leaves. "Let us sit there awhile, and we can talk."

Dainon followed him and both sat cross-legged. "There is so much I do not understand."

"I know. We have spoken of the *Seruani*, but you should know—I am *Seruan*." When Dainon stared at him, Arrio gave him a smile tinged with sorrow. "I do not know which of my parents was *Seruan*—nothing was known of my father, and though my fathers made extensive inquiries, they could find no one who knew my mother."

"You wish you had known them," Dainon said, his heart going out to Arrio.

Arrio nodded. "Of course. Please, do not think me unhappy with my family. I love my fathers, but...." He stared out at the ruins. "I have so many questions. What was she doing here? Where was my father? Where is he now? Does he know I exist? What gifts did they possess?"

"Do you... do you have gifts?" He wanted to know more about Arrio.

Arrio regarded him thoughtfully. "I do not speak of such things with anyone, save for my fathers, but my senses tell me it is right to share with you."

There it was again, that feeling of something waiting to be set free....

Dainon repressed a shudder and focused on Arrio. "I am honored."

"There are times when I see things in dreams, events yet to happen. My *papa-turo* is helping me to recognize those dreams that have import, but it is not easy. He tells me to write down what passes in my dreams when I awaken, but I do not always do this." He smiled. "I am a poor student."

Dainon chuckled. "Even knowing you for such a short time, I doubt that." Arrio was clearly very intelligent.

Arrio laughed. "You are too kind." He leaned back, his weight on his arms, and the motion stretched out his lean body.

Dainon tried hard not to stare. "That is an amazing gift."

Arrio laughed once more. "It is certainly less strange than my other ability."

"Which is what?"

Arrio hesitated, his gaze locked on Dainon. Finally he let out a heavy sigh. "I am able to use my senses to locate various... resources."

"What kind of resources?" Dainon's interest was piqued.

Arrio shrugged. "Water, oil, minerals, precious stones.... Such knowledge is then shared with those who have need of it: those who supply the kingdom with oil for cooking and heating, those who make jewelry, farmers who wish to irrigate their land...." He peered at Dainon. "You think me strange?"

Dainon thought him truly wonderful.

"Not at all," he stressed. "I find your gifts awe-inspiring."

Arrio's face flushed. "There are many in Teruna who possess more astounding gifts than I."

His humility was endearing.

"When I first heard the tales about Teruna, I thought them unbelievable, I must admit."

Arrio nodded. "I can understand that reaction. How should one react to tales of power and magic?"

Magic....

Dainon got up and walked toward the part of the ruins that had been cleared of plant life. A white stone altar, its surface cracked, sat at one end of the temple. He crouched low to peer at a carving on its side. Three hands, each clasping the wrist of the next to form a circle.

Where have I seen this?

Then it came to him. "There is a hanging behind the thrones in the audience chamber," he said slowly, "that bears this same image."

Arrio rose and joined him, bending to run his fingers over the carving. "This represents the Bond of Three. Once, long ago, it was a symbol of the *Seruani*, a symbol of great power. *Papa* found reference to it in ancient scrolls." He shivered. "People still speak of what came to pass the day of my fathers' wedding. That moment when they joined hands, the strange light that surrounded them...."

When they joined hands....

Dainon could not repress the shudder that coursed through him.

"Dainon? What is wrong?"

He straightened, Arrio copying him. He faced the prince, his stomach clenching. "I am a simple man, a warrior. I have no gifts, but... I have... felt such power."

Arrio stared at him. "Tell me," he said quickly.

Dainon swallowed. "I felt it for the first time the day I met my wife. Our hands touched, and there was... something, so powerful, it shook me."

"What do you think it meant?" Arrio's blue eyes never left him.

Dainon's heart stuttered. "I believed once that it was a sign that I had met my soul mate, but now...."

"You no longer believe it?"

Dainon's throat tightened. *I cannot tell him. He will think me mad.*

"Dainon." Arrio moved closer, until Dainon could feel the heat of his body. "Tell me," he whispered.

"I... I felt it again."

"When?" Arrio demanded.

"The day we met. On the beach. When your hand touched mine."

Arrio's eyes widened. "Was that the only time?"

Dainon shook his head. "When I held you after our race. The same pulse of energy, jolting through me."

Arrio shifted closer. "Touch me again." His voice was low, demanding.

"What?" Dainon's head was spinning, his skin tingling.

"Now, Dainon. Touch me now."

Heavens help him, he could not ignore Arrio's demand.

Dainon slowly put his arms around Arrio and drew him close. Arrio brought his hands to rest on Dainon's shoulders and....

That same lightning rocketed through him, only stronger than ever, and Dainon trembled at its power.

"Kiss me."

Dainon did not hesitate. He brought his mouth to meet Arrio's, lips parting, tongue plunging deep in exploration, lost to everything but the urgent desire to kiss him.

Arrio moaned softly, feeding the sound between his lips, his hands moving to cup Dainon's head, pulling him deeper. Dainon marveled at the taste of him, the feel of Arrio's body against his, the rightness of having Arrio in his arms....

The feel of Arrio's hard length pressing against his own thickening cock.

He staggered back, releasing Arrio and staring at him in consternation, fighting to regain his composure. *By the Maker....*

Arrio breathed deeply, his chest rising and falling rapidly. "You stopped." He tilted his head. "Did you feel it again?"

"Yes," Dainon whispered. His body still tingled, his shaft hard.

"What do you think it means?" Arrio appeared calmer.

"I do not know." Except Dainon knew that to be a lie.

"Do you find me attractive, Dainon?"

The change in direction made him his head reel. "I... I am not attracted to men." His heartbeat raced.

Arrio smiled. "That is not what I asked. Let me try another question. Have you ever found another man attractive?"

Dainon opened his mouth to tell Arrio *no, never*, but the words died on his lips.

Arrio's eyes gleamed. "Who was he?"

I had all but forgotten him. "He was a warrior. It was years ago," he added, as if that mattered.

Arrio nodded. "Did you act on this attraction?"

"No!" Dainon gaped. "I would never have done such a thing."

"Why not?" Arrio asked simply. "Were you still with your wife?"

"It was after her death, but...." Dainon struggled to explain himself. "He was lower in rank than I. To have acted in those circumstances would have been wrong."

Arrio's face lit up. "Ah, but what if he had not been? What then? Would you have pursued him?"

Dainon knew the answer, but he could not give voice to it.

No, I was too focused on my grief.

Arrio caressed his cheek, soft as a whisper. "I have to confess. I find you very attractive." He bit his bottom lip. "Though I should not have revealed that."

"Why not?" Although Dainon had known Arrio but a short time, the prince did not strike him as one who held back when it came to sharing what was on his mind. The thought made him smile inwardly. He liked Arrio's candor and enthusiasm.

"My *papa-turo* told me to stop pushing, to let you set the pace."

Dainon stilled, Arrio's hand cupping his face. "You spoke of me to your father?"

Arrio nodded. "Except he already knew, of course."

The confession made Dainon's heart sink. *How can I look them in the eye again?*

"Will you answer my question now?"

"Ask," he said quietly. *Please, do not ask me why touching you should cause such a reaction in me.* The logical implication was there, but Dainon was not ready to face it.

"Do you find me attractive?"

If I answer truthfully, what will happen?

More importantly, why did it feel as though the truth would catapult him into an unknown world of powerful, overwhelming sensations?

Dainon inhaled, drawing in his courage. "Yes." He tensed, awaiting Arrio's reaction, but to his relief, the prince simply nodded. When Arrio relaxed, it became obvious that he shared Dainon's relief.

He is as nervous as I. The realization eased Dainon's tension.

"Thank you for being honest," Arrio said at last. "And for giving me a goal."

The skin on Dainon's back prickled. "Goal?"

Arrio grinned. "Did you imagine you could tell me you feel something for me and that I would do nothing with such knowledge?" He leaned forward and kissed Dainon slowly on the lips. When he drew back, that grin was still in evidence.

Dainon had a feeling his fears of unleashing a primal force had just been realized.

Arrio laughed heartily. "But enough of such things. Would you like to see more of the city?"

Dainon restrained himself from sagging with relief. "That would be good."

What have I done?

He could not decide whether the knots in his belly were due to fear or anticipation.

KEI LOVED the city of Teruna. The streets were cobbled and wide, filled with noise and color. And there were so many people. After his quiet, two-day journey, the bustle and activity around him were truly welcome. He'd entered the city through a huge gateway in the white stone wall, and decided to get off his horse and lead her through the streets that led up toward the palace.

Everywhere he looked there were happy faces, not that he had need to see their expressions. The colors surrounding every person he encountered were evidence enough. Teruna was alive with love, joy, and peace, and it gladdened his heart to see it. Now and again he glimpsed someone who was ill or saddened, but on the whole, the city was a sea of cream, gold, deep blue, and white. He knew from experience that such colors were positive. When he'd shared with Sorran the belief that he was going mad because he was seeing things, his relief at Sorran's response had been overwhelming.

Sorran saw the colors too.

Joy bubbled up inside him to see such happiness around him. *I think I shall stay here awhile.* He was in no hurry to return to his palatial prison, for that was what life in Vancor had amounted to. He harbored the hope that making this journey would provide the catalyst for change once he returned.

Kei strolled through a stone archway and found himself in a wide square, full of stalls where vendors sold all manner of merchandise. He marveled at the vibrant colors of silks and woven fabrics, the delicate wood carvings, and the aromatic spices. He watched as a man sketched the scene before him, capturing the essence of the city on thick parchment. Kei stood still, gazing at the wondrous view.

Then he froze, his brain unable to process what he was seeing.

Two men were walking away from him toward the street that led up the hill. They were roughly the same height, nothing remarkable about them....

Except they had no colors.

Kei blinked. He blinked again. The men were about to pass from his view, but one more glance was enough to confirm he had not imagined it. They stood out against the backdrop, no colors lapping around them.

In his entire life, Kei had never met one person whose aura was not visible to him, and this new phenomenon left him shaken and apprehensive.

What does this mean?

Then he realized there was someone close by who could answer such a question.

Kei climbed onto his horse and maneuvered through the busy streets, winding his way up the hill to the white palace whose walls glowed in the late afternoon sun. When he reached it, he dismounted and tethered his horse to a post before walking up to the huge door bracketed by two guards. Before he got halfway, however, one of the guards approached him.

"What is your business here?"

Kei stilled. "I am here to see Prince Sorran." He fought the urge to demand to see Sorran, his mind still in confusion from his experience in the square.

The guard arched his eyebrows. "Indeed. For what purpose?" He smirked. "You cannot simply walk into the palace."

Kei gave him a patient smile. "Prince Sorran will see me."

The other guard chuckled. "Oh, he will, will he?" He glanced at his fellow guard and grinned before returning his attention to Kei. "And why should he want to see you?"

Kei had never encountered such an attitude. "Because I am his brother?" He tried hard to school his features.

The guard stared at him. "Prince Sorran does not have a brother."

"Yes, he does," the other guard contradicted him. "He lives in—"

"Vancor," Kei interjected, his patience beginning to wear thin. When both guards stared at him, he huffed out a breath. "I have a solution. One of you will escort me to the royal audience chamber or wherever you wish to leave me, while someone goes to my brother and informs him that Prince Kei is here. You may remain with me until Prince Sorran arrives." When they hesitated, he pulled himself upright and speared them with an intense gaze. "Although you may not wish to do so when my brother hears how I have been treated."

One of the guards regarded him carefully and cleared his throat. "I shall escort you," he said slowly.

"Thank you. And would someone take my horse to the stables? I am sure Timur will take care of her." Kei watched their expressions change. He had never met the head of the stables, but he had listened to enough of Sorran's tales.

"See to his horse," the guard barked. He gave Kei a nod, not meeting his gaze. "Follow me."

He led Kei through the gate, across a courtyard, and up to the door of the palace. Kei followed him through cool, stone-flagged hallways until they reached a small chamber. The guard gestured to the stone bench against the wall. "Wait here, please." He disappeared from view, and Kei sagged against the wall, his cloak across his knees. He put the guards from his mind and focused on the two men in the square.

What does it mean?

He held on to the hope that Sorran would be able to help him.

"Kei? What are you doing here?"

Kei snapped his head up to see Sorran in the doorway, a look of sheer delight on his face. Kei sprang to his feet and lunged across the chamber to throw his arms around his brother. "I am so happy to see you," he murmured into the soft fabric of Sorran's robe. He clung to Sorran, tremors rippling through him.

"Peace, Kei," Sorran said quietly, stroking his back. "What ails you? And how do you come to be here?"

Kei breathed in Sorran's familiar scent, unwilling to speak until he was composed once more. When calm had returned, he straightened and stepped back. "I wanted to see you," he replied with a smile.

Sorran shook his head. "I had not been informed of your visit." He paused, his eyes widening. "You came alone?" When Kei nodded, Sorran stared at him. "How did you get our mother to agree?"

"I will tell you all, I promise."

Sorran smiled. "My little brother has grown up." He put his arm around Kei's shoulders. "Come with me. Tanish and Feyar will be delighted to see you. And you will finally meet Arrio." He guided Kei along the corridor. "We have a guest staying with us, a visitor from Kandor on a diplomatic mission."

"Good," Kei responded absently. "But I need to talk to you." The strangeness of what he'd encountered lingered still.

Sorran stopped before a huge ancient wooden door guarded by two warriors, and laid his hands on Kei's shoulders. "I was right: there *is* something troubling you."

Kei shook his head. "Not now. It can wait. Let me greet my brothers-in-law and my nephew first." He had heard so much about Arrio over the years, and had often wondered why they had never met. Sorran had always claimed the timing had not been right.

"Very well." Sorran lowered his hands. "But once that is done, you and I shall talk." He gave the warriors a nod, and they pushed open the heavy door. Kei followed Sorran into a large chamber, one side nothing but long windows that let in the light. At the far end stood three thrones, but there was no one in sight.

"They are in Tanish's private audience chamber," Sorran explained, walking toward a door to the right of the thrones, outside which stood one guard.

"Do you need all these warriors?" Kei saw few around the palace in Vancor.

Sorran laughed. "No, but when Tanish informed the royal guard that they were no longer required, Deron, their captain, said that would only take place once he was in the ground. Until then, he served the king, and that meant the king would have bodyguards."

"Such loyalty."

Sorran nodded. "Tanish trained with Deron when he was your age—they are more than king and captain." Another nod to the guard and the door opened for them.

"By the heavens, that guard spoke truly. It *is* Kei!" Feyar came toward him, arms outstretched, and Kei stepped into the warmth of his embrace. "What are you doing here, cub?"

Kei's heart eased to hear the familiar endearment. "Do you not think it is time I paid a visit?"

"Yes, but usually a royal prince arrives with an entourage, not alone." Tanish rose from his chair to greet Kei with a broad smile. Kei left one embrace for another, and Tanish held him close. "What is my favorite brother-in-law doing so far from Vancor unaccompanied?"

Kei laughed at their habitual joke. "Your *only* brother-in-law grew tired of waiting for the Terunans to come on a visit." He glanced around the chamber. "But where is my nephew?"

Feyar led him over to the window. "Arrio and our guest Dainon have been exploring the city. They should be here soon. Let me see if there is any sign of them." He peered down into the courtyard below and pointed. "There they are."

Kei followed his finger—and for the second time since he'd arrived in Teruna, he froze. The two men walking toward the palace were roughly the same in build as the men he'd seen in the square. Not that Kei needed to see their faces. One thing had not changed—they had no aura.

As Kei watched, the two men disappeared from view as they entered the palace.

"Sorran," he whispered, leaning heavily on the sill and fighting the dizziness that threatened to overwhelm him.

Sorran was at his side in an instant, his arm darting out to support Kei, who leaned against him. "You are ill," Sorran said quietly.

Kei shook his head. "My nephew and your guest—Dainon?— they… they have no colors," he whispered.

Sorran stiffened. "You frighten me, brother. Of course they do. I have seen them, many times."

Kei clutched Sorran's arm and stared at him, his heart pounding. "Truly? You see them?"

Sorran nodded slowly, and then his eyes widened. "But you do not. Why should this be?"

The door opened, cutting off Sorran's next words, and the two men entered. Kei stilled as he watched his nephew draw closer, taking in little of Arrio's physical appearance. What held Kei captive was a pair of deep blue eyes.

I have seen those eyes before.

Then it came to him.

Kei was staring at his destiny.

CHAPTER
EIGHT

ARRIO STARED in confusion at the young man in Sorran's arms, his senses suddenly alert. He had never seen him before, and yet there was something familiar about him. Those dark eyes, so dark they were almost black, reminded him of....

With a shock, Arrio looked from Sorran to the young man and back to Sorran again.

Can this be Kei? It could be no one else. Arrio noted the protective stance of his fathers, their preoccupied expressions, and it became clear to him that all was not well.

He left Dainon at the door and crossed the floor with long strides, eager to meet his uncle. Kei's eyes widened as Arrio approached and he straightened, though Sorran did not move from Kei's side.

"Uncle?" Arrio came to a halt a few feet from him. "I am Arrio."

Kei glanced at Sorran, who nodded and moved to stand next to Tanish. Kei held out his hand in greeting. "It is good to meet you at last."

Arrio regarded the outstretched hand in dismay and lifted his gaze to meet those beautiful eyes. "No," he said simply.

Kei swallowed hard. "No?" he repeated, lowering his hand.

Arrio gave him a hopefully reassuring smile. "I have not waited this long to meet you to be content with merely clasping your hand in mine." He held his arms wide and waited, his heartbeat racing.

Kei smiled. "You are as my brother described."

Arrio laughed. "Is that a good thing?"

Kei hesitated a moment longer, then walked forward to meet him in a firm embrace.

The moment Arrio held Kei close, his body reacted. Kei was warm, and a musky aroma emanated from him, a scent that stirred Arrio's senses.

He wanted to linger, to drink Kei in, but knew that to do so would attract attention. Reluctantly he released Kei and stepped back.

Kei's gaze locked onto his, and those dark eyes widened. His lips parted, but no sound came forth.

What rocked Arrio was the desire burning in him to kiss those lips, to feel Kei's body mold to his, to drink in more of that heady scent that seemed to permeate his very being.

What is happening to me? He could not contain the tremors that coursed through his body.

Kei's sharp intake of breath told him Arrio's reaction had not gone unnoticed. He stiffened, and Arrio hastened to reassure him.

"Peace, uncle. I feel it too," he whispered, moving a little closer.

Kei became still. "Truly?"

Arrio nodded and was relieved to see a little of the tension bleed from Kei's body. Arrio's heart slowed at last to its normal pace.

Behind him, Dainon cleared his throat, and Arrio took a deep breath. Shame flooded him.

I could not have been more obvious. What must he think of me? The day I speak of my attraction to him, I stand in plain sight of him, unable to hide my attraction to another.

His physical reaction to Kei confused him. Everything in Arrio told him he was meant to be with Dainon, yet here was this prince who pulled from him such strong emotions that Arrio trembled. He stepped back and his tremors eased.

By the Maker, what is this? Arrio could not break eye contact with Kei, and it appeared the prince was similarly afflicted. When Dainon coughed, the spell was broken, and Arrio looked around him in confusion. Dainon regarded him with grave eyes, and Arrio flushed under the weight of such intense scrutiny.

Tanish beckoned to Dainon. "Come meet Prince Kei, Sorran's younger brother." His eyes twinkled. "Who has surprised us all." Kei flushed and Tanish laughed. "I speak in earnest. I never thought to see the day your mother would let you undertake so bold an enterprise."

"I can only think Kei has bewitched her." Sorran grinned. "As we speak, there is a duplicate Kei in the royal palace and she is convinced he is the real prince."

Kei laughed heartily, plainly recovered from his shock, and Arrio was once more transfixed. *What is it about you?* He looked Kei up and down, taking in more of his physical appearance. "Apart from your build and your eyes, you do not resemble my *papa-turo*." They shared the same olive complexion, but where Sorran was smooth-skinned, Kei appeared to be the opposite. The long black robe he wore revealed enough of his chest for Arrio to see the thick layer of hair that covered it. Kei was bearded, his black hair short and sleek.

Kei smiled. "My coloring is that of my mother, but the rest? My father is to blame."

Sorran snorted.

Arrio had no complaints. He liked what he saw.

Dainon finally moved from his position and walked over to stand before Kei, head bowed. "Your Highness."

Kei bowed in return. "I am happy to meet you, Dainon. I too am a visitor to Teruna."

Dainon raised his head and gave Kei a smile that did not meet his eyes. "I am sure all here are delighted to share your company." He took a step back, flashing a glance in Arrio's direction.

Arrio swallowed.

"Nephew?"

Arrio regarded Kei, who smiled at him, those dark eyes catching the light. Arrio returned his smile, a feeling of uncommon shyness stealing over him. "I have thought of you as my uncle for so long, but now that we meet, it feels… strange to call you thus."

Sorran chuckled. "Then you are Kei and Arrio. You share no blood, after all."

Arrio hardly heard him. Kei was enchanting, and once again Arrio found it difficult to drag his attention away.

Dainon cleared his throat. "If you will all forgive me, I must take my leave of you."

Tanish nodded. "Of course."

Dainon bowed to him, and after darting another glance in Arrio's direction, he left.

When the door closed behind him, Tanish sighed. "I fear this will end badly."

Arrio's heart beat strongly. *Does he see what happens here?* Then he latched on to the more likely significance of his *papa*'s words. Tarrea was not a young horse, and Dainon's concern for her clung to him like a shroud.

"What is wrong?" Kei asked. "Why does Dainon look so… burdened?"

"His mare is gravely ill," Feyar told him. "He goes to be with her."

"Mare?" Kei appeared stricken. He turned to Sorran quickly. "May I go too?"

Sorran nodded instantly. "Yes, go. It may be that you can help."

"I will show you the way," Arrio blurted out.

Tanish and Feyar nodded, but Sorran gazed at him, eyes bright with a knowing expression.

Arrio led Kei from the chamber, silently cursing Sorran's ability to see what Arrio did his best to hide. The thought crossed his mind that he was about to be in close proximity to two men who stirred his senses: one who appeared equally affected, and the other no doubt confused by Arrio's actions.

Arrio could not explain what was happening to him, but he could not wait to see what would come to pass.

DAINON STRODE toward the stables, trying to ignore the roiling in his gut. He told himself it was concern for Tarrea, but he knew it to be a lie. The reason for his state was standing in Tanish's private chamber, talking with Kei, clearly captivated by him, and the realization only served to exacerbate Dainon's anxiety.

Why is Arrio toying with me?

Dainon did not know what to think. His solitary world had been rocked to its core when he'd encountered Arrio on that beach. He'd been brought to the point where he had to face reality: he was attracted to a man. Except he knew it went beyond mere attraction. It seemed as though there were forces at work, pulling the two of them together. He'd finally arrived at the realization that he wanted Arrio. And then in walked Kei.

Dainon was not blind. Arrio was fascinated by the young prince, something Dainon understood only too well. What made his heart ache was the thought that somehow Kei's arrival had changed things. The irony did not escape him.

Arrio breezes into my life, turns it upside down, brings me to the point where I can no longer deny I want him—only to discard me in favor of another.

He knew he was overreacting. Arrio had not discarded him—had he? But some inner sense told Dainon that something had shifted, and he did not know what to do.

Footsteps behind him made him falter, and a glance over his shoulder revealed Arrio and Kei, moving swiftly to catch up to him. Inwardly he groaned.

Is it not enough that I have already seen the connection between them? Must they follow me to flaunt it?

He strode into the stables, pushing his confusion from his mind. It was time to think of Tarrea. The evening approached, and the stable boys were at work, grooming the horses and feeding them.

As Kei and Arrio followed him into the stables, all the horses appeared at the doors to their stalls, whinnying. At first Dainon thought they were greeting Arrio, but it soon became clear that they were focused on Kei. The prince walked to each horse, patting and stroking, whispering to them in greeting, and as he passed by, they turned their heads to follow him, still whinnying.

"By the heavens." Timur joined Dainon and Arrio, his gaze fixed on the scene before them. "I have never seen such a thing." He moved closer to Arrio. "Who is he?" he asked in a whisper.

"Prince Kei, my *papa-turo*'s brother."

Timur's eyes widened. "The boy has a way with horses, that much is evident. I know of no other who has such a connection with them." He turned to Dainon, his expression growing somber. "Your girl is worse."

Dainon's heart plummeted. He knew Tarrea was nearing the end of her days, but he had thought to have more time with her. "Tell me," he demanded urgently, following Timur into a stall at the far end of the yard.

Tarrea lay on her side, but as he watched, she struggled up and pawed at the ground.

"Can you tell if she is in pain?" Arrio asked Timur, his gaze focused on Tarrea. Dainon heard the concern in his voice, and for a moment, he forgot his previous… *annoyance? Disappointment?* Dainon could not quantify his emotions where Arrio was concerned.

One minute he takes my heart and twists it, and the next, he makes me want to—

Timur stood beside Tarrea, and Dainon focused on him. "Dainon says her heart beats faster than normal," Timur told Arrio, gently stroking down Tarrea's neck and smoothing her mane. He gazed at her, his forehead furrowed. "Her breathing has quickened too. She sweats frequently and she has no appetite. The old girl cannot get comfortable in any position, and she lies down far too frequently."

As if to prove his point, Tarrea lay down on the straw, and Dainon knelt beside her. Tarrea flared her nostrils and curled her lips.

"Easy there," he crooned, stroking her soft nose. It hurt him deeply to feel so helpless.

"May I see her?" Kei stood in the doorway. "I may be able to help."

It was on the tip of Dainon's tongue to refuse him, but he realized quickly how immature a reaction it would be. *He is not to blame for Arrio's attraction.* Dainon nodded, and Kei came slowly into the stall to kneel at Tarrea's side. She lifted her head from the straw to peer at him, but Kei made a soft noise and she lowered it again.

Timur caught his breath. "So you speak horse, Your Highness?" His smile was sad. "An amazing skill in one so young."

Kei glanced in his direction. "I have a... rapport with animals," he said quietly.

Dainon listened in astonishment as Tarrea's breathing eased with Kei's gentle stroking. "That much is evident, Your Highness."

Kei paused and turned to regard him, those dark eyes unreadable. "Kei. I am Kei."

Dainon nodded. "As you wish."

Kei tilted his head. "I must ask something of you, but I fear it will cause you pain."

Dainon's heartbeat raced. "Ask, Your—Kei."

"Your horse is nearing her time. If we do nothing, she will slip from us, but not without pain."

"Go on." Dainon's throat tightened at hearing confirmation of his fears.

"I can do one of two things," Kei said quickly. "I can ease her pain, so she will not suffer, or...."

"Or what?" Dainon seized on the note of hope in Kei's voice. The prince's youth did not matter—in that instant Dainon trusted Kei with all his heart.

Kei met his gaze. "I can attempt to heal her of what ails her. I cannot prevent her death, but I can postpone the inevitable. You would have more time with her, and she would be free of pain." His voice rang with confidence.

"Heal her?" Timur stared at him. "You... you can do that?"

Kei smiled. "It is a possibility. I have done so before."

From behind Dainon came Arrio's quiet gasp.

Dainon knew his answer. He was not ready to lose Tarrea. She would take with her his memories of Merron, laughing as he clutched her legs, Tarrea showing infinite patience with the little boy. "Heal her, if you can."

Kei nodded, a knowing look on his face. He stretched out his hands and moved them over Tarrea, keeping a scant distance between them. Kei wore an expression of intense concentration as he slowly proceeded to map out every inch of her. When he reached her belly, he paused, his brows scrunching up. He held his hands still above her and closed his eyes. "Here," he whispered, bringing his hands together. "There is… something here."

Tarrea let out a soft neigh as if in agreement.

"What is it?" Dainon asked, both Arrio and Timur echoing his question.

Kei frowned. "Silence. I need to concentrate." He straightened his back and held his arms out, hands still hovering over Tarrea's belly.

The silence that fell went beyond the stall. Dainon could not hear a single sound from the stables.

Kei's breathing sped up. "There is… a mass." His hands trembled as he stretched out his fingers, only to curl them into his palms, repeating the motion over and over.

Dainon could not keep silent. "What are you doing?"

Kei shuddered and drew in a deep breath. "Shrinking it, I hope, until there is nothing left."

Dainon stared at him in awe, but Kei was oblivious to him. Long minutes ticked by, still no sound penetrating from beyond the stall.

At last Kei sat back on his haunches, his face drawn and tired. "It is gone," he said in a low voice.

As if in response to his words, Tarrea got up and tossed back her mane before lowering her head to drink from her water trough.

Kei reached into a nearby bucket and grabbed a handful of oats. He held them out to her, and Tarrea ate from his hand while he stroked her neck and behind her ears. "Yes, my beauty. You need to get your strength back." He smiled when not a single oat remained.

Dainon choked back a sob. When Kei snapped his head in Dainon's direction, Dainon did not hesitate, but grabbed Kei, pulling him into his arms. "Thank you," he whispered. "Thank—" The words died on his lips when a familiar jolt left him shaking, his skin tingling and the hairs on his arms standing to attention.

No. No. This… this cannot be. Ice spread from Dainon's core, and waves of dizziness rippled through him, his joy at Tarrea's recovery forgotten for the moment.

Kei stared up at him, eyes wide, his face draining of color, lips parted in a sharp intake of breath.

With an effort Dainon released him, unable to take his eyes from Kei's shocked expression. "Thank you," he repeated. Inside his head was chaos. *How can this be?* Two men, both shaking his world to the core.

Kei continued to stare at him, visibly trembling as though he sensed Dainon's inner turbulence.

Timur came closer, stroked Tarrea, and placed his hand on her belly. "By the Maker. You did it. Look at her." He wiped a hand over her flank. "Dainon, her blanket. She's covered in sweat."

With a supreme effort, Dainon stepped aside, picked it up, and threw it over her back.

Kei's breathing hitched. "What is that?"

Dainon turned to see Kei pointing at the blanket, where the image of a bear had been stitched. "That is the emblem of Kandor," he said, still working hard to regain his composure. The jolts of energy that had left him trembling had abated, and with each passing minute, he grew more convinced that he had imagined it. *It must be so.* For if not, then….

Dainon did not want to think what the significance might be.

Arrio regarded them with wide eyes, shaking his head slowly as though in disbelief. "Kei, you possess a great gift."

When silence greeted Arrio's words, Dainon turned to look at Kei, who stood very still, his gaze fixed on the blanket, Arrio's praise seemingly unheard.

"Dainon." Kei's voice was quiet. "What is your occupation in Kandor?"

Something prickled Dainon's consciousness. "I am a warrior. Why do you ask?"

Kei's mouth fell open, and he reached up to touch his parted lips. "Warrior?"

Dainon attempted a smile. "Do you wish to see my sword?" He had meant the remark humorously, but to his consternation, Kei's eyes bulged and he stumbled back against Arrio, who put out his hands to stop Kei's fall. A jolt shook Kei as their bodies came into contact, and he jerked, shifting out of Arrio's reach.

Dainon darted forward, his heart pounding. "Kei? What ails you?" The prince's chest heaved and his breathing grew erratic. Before Dainon could reach out to grab him, Kei straightened and lifted his chin high.

"It is naught. I shall leave you with Tarrea and rejoin my brother." His voice shook, belying his statement.

Before Dainon could utter a word, Kei had fled with a swiftness that left him staring, greatly discomforted.

"Is the lad ill?" Timur asked, his hand resting gently on Tarrea's back.

Arrio met Dainon's gaze but remained silent.

All is not well with Kei. Dainon was sure of it. No matter what the prince said, Dainon felt it with every fiber of his being. And he could not escape the conclusion that whatever had affected Kei so strongly, he was the cause of it.

That was enough to bring him to a decision.

"Can you see to Tarrea?" he asked Timur.

"Certainly." Timur glanced toward the door where Kei had left, and cocked his head to one side. "Yes, see to the boy. There is something not right there."

Dainon gave a quick nod to Arrio and hurried from the stall.

CHAPTER
NINE

KEI RAN to the palace, unable to remember the path he had taken to the stables. His heart was beating wildly, so fast that he feared it would burst. The one thought that repeated in his head over and over was that he had to see Sorran. He clutched at the hope that his brother would know what was happening to him. When he spied a familiar door, relief flooded through him and he headed for it.

As he neared it, the door opened and Sorran appeared. His eyes widened when he saw Kei. "What is wrong?" he cried out, hands outstretched to catch Kei as he stumbled into him.

Kei collapsed, his legs buckling beneath him, and groaned when his knees connected with the hard stone floor.

Sorran encircled him with strong, capable arms, helping him to his feet and supporting Kei while he leaned against him, shivering. "I have you, brother," Sorran murmured, and Kei became aware of a sense of peace that filtered through the layers of panic, soothing him until he breathed more easily. "That is better." Sorran stood still, holding Kei close, his hands gentle on Kei's back.

It was only then that Kei realized where that peace came from. "You… are doing this?" He rested his head against Sorran's shoulder, grateful beyond measure for the wondrous gift.

"You do not recall my soothing you like this when you were younger?"

Kei shook his head, although something stirred in his memory, and he knew Sorran spoke the truth. Waves of calm continued to flow over and through him, until his heart beat as normal and his breathing was regular. He straightened, composed once more. "Thank you," he said quietly. "I am sorry if my state alarmed you."

Sorran held him at arms' length, his gaze focused on Kei's face. "We need to talk, clearly."

Kei could only nod. Sorran guided him along the corridor to a doorway, and suddenly Kei caught a scent of flowers and the faint chirping of birds. When Sorran led him into a garden where light, color, and perfume assaulted him from all sides, Kei welcomed the sensory overload. Anything to blot out his own internal confusion.

Sorran gestured toward a stone bench beneath a wide-spreading tree whose bronze leaves reflected the afternoon sunlight. "Let us sit here."

Kei sank down onto the cool surface and then leaned forward, his head in his hands. "I am going mad," he whispered.

Sorran laid a hand on his shoulder, and Kei jumped. "Peace, Kei."

Kei inclined his head to peer at Sorran, an idea occurring to him. He grabbed Sorran's hand. "Tell me a lie," he demanded.

"Why would I do such a thing?" Sorran's brows knitted.

"Do not wonder at my request, but simply do as I ask." Kei steeled himself, praying his fears would not be realized.

Sorran sighed. "Very well. I… I do not love Tanish and Feyar." He regarded Kei with watchful eyes.

Kei's reaction was instantaneous. He knew it to be a lie, not because he knew the truth, but because his gift told him so.

Then what happened just now? Why did I sense… nothing? His heart plummeted at the recollection, and realization settled over him. *I am not going mad.* He let go of Sorran's hand and groaned.

"Kei, speak to me. What ails you?"

Kei straightened and clasped his hands together. "I hoped that my gift had failed me, but no. All is as it should be."

Sorran sighed with exasperation. "You speak in riddles. Tell me."

Kei looked him in the eye. "I cannot tell if Arrio and Dainon speak truth."

"What do you mean?"

"Simply that. When they speak, I feel… nothing." He fought to keep calm. "I thought my gift had left me. That is why I asked you to lie to me."

"To see if your gift had deserted you, but clearly it has not." Sorran regarded him thoughtfully. "You cannot use Truthspeak in their presence. Coupled with that, they have no auras—that *you* can perceive, at any rate."

Kei nodded. "I feel so lost. What is happening to me?"

Sorran's gaze grew more intense. "Have you shared everything with me?"

I should have known I could hide nothing from him. Had it not always been so?

"When I was younger, I had a dream."

Sorran smiled. "You saw something in a dream that has come to pass, something that connects with them." He relaxed visibly.

"Yes," Kei sighed. He took a moment to focus his recollections. "Only certain elements of it have remained with me, and I had not thought them to be important. They were so random, there could be no connection between them." He shivered. "Until now."

Sorran tilted his head. "And now?"

Kei shared with him that first sight of Arrio's eyes, and the image of a bear with a sword. Sorran fell silent and Kei stared at him. "Do you know what it means?"

Sorran gazed at him. "Yes. More importantly, so do you, but for some reason, you are fighting it. Why?"

Kei swallowed. "What... what do you mean?" His pulse raced and his chest tightened.

"Kei." Sorran's eyes were full of love. "You cannot deny what you know to be true. Be still, open yourself to your gifts, and accept what your senses tell you."

"But I cannot accept that. It cannot be true." Kei gaped at Sorran, his heartbeat speeding up. "Both of them?"

"Is it so strange a thing to accept that both should be your destiny?" Sorran smiled. "You accept readily enough that I was meant for Tanish and Feyar. Why then is it so difficult to accept your own destiny?"

"But I know nothing about them."

Sorran laughed. "You have heard tales of Arrio since you were a little boy. In that respect you have the advantage. *I* walked into the royal audience chamber and knew Tanish was mine before we had exchanged a word. When I first laid eyes on Feyar, I knew." He stroked Kei's cheek. "They are meant to love you, brother. Accept it."

Kei closed his eyes and focused inward. He gave up any notion of resistance and opened himself up to his senses. In that moment, something inside him shifted and his thoughts clicked into place. Slowly he opened his eyes and regarded Sorran in wonder. "It is true, then."

Sorran's smile widened. "You see it."

Kei nodded. With each passing moment, the realization grew more solid and his fears seeped from him. "Do I tell them?"

Sorran's reaction was swift. "No! Arrio might accept it, but Dainon? He is not ready. No, now is not the time. You will know when it is right."

Kei recalled his exit from the stables. He put his head in his hands once more. "Dainon will think me such a *temura*."

Sorran chuckled. "Dainon has probably never seen a *temura*, but doubtless Kandor has similar creatures." The tiny animals dwelt in burrows in the Vancoran palace grounds, unspeakably cute but timorous to the point that they froze whenever anyone tried to approach them. It had taken Kei years to get near enough to pet them, and only then because he went armed with vast quantities of their favorite fruit.

"Then what should I do?" Kei asked.

"Spend time with Dainon and Arrio," Sorran advised. "*You* know what is to come—they do not. So be patient."

Kei liked that idea. Then he sighed. "Time is not on my side. Mother will expect me to return to Vancor."

Sorran rose. "Leave our mother to me. I will send a messenger to Vancor, to inform our parents that you will remain with us for a while longer." He patted Kei's shoulder. "Stay here and enjoy the peace. Join us when you feel ready."

"Thank you."

Sorran nodded and left him.

Kei surrendered himself to the tranquility of the garden, letting the sounds of trickling water and birdsong and the sweet perfume permeate his senses.

I am destined for two men.

Only then did the implications occur to him, and the realization sent heat racing through him. *In a world full of men, I am destined to share my life with two who were made to be with me.* His fear of intimacy evaporated. *I can truly be with them, in every sense of the word.* One sense in particular.

Kei's future had suddenly changed direction, and he was eager to find what lay ahead for him.

DAINON ENTERED the audience chamber. One glance was enough to tell him Kei was not there. His heart sank. *Where is he?* Kei had seemed tormented. Dainon did not know what had caused him to flee as he did, but Kei's hasty departure raised questions.

Was it me? Did he too feel that jolt when we touched? Am I to blame? He had to know.

Dainon turned and exited the chamber, scanning up and down the corridors for any sign of Kei. It was only when he'd begun to search for Kei that Dainon had realized how big the palace was. It appeared to be a never-ending maze of corridors.

When he caught sight of Sorran at the far end of one of the numerous passages, he sighed with relief and headed for him. *Sorran will know where he is.* "Your Highness!"

Sorran halted and turned to face him, and Dainon came to a stop in front of him. "Dainon, you seem disturbed. What is wrong?"

"Have you seen Prince Kei?"

Sorran became still. He nodded slowly, his expression neutral. "I left him in the royal garden. He may still be there."

Dainon recalled its location. "Thank you." He bowed his head once and took his leave. When he emerged, blinking into the bright sunlight that filled the walled garden, he took a moment to stop and breathe in the fragrant air. His anxiety felt at odds somehow with the peaceful atmosphere that pervaded the space.

"It does not surprise me that my brother and brothers-in-law like to spend time in this place." Kei's voice was soft, devoid of the agitation that had been so obvious a short time ago. He sat under a tree whose spreading branches provided shade from the sun.

Dainon approached him slowly. "If I am disturbing you, I will take my leave."

Kei smiled. "You are no disturbance. Come, sit with me."

Dainon obeyed, relieved to see the change in him. He leaned against the thick trunk of the tree, hands clasped, momentarily at a loss for words.

"Tarrea is a beautiful horse," Kei said. "Your love for her is evident."

"She has been mine since she was a foal." His throat tightened at the thought of what might have been. "Thank you again for what you did."

To his surprise Kei placed a small hand over Dainon's. "Peace, Dainon. She is yours for a little while longer." His fingers curled around Dainon's. "Not much longer, however, but she is free of pain. Let her rest now."

Dainon could not repress the shiver that ran down his spine at the touch of Kei's hand to his. When Kei turned to gaze directly at him, Dainon found his words. "I came to find you because I feared I was the reason you fled the stables."

Dark eyes focused on his. "I am sorry if I alarmed you. Be assured, all is well."

Then why did you run? And why was Dainon's heart racing as he gazed upon Kei's beautiful face?

Then a realization struck him. For the second time in his life, Dainon thought another man beautiful. And more than that—another man who sent his thoughts into confusion and made his body react.

What are you doing to me, Prince Kei?

"I will leave you to enjoy the tranquility of this spot." Kei released his hand. The slight tremor that had thrummed through Dainon at his touch was suddenly no more, and he found himself regretting its departure.

Kei rose to his feet and stood before Dainon, close enough that Dainon caught his scent: a spicy aroma that seemed to pour off him, invading Dainon's nostrils and stirring his senses. *By the heavens, he smells good.* Spice, musk, soap, and underneath it, a scent that made him think of—

Dainon froze, shaken to the core by the image that had filtered through his mind.

Kei, in my bed. He swallowed hard, his shaft twitching into life at the thought of Kei, naked, stretched out beneath him, belly taut, legs spread, while Dainon—

No. No. No.

He opened his mouth to say something, *anything* that would excuse him from Kei's presence, but was robbed of all speech when Kei leaned closer and kissed him on the mouth, no hesitation on his part. Dainon stiffened for a second before reacting instinctively, curling a hand around Kei's nape and pulling him deeper into the kiss, his tongue parting Kei's lips.

Dainon was lost in that kiss, drowning in the sheer pleasure that coursed through him, that made his body sing.

Kei's soft moan brought Dainon to his senses. He broke the kiss and lurched to his feet, backing away.

Kei stared at him, his breathing rapid. "Did… did I do something wrong?"

"No," Dainon assured him, "but I must go. My apologies for leaving so swiftly." Without waiting for a reply, he left the garden with long strides, not missing the startled sound that came from Kei. Dainon made his way through the palace, passing servants who bowed to him and guards who acknowledged him with a nod. He barely registered them, not altering his pace until he reached the sanctuary of his chamber. He closed the door behind him and then sank to the floor, cradling his head in his hands.

What is happening to me?

Two of them. Two men who aroused him. Two men who sent him plunging into confusion.

He had not imagined the connection he had seen between Arrio and Kei, and *that* made sense. They were of a similar age. But Dainon could not deny there had been a connection between himself and Arrio. Yet that did *not* make sense. And now this, an insane moment of rampaging desire, where all he could think about was the urge to take Kei.

He put from his mind the pulses of lightning that had zapped through him with both princes—there had to be an explanation. *It does not matter that I am attracted to both of them.* Dainon could not deny what his body was telling him, but that did not mean he had to act on it.

He forced himself to take several deep breaths in an effort to compose himself. He got up from the floor and sat on the edge of the bed, trying to look at the situation calmly and logically.

Arrio says he is attracted to me. Kei is plainly attracted, else why would he kiss me?

In a burst of clarity, Dainon accepted what he knew to be the painful truth. It did not matter how attractive he found the two young men. It did not matter if they thought themselves attracted to him. Nothing could come of it. He was in Teruna for a short time, and then he would return to Kandor, his mission completed. Arrio and Kei would forget all about him and lose themselves in each other, which was how it should be. He was twice their age, when all was said and done. He told himself they were too young to know what they truly wanted.

Calm restored, Dainon got up and walked out onto his balcony, breathing in the warm, fragrant air. *I am right to put this from my mind. Nothing can come of it. I was mad to think that it could. This is for the best.*

Dainon repeated the litany until he had convinced himself of it. Even if the ache in his heart said otherwise.

ARRIO GAZED after Dainon, putting aside his own confusion as concern spread through him. Both Dainon and Kei had appeared agitated, and Arrio had wanted to run after them.

Why do both of them affect me so strongly? Arrio could still feel the vibrations that had jolted him when he had clasped Kei to him.

"Arrio!"

Timur's sharp cry broke through Arrio's internal musing, and he turned to find the bear regarding him with a smirk. "And where were you?" Timur grinned and patted his arm. "I have repeated your name three times."

"My apologies," Arrio said, flushing. "I was lost in my thoughts."

"And which of them were you thinking about?"

Arrio gaped at him. "I...."

Timur laughed, a deep, rich sound that rolled out of him. "Ah-ha. I knew I was right. Can it be that Prince Arrio has finally found a man who stirs his interest?" He shook his head. "That will break Oren's heart, you know."

Arrio snorted. He was aware of the stable boy's infatuation with him—it was difficult to miss when Oren followed him around the stable, never once taking his gaze off Arrio. "Oren will live. And I am not discussing this." How could he, when in his own mind, there was nothing but confusion? He brought his attention to Tarrea. "She is truly improved?"

Timur smiled as he stroked the mare's neck. "I never saw such a thing before. It was like magic." He flicked a glance in Arrio's direction. "So, Prince Kei is *Seruan*, then? Like his brother?" Arrio nodded, and Timur shook his head once more. "You would think nothing could surprise me, having a *Seruan* for a husband, but...." He sighed. "Amazing."

Arrio caught sight of Timur's left hand. He grasped Timur's wrist and stared at the heavy gold ring, its surface etched. "Is that new? I do not recollect seeing it before."

Timur's face glowed. "Erinor gave it to me last night, his gift to celebrate our eighteen years of marriage." He held out his hand so Arrio could examine it more closely. "The words are something your *papa* gave him, apparently. He says it reads 'You are my heart.'" Timur regarded the ring, his smile lingering. "Appropriate, since he is mine."

Arrio's throat thickened to see the love in Timur's expression. "And what did you give him?"

Timur's neck and cheeks flushed. "None of your business," he said gruffly.

Arrio laughed. Impulsively, he grabbed Timur in a brief embrace, breathing in the smell of leather, straw, horses, and sweat. It was the smell of his childhood, reminiscent of the many hours he had spent in the stables, watching Timur at work. He released Timur and peered again at the ring. "It is beautiful work."

Timur nodded in agreement. "It was made by your friend Parina."

Arrio beamed. "She is truly talented." Parina was a gifted jeweler, and Arrio loved to frequent her workshop, watching in fascination as she took gold, silver, and precious jewels, and fashioned them into beautiful pieces. Then a thought occurred to him. "I should take Dainon and Kei to see her stall."

"And which of those two will leave there bearing a promise ring from you?" Timur gave him a knowing glance. "Or will it be both of them?" Arrio gave him a startled glance, and Timur laughed heartily. "I knew I was not mistaken."

Arrio silently cursed Timur's eyes. "You see too much," he growled. "And we shall not talk of this." He tilted his head. "Unless you wish to tell me what you gave Erinor as your gift."

"Still none of your business. I will say, however, that it made him very happy." Timur winked. "Now off with you, pup, and let me work. Go find your men." He grinned and shook his head. "History repeats itself. I cannot wait to hear what your fathers will make of this." When Arrio glared at him, Timur held up his hand. "Peace, Arrio. You know me better than that. My lips are sealed."

Arrio kissed his cheek and exited the stall.

My men.

What astonished him was the feeling of rightness that spread through him.

Chapter TEN

"WHAT ARE your plans for tomorrow?" King Tanish asked Arrio as they finished their evening meal and the dishes were cleared away. "Where do you intend to take our guests?"

"I was about to ask the same question," Kei said, his eyes bright. "I am impatient to see more of Teruna."

Dainon said nothing. He knew he had been quiet throughout dinner, but he did not think his hosts would notice. Kei had been regaling them with news from Vancor. As he talked, it had become clear that Kei had little experience of the world beyond the palace. Dainon could understand why the thought of discovering Teruna would excite him. Kei's natural exuberance was an attractive trait, and the genuine pleasure he took from each new encounter was endearing.

The thought made him sigh internally. *Yet another thing that endears Kei to me.*

"I had intended to take you both to meet our royal jeweler," Arrio told them, "but when I went to check with her an hour ago, she told me something that has forced me to change my plans." He gave Dainon an apologetic glance. "I am sorry, but I will have to find you another guide for the next few days. I too have a mission."

Dainon's heart sank. *He is going somewhere?*

"Are you going to tell us of your mission?" Feyar asked dryly. "Or is it a secret?" His lips twitched with amusement.

Arrio smiled. "No secret. I need to go… prospecting." His gaze flickered briefly in Dainon's direction, and in that moment, he recalled Arrio speaking of his gift.

"What does that mean?" Kei furrowed his brow.

King Tanish straightened, but Arrio gave him a reassuring glance. "Dainon already knows, *Papa*, and I see no reason why Kei should not be told. He is family."

"Agreed." King Tanish met Dainon's gaze. "No one outside the palace knows of Arrio's gift. Whatever information he gives us, we pass on to those who have need of it."

"And similarly, if resources are required, those concerned let us know," Sorran added. "We simply tell them that information is shared with us and that we in turn pass it on. No one is to know where it comes from."

"You feel there are those who would take advantage of him," Dainon surmised.

King Tanish nodded. "It is a system that has worked well for the last five years since Arrio realized what he could do."

"I am no clearer," Kei said quietly. "Arrio is gifted? As I am?"

Arrio reached across the table, took his hand, and squeezed it gently. "I will explain everything later, I promise."

Dainon's chest tightened at the look that passed between them. It only served to confirm his earlier thoughts.

"I take it the objective is gold and other such resources?" Feyar asked Arrio, who nodded. "Then shall I inform Deron that he needs to be ready early tomorrow morning?"

"Yes, *Papi*. Have him pack enough provisions for three days at the most. I will leave at dawn."

"Deron?" The name was familiar to Dainon.

"He is the captain of the royal guard who accompanies Arrio when he makes such journeys. He acts as bodyguard."

"No," Dainon blurted out, the word slipping from his lips before he had time to think. When those around the table jerked their heads in his direction, he took a moment to breathe. "I will accompany Arrio."

Arrio stared at him, lips parted, his eyes shining. "Truly?"

Dainon nodded. "Deron can remain at his post. After all, this is a mission for which I am eminently suited."

Sorran smiled. "That much is true." He gazed at Arrio. "You agree to this?"

Arrio nodded. "As long as Dainon realizes what he is agreeing to. I had thought him too fond of his bed to abandon it for two nights sleeping under the stars." He flashed Dainon a mischievous grin that reminded him of the day they had met. The thought of spending three days with Arrio warmed him.

"I think I can cope." Dainon returned Arrio's grin, his earlier apprehension slipping.

"Can I come too?"

Dainon bit back a groan at Kei's quietly uttered request, and his heart sank further when Arrio's face lit up.

Sorran was smiling too. "If Arrio does not mind," he said.

"I do not mind at all." Arrio's grin had not dimmed. He and Kei regarded each other, and Dainon imagined he saw something pass between them.

His stomach churned. *They are meant to be together. They are clearly attracted to each other.* With that thought he saw the next three days spreading out before him—the two princes deepening their connection while he remained on the outside, shut out.

It was more than Dainon could bear. *Deron can accompany them after all.*

"It seems you will have two princes to protect," King Tanish informed Dainon with a smile. "The future kings of Teruna and Vancor will be in your more than capable hands."

Dainon knew where his duty lay. He shoved aside his own feelings of dismay and bowed to King Tanish. "I shall guard them with my life." He pushed back his chair and rose. "In that case I will take my leave of you and get some sleep." He wanted to be alert for the journey.

A journey I now dread.

"Very well. Deron will see to the provisions," Sorran told him before turning to Arrio and Kei. "If you are going to leave here at dawn, then you should follow Dainon's example and go to bed."

"We need less sleep than Dainon," Arrio said with a gleam in his eye, winking at Dainon. It was obvious the remark had been uttered with humor, but it had only served to reinforce the difference in their ages.

As if I needed a reminder.

Dainon had had enough. "Good night," he said, bowing his head, then leaving the room. Once outside in the hallway, he stood still and drew in a deep breath, his hands clenched at his sides in tight fists.

I have agreed to this. I will protect them.

The idea of being in such close proximity to them held all the promise of torture.

"COME IN," Kei told Arrio, standing aside to give him entry to the chamber. He had found it difficult to contain his excitement ever since Arrio had mentioned his "prospecting." In all their visits to Vancor, not once had his brother and brothers-in-law seen fit to mention that Arrio had gifts. They had regaled him with humorous tales, but never a word of this.

Kei's chamber glowed in the warm light from the candles that had already been lit. He closed the door and joined Arrio where he stood by the open window, looking out over the city. The moon bathed the city's walls in its light, causing them to appear blue.

"Teruna is beautiful," Kei said with a sigh. "But like this, in the moonlight? She has an ethereal beauty that makes me ache to see it."

"It makes me happy that you feel this." Arrio faced him. "But I promised you answers."

Kei nodded and gestured to the bed. "Shall we be comfortable while we talk?"

Arrio nodded and followed him.

Kei's heart pounded as he stretched out on his side, regarding Arrio, who copied him. Having him so close made Kei's pulse race. He yearned to bare his soul, to tell Arrio all he knew, but Sorran's advice rang in his ears. He would always follow his brother's counsel, but there was more to it than obeying Sorran. Everything in Kei told him the time was not right, and he had learned to trust his instincts.

"So," Arrio began, propping up his head with pillows. "It seems we both have gifts."

Kei said nothing, waiting.

Arrio regarded him in silence, studying him carefully. Finally he nodded. "I have dreams where sometimes I see things that have yet to happen."

Kei gaped, and something inside him eased at Arrio's words. "I too have such dreams."

Arrio relaxed visibly. "By all that is wondrous." Then he laughed. "I should not be surprised to learn this about you. After all, you are my *papa-turo*'s brother."

"*Papa-turo*—what does that mean?"

"Tanish tells me *turo* was an ancient word for teacher," Arrio informed him. "And since Sorran is the one who teaches me to use my gifts, it seemed fitting."

That made Kei smile. "He teaches me too."

"We are both lucky, then," Arrio said, peering at Kei. "I have already seen your connection with animals, and your ability to heal them. Do you see colors, as Sorran does?"

Kei's heartbeat sped up. "Sometimes," he said slowly, hating the way the lie tasted in his mouth. He could not admit the truth, however. "But not with everyone I meet." That much was true at least.

"I cannot," Arrio admitted, his voice tinged with sadness. "I would love to be able to see what you both see."

Kei reached across to clasp Arrio's hand in his. "But you have another gift, yes? One that intrigues me."

Arrio smiled. "This is true. I am able to locate natural resources, be they oil, water, stones, minerals…."

"How do you find them?" Kei was fascinated.

Arrio rolled onto his back, Kei's hand still wrapped around his. "It is difficult to explain. They… pull me, I suppose is as good a way of describing it as any. It feels like an itch that I cannot scratch, and the closer I get, the worse it becomes." He grinned. "As with any itch, the trick is not to scratch it."

Kei laughed. "So tomorrow you look for gold?"

Arrio nodded. "But I already have an idea where to look, hence the time period. The mountains to the north of here are more than a day's ride away, and I have located seams of gold there in the past. Once a mine has been set up, they work it until it is exhausted, and then I set about finding a new seam."

"But surely anyone can mine for gold," Kei pointed out.

"Of course they can, and there are always those who are greedy for gold or precious stones. They are free to seek wherever they choose. But what I discover is not shared with such people, and those who are given the locations are careful to keep such knowledge to themselves."

"And what about resources like oil?"

"All the oil for the kingdom is supplied by a royally appointed company," Arrio said. "Tanish created it so that everyone pays the same price."

"Yet no one knows about your gift?"

"Only my fathers. You and Dainon are the first to learn of it. Not even Timur knows."

Kei stared at him. "Then I am truly honored." In the face of such honesty, he did not feel he could hold back. "I… I have one last gift."

"Oh?" Arrio widened his eyes. "Tell me!"

"It does not work with everyone, but… when I lay my hand on a person, I can tell if they are telling me the truth."

Arrio let out his breath in a slow exhale. "Truthspeak? You are gifted in Truthspeak?" Kei nodded shyly, and Arrio rolled onto his belly and, propping himself up on his elbows, he rested his chin in his hands. "Sorran has spoken of this. How does that feel?"

Kei considered how best to answer. "It is as if their thoughts are transparent."

Arrio stared. "You hear their thoughts?"

"Yes."

He sighed. "My heart goes out to you."

It was not the response Kei had expected, and the note of genuine sympathy in Arrio's voice made him choke back sudden tears. Arrio reacted instantly, shifting closer and putting his arms around Kei.

"Sweet Kei. You see everything. You cannot shut them out," Arrio murmured. "That is not a gift—that is a torment."

Kei could not hold back his tears any longer. "Yes," he whispered. Arrio's arms tightened around him, and Kei buried his face in Arrio's robe, breathing in his scent. Soothing sounds fell from Arrio's lips as he held him, providing Kei with some much-needed comfort. Arrio rubbed down Kei's back, his touch gentle and slow, no need for words between them. Kei's tears finally abated. "I am sorry," he said quietly. "I was—"

"You have no need to apologize," Arrio said, stroking his hair. A comfortable silence fell once more between them, Arrio's gentle caresses creating an almost hypnotic effect. When Arrio cleared his throat, Kei steeled himself for the question he knew was coming. "You said Truthspeak does not work with everyone."

Kei wiped his eyes with his hand and sniffed, his head resting on Arrio's shoulder. "That is true. There are… a few whose thoughts are hidden from me." *Such as you and Dainon.*

"Then I thank the Maker for them. It gladdens my heart that you find some relief from this." Arrio kissed Kei's temple. "Does it feel better to have shared with me?"

"Yes, truly." Kei felt lighter. He eased out of Arrio's arms and sat up. "Thank you."

Arrio sat up with him. "I am glad we know more of each other's gifts. I do not wish to hide from you, and it is good to share our secrets."

Kei's throat tightened, but he did not contradict him. *Not all our secrets.*

Arrio yawned. "Now we should sleep. Tomorrow you share an adventure with me." He smiled. "I am very happy that you and Dainon will be with me."

Kei nodded, unable to give voice to his thoughts. He had seen Dainon's expression when Arrio had agreed to both of them accompanying him. *I am not certain Dainon is happy.* As for Kei, he found himself torn. He wanted to know more about both men, but the idea of hiding what he knew made him apprehensive.

Can I keep this knowledge from them? Am I that good a liar?

Kei thought not.

CHAPTER
ELEVEN

DAINON HAD to admit, the genuine joy Kei found in his surroundings was a delight to behold. Their journey so far had been punctuated by frequent stops so Kei could take it all in, but far from proving an annoyance, it was obvious that both Dainon and Arrio loved watching him.

"His life in Vancor must have been so restrictive," Arrio murmured as they gazed at Kei. He stood in the middle of a field of wild flowers that reached up to his waist, surrounding him in a sea of lilac and white. His face was alight with sheer wonder as he stroked his fingers over the flower heads.

"I am not surprised that he takes such joy in each new discovery," Dainon added. Every twist and turn of their path revealed yet more beauty to stun and amaze him. Not that Dainon was immune to the breathtaking scenery. "I must admit, there is nothing as glorious as this in Kandor." His next words died on his lips, and he stared, mouth open.

Arrio followed his gaze and caught his breath. "By the Maker. Look at him."

Kei held his arms wide, and hundreds of butterflies, their wings a shimmering blue the color of a summer sky, hovered about him, alighting on his fingers, his arms, his shoulders, even the top of his head. They created a mesmerizing cloud of fragile, gossamer beauty that shifted incessantly, so many that briefly Dainon lost sight of Kei's face.

He did not miss Kei's low cries of pleasure, however.

"How beautiful he is," Arrio whispered. "He is as one with them, a part of nature."

Dainon could not miss the awe in Arrio's voice, and in spite of his own misgivings about their journey, he had to agree: Kei was truly beautiful.

A sound reached them—a growl carried on the breeze. The butterflies rose up, and with a mass fluttering of silken wings, they were gone. The sorrowful expression on Kei's face was heartbreaking. Slowly he walked toward where Arrio and Dainon stood with the horses, his dark eyes lowered. When the growl grew louder, he snapped his head up. "What is that?"

"That was to be my question also," Dainon stated, turning to Arrio. "A wild animal?

"Possibly a bear or a lion," Arrio said. "There are bears dwelling in the forests nearby, and lions live up in the mountains." He grinned. "Now you know why I never travel here alone." He peered toward Dainon's horse. "You did bring your sword?"

Dainon laughed. "Of course." He scanned the land around them. "That sounded as though the perpetrator was close." He was not afraid; he knew his skill with a sword would be more than a match for any creature that came too close.

Kei looked at them both. "Bears? Lions?" His grin matched Arrio's.

Dainon swore internally. "I know you have a gift where animals are concerned, but you are *not* to go looking for bears or lions, do you hear me?" He reached for his sword where it was strapped to his saddle bags, but Arrio stopped him.

"Peace, Dainon. The wind deceives us." Arrio smiled. "And Kei? Dainon speaks wisely. I have heard tales of your... exploits from my fathers. You will exercise caution while you travel with us."

Kei huffed out a sigh. "Very well."

Dainon thought it an adorable reaction. *He is still so young.*

A growl of a different kind rolled out, and Dainon flushed.

Arrio laughed. "I think that is our signal to stop for the night and eat." His eyes shone. "Someone is hungry."

"Where shall we make camp?" Dainon asked. "Do you have a spot in mind?"

Arrio nodded. "Another hour's ride from here, there is a river, and trees that will provide shelter." He gazed up at the cloudless sky. "The night will be cold, so we will put up the tent and light a fire."

"And food?" Kei inquired. "What shall we eat?"

Arrio chuckled. "Wait and see."

They mounted their horses and Arrio led the way, maintaining a steady pace. Dainon reached down to pat his stallion on the neck. "You're a good horse," he said, his voice low. It had pained him to leave Tarrea in the stables, but he had to agree with Timur that such a journey was not advisable. *She has probably undertaken her last journey.* Dainon doubted he would return to Kandor with his beloved mare. His heart quaked at the thought, but he clung to the one thing that brought him a small measure of peace. *At least she will end her journey free from pain.* Not for the first time, his gaze focused on the young man who rode ahead of him. *Thank the Maker for Kei.*

The day had been less painful than he had anticipated. They had ridden in silence for the most part, except for Kei's enthusiastic outbursts when something else caught his attention. In fact, the more time Dainon spent in Kei's presence, the more endearing he found him.

Perhaps this excursion will not be as difficult as I had thought.

ARRIO SAT on the river bank, enjoying the performance.

Dainon stood on a boulder, staring into the crystal-clear water, a spear in his hand. "Are you sure about this?"

Kei giggled. "I am certain Arrio makes fishing sound easier than it is." He regarded Dainon with eyes that danced with amusement. "You said you wanted to try."

Dainon flashed him a look. "How difficult can it be? See a fish, stick a spear in it." When Kei giggled again, Dainon glared at him. "What about your task? I do not see a fire burning."

"Be patient with me," Kei said, his tone coaxing. "This is only the second fire I have ever built, and the first one took me long enough to get it to light."

Dainon said nothing, but simply pointed toward the pile of sticks and logs with a firm stare.

Kei smirked. "Yes, Dainon."

Yes, Arrio was definitely enjoying himself.

"Dainon," he said patiently. When Dainon turned to regard him, Arrio grinned. "In order to catch the fish, you need to be standing *in* the river."

Dainon heaved a sigh and stepped down off his boulder into the cold river. The water rippled around his calves, and he peered into it, arm poised, spear held aloft.

"There!" Arrio yelled, pointing to where a large silvery fish caught the sunlight that filtered through from the surface.

Dainon stabbed into the water, missing it, only to raise the spear and thrust it again.

"Did he catch it?" Kei called out from where he knelt by the pile of wood, an edge of laughter plainly audible.

"No, he did *not*," Dainon growled. "And if you call out again, you can get in here and catch our dinner yourself."

"Oh no," Kei responded swiftly. "I may like eating fish and fowl—that does not mean I can stomach the idea of killing it. How you can kill something that has a face is beyond me." He grinned at Arrio, who had to fight hard to hide his smirk.

Arrio brought his attention back to Dainon, who was stalking yet another unsuspecting fish. He tried not to laugh when Dainon missed it again. "You need to put more power into your thrust," he said, schooling his features.

Dainon lifted his eyebrows. "More power?" He aimed the spear at the glittering surface, waited until another victim swam into view, and then launched himself at the fish, missed—and fell headlong into the river, spluttering.

Arrio caught his breath and gaped as Dainon staggered to his feet, his short tunic clinging to him. He gave Arrio a baleful stare, which proved too much for him to bear. Arrio took one look at the wringing wet warrior and burst into a peal of laughter.

Dainon flung his spear at the river bank and heaved himself out of the water, growling.

"Arrio, he sounds like one of those bears you were speaking of," Kei said with a chuckle. "A very wet bear."

Arrio stared in disbelief as Dainon strode over to where Kei knelt and scooped him up, putting him over his broad shoulder. Kei squealed and squirmed, but he could not wriggle free. "Dainon! Put me down. Put me down, now!"

Dainon reached the bank in three long strides. "Certainly," he said with a grin—and dropped Kei into the icy water.

"B-By the h-heavens," Kei stuttered. "How c-can the air be so warm and yet the w-water so c-cold?" Kei's robe rose up around him like a skirt, and he struggled to stand, the fabric clinging to his slim body. He glared at Dainon, who observed him from the safety of the river bank, laughing heartily.

"Is it cold?" Dainon asked with wide eyes. "I had not noticed." He gave Kei a wicked grin.

"Now, children," Arrio said amid his own bursts of laughter. "How old are you both?" He watched as Kei heaved himself up onto the bank. Arrio sighed. "Get out of those clothes. It's warm enough that you will soon dry off."

Kei did so, shivering and mumbling under his breath something about how *he* wasn't the child there. Dainon pulled his tunic off, still grinning.

Arrio watched them, shaking his head. He untied his own robe before removing it and placing it on the ground. The warm breeze felt pleasant against his bare skin. "Now watch a master at work." Naked, he picked up the spear from where Dainon had flung it and stepped into the water, repressing a shudder. He was not about to give Dainon the satisfaction of seeing him shiver.

"Wait—you fish naked?" Dainon said with yet another glare.

"Of course," Arrio said innocently. "I would not want to fall and get my robe wet." He did his best to keep a straight face.

"Funny that you did not think to give me that same advice," Dainon retorted with a glint in his eye.

"Truly? I was sure I did." Arrio gave him a sweet smile and then concentrated on his task. He aimed his spear, and seconds later a fat fish was wriggling on the end of it. Ten minutes later, three fish lay on the bank. Arrio had brought a swift end to their suffering. He faced the two men with another smile. "Dinner?"

Dainon's eyes bulged, but then Arrio heaved a sigh of relief when his face creased into a broad smile and he laughed. Arrio joined him, taking the opportunity to observe Dainon's muscles, his lean belly and muscular thighs, and his cock that thickened even as Arrio watched.

What I would give to have those strong arms around me while I sleep, to share the heat of his body.

There was more of Dainon that Arrio ached to share, but he had not missed the fact that Dainon seemed more subdued since they had shared a kiss or two. Arrio was not certain if he had done something to bring about this change, but he knew he was not imagining Dainon's new reticence.

We shall see what this journey brings.

The other object of his desire stood on the bank, naked, eyes closed, face upturned toward the sun, arms held out in worship. Arrio caught his breath at his first view of Kei in the nude. He stared at the thick layer of black hair that covered Kei's chest, leading down in a trail to his cock, above which sat a thick bush of curls. His thighs were covered in the same black down.

Then Arrio's breath stuttered in his chest when Kei's gaze met his. Kei slowly lowered his arms to his side and turned to face Arrio head-on, chin lifted high, those dark eyes watching him, that concave belly making Arrio ache to use it as a pillow, to fall asleep listening to the beating of Kei's heart.

Kei's eyes widened and his lips parted, his tongue darting out to lick them.

In that moment Arrio wondered if Kei could read his thoughts, and heat raced through him at the realization that he *wanted* Kei to see his desire.

Arrio knew he was hoping for more than Dainon. He wanted them both.

KEI PATTED his belly with a sigh. "That was delicious." Dainon had cooked the fish to perfection on wooden spits over the fire, after stuffing their cavities with wild garlic and other herbs he had found. "Where did you learn to cook like that?"

Dainon smiled. "I may not be able to catch a fish with a spear, but I have cooked a few in my time. I learned about wild herbs when I was out on patrols. Anything to improve the taste of some of my catches."

"I am impressed." Arrio took his last mouthful of fish and hummed with pleasure as he chewed it. He gazed with exaggerated regret at the empty spits. "No more?"

Kei laughed. It had been a wonderful end to an amazing day. He was relaxed, his belly was full, and his mind was at peace. Even his impromptu bath in the icy river seemed amusing from his position next to the fire that Arrio had finished. The night was cold, but the heat from the flames overcame it. Kei closed his eyes and drank in the sounds that filtered through the trees surrounding them. He caught the cries of birds and the distant roar of unknown animals, but one glance at Dainon's relaxed features wiped away his fears.

He will protect us. Kei knew that with every fiber of his being.

"Have you been on many patrols?" he asked. "And if Kandor was at peace, what did you do?"

"I trained warriors in skills for survival," Dainon said. "How to forage for food. How to track, both animals and men. How to light a fire. Basic skills."

Kei chuckled. "I had need of someone with your skills my first night away from Vancor. I managed to put up my tent, but the fire was another matter. If the night had been warmer, I would have given up."

"But you did it," Dainon said with a smile. He nodded to a point over Kei's shoulder. "And you did well this evening."

Behind them was the tent Arrio had brought and Kei had erected. It was a simple affair, its flaps drawn back to let the warmth of the fire in. The layers of fur that had been spread on the ground inside appeared soft and inviting. They would be warm enough. If the furs were not up to the task, then the close proximity of their bodies would accomplish that—it was not a large tent.

"How far are we from our destination?" Dainon asked, clearing away the fish skin and bones that remained.

"If we rise early, it should take perhaps a few hours before we reach the mountains where I last found gold. Once I have located a rich seam, all we need do is mark it on the map. We can travel back to this place to camp once more, and the following morning we will leave for Teruna." Arrio placed more sticks on the fire. "I will build up the fire to keep it burning as long as possible. That will keep any… visitors at a distance."

"Visitors?" Kei knew it was reckless, but he wanted to see what made the noises that rumbled through the night air. When there was no reply, he glanced over to where both Arrio and Dainon were regarding him with amusement. "What have I said?"

Arrio laughed. "All these years I have listened to tales of my uncle Kei. I have laughed until I cried at some of them, and I was certain they were exaggerated for my entertainment. But now I see everything my *papa-turo* told me about you is true. The way he described you made me long to meet you. I am so happy that you made the journey to Teruna."

Kei glowed. "I too am happy to finally meet you." He ached to say more, to add that meeting both of them had brought him joy, but fought the urge. Arrio might have proved receptive, but Dainon was an unknown quantity. Kei had been unable to resist kissing him in the garden, out of a desire to see the outcome, but Dainon's swift exit told him much.

He is not ready for such knowledge.

Dainon cleared his throat. "Then it is time we got some sleep. Arrio needs to be rested if he is to use his gift to the full tomorrow." He glanced toward the tent. "Perhaps I should sleep out here in the open. There is not much room in there."

Arrio's eyes gleamed. "I will not have it. And if there is little space, then we will have to huddle together under the furs. We will certainly be warm." He rose to his feet and slowly unfastened his robe. "Skin against skin is the best way to share body heat. Is that not correct, Dainon?" Arrio folded his garment and placed it on the ground, a safe distance from the fire. He stood there, the firelight playing over his body.

By the Maker, he is so beautiful. Kei could not take his eyes off Arrio, noting the way the light rippled over his muscles and toned flesh. His sac was in shadow, but Kei glimpsed the heavy-looking orbs that hung below Arrio's long shaft. Kei's fingers ached to touch it, to stroke along its length.

Then Dainon coughed and got to his feet, removed his tunic, and revealed that hard, furry body. A mat of hair covered his wide, firm chest that Kei longed to run his fingers through. Two men, so different in their appearances, and yet both stirred Kei's senses. The prospect of spending a night naked under soft layers with them was enough to have his cock stiffen inside his robe.

"Kei?"

Arrio was watching him, those deep blue eyes locked on his.

Swallowing, Kei stood, and with trembling fingers, he undid the tie around his waist. He slipped the robe from his body, shivering as the cool night air came into contact with his bare skin. He was conscious that his shaft had lengthened and stiffened in spite of the breeze.

Kei knew his hardness had nothing to do with the cool air and everything to do with the two men he gazed upon.

"Time for sleep," Arrio said with a smile, his gaze flickering down to where Kei's erect length rose.

Heavens help me.

CHAPTER
TWELVE

KEI MOANED softly when Arrio's tongue flicked his nipple, sending shudders through him.

"He likes it," Dainon said with a chuckle before leaning in to claim Kei's mouth in a kiss full of heat. Kei curved his hand around Dainon's head to pull him in deeper, feeding soft cries between Dainon's lips while he pushed at Arrio's head in an attempt to get him to move lower.

Arrio laughed against Kei's belly, tickling him. "I cannot imagine where he wants me to go," he said, his breath hot against Kei's skin.

Dainon broke the kiss and stared at Arrio, licking his lips. "Do it. I want to watch you take him in your mouth."

Kei groaned and let go of Arrio. He reached down to grasp his shaft, holding it out in anticipation of those full lips around it, that hot, slippery tongue flicking the head. "Please," he begged.

Arrio and Dainon locked gazes, and something passed between them. Then Kei arched his back when Arrio's mouth met his cock. *Oh. Oh, sweet Heavens.* Dainon moved his hand down to Kei's sac, cupping and squeezing his testicles before sliding a finger purposefully toward his entrance. When he slowly sank it deep into Kei's channel, a full-body shiver coursed through Kei, and he tightened his grip on his shaft in an effort to stop what he knew was about to happen. Lightning lit up every nerve in him, every inch of skin tingling as his swollen cock throbbed—

Kei opened his eyes, gasping, heart hammering as he spilled over his hand, body shaking from his climax. His shaft jetted pulse after pulse of seed until he lay limp, his hands covered with the evidence of his dream. He fought to draw breath into his lungs, conscious of the men sleeping beside him. When at last he had his breathing under control, he lay there, torn between the ecstasy he had experienced and the deep-seated regret that it had not been real. It did not matter that his senses were telling him to be patient, that one day what he dreamed would become reality.

Kei had never had a dream like it, and he was hungry for more.

"You make such a beautiful noise when you spend," Arrio whispered into his ear. Kei caught his breath and became rigid. Arrio shifted closer and suddenly there was his hand, holding a towel. "Here. Wipe yourself." His breath tickled Kei's ear. "You do not want to spend what is left of this night sleeping in a wet spot."

Kei took the towel and removed all traces of his seed. He put it aside and rolled over to face Arrio, his face heated. He could hear Dainon's breathing, slow and regular, evidently asleep. *Thank the Maker.* It was bad enough that Kei had awoken Arrio.

Arrio lay on his side, head nestled in the crook of his arm. "Was it a good dream?" he whispered, reaching out to stroke Kei's hip, his hand slipping beneath the layer of fur.

"Yes." Kei was not about to share his dream. *Please, let me not have said their names aloud.* When Arrio said nothing more, he breathed more easily. "I am sorry if I awoke you." He kept his voice to a whisper.

Arrio gently traced the line of Kei's hip, moving higher to stroke along his arm. "I was not asleep. I was lying here thinking about you."

Kei's chest tightened. "You... you were?"

Arrio caressed his cheek. "How could I sleep, when I lie between two beautiful men? I listened to your low moans, felt you move against me as you touched yourself, and all I could do was...."

"What?" Kei held his breath, his body taut.

"Wonder what it would be like to kiss you."

By all that is holy. Kei wanted that too.

He shifted closer until their bodies were pressed up against each other and he could feel the heat of Arrio's length searing his belly. Kei reached out and cupped Arrio's cheek. "Then kiss me," he whispered.

Arrio's breathing hitched. Before Kei could think, his mouth was taken in a kiss that held the promise of so much passion, it made Kei yearn for it. Arrio plunged his tongue between Kei's lips, and Kei opened for him, unable to lie still while Arrio claimed him without hesitation. He wanted to moan with pleasure when Arrio pushed him onto his back and rolled on top of him. Instinctively Kei spread for him, shuddering at the feeling of Arrio's hot, heavy cock slowly rubbing against his already half-hard shaft. Kei's heartbeat raced, his breathing quickening as he clutched at Arrio's back, fingers digging into the muscle. Arrio buried his face in Kei's neck, his breathing rapid and harsh, urgent with arousal while he rocked gently against Kei's body.

When Dainon made a soft noise, Kei froze, and sanity was restored.

He pushed gently but firmly at Arrio's shoulders, forcing him to roll back to his position next to Kei. Arrio's breaths were labored, as were Kei's, his body trembling. "Why… why do you stop?" Kei could hear the confusion in Arrio's voice.

How can I explain? How do I tell him that this cannot be? Not yet, and not like this.

In a burst of clarity, Kei knew with every sense he possessed that it was wrong for Arrio to take him. *I am destined for both of them. And when the time comes, it will be the three of us.* How he came to know this, Kei had no idea, but as always, he trusted his instincts—even if those same instincts had resulted in him spreading his legs to accept Arrio's cock.

He shivered at the thought. *Desire, arousal, lust—how truly powerful they are.* Arrio had wanted him….

Arrio….

Kei stroked Arrio's chest. "As one who is similarly gifted, will you trust me?"

Arrio stilled beside him. "Your senses bade you stop?"

Kei nodded. "More than that, I cannot tell you. But know this… I have never shared my body with anyone."

Silence fell, followed by Arrio's slow intake of breath. "Neither have I."

Something inside Kei clicked into place, some inner sense that they were back on the right path. *This is as it should be.*

Arrio placed his hand over Kei's. "I trust you." Kei sighed with relief when Arrio pressed his lips to Kei's in a chaste, lingering kiss. Then he brought his mouth to Kei's ear. "But you will be mine. This *I* know."

"I will," Kei acknowledged, unable to repress the shiver that coursed through him. A gust of wind shook the tent, and he shivered again, this time with cold.

"Come here." Arrio wrapped his arms around Kei, enveloping him in warmth. "You shall sleep in my arms."

Kei settled against Arrio's body, content and at peace once more. Dainon's breathing, slow and hypnotic, pulled him into a deep sleep.

DAINON AWOKE with the dawn and stretched beneath the soft layer that covered him. Without turning his head, he knew his two companions still slept—their breathing was slow and even.

What would I give to sleep with them curled up around me?

The thought shocked him into stillness. Shame spread through him at the memory of undressing the previous night. He had yearned to suggest that he sleep between them, but in the end, his nerve had failed him. Dainon was accustomed to being a leader of men, confident and bold, and yet around Arrio and Kei, he was plagued with uncertainty.

When I am with them, I do not recognize myself. He could not deny his attraction to them, and the simple recollection of their lips against his was enough to send a pulse of heat through his body. What shook him most was the realization that he wanted *more*. His skin prickled at the thought of sliding his shaft deep into Kei's tight little body, and something primal unfurled deep in his belly to think of Arrio sinking his long cock in Dainon's hole.

That sent a jolt through him. Dainon was a warrior, the aggressor, and yet he could envision himself submitting to Arrio, bending over for Arrio to take him roughly….

Dainon stifled a groan and flung his arm across his eyes, as if that would blot out the images that invaded his overheated brain. His imaginings went far beyond the simple attraction he had experienced toward another warrior. He had thought Caro good-looking, and perhaps if Dainon had allowed himself to take it further, they might have—

No, we would not have. He knew that now. He had been too bound up with grief, and added to that was the impediment that such couplings were deemed unsuitable.

Then what has changed? What has caused such a climatic shift in me?

There could be only one explanation—*or should that be two?*—and both of them slept beside him.

His thoughts went to Kei. If he had found the young man endearing before their brief dip into the river, that was as nothing compared to how he felt after. Kei's playful nature lightened Dainon's heart, and he had found himself studying the prince during their evening together. The more time he spent around the two princes, the more delight he took in their company. That first kiss he had shared with Kei lingered still in his memory, as did the feel of Arrio in his arms after their race.

I would have that again. And more. Dainon lay still in the quiet of the morning and let his mind wander, free to imagine the taste of Kei's lips, the feel of Arrio pinned between them, rocking back onto Dainon's cock before pushing deep into Kei's passage. *Heavens, I want them both.*

Dainon pushed back his fur blanket and sat up, conscious of his rigid shaft that poked up at his belly. He turned to gaze at his companions and—

Oh sweet Heavens. Look at them. Dainon regarded the pair, his heart aching.

Kei lay in Arrio's arms, his head resting upon Arrio's bronzed chest. The layers that had covered them had been pushed lower, and Dainon could see Kei's thigh lying across Arrio's body, his hand resting protectively over where Arrio's heart beat. Arrio's hand lay on Kei's thigh, and the scene was one of such beauty and tranquility that Dainon struggled to breathe.

They look so... perfect together, as though they were made for each other. Their bodies interlocked, and as Dainon watched, Arrio murmured in sleep and pressed his lips to Kei's head.

Dainon wrinkled his nose. Something pervaded the air, a familiar smell of.... He stared at them, his heart sinking as he realized what had stirred his senses. Dainon was accustomed to the scent, so reminiscent of the barracks, the bathing area, the early mornings on patrol when warriors awoke hard and needing relief.... He gazed at Arrio and Kei in dismay.

They shared their bodies while I slept.

The depth of his dismay disturbed him.

Why should it distress me so? They are of a similar age, and any fool could see there is a connection between them. Yet the knowledge that the princes had enjoyed an intimacy that Dainon would not dare suggest weighed heavily on him.

He got up and crept out of the tent, the cool morning air wafting over his body, pebbling his skin. He walked slowly to the river, knelt on the bank, and scooped up the icy water in his cupped palms, dousing his head, face, and neck. He shook his hair to rid himself of the last drops and then stood there in silence, drinking in the sights and sounds around him.

Anything rather than think about Arrio and Kei.

Dainon put on his tunic and set about relighting the fire. Once he had it burning away merrily, he filled the metallic pot that Arrio had brought along with clean water. From Arrio's saddlebags he withdrew the pouch that held aromatic leaves, and after removing a handful, he dropped them into the pot and set it carefully on crisscrossed sticks, the flames licking at its base.

He lost himself in the mundaneness of simple tasks: feeding the horses, providing them with fresh water, slicing up chunks of fruit that Kei had brought along. Dainon's activities occupied him, but did not take away the sting.

"You have been busy."

Dainon stiffened as Arrio's voice pierced the quiet morning. He replied without turning around. "Breakfast is prepared and the brew is almost ready. Once we have eaten, we can be on our way." He awaited Arrio's response, but when silence greeted his words, Dainon twisted to peer over his shoulder.

Arrio stood by the tent, his robe clutched around him. His brow was creased. "Is all well with you, Dainon?"

Dainon forced a smile. "All is well. I am eager to see what this day brings." He went back to his task of slicing thick pieces of bread. "Is Kei awake?"

"He stirs, but not fast enough for my liking." Arrio gave a low chuckle. "Perhaps he needs another dip in the river to awaken him."

Dainon did not respond. He had loved the playful episode of the previous day, but the morning's discovery had robbed him of all joy. It had taken his recent revelations to bring home to him the futility of his situation. No matter how much he might want to take things further, he knew in his heart that it was not to be.

I do not belong here. I do not fit here. Why begin something that can only end in misery when I have to return to Kandor? And more misery when they realize they only need each other?

All Dainon wanted was to find the gold, return to Teruna, and see how far King Tanish and his ministers had gone along the path of providing aid for Kandor. Then Dainon would go home and leave this painful situation behind him.

This is not for me. They *are not for me.*

As THEY drew closer to the mountains, Arrio became aware of the familiar sensations that tickled up and down his spine. *We are nearly there.*

Kei looked across at him from his mount and grinned. "Do you itch yet?" he asked with a knowing look.

Arrio laughed. "Oh, I do indeed." It delighted his heart that Kei had remembered.

Behind them, he caught Dainon's cough on the breeze. For the seventh or eighth time that day, Arrio found himself wondering what had changed. Dainon had been quiet and aloof with him all morning. Then he considered this: *Not only with me—with Kei too.* The thought saddened him. He yearned to stop and take Dainon aside, to demand to know what was wrong, because plainly all was not well. But each time he approached Dainon, the warrior picked up a little speed and Arrio found himself alone.

It was only when he took a moment to consider the morning's events that a possible reason for Dainon's aloofness occurred to him. *How must we have appeared to him when he awoke?* Arrio was not stupid. He knew Dainon had finally accepted his attraction to men, and perhaps the sight of Kei in Arrio's arms had kindled a small amount of jealousy in Dainon's heart.

He stared at the warrior's back, noting his rigid posture, and sent him a silent message.

I would sleep in your arms in a heartbeat. All you have to do is ask. Arrio was a prince, but in such matters, he knew he could not demand that of Dainon. The impetus had to come from Dainon himself.

It was evident from Kei's expression that Dainon's attitude had hurt him, and Arrio compensated by talking with him, swapping tales of Teruna and Vancor. Kei had relaxed, and the two of them had passed the hours in pleasant conversation. By the time the mountains were in sight, Arrio felt completely at ease with him, as if they had known each other all their lives.

Something good came out of Dainon's foul mood. Arrio prayed that the warrior would put aside his jealousy soon. He wanted the Dainon who had encountered him on the beach, the Dainon who had swum with him, who had kissed him and made him ache for more.

The Dainon who rode with them was like a stranger.

"What are we looking for?"

Arrio snapped his head up. It was the first time Dainon had spoken in an hour. Arrio overcame his shock quickly. "There are many caves up ahead. A few of them have been mined in the past, but not all of them are suitable. My task is to seek out a cave that has a seam rich enough to make it viable for mining."

"How long does a mine last?" Kei asked.

"That depends on how hard the miners work it," Arrio replied. "Gold is used for jewelry, decoration, and as currency. Care is taken not to overwork it, however." He resisted the urge to scratch as they drew near to the caves that were situated in the foothills of the mountains. Arrio pointed to a cave whose entrance was blocked with wooden slats. "When a seam is exhausted, the mine is shut down to prevent accidents." He clicked with his tongue to move his horse forward.

"What kind of accidents?" Kei gazed at him with wide eyes.

"Sometimes the gold is many feet below the surface. The miners dig a series of deep shafts, down which they descend, and then they dig tunnels. Accidents have happened where a miner has fallen down a shaft. To seal off a mine thus tells any future prospectors that its gold has been retrieved and that entrance is forbidden." Arrio brought his horse to a stop before a cave opening. Without a word he climbed down and walked slowly over to the entrance, a split in the rocks that was wide enough for perhaps two men to walk through it.

"Can I come too?" Kei pleaded, clambering down off his mount and hurrying to Arrio's side.

Dainon dismounted and tethered the horses to a tree. "My advice is caution. You do not know what lies beyond this point."

Arrio grinned. "Yes, I do—gold." He patted Kei's arm. "You will be safe with me." He glanced at Dainon. "We will not be gone long. And if we have need of you, we will shout."

"Will there be enough light in there?" Dainon asked.

Arrio smiled. "I do not intend to venture too far into the cave. There will be light enough that penetrates from the exterior."

Without waiting for Dainon to reply, Arrio stepped into the cave, the air cooling almost immediately. The interior was not very large, maybe seven or eight feet surrounded on three sides by rock. The space stretched up perhaps ten feet.

Kei was close behind him. "Will we see the gold?" His whisper echoed in the stillness.

Arrio chuckled. "No, but I do not need to see it." He came to a halt in the center of the space and held out his hands. He closed his eyes and focused inwardly. Almost instantly his skin began to crawl, until all the hairs on his neck and arms were standing on end. Slowly he moved toward the wall of rock and placed his palms against the surface. A tingle shot along his arms and shuddered its way down his spine.

"What is happening?" Kei asked breathlessly.

"My body feels as though every inch of my skin is itching, and I ache to scratch."

"What does that mean?"

Arrio laughed, the sound rolling out of him and rebounding off the rock. He took a step back, his hands falling to his sides. "That my fathers, the miners, and my friend Parina will be very, very happy." He knew with absolute certainty that beneath his feet was the richest seam he had ever encountered. He clasped Kei to him in a fierce embrace. "I am happy to have you here with me." It felt right to have Kei at his side.

"I am happy to share this moment."

"Arrio? Kei?" Dainon's voice pierced the gloom.

"Let us go out before he comes in after us," Arrio suggested. He hoped the discovery would lighten Dainon's mood.

Kei sighed. "I wish I knew what ails him. He is not himself today."

Impulsively, Arrio grabbed Kei in another hug. "I feel it too. Let us hope our journey home is an improvement." *Perhaps a change in our sleeping arrangements might be the solution.* Arrio would see what the night brought. He let Kei go, and they stepped out into the bright sunshine.

Dainon heaved a visible sigh. "I think we should leave this place. Something or someone watches us." He went over to his horse and pulled his sword free.

Arrio froze. "Truly?"

Dainon nodded, scanning their surroundings. "I trust my instincts." He beckoned to them. "Quickly."

Arrio complied. He too trusted Dainon's instincts. As he reached his horse, a loud growl rent the air, making him shiver.

"What is that?" Kei whispered, standing still.

Before Arrio could reply, the trees and bushes a few feet away shook violently. Arrio only had time to register a huge, dark shape with teeth and claws making straight for him before those claws sliced down his arm, sending him sprawling to the ground. He clutched at his blood-soaked arm, dizziness overwhelming him. He lifted his head weakly to see a black bear on its hind legs, towering over him, his blood dripping from its claws.

Dainon launched forward, sword in hand, ready to run it through, when Kei's voice rang out.

"Do not kill her!"

CHAPTER
THIRTEEN

KEI LURCHED toward the bear, hands outstretched, his heart quaking. The creature had not moved, her huge paws raised, her mouth wide. A roar thundered out of her, and Kei tried not to shiver at the sight of all those teeth.

"Get out of the way before you are hurt!" Dainon's voice cracked, his panic evident. "Move, Kei, and let me kill it."

Kei kept his eyes locked on the bear. "Lower your sword," he commanded, keeping his voice low. "Go to Arrio and tie something around his arm to slow down the bleeding." When nothing stirred in his peripheral vision, he let out a growl. "*Now*, Dainon. The bear will not harm me, and Arrio needs you." He edged a little closer, making a low humming noise in the back of his throat. *You will not harm me, will you?*

Something in Kei's manner must have broken through Dainon's panic. To Kei's profound relief, Dainon stepped behind him and knelt at Arrio's side.

Kei yearned to look, to see how badly Arrio was hurt, but he knew he could not. "How is he?" he asked, his focus still on the bear, who had not taken her eyes off him, but had not moved.

"He is pale. There are three deep gashes down his arm and there is a lot of blood."

As if in reply to this, Kei caught Arrio's low cry of pain, and it tore at his insides.

"Use your training. Stem the flow of blood." Kei forced as much authority into his voice as he could manage. "Easy there," he crooned, taking another step toward the bear. "They are safe. Be at peace." He heard the tear of fabric.

The bear swayed, her paws lowering, and Kei caught her plaintive whine.

Thank the Maker. "All is well," he told her softly, his voice low and even. "They are safe."

"Who is safe?" Dainon whispered from below his field of vision.

"Her cubs. We came too close to her children and she attacked. Arrio was obviously nearest." He resumed his low humming, and the bear dropped back onto all four paws. "That is the way. Good girl." Kei took a deep breath. "I could not let you kill her," he whispered to Dainon. "She was only protecting them. If you had killed her, they would not have survived without their mother."

"How... how do you know all this?" Kei could hear the wonder in Dainon's voice.

"It is what my gift tells me," he replied. He heaved a huge sigh of relief when the bear turned and lumbered out of sight, retreating the way she had appeared. Tremors shook Kei as he sank to his knees, violent shivers racking his body. Then he remembered Arrio. He crawled across to where Arrio lay in Dainon's arms, his face almost white, his breathing ragged. Dainon had torn a piece from the bottom of Arrio's robe and tied it around his arm, the blood already soaking through it.

"You... you did it," Arrio gasped, struggling to raise his head to look at Kei.

"Be still," Kei bade him, "and let me see." Gently he untied the makeshift bandage and handed it to Dainon. Something pushed at him, some innate sense that would not be silenced, and Kei knew better than to fight it. He shivered at the sight of those deep cuts, their edges white.

"We are too far from Teruna to do anything but try to stop the bleeding," Dainon said urgently.

"Help me to lie him down, and then fetch one of the water bags," Kei said quickly. Dainon gently disengaged Arrio from his arms and laid him on the ground. Kei took Arrio's arm in one hand, wincing inwardly when Arrio let out a moan of pain. Kei held his other hand over the gashes and closed his eyes.

Arrio cried out, and the sound tore at Kei's soul, but he persevered.

"You are hurting him," Dainon insisted, returning with the water.

Kei's senses told him otherwise. He heard the hint of a tremor in Dainon's voice and sought to distract him. "You do not strike me as a man who allows himself to panic, and yet I heard it plainly."

There was a moment of silence. "You are right," Dainon acknowledged quietly. "All I could think of was that Arrio was hurt. And yet if it had been any other man, I do not think I would have reacted in the same manner." He paused. "Except if it had been you."

Kei liked his response. *Dainon begins to see that we are important to him.* Yet it was not enough. *He is not ready to learn the truth.*

He moved his hand through the air above Arrio's arm, aware of the heat radiating from him, growing more and more intense. Arrio's cries softened into low whimpers, and Kei's heart soared. He prayed silently to the Maker, all his senses focused on Arrio.

"By all that is holy."

Dainon's awed whisper had Kei opening his eyes. Dainon stared at him, mouth open, before glancing down to where….

Thank the Maker. Arrio's color had returned and his breathing was more even. Dainon trickled water onto the bandage and gently wiped away the blood from his arm—his unblemished, perfect arm.

Kei stared at it, unable to process what he was seeing. No scars, not even a scratch, marred Arrio's bronze skin. *I did that.* Gratitude coursed through him, silent words of thanks for his gift.

Arrio peered at it, his eyes wide, before raising his chin to lock gazes with Kei. "You healed me."

Kei nodded, swallowing, a wave of fatigue rolling over him. He could not speak, his throat tight. When he tried to stand and his legs gave way, both men caught him.

Arrio put his arms around him. "Have you ever healed someone before today?"

"You are my first," Kei whispered. His head was spinning, his face tingling, and a slow tide of gray dots rose up to take his vision. He was aware of Arrio's and Dainon's voices growing fainter, as though they spoke from miles away. Then everything slipped away from him as suddenly the world became black.

WHEN HE opened his eyes, he was in Arrio's arms, with Dainon kneeling beside him, brow furrowed.

Arrio gazed at him, his face glowing. "Welcome back." He cupped Kei's cheek with such tenderness that it made Kei's heart ache.

"What… what happened?" Kei struggled to sit up, Arrio assisting him.

Dainon brought him a cup of water, and he drank it greedily. "You lost consciousness," Dainon informed him. "We can only surmise that healing Arrio took its toll on your body." He peered intently into Kei's eyes. "How do you feel?"

"I feel fine," Kei insisted. "Can I stand?"

"Only you know the answer to that question," Dainon said, that frown still in evidence. He and Arrio stood on either side of him, supporting him as he got to his feet, his legs a little unsteady.

Kei regarded the two men. "Are we done here?" The dizziness he had experienced was fading, but he was left feeling weak.

"Most definitely," Arrio said. "We are going back to the riverside to camp there tonight. And you will ride with me," he added firmly.

Kei snorted. "I am more than capable of sitting astride my horse." As if to prove his point, he took a step toward his mount, and the world slipped sideways a little.

Dainon's strong arms were there in an instant. "It is no sin to need help, Your Highness." Dainon spoke softly into his ear.

The use of his title made Kei's gut clench. "I faint, and suddenly I am no longer Kei?"

Dainon's body stiffened against Kei's. "Forgive me, but I had forgotten that I am here in a formal capacity as your protector."

Kei turned slowly in his arms. "Then as my protector, I command that you use my name." A wave of recklessness overcame him, and he reached up to cup Dainon's head. "And we are past such formalities, you and I." Unable to stop himself, Kei drew Dainon close until their lips brushed softly in a chaste kiss. His heart sang when Dainon did not pull away, and his arms tightened around Kei's body.

The sound of a throat clearing shattered the intimate moment.

Arrio regarded them from his horse, smirking. "It seems you are feeling better," he said to Kei, "but I am taking no chances." He held out his arms. "Dainon, help Kei up to sit in front of me. Can you lead his horse?"

Dainon seemed as if he was going to argue, but eventually he nodded. "Very well." He sighed. "I am learning that once you have made up your mind, there is little anyone can do to change it." He lifted Kei and helped him straddle the horse's back.

Arrio laughed. "You learn fast." He waited until Dainon had mounted his stallion and tethered Kei's horse to his saddle. "Let us leave here quickly, lest we disturb the mother and her cubs again." He clicked his tongue and pulled gently on the reins, and his horse moved off, Dainon riding ahead of them.

Kei leaned back against Arrio's chest, loving the feel of his arms around him. He did not want to think about the heart-stopping moment when the bear had sliced his arm. "What about you? Are you recovered?" he asked.

A chuckle tickled his ear. "By the time you regained consciousness, I was fine. Your hands are truly magic. I was more concerned about you." A pause. "Dainon was worried about you also."

Kei said nothing. He had felt Dainon's concern roll off him in waves, and that had spoken louder than words.

"Your kiss seems to have healing properties too. He appears more relaxed than earlier." Arrio paused. "That is not the first time you and he have shared a kiss. And do not deny it. I *know* this. My senses do not lie. Have you shared everything with me?"

Kei opened his mouth to say *yes*, but closed it when some inner voice spoke up. *Be truthful with him.* Kei was learning to listen when that voice spoke. "Not entirely."

Arrio's sigh tickled his neck. "I sensed as much. I do not know what happened back there, but I do know you did more than heal me."

Kei turned his head to look at Arrio. "What do you mean?" His heartbeat sped up.

"Only that I feel you. I am… aware of you, as I never was before. Now, why should that be?" He kissed Kei's cheek. "Could it be that you have an idea why?"

Kei breathed out a sigh. "We need to talk." He stared ahead to where Dainon rode before them, his back straight. "Tonight, when Dainon is asleep."

"Very well." Arrio's arm tightened around his waist and his lips brushed over Kei's ear, making him shiver. "I shall never forget this day."

Kei had a feeling that once Arrio knew the truth, that statement would prove to be more profound than he realized.

ARRIO WAITED until he was certain Dainon was asleep before picking up the layers of fur and moving silently out of the tent, Kei accompanying him.

As they neared the fire, Kei shivered. "It is a cold night." The black sky was strewn with stars, and the moon shone bright and full, no clouds to hide it.

Quickly Arrio spread the layers on the ground beside the fire. "I will have you warm soon enough." He grabbed more wood from the pile Dainon had placed nearby, and layered it on top of the fire. Then he pulled back one of the furs and lay on his back, his arm wide in invitation. "Come lie with me under here. We shall be warm together."

Kei stretched out beside him, his nude body pressing up against Arrio's side. Arrio covered them and then slipped his arm under the soft fur to pull Kei even closer. It was not long before Kei's shivers died away, and he put his arm across Arrio's chest with a low sigh of contentment.

Arrio took a moment to enjoy the feel of Kei's body so close to his, the softness of his beard as it grazed his chest. Kei seemed at peace, as though he was born to be in Arrio's arms. He suffered a brief pang at the thought of Dainon lying several feet away from them, soundly asleep. Arrio had yearned to curl up around him, to fall asleep sharing the warmth of Dainon's body, but he had forced himself to be practical. There was less chance of disturbing him if they slept apart.

They had ridden back to the river in silence, but it had not been oppressive. Arrio had been lost in his own thoughts, filled with awe for what Kei had done. When they had made camp, Arrio had suddenly become aware of his hunger, and had dined well on the bread and cured meats they had brought for the journey. Dainon seemed to have retreated into himself, his furrowed brow an indication of deep thought. When he had suggested an early night, Arrio had fought hard to maintain his composure.

Arrio had questions, and only Kei could provide the answers.

He listened to the crackle of the fire and the whistle of the wind through the trees. When Kei remained silent, Arrio stroked his arm. "It is time to share with me."

Kei sighed softly. "May I ask you something personal?"

"Of course." Arrio had no desire to hide from Kei.

"How is it that you have lived twenty-one years and yet you are still a… virgin?"

Arrio sighed. "You of all people may be able to understand my reasons for remaining so. When I was sixteen, I realized for the first time that while there were many beautiful girls in Teruna, none of them stirred me. It took a walk through the city to bring home to me where my appetites lay. There was a wrestling bout in the square, an exhibition of skill, and several pairs of men took part. They wore nothing, their bodies glistening with oil."

"And you liked that."

Arrio chuckled. "I went straight to my fathers and announced my discovery that men made me hard."

Kei snorted. "I see now that little has changed. You like to speak your mind."

Arrio kissed his forehead. "And I see no reason to change. Prevarication wastes time. But to answer your question, my *papi* spoke to me of those *Seruani* who instruct others in the pleasures of the flesh. He asked if I wished to have such instruction."

"Such instructors exist in Vancor also," Kei said. "So you did not accept Feyar's suggestion. Why?"

Arrio rolled onto his side to face Kei. "Some... sense in me bade me wait. I knew somehow that when I finally shared my body with another, it was to mean something."

He heard the hitch in Kei's breathing. "You knew the timing was not right."

"Yes," Arrio breathed. He exulted in the knowledge that Kei truly understood. "That is not to say there have not been moments when I have silently cursed my senses, nights when I have ached to know what I am missing. I recall one such night when I could not sleep. I went down to the stables to saddle up a horse and go for a ride. As I passed one of the stalls, I caught sounds, grunts and moans, so I peered inside." The memory of the two grooms fucking in the empty stall sent a flush of heat through him. "They did not see me. They were lost in each other. But watching them together made me ache for what they had."

Kei nodded. "I too have watched men making love. And yes, I know what you felt. I took a young man from the royal harem to be my first, but one touch of his hand was enough to tell me this could not be."

In a burst of clarity, Arrio saw the truth. "His thoughts would have been as bare to you as his body." It was as if he were *there*, feeling Kei's horror as the nature of his gift dawned on him. Then the import of his realization hit him. "How can you be with any man, if that is what awaits you?" His heart went out to Kei. "I see now why you stopped me last night." Sorrow filled him as he recalled telling Kei he would be Arrio's.

"Peace, Arrio. I am not finished." Kei sat up and drew his knees to his chest, hugging them. "I need to share something with you."

Arrio sat up also, facing Kei. "Speak," he urged. His body tingled and his heartbeat raced.

"Years ago I had a dream. I knew upon waking that it had import, and the dream recurred many times as I grew up. But the two images I retained from it did not make sense." He paused. "Do you not think it odd that we have never met until now?"

Arrio stared at him, a memory surfacing. "I once asked Sorran why they never thought to take me with them on their visits to Vancor. He simply said the timing was not right." The skin on his back prickled, and it had nothing to do with the cool night air.

Timing. We are meant to be here, to be speaking thus. He shivered.

Kei nodded once more. "We were destined to meet in this manner."

To hear an echo of his own thoughts sent pinpricks up and down Arrio's spine.

"So imagine my shock," Kei continued, "when I entered the royal audience chamber, to be confronted by one of the images from my dream."

"What image?" Arrio whispered, his skin pebbling.

"I had seen a pair of deep blue eyes. I had no idea of their significance, until I met you—and there were those same eyes, staring at me."

In that moment Arrio recalled the way his body had reacted to Kei, that first moment when they had embraced. Moreover, he could still see Kei's wide eyes, his parted lips. "You dreamed... of me?"

Kei nodded slowly, not breaking eye contact.

"Then you and I—"

"Are destined to be together," Kei finished, his chest rising and falling rapidly.

The words hung there between them. Arrio did not need to be gifted with Truthspeak—his heart knew Kei spoke the truth. *He is truly mine.*

Then why do I feel so heavy?

Something tugged at Arrio's consciousness. Some sense told him there was more to come.

"I do not understand," he blurted out. When Kei's face fell, Arrio hastened to reassure him. "What you are telling me makes sense. I feel the... rightness of it, and believe me, my heart rejoices that we are meant for each other."

Kei's posture relaxed and he breathed out a sigh.

"But what it does not explain is...." Arrio broke off and glanced toward the tent where Dainon lay sleeping. He swallowed hard. "Him," he said softly. Arrio did not dispute Kei's vision, but neither could he dismiss what his senses told him: that he and Dainon were also meant for each other. *How can I be meant for both of them?*

Instantly Kei shifted until he knelt beside Arrio, his hands cupping Arrio's face. Kei stared at him. "Wait. Please, let me finish." Arrio took a deep breath and nodded, and Kei sighed. "The second image was a bear, carrying a sword." He released Arrio and sat back, regarding him in silence.

Arrio frowned, his thoughts flung into confusion. "A bear? That does not ma—" Then it hit him. *The stable. The emblem of Kandor. Dainon, the warrior.* He stared with wide eyes. "By the Maker," he whispered, as the veil was lifted from his sight. "Three of us." His skin prickled all over, and he closed his eyes, focusing inward. A sense of calm pervaded him, a peace he had seldom encountered, and in that moment, he knew. "You speak truth." With Kei's explanation, everything slotted into place, with a click so solid that it shook Arrio's world.

They are both my destiny.

"And yet there is more."

Arrio opened his eyes. "More?" *What more could there be?*

Kei smiled. "When I told you that Truthspeak did not work all the time? In all my years, there have only been two people for whom this is the case."

Arrio wanted to laugh and cry with happiness as the implications of Kei's revelation sank in. "Dainon and me."

Kai nodded, his face alight. "I was so confused at first. I thought I was going mad. What made it worse was the first time I glimpsed the two of you in the square, I knew you were different. In a sea of people, you were the only two whose colors were hidden from me."

Arrio could not contain the joy that bubbled up inside him. He pulled Kei down onto the fur and clasped him to his chest, gazing up into Kei's eyes. "Then we are truly meant to be." He caressed Kei's cheek, his heart filled with wonder. "You are mine," he whispered, before pulling him down into a kiss. Arrio did not hold back. He poured his heart and soul into that kiss, imbuing it with all the passion and desire he had locked away inside him for so long.

Kei ran his fingers through Arrio's short hair, soft moans escaping him as he returned the kiss. Arrio exulted in the knowledge that the two of them were meant to be.

When Kei stilled next to him, Arrio froze and looked him in the eye. "What is it?"

Kei exhaled slowly and sat upright beside him. "We cannot do this. Not without Dainon. And before you argue with me, look within your own heart. You know I am right."

Arrio said nothing but inclined his head in Dainon's direction. "Then tell him. Share with him as you did with me." All he could think of was the three of them, locked in passion. *By the heavens, yes. I want that.* He yearned for it, for the start of their journey together. "*Tell* him, Kei."

Kei shook his head. "I... I cannot. He is not ready."

Arrio wanted to scream to the heavens with frustration. "But how can you know that?"

Kei fell silent for a moment. "Arrio, I have spent my life being guided by what I glean from people's auras and from Truthspeak. Right now I am trying to navigate my way with neither of those gifts. I knew that it was right to share with you."

"But how could you, without your gifts?"

Kei smiled. "Oh, Arrio, you are like an open book. Every thought, every emotion, is *here* for me to see." He stroked Arrio's face. "I do not have to guess with you. But Dainon? His thoughts are not so transparent. He schools his features. And...." He hung his head. "I do not know what to do, because I cannot see which way to go."

Arrio's heart sank. "Then what do we do? Wait? And for how long?" He sighed. "I do not know how much longer I can wait, knowing you are both mine. Knowing how much I want you both."

Kei chuckled. "You have waited this long, Your Highness. You can wait a little longer. Unless you are telling me that after twenty-one years, you have suddenly lost the use of your hand?" Before Arrio could respond, Kei continued. "I do not think we will have long to wait."

"What tells you this?"

Kei smiled. "He is here, is he not? *I* am here. Fate has brought the three of us together. *That* is what gives me hope. So we will wait."

Arrio made a decision. "I will speak with my *papa*. Dainon may find he has to stay longer in Teruna than he had planned." He grinned.

Kei laughed quietly. "Why, Prince Arrio, you are evil." He glanced toward the tent. "But now we must sleep. Who knows? Tomorrow may be the day we share what we know with Dainon."

"I pray it is so." Reluctantly Arrio sat up. He banked the fire, then gathered up their furs and took Kei's hand. "For years I have watched my fathers, seen the love between them. So many times I wished for a love like theirs. To know I am to share my life with you and Dainon brings me great joy. Please, forgive me for being eager for my new life to begin."

Kei kissed him slowly, his arm around Arrio's waist. "I too am eager." He glanced down at their bodies with a rueful smile. "As is evident." Arrio had no need to look down—he could feel Kei's length against his own, both of them hard. "But soon we three will become one, and I can wait for that."

Arrio nodded. "Then let us sleep and see what tomorrow brings us." He vibrated with excitement, so much that he felt sleep might be difficult. In the space of one fireside conversation, everything had changed. He had grown up in a family where he had accepted the mystical and the wonderful as part of life, but he knew now that he had been on a path leading to this moment.

He led Kei by the hand to the tent where their soon-to-be lover slept, unaware of what awaited him.

Let it be soon.

DAINON WAITED until both Kei and Arrio were sleeping before slipping from beneath his fur layer. He got up as silently as possible, wrapped the soft covering around his body, and crept out of the tent. He walked over to where the fire blazed away, staring at its flames with a heavy heart.

Dainon had not caught the words that had passed between the two princes, but what he had seen had been enough. He had watched them, the firelight dancing over their naked bodies, the blueish moonlight falling on them, illuminating their forms.

He had awoken as they left the tent, and it had taken all his effort to lie still. He had remained that way until curiosity got the better of him. When he had peered outside, his heart had stuttered at the sight which befell him. The two of them lying together naked on furs beside the fire, Kei at Arrio's side, locked in a kiss.

It is true, then. They are together. Dainon did not need to see more. When they had stilled, he had lain down hastily, his heart pounding, lest they turn in his direction and catch him observing them. Minutes later they had crept back into the tent and Dainon had feigned sleep.

The fire warmed his body but inside he felt cold. They had walked into his life and turned it upside down. He knew he had fallen for Arrio, only to be swept up in a tide of confusion when Kei had kissed him—

Twice. He kissed me twice.—and Dainon had found himself attracted to him. But standing there by the fire, alone in the blackness of the night, Dainon thought back on the days since Kei's arrival. He recalled the times Arrio and Kei had been together, recalled how they had acted, the obvious connection between them. He put aside his own feelings and assessed the situation with cool logic.

They are two princes, whereas I am but a warrior.

They are of a similar age, whereas I am twice theirs.

They fit together. They belong together. And I was always here as a visitor. Kandor is my home. My duty lies there.

His heart aching, Dainon knew what he had to do—and that it would break his heart.

Chapter
Fourteen

"He saw us by the fire last night. That is the only explanation for his... retreat from us," Kei whispered as he climbed down from his horse and tethered her to a tree next to the brook where they had stopped. She reached down, stretching her long neck to drink from the cold water. Kei's gaze flickered to where Dainon stood several feet away, patting his stallion's neck and talking softly to him.

Arrio feared Kei was right. Dainon had been quiet all morning, barely exchanging a couple of words with them, seemingly deep in his own thoughts. Arrio forced out a low groan. "Then what should we do?" He could not begin to imagine what Dainon thought of them.

Kei's gaze was still focused on Dainon, his forehead creased in a frown. Then he let out a heavy sigh and looked Arrio in the eye. "We tell him."

Arrio arched his eyebrows. "*Tell* him? Were you not the one saying, 'No, no, we cannot share this with him.'?"

"Arrio, I know what I said, but... I cannot see what we should do. I only know that he seems so... alienated." He caught his breath. "*Look* at him." The plaintive note in Kei's voice made Arrio's heart ache.

He turned to regard Dainon, and his stomach churned to see the warrior's stony expression. Dainon avoided their gazes, leaving his horse and sitting beneath a tree, his water bottle in his hand. *He has shut us out.* Not that Arrio blamed him.

In that moment he knew what he had to do.

Arrio held out his hand to Kei. "It is time."

Kei's face fell. "Truly?"

"We cannot leave him to his own conclusions. If we are meant to be, we must share that knowledge with him. If we continue to vacillate, indecision will tear us apart before we have the chance to be together." He waited, hand outstretched, and finally Kei took it. Arrio led him to where Dainon sat, drinking from his water bottle.

Arrio joined him, sitting cross-legged and facing him, the dappled sunlight making patterns on the ground, and Kei sat by his side.

Dainon did not react at first, but after a moment, he gave Arrio his attention. "You wish to say something?"

Arrio nodded, his gut clenching. "You are upset with me."

Dainon studied him carefully. "I have no reason to be upset with you—do I?" He lifted his eyebrows and met Arrio's gaze.

The coolness of his tone sent shivers tripping through Arrio's body. "We do not want you to be unhappy. You are... important to us."

Dainon huffed and stared out across the fields dotted with wild flowers. "I am merely your bodyguard."

Shock hit Arrio at his core. "You are more than that and you know it." Beside him, he caught Kei's soft gasp.

Dainon slowly turned his head to spear Arrio with a look that made his heart quake. "And how would I know that?" There was steel in his voice. "You kiss me, touch me, bring me to the point when I can no longer deny that I want you, and then Kei arrives."

Kei's breathing hitched and he squirmed in obvious discomfort.

"And then everything changed," Dainon pressed on, his focus on Arrio. "It was as if I no longer existed. I see you together, and all it does is reinforce what I know to be true. Why would you want to be with someone twice your age and with no experience in how to please a man, when you can be with Kei?"

"But we never wanted it to be the two of us. We want to be with—"

Dainon's eyes flashed. "Do you think me blind? I see the two of you, unable to keep your hands off each other. Sneaking out at night when you think I am asleep, so you can...." He swallowed hard, his hands clenched into fists.

Arrio's heart sank. "So you did see us."

Dainon snorted. "Did you think you could leave the tent without waking me? I would be a poor warrior indeed if I had slept through that. And you should take more care when you...." Dainon drew in a deep breath. "As I said, I am not blind."

"This is all my fault," Kei broke in. "I should have told you—"

Dainon froze. "Told me what?"

Kei blinked. "I... I cannot." He looked to Arrio, his eyes pleading.

Arrio grasped Kei's hand and held it tightly. "I know these are unfamiliar waters for you, but everything tells me it is right to share this with him. I trust my own judgment, but it is clear you do not."

Kei widened his eyes. "I... I do."

That was all Arrio needed to hear.

He turned to Dainon. "Kei had a vision. He saw you and me in a dream, and when he met us, he understood the truth of it." He paused, inhaling deeply and not breaking eye contact with Dainon. "The three of us are destined to be together."

DAINON'S HEAD spun. "Together... as in the way your fathers are together?"

Arrio nodded. Kei regarded him with large eyes, so still it was as if he had been frozen.

Dainon closed his eyes, seeking a moment to frame his thoughts. He fought to keep his emotions in check, to retain some measure of objectivity. When he was calm, he opened his eyes and regarded the two men who faced him, their expressions anxious.

"I do not think you realize how huge a shift you wrought in me," he said slowly. "You brought me to the point where I had no choice but to acknowledge my attraction to you both, something I would never have believed possible before I came to Teruna. More than that—I wanted you. I saw us in my head in ways I have never countenanced, but which left me aching with desire."

Arrio opened his mouth, but Dainon held up a hand to silence him.

"So, it was one thing to awaken that desire in me. It was another to see the two of you together and feel as though I was somehow locked out."

"We are truly sorry—" Kei began, but Dainon interrupted him.

"But now this? You speak of visions and dreams. You declare that it is Destiny that has drawn the three of us together. You act as though I should accept what you say and submit to the will of whatever force seeks to bind us." Dainon paused to draw breath. "You will both have to pardon my skepticism. Thank you for sharing what you clearly feel to be true, but... I do not fully believe you."

A heavy silence fell. Arrio gazed at him with such dismay that Dainon yearned to comfort him, but he knew he could not. *Better to say what lies on my heart.*

"But… my visions…." Kei's voice cracked.

"I do not doubt your belief in your visions," Dainon said, "but your words do not match your actions." *If it is as you say, why did you share your body with Arrio? Why sneak out to lie with him by the fire?* Dainon lowered his head. He could not bring himself to reveal his thoughts, although his heart ached to believe that Kei spoke the truth.

"If it is as you say," Arrio said at last, "then is there any hope for us?"

The pain in Arrio's voice cut him like a knife.

Dainon raised his chin and looked at them. "Thank you for being… open with me." It was on the tip of his tongue to say *honest*, but he could not do so. "You have given me much to think about." That much was true. Dainon had an idea that their conversation would replay in his head over and over, once he was back in Kandor.

How could I forget this?

Dainon rose. "But now it is time for us to complete our journey. If we leave soon, we can be in Teruna before nightfall." And without another word, he walked over to his stallion, slipped his water bottle into his saddle bags, untethered the reins, and mounted.

He waited until Arrio and Kei were astride their horses, and then he led them along the path, his heart sore and his head spinning.

I want to believe them. But he knew he could not bear it if he allowed himself to do so, only to have them treat him in the same fashion as before. He thought back to his decision of the previous night. Nothing had changed.

My way is better. Dainon repeated the phrase over and over in his head. If he said it often enough, he might come to believe it.

KEI GLIMPSED the white walls of the city, glowing in the late-afternoon sunlight, and sighed with relief. *It is nearly over.* The last part of their journey had been fraught with tension. Dainon had ridden ahead, his back rigid. Kei had ached to ride up to him and talk with him, but he knew it would be to no avail. Dainon had shut his ears to them.

Arrio brought his horse alongside Kei's. "I feel your pain and distress, but we made the right decision." He kept his voice low.

Kei stared at him. "How can you think that?" He glanced forward to where Dainon rode, his posture stiff and unyielding. *We have only made matters worse.*

Arrio sighed. "It is better, now that everything is out in the open. Now it can be addressed."

"But Dainon does not want to address it." That much was obvious.

Arrio smiled. "*Now* he does not, it is true, but it will not always be so. I have had time to think on this, and I am not worried."

"How can you not worry?" Kei gaped at him in disbelief.

"Because, *terushan*, you have seen this. We *will* be together." When Kei continued to stare at him, Arrio sighed once more. "I trust your gifts, but also I trust my own feelings. This *will* come to pass. We have been truthful with him. All we can do now is leave him to think about it."

Arrio's faith in Kei's gifts sent warmth flooding through him. "You truly believe this."

"I do."

Kei bowed his head and sent up a silent prayer of thanks for the beautiful man at his side. Then he corrected himself. *The beautiful men. I should have the strength of my own convictions.*

Arrio's words came back to him. "*Terushan*? What does that mean?"

Arrio flushed. "It is an ancient word my fathers use. It means, my love. And one day it shall be my *terushani*—my loves." And with that he squeezed with his legs and the horse trotted ahead.

Kei stared after him, lips parted, eyes wide. *My terushani.*

The word tasted good on his tongue.

DAINON GOT down off his horse and led him under the stone archway to the stables. Arrio and Kei were behind him, both silent. He was grateful their excursion was at an end. The air had been thick with tension, but Dainon knew the fault for that lay with him.

Was I too harsh with them? He had no idea how they had expected him to react. *Did they think I would take them in my arms and accept what they told me without reservation, without a second thought?* Dainon doubted there was a man alive who would do that when presented with such a fantastical concept.

Yet he could not deny that some part of him yearned for it to be so.

The stables were bustling with activity, all the grooms engaged in their duties.

Timur emerged from a stall, accompanied by a slender man in a red cloak. He caught sight of Dainon and his face fell.

In that moment Dainon knew. He approached Timur with a heavy heart. "She is gone."

Timur nodded. "She went last night in her sleep. I am sorry, Dainon. I know she was dear to you." He inclined his head toward the man cloaked in red. "This is my husband, Erinor."

Erinor bowed his head. "My condolences, Dainon."

His words barely registered. Dainon turned to Kei, his throat tight. "You said she would live longer."

Kei appeared stricken. "I said she was near her time, and that I was only postponing the inevitable. I took away her pain."

Dainon closed his eyes, fighting the urge to growl. *So much for your gifts, Your Highness.* Why should he believe in those same gifts that spoke of their destiny?

"She did not suffer at the end," Timur said, his words almost gentle.

Dainon swallowed. "And I was not here when she passed." He grabbed his saddle bags and gave a nod to Arrio and Kei. "If you will excuse me." He turned and exited the stable, heading for the royal audience chamber, his chest constricted. He could not think about Tarrea, not when he had a task to do.

I will mourn her later.

Dainon approached the two guards at the door to the chamber and drew himself up to his full height. "I would speak with the king."

One of them nodded. "Wait here." He entered the chamber, leaving Dainon in the hallway.

The remaining guard peered at Dainon. "His Highness is safely returned from his journey?"

"His Highness has returned unscathed," Dainon said. It was then that he recalled the bear's attack. The excursion might have ended very differently had it not been for Kei's gift.

The thought sent a pang of guilt through his belly.

Either I believe in his gifts or I do not. He had seen it with his own eyes, seen the blood wiped away to reveal Arrio's arm free of the horrible gashes. *Why then can I not believe him when he speaks of my destiny?*

The door opened and the guard reappeared. "His Majesty will see you now."

Dainon thanked him and hurried into the chamber, crossing the room in long strides. At the far end, King Tanish stood with Feyar and

Sorran, the three men deep in conversation. Two royal guards stood on either side of the door to the chamber.

Dainon approached the king and his consorts, and knelt before them. "Your Majesty. Your Highnesses." He bowed his head.

"Rise, Dainon," the king bade him. "We are pleased to see you with us once more."

Dainon stood, his head still bowed.

"Your timing is uncanny," Sorran said. "We were going to send for you. The guards informed us of your return. You have our thanks for bringing Arrio and Kei home safely."

Dainon raised his head. "May I ask if you have come to a decision regarding Kandor's request for aid?"

King Tanish lifted his eyebrows. "Your timing is indeed uncanny." He held out his hand, and Feyar placed in it a scroll, secured with a wax seal. "This is our reply to King Rohar."

"May I be permitted to know if it is good news?" Dainon, asked, his heart pounding. He knew he was overstepping the mark, but he needed to know.

The king smiled. "We think your king and his council will be happy when they read our proposals."

Dainon straightened. "Then for the sake of Kandor, I should return there at once, to share this news."

"You mean to leave now?" Feyar frowned. "But surely you need to rest."

"I am more than capable of undertaking this journey." Dainon's breathing quickened. *Say the word and I am gone from this place.*

"We have heard about your mare," Sorran said, his voice soft. "Our condolences."

Dainon acknowledged his words with a short bow of his head. "Then you will understand why I must leave immediately. It will be a longer journey."

Feyar gaped. "You cannot mean to return to Kandor on foot."

Dainon was prepared to do whatever it took to get him out of Teruna.

"I will start off now. I am sure there will be merchants traveling that way who will have room for me."

"Dainon, wait." Sorran glanced at his husbands, exchanging a look with them before turning back to Dainon. "The stallion you rode while you stayed with us. Fiore? He is yours, with our gratitude."

Dainon stared. "I... I cannot accept such a gift."

"Nonsense." The king walked over to him. "You protected our son and Sorran's brother. You have carried out your mission with honesty and integrity. And Arrio has already told us that you and Fiore worked well together. Accept this gift from us, as a sign of the future cooperation between our two kingdoms."

Dainon's throat seized. "I thank you all for such a magnificent gift. I will take care of Fiore."

"And who knows?" Sorran smiled. "One day Teruna may see Fiore—and you—again."

Dainon did not think so. His duty lay in Kandor.

He bowed once more. "Then if you will put the scroll in my keeping, I will deliver it to my king immediately, once Fiore has had some rest."

King Tanish placed the scroll in his hands, then clasped Dainon's shoulders. "May the Maker go with you, Dainon." He released him and stepped back.

Dainon swallowed past the lump in his throat. "Your Majesty."

Sorran addressed one of the guards. "See to it that Fiore is prepared, and have provisions for Dainon's journey sent to the stables as swiftly as possible. Thank you."

The guard bowed and exited the chamber.

"I wish you a journey free from incident," Feyar said with a smile.

Dainon thanked him. "You have been generous, gracious hosts." He turned to leave them, but Sorran stopped him, a hand to his arm.

"Dainon, I look forward to meeting you again."

Dainon opened his mouth to refute the possibility, but the words died on his tongue when he gazed at Sorran. His confusion was compounded further when Sorran smiled.

"Teruna has not finished with you yet."

Dainon gave a last bow and left the chamber, his heart pounding as he recalled how Sorran's words rang with confidence.

What does he see in my future?

Then he dismissed it. *It does not matter. Teruna will not see me again.*

ARRIO MADE his last notation on the map. "There. I will give this to my fathers, ready to be passed to those who need it."

"I think you should draw a bear on that map too," Kei said. "She must dwell near the cave, and if they start mining...."

Arrio nodded. "I will make sure they are told. And now let us go to talk with my *papa-turo*. He will ensure Dainon remains with us a little longer." He led Kei from his chamber and through the cool hallways.

Kei could not forget the look on Dainon's face. "I felt his sorrow at Tarrea's passing."

Arrio nodded. "My arms ached to hold him to me, to let him know we shared his grief."

"Do you think more time is all he needs?" Kei was less certain.

"Once he has had time to reflect, I am sure he will see things differently."

Kei prayed Arrio was right.

The guards pushed open the door to the audience chamber, and Arrio entered, Kei at his side. Arrio's fathers stood close together, and something about their stance sent ripples of unease skating down Kei's spine. When Sorran looked across to them, his careful expression only added to Kei's disquiet.

"*Papa-turo*," Arrio said instantly, "we need your help. Dainon must stay with us a while longer."

The three men exchanged glances, and Sorran cleared his throat.

"Dainon has already gone."

CHAPTER
FIFTEEN

ARRIO STARED at his fathers. "But… how can this be? When? He left us in the stable but a short while ago. He cannot be gone. And gone where?"

Kei stood at his side, his face pale.

"He has returned to Kandor," Feyar said. "Where else would he go, now that his mission is complete?"

"I do not understand. He left us?" The undercurrent of misery in Kei's voice tore at Arrio's heart, and he knew he had to do something. He could not let his *terushan* suffer.

"Kei, go to the garden, and I will come to you." Sorran spoke softly, but in a tone that made it clear he expected no argument from his brother. "We shall talk more of this."

Kei's lips parted, his eyes wide, but then he bowed his head. "As you wish." He glanced in Arrio's direction, his lips pressed together, before leaving the chamber.

Arrio was not about to waste valuable time. "I will ride after Dainon." He could not have traveled far.

"You will do no such thing."

Arrio stiffened at the rebuke in his *papa*'s voice. "You do not understand. He cannot leave. He is ours."

King Tanish arched his eyebrows. "*We* do not understand?" His tone softened. "Sorran shared Kei's vision with us, my son. We, of all people, know how you feel."

"But how can he leave without a word to Kei and I, especially after we—" Arrio snapped his mouth shut.

Sorran's eyes gleamed. "After what? Tell me, Arrio. What did you do?"

Arrio heaved a sigh. "We shared Kei's vision with him. We felt he needed to know."

The chamber fell silent, and Arrio became aware of three pairs of eyes focused on him.

"So," Sorran began, "you went against everything I advised. I urged caution, but of course, you know better, as you always do." He shook his head. "Our headstrong, confident Arrio."

"I do not feel so confident now," Arrio murmured. "*Papa-turo*, can you see if… he will return?"

Sorran walked up to him and held out his arms. Arrio stepped into the warm circle of his embrace, never needing it more than in that moment. Sorran held Arrio close and spoke into his ear. "If what you have told him does not convince him that his place is with you and Kei, then it is over." Arrio's heart lurched in his chest, an ache spreading through it. Then Sorran kissed his temple. "Trust your instincts, my son, and do not lose faith. Now is the time for patience." He cupped Arrio's chin and lifted it to look him in the eye. "Look within. What do your senses tell you?"

Arrio closed his eyes and concentrated. After a moment, he relaxed. "That I should listen to my *papa-turo*, who is a wiser man than I." He opened his eyes and regarded Sorran. "You give good counsel." He glanced toward the door. "And Kei has need of it. I feel his pain. Should I go to him?"

Sorran shook his head and took a step back, releasing him. "No, let me speak with him first."

"Stay with us and tell us of your excursion," Tanish said. "We have yet to hear of this."

Sorran chuckled as he walked to the door. "I too would like to hear of this. I have no doubt the three of you had an adventure." He grinned at his husbands. "Be sure to relate it all to me later."

When the door closed behind him, Arrio turned to his fathers, his arm outstretched. "I have such a tale to tell you."

KEI SAT beneath the spreading tree, doing his best to let the garden's tranquil ambiance work its magic, but it was to no avail. His emotions were in turmoil. The last thing he had expected was that Dainon would leave. Facing up to the possibility that he might not return sent tendrils of panic unfolding in Kei's belly.

"You need to put aside your internal conflict and focus on what your gifts tell you."

Kei gave a start. "I did not hear you enter." The daylight was fading, and light from within the palace spilled out through the windows that overlooked the garden, illuminating the white stone path where Sorran stood. The buzzing of crickets filled the evening air.

Sorran joined him on the bench. "That does not surprise me. The clamoring inside your head would drown out any other noise." He tilted his head and gazed at Kei. "Share your thoughts with me. I may be able to give you guidance."

"I want to go home," Kei blurted out.

Sorran widened his eyes. "Why in the name of heaven would you want to do that? You have spent most of your life anxious to escape Vancor, and now you wish to return to your palatial cage?"

Kei said nothing. *How can I reply to that, when what he says is true?*

Sorran narrowed his eyes. "I see. The first time things do not go well for you, you decide to run away from them? And this from a man who would be king some day?"

Kei set his jaw. "I have done what I set out to do. I wanted to see more of the world, and I have seen it. I can return now."

Sorran shook his head. "No, Kei. You would not be happy, not now that you have had confirmation that your visions are true. Not now that you know what awaits you."

"But can I trust my visions?" Kei's stomach roiled.

Sorran sighed. "I think you need to stay here a while longer."

"Perhaps I should discuss that with Arrio, to see what—"

"No!" Sorran's vehement outburst startled Kei and he jumped. Sorran gave him an apologetic glance. "I am sorry. What happened to my confident brother? The Kei I knew was not so indecisive."

Kei bowed his head. "That Kei knew what people were thinking. He saw it in their colors, in their thoughts." He raised his head to meet Sorran's gaze. "*This* Kei is acting in the dark."

Sorran fell silent, studying Kei so closely that the skin on the back of his neck prickled. "Most people do not have the benefit of Truthspeak or auras to help them navigate their way through life. And though you may not see it that way, this situation is a blessing."

"In what way?" Kei frowned, genuinely perplexed.

Sorran smiled. "For the first time in your life, you see things the way everybody else sees them. They have no gifts to guide them, to show them what the future holds. They have to trust that life will be kind to them, and if it is not, that they will be able to cope with what it throws at them. You get to experience how *they* feel, Kei. This is a good lesson for a future king."

Kei studied the ground at his feet. "So you are saying I should accept that I cannot see what will happen, but I should trust what my visions have revealed thus far?"

"Yes." Sorran gripped Kei's chin, forcing his head up. He beamed at him. "Trust what you saw long ago, and forget about what is hidden from your sight now." He let go of Kei's face.

Kei bowed his head once more. "Then I will wait and see if Dainon comes back to us."

Sorran's arm around his shoulder was a comfort. Kei leaned against him, drawing strength from his brother's presence. Kei closed his eyes and sent out a silent message.

We are yours, Dainon. We will never belong to another. Come and claim us.

He prayed that wherever Dainon was, he heard Kei's words.

DAINON WAITED outside the throne room, the scroll in his hand. He had barely had time to take his bags from the stables to his house in the barracks before word reached him that the king had sent for him. *He has eyes everywhere.*

Dainon yearned for a bath to wash away the dust and sweat of his journey. He knew he had pushed Fiore to his limits, stopping only to give him rest, food, and water before forging on. Dainon was beyond tired. Sleep had proved elusive, and when it had come, it had brought dreams that made his heart ache. He told himself that with every mile he put between him and Teruna, the images in his head would grow more indistinct, Arrio and Kei's voices fainter, but it had not been the case. They were still there inside his head, as real and as beautiful as ever.

I cannot think of them. I have to put them from my thoughts.

Throughout the journey, Dainon had been at war with himself. He told himself that it was better to be without them. *Then why do I feel worse?* He told himself that Arrio and Kei were happy, that they were getting what they wanted—each other. They did not need him.

But that is not what they said, is it?

By the time Dainon had reached the palace, he was as miserable and confused as the moment he had left Teruna's borders, his mind in conflict.

The guard opened the door, and Dainon entered, not surprised to find the king was the room's only occupant.

King Rohar sat on his throne, his back straight, eyes focused on Dainon as he approached. "You have news?"

Dainon halted before the throne and dropped to his knees before his king, his hand outstretched, offering the scroll. "Teruna's reply, Your Majesty."

King Rohar was on his feet in seconds. He crossed the space between them and took the scroll. "Rise, my faithful warrior." He pointed to a leather and wood chair below the long window that looked out over Kandor. "Sit, rest." The king broke the seal and unfurled the scroll. He glanced at the parchment and looked up sharply. "Do you know what this contains?"

"No, Sire. It was given to me sealed, and nothing was revealed to me." Dainon sank into the chair, the wide strip of leather supporting him comfortably.

The king sat on his throne, reading the document and nodding every now and then. Dainon wanted to close his eyes but dared not. There would be time enough to rest when the king was done with him. He lowered his gaze to the floor and waited, grateful for the respite from his traveling.

"By the heavens, I had not expected this."

Dainon raised his chin. The king had lowered the scroll to his lap, his face alight.

"King Tanish must be a very wise ruler." King Rohar tapped the document. "I will share this with you, because it may be that you can provide me with more information."

Dainon bowed his head once. "You honor me, Sire."

"King Tanish proposes a voluntary migration. He will provide incentives for Terunans to come to Kandor, with greater financial rewards for those who possess skills that would be of use to us. The number of people he suggests that might welcome such a move is amazing."

Dainon recalled his first conversations with Arrio. "Teruna's population is expanding, Sire. I am sure there are many who would relish the opportunity to begin a new life in Kandor."

"Tell me about the Terunans." The king leaned forward, his eyes bright. "What are their beliefs? Does their culture differ greatly from ours? Did you meet any *Seruani*? Would integration be problematic?"

For the next thirty minutes, Dainon recounted his experiences among the people of Teruna, and as time passed, the king's smile widened.

"By all that is wonderful, you have done well, Dainon."

Something gnawed at Dainon's insides. "Your Majesty, there is a point I feel I must raise."

"Speak." King Rohar's expression sobered.

"In Teruna, marriage is for all who wish it." When the king frowned, Dainon plunged ahead. "Men marry with men, women with women. And there are marriages between three people." He paused, uncertain as to how his words would be received. "Provision would have to be made under the law for such… relationships. Your Majesty would need to discuss this with the royal council before King Tanish's offer could be accepted."

The king studied him carefully. "You speak wisely, Dainon. And you are right to bring up this matter. It may be that I will have need of you once more when these proposals are brought before the council for deliberation." He smiled. "But that is in the future. Now you must rest and put your journey behind you." He rose to his feet and walked over to where Dainon sat.

Dainon stood to attention, but the king patted his arm. "Welcome home, warrior. Kandor is grateful." He tilted his head to one side. "Now that I see you more clearly, I realize that this mission has taxed you greatly." His hand came to rest on Dainon's shoulder. "Is all well with you?"

"Sire, I am merely tired. I am sure that once I have rested and eaten, I will seem more like myself."

"Take as long as you need. I do not expect you to take up your duties until three days have passed." When Dainon opened his mouth to object, the king frowned. "I am serious. Take the time, Dainon. And your king is not blind. There is more than tiredness in your face."

Dainon stared at him, aghast. *Do I wear my hurt and confusion where all may see it?* Finally he bowed his head. "I will obey you in all things, Sire." He straightened and exited the throne room. He made his way through the palace, out into the courtyard that housed the stables, and through the gate that led to the barracks. The complex was comprised of a training yard, a bathhouse, rooms set aside for fitness and massage, the physician's rooms, and the two-story gray stone buildings where the warriors slept. Dainon had a small house set apart from the barracks, as befitted his rank. He had dwelt there since his marriage, and although he should have given it up after his wife's death, nothing had been said and he had remained there.

Dainon nodded in passing to his fellow warriors before retreating into his house and closing the door behind him with a solid clunk. He gazed at his surroundings, the house that had ceased to be a home so many years ago. The place was clean but sparsely furnished. A low couch by the fire doubled as Dainon's bed. It had been years since he had slept in his bed—there were too many memories to contemplate such a thing. He had thought many times of having it removed, but the idea distressed him.

Perhaps it is time for me to cast off my memories. If he had learned anything from his visit to Teruna, it was that he had changed.

And they changed me.

He bowed his head and clenched his hands into tight fists at his sides, willing himself not to think of Arrio and Kei, but to little avail. He could still hear Arrio's voice, softly telling him that the three of them were destined to be together.

How easy it would be if that were true.

Unfortunately life rarely worked like that.

What stuck in his mind most was the way they appeared to believe that he would capitulate, accept what they told him at face value, and throw himself into a new life with them.

Is that how they think the world works? Their "vision" took no account of Dainon's duty to Kandor. It seemed to skim over the fact that he had never known a man, and that until they had crossed his path, he had never entertained thoughts of taking another man as longingly as he yearned to take them.

And still they affect me. They are days from me, and yet they invade my thoughts.

Dainon pulled his clothes roughly from his body, aware of the hurt inside him. He knew what lay at the heart of it. It might have begun when he saw the connection between Arrio and Kei, saw how he… faded as their attraction flourished, but that first morning by the river had cut him deeply. He could have confronted the pair with the truth, but there seemed little point. Dainon had seen them curled up in each other's arms, the air still bearing the scent of seed and sex.

They lay beside me and made love. And they compounded the hurt by sneaking away to lie once again in each other's arms.

They made me want them, and yet they did not want me.

That was what plagued him. *That* was what he found so difficult to forget.

Dainon grabbed a short robe and a towel, and left the house to find a way to rid himself of his aches and pains.

DAINON PEERED around the door to the room where warriors received massages, and withdrew when he saw it was occupied.

"Dainon!"

He halted at the sound of a familiar voice and looked once more into the room. Garron lay on his side on the massage table, propped up on his elbow, beckoning him. "Get back in here. Where have you been?"

Dainon closed the door behind him and approached his fellow warrior. "On a mission for the king."

"I thought it must have been something from on high when nothing was posted. Well? How did it go? Did you accomplish whatever it was that you set out to do?" Garron grinned. "Or can you not discuss it?"

Dainon smiled. "I always said you had brains." He had spent an hour in the pool, letting the waters soothe away his bodily aches, at least, and he felt refreshed.

A pity my spirits could not be so easily revived.

The door opened, and when Dainon saw who entered, he gave Garron a weary but knowing smile. "I will leave you to Caro's tender ministrations." He turned to leave.

"Wait, Dainon. You need not leave. Caro is here to give me a massage. You will not disturb us."

Caro acknowledged Garron's words with a nod.

Dainon closed the door again with a patient sigh. "Garron, you need not lie to me. I understand."

Garron's eyes grew wide, and beside him, Caro paled. "What… what do you understand?" Garron said at last.

"I have eyes, do I not?" Dainon let out a sigh of exasperation. "Caro is your lover." When Garron's breathing hitched and Caro's pallor grew, Dainon groaned inwardly. He approached the table and knelt beside it, his gaze fixed on Garron. "I have known this for many years, my friend. I have not given away your secret, nor will I. Who you choose to love is no one's business but your own."

"You… know about us?" The tension in Garron's body eased, and Caro relaxed visibly.

Dainon nodded. "And you need to hear me now. The time may come, and soon, when you two no longer have to hide your love."

Garron arched his eyebrows. "Truly? How… how can that be? It is against the law."

"And laws can be changed."

Garron snorted. "I think you are drunk." He glanced at Caro and froze.

Dainon followed his gaze and caught his breath at the look of longing in Caro's eyes, so fierce, it made Dainon's heart ache.

"By the Maker," Caro whispered. "I could dwell in his home without having to sneak in when all are asleep and leave before dawn?"

Dainon nodded slowly. "Better still. Suppose you were able to marry?"

Garron laughed bitterly. "Now I *know* you are drunk."

"No, *amari*, do not laugh," Caro begged, and Garron flushed.

"What does that mean? *Amari*?" Dainon wanted to know.

Caro held his chin high. "It means *beloved* in ancient Kandoran. I came across it many years ago. I did not think any would recognize its significance if I used it." He moved to stand beside Garron and gently stroked his back. "My heart leaps at the thought that I can stand beside you, show everyone how much I love you, that two warriors *can* love one another."

Garron sat up on the table and studied his lover's face. "Mine too," he whispered before cupping Caro's nape and pulling him slowly into a tender kiss. Caro did not resist, but put his arms around Garron's neck and surrendered to the kiss.

Dainon crept out of the room as quietly as possible, changing the sign on the door to read Occupied.

He walked slowly to his house, lost in a sea of conflicting thoughts. If what King Tanish proposed came to pass, then Kandor would change beyond recognition. Dainon knew there would be resistance at first, but he focused instead on the new possibilities that would open up for Kandorans everywhere.

Not for me, however. The realization weighed heavy on his heart.

Dainon did not believe for one second that his brief sojourn in Teruna had paved the way for him to explore a relationship with another man. That was not to be.

His heart had already been claimed by two men who were destined to be together, in spite of what they believed to be the truth.

If I could have loved again? It could only have been them.

CHAPTER
SIXTEEN

ARRIO OPENED his eyes and blinked. "Kei? What is wrong?"

Kei sat at the end of his bed, his legs curled up under him, the moonlight making his white robe glow. "I could not sleep, and your door was open, and I thought—"

"Peace." Arrio threw back the covers. "Get in." Dainon had been gone for a week, and if he were honest, Arrio had expected to find Kei in his chamber a lot sooner.

Kei shrugged off his robe and climbed in, snuggling up against Arrio's side.

Arrio shivered at the first touch of cool flesh against his. "Why are you cold?"

"I took Ranor for a ride, thinking it would help." Kei wrapped his arms around Arrio and buried his face in Arrio's neck. "You smell wonderful. All warm and safe." He fell silent, and Arrio put an arm around him, drinking in Kei's spicy aroma. The scent crept into his nostrils and played with his senses, until his shaft began to thicken.

"This is not a good idea," Arrio murmured into Kei's hair, catching the smell of salt and sea air.

"Why not?" Kei asked with a yawn, releasing Arrio and turning in his arms until Arrio's chest met his back, the soft curve of Kei's buttocks meeting his groin, where his cock rose eagerly to greet them.

Arrio sighed. "Because I thought we were serious about waiting."

Kei twisted his neck to peer at Arrio. "We were. That is to say, we are." He pulled Arrio's arm over his waist and covered Arrio's hand with his own. "This feels better. I could not sleep in that bed a moment longer."

"Why not?" Arrio did his best to ignore his interested shaft.

Kei sighed into the pillow. "I miss him. I know that makes no sense, as we never shared a bed, but… I close my eyes and he is *there*, so real, I can almost reach out and touch him."

Arrio said nothing. There was no point. He had felt the same every night since Dainon had left. "Do you feel he will return?"

Kei hesitated before responding. "I cannot see. My heart tells me yes, he will come back to us. My head has other ideas."

Arrio stared at the ceiling. "I do not know if I can wait for him to make up his mind."

Kei rolled over to regard him with wide eyes. "Why, what would you do?"

"Go after him." Even as he said the words, he knew he would never do such a thing, not if it meant going against his fathers' advice.

Kei arched his eyebrows. "And what would that accomplish? We have a saying in Vancor: 'A man convinced against his will is of the same opinion still.' If he does not wish to return to us…."

Arrio swallowed hard. "I wanted him, Kei, with every fiber of my being. I pursued him when I should have backed away. Perhaps I tempted him beyond his endurance, but I had to know if—"

"I know." Kei stroked Arrio's cheek. "I felt the same desire that you did. But we must be patient."

Arrio set his jaw. "Patience is not one of my virtues, so my fathers tell me."

Kei caught hold of his chin and stared at him. "We have to believe he will return. To do otherwise will drive us to despair."

Arrio gazed into Kei's dark eyes and finally let out his tension in a sigh. "You are right, of course."

Kei kissed him, and he closed his eyes, losing himself in Kei's scent, the feel of his skin against Arrio's. When they parted, Kei turned away from him and sank back into his arms. "He will come back to us."

Arrio kissed Kei's shoulder. "Well, until he does, you are welcome to share my bed. As long as you do not tempt me beyond endurance."

Kei chose that moment to wriggle, his bottom pressing up against Arrio's rapidly hardening length. Arrio let out a groan and Kei stilled. "Is that too tempting?"

"Yes," Arrio forced out through gritted teeth. He became still when Kei froze in his arms.

"Perhaps you are right. Perhaps I should sleep in my own bed." Dejection was evident in his voice.

Arrio stopped Kei's words with a kiss, loving the way Kei melted into it, a soft murmur of pleasure escaping his parted lips. When he drew back, Arrio caressed Kei's cheek. "You are mine, Kei. I believe that with all my heart. But Dainon is ours too. Your senses tell you that we should wait until the three of us can… be together." He paused and kissed Kei once more. "I can wait for that," he said quietly. "And in the meantime, I want to fall asleep with you in my arms."

Kei's sigh of happiness said it all.

Arrio curved his body around Kei and put his arm around him. "Sleep, *terushan*. Tomorrow brings us one day closer to Dainon's return."

"Let it be so." It felt like a prayer, and Arrio hoped someone was listening.

"TERUNA IS so beautiful." Kei stood on Arrio's balcony, looking down at the city.

Arrio joined him. "I have the best view." His corner chamber had two balconies that overlooked both the city and the palace grounds. From where Kei stood, he could hear birds singing in the garden below and the faintest trickle of the fountain.

Arrio put his arms around Kei's waist and rested his chin on his shoulder. "I am glad that you finally found sleep," he murmured.

Kei closed his eyes to the view and let Arrio's presence fill his senses. Waking up in his arms had been heavenly. "Do you think anyone would mind if we shared a room while I am here?" Having Arrio so near had been a balm to his soul. For the first night since Dainon had departed for Kandor, Kei had slept well, if only for a short time.

"By 'anyone,' you mean my fathers and your brother," Arrio said with a chuckle. "I do not think they will object. I will ask my *papa-turo*."

"Ask me what?"

Both of them turned their heads at the sound of Sorran's voice. He stood at the chamber door. "May I enter?"

"Please." Arrio relinquished his hold on Kei and stepped to one side. "Kei wants to share a room with me. I thought that since he likes mine so much, he could share it. That is, if you, *Papa*, and *Papi* have no objections," he added quickly.

"I will speak with them on the matter." Sorran joined them on the balcony and drew in several deep breaths. "This was my room when I first came to Teruna. I have always loved it."

Arrio widened his eyes. "I did not know that." He gazed at his chamber, smiling. "How did it come to be mine? I do not remember."

Sorran returned his smile. "You were three, nearly four years old, I recall. Until then you had shared your room with Emena, a nursemaid who looked after you. We decided it was time you had a room of your own, and we let you loose in the palace to choose for yourself."

Kei giggled. "You let him loose? Your choice of words is interesting."

Sorran laughed. "Arrio was like a small tornado at that age. It made us all breathless keeping up with him. He ran through the corridors, pushing open every door, until he came to this one. When he had stomped his way over every inch of floor and tried to climb up onto the balconies, he declared this was his room."

"You gave me a room with balconies? I was a baby!" Arrio stared at his father. "I could have fallen."

Sorran snickered. "Feyar scooped you up in his arms and let you see what lay below the balconies. Then Tanish picked up a carved stone figure from a shelf and dropped it over the edge." He shook his head. "Your face as you watched it smash into pieces…. Apparently it was enough to make you decide never to climb them again."

When Arrio gave a mock grimace, Kei laughed. "You must have been an adorable child."

Sorran snorted. "He had his adorable moments, yes. A pity there were not more of them." He winked. When Arrio's mouth fell open, Sorran grinned. "You wish me to lie to your future husband? Bearing in mind that I would be lying to my *brother*?"

Arrio huffed. "Did you seek us out for a reason?"

Kei rubbed Arrio's back, smiling. He sensed no real hurt in Arrio. What made him smile was Sorran referring to him as Arrio's future husband. Then his smile faltered. *One of my future husbands.* He wondered what Dainon was doing at that moment, if he was thinking about them.

Sorran's hand on his arm returned him to the present.

"I came here to talk to both of you." Sorran gestured to the table. "Sit with me?"

Arrio's gaze flickered in Kei's direction as they followed Sorran and sat. "Is something wrong?" Arrio's expression grew more serious.

"No, but I felt it was time to bring up a subject that needs to be discussed." Sorran cleared his throat. "When I came to Teruna, my father and King Feolin, Tanish's father, decided that Tanish and I would be married."

"I know this," Arrio said, but Sorran held up his hand.

"Let me finish, please." He regarded Kei keenly. "I was your age, maybe a little younger. When my father announced to everyone present in the king's private chamber that I was a virgin, it was decided that I should receive instruction."

Kei stared at him. "You have never spoken of this." Judging by Arrio's expression, it seemed to be the same for him.

Sorran flushed. "That is because my instructor was a *Seruan* named... Feyar."

Arrio straightened in his chair. "*Papi* gave you lessons in how to please *Papa*?" He grinned. "I see now why you have never mentioned this."

Sorran smiled. "It must be said that neither of them was very happy about it, but he was the best choice. He and Tanish had been lovers since Tanish was seventeen." He coughed. "But this is why I am here. I had no experience, but my future husbands did." He gazed at them. "So, I wondered if you wanted some advice...."

Kei saw the light. *No. No.* "I do *not* want my *brother* giving me advice on how to...." He shuddered. The idea made him want to curl up into a tight little ball.

"I thought it best if I was the one talking about this with you," Sorran said simply.

Kei gaped. "Best? How could it be worse?"

Sorran locked gazes with him. "It could be with our mother," he replied dryly.

Kei's testicles chose that moment to climb up into his body. "You are right." He shivered. "I do not want to imagine how *that* conversation would go."

"*Papa-turo*, while you are correct in your assumption that neither of us has any experience," Arrio said, reaching across the table to clasp Kei's hand in his, "we would rather make our own discoveries." He gave Kei a sideways glance and grinned. "It would be more fun that way."

Kei grinned back at him.

"And we will not be... experimenting while Dainon is not here," Arrio concluded. His hand tightened around Kei's.

Sorran sat back in his chair. "You are waiting for him. Such a decision requires great will power." He bowed his head and then smiled once more. "I am impressed."

Arrio huffed. "I will be more impressed if I can hold out for as long as it might take." He glanced at Kei and then back to Sorran. "Make no mistake, I want both of them—but some things are worth waiting for."

Kei caught his breath at Arrio's words. He lifted their joined hands and kissed Arrio's fingers. Then he faced his brother. "My prayer is that Dainon returns to us soon. I do not know when that might be, but I will trust what my instincts tell me. He *will* return."

Sorran gave a slow nod. "You would do well to trust your instincts in this." He smiled and rose. "I am glad we could talk." He turned to Arrio, his eyes twinkling. "I will share one thing that life with your fathers has taught me."

Arrio gave an exaggerated gulp. "Yes?"

Sorran grinned. "Sex is fun." And with that he left them at the table and exited the chamber.

Kei gazed at the door. "That is something I would rather not contemplate."

"What, that sex can be fun?"

Kei shuddered. "No—that my older brother is still having sex."

The door opened and Feyar looked around it at them. "Can we talk?"

Two voices rose in unison. "No!"

SORRAN STOOD naked on the balcony, thankful that their chamber was the highest in the palace and could not be overlooked, except from the roof. He knew without turning that his husbands were moving to join him. Sorran gazed up into the night sky, the moon full and not a cloud to mar it. "Are we getting old?"

Feyar chuckled and kissed his back, making him shiver. "What brought this on?"

Tanish stood to his left, reaching across to stroke Sorran's chest. "Who is old here?"

Sorran laughed quietly and leaned on the balcony, gazing down at Teruna. "I was thinking today about when we first met, and the first time we made love."

"What made you think of that?" Tanish asked, rubbing Sorran's shoulders.

"I went to speak with Arrio and Kei, to see if they needed some advice, and—"

"Ha!" Feyar laughed. "That explains it. Little wonder they did not want to talk to me, if you had already been there before me."

"They did not want my advice either," Sorran admitted. "But thinking about back then... we were so young."

"And forty-one feels old?" Feyar snorted. "I am two years away from fifty, and Tanish is four years behind me. You are as old as you feel."

Sorran sensed movement behind him, and then Tanish slid his hand down Sorran's spine, taking his time. He curved his body around Sorran's and kissed his shoulder. "Feyar is right," he whispered into Sorran's ear. "And we are not getting old."

Sorran gasped as two oiled fingers penetrated him, two strong hands spreading his cheeks. He widened his stance, and those long fingers slid deeper, nudging his gland. Sorran gripped the edge of the balcony, the stone rough against his palms, and arched his back.

"For example," Tanish said, his voice husky, "we are not too old to fuck you on the balcony." His fingers glided in and out of Sorran's passage, moving faster, until Sorran was panting, moaning softly, and pushing back to take them as deep as possible.

"Our *dorishan* wants to be fucked, Feyar." Tanish let out a throaty chuckle.

Feyar let go of Sorran's buttocks and leaned forward to whisper in Sorran's ear. "Twenty years or more since the day we first took you, and you are still our sweet one, your tight hole made for only us."

Sorran groaned. "Then take me. Take me now." He held his breath as Tanish guided his slick cock into position and then grunted when he buried his shaft to the hilt in Sorran's body.

"Spread your legs wider," Tanish growled.

Sorran complied, his breath quickening when Feyar crawled between them to sit up and take Sorran's cock into his mouth, his hands moving around to spread Sorran once more for Tanish. Sorran rocked between Feyar's talented mouth and Tanish's hard length, Tanish's hips slamming into him with every thrust.

"And we are not... too old to... make love all night long," Tanish ground out between thrusts.

"Who is old?" Sorran cried out as Tanish brushed over his gland again and again with the head of his cock, and Feyar lapped up the precome that leaked from his slit before taking him deep into his throat.

Sorran held on to the balcony and gave himself up to the sheer joy of being fucked by his husbands, their mingled moans and soft cries rising into the night.

Sorran had never felt so young.

DAINON PACED up and down outside the council chamber, his stomach churning.

Why does the council wish to see me?

He knew the king had spoken of such a thing when he had first returned from Teruna, but two weeks had passed since then. With each new day, Dainon immersed himself in his life at the barracks and tried to forget the two princes who both attracted and hurt him. He told himself on a daily basis that they were happy without him, but there were so many things that he could not forget: the feel of their lips on his; the sight of them by the river in all their naked glory; the conversations that delighted and enthralled him; Kei and his shimmering cloud of butterflies; Arrio walking out of the sea....

Will I never forget them?

He told himself that in spite of what Kei believed, Dainon's destiny lay in Kandor, and that he had had no choice but to return there.

The door opened and a guard appeared. "You may enter."

Dainon gave a nod to the guard, took a deep breath, and strode into the chamber, his back straight, his gaze focused ahead. In front of him was a long table, around which sat nine men, the king in the center. Before the table was one chair.

Dainon needed no instruction to know where he was to sit.

On either side of the room stood a guard. Dainon gave them a glance and suppressed his reaction when he saw they were Garron and Caro, their faces impassive as they stood at attention. The coincidence sent a shiver down his back. He bowed to the council and waited, his heartbeat racing.

"Sit, Dainon." The king gestured to the chair, and Dainon sat, holding himself straight. King Rohar addressed him. "Today marks the final day of our deliberations over the proposal from King Tanish. We are all agreed that this migration will take place, and as soon as possible. However...." The king paused and locked gazes with Dainon.

Something is coming.

"I summoned you here because you have been to Teruna. You have valuable knowledge of its people and their customs." He paused, and Dainon felt a jolt of apprehension. "If we are to make the Terunans feel welcome, we must do our best to accommodate them. In my opinion, that will mean changing our laws."

Dainon's breathing quickened. *Our conversation.* He ached to glance at Garron as it slowly dawned on him what was coming. *Now I know why I am here.*

The king broke eye contact, and immediately a rumble of voices filled the air.

"What laws need we change?" a minister demanded. "And why has there been no mention of this prior to this meeting?"

"There is nothing that requires change on Kandor's part," an elderly minister said with a scowl.

Dainon was amazed at the way the ministers spoke in the king's presence. *Have they no respect?*

"Why should we change a single word? If they want to live here, they must abide by our laws," another minister called out.

"I disagree." King Rohar spoke quietly, but with those two words, the room fell silent. He met Dainon's gaze. "What is your opinion, Dainon?"

It felt as though eight pairs of eyes were burrowing into his flesh.

"I agree with Your Majesty," Dainon said, his voice faltering at first, but when the king nodded, smiling, he gave an inward sigh of relief. He cleared his throat and forged ahead. "Our laws forbid relationships between two men or two women. If that law remains in place, King Tanish may provide all the incentives he wishes, but the people will not come here."

"Why not?" The question was echoed by three or four ministers.

"Because in Teruna there are such relationships, and not just between two people, but sometimes three. The bond of three is seen as holy by many, and dates back to Teruna's earliest times."

The oldest minister coughed. "Then perhaps it would be better if they stayed in Teruna. We don't want people like... that coming here."

Dainon heaved a sigh of relief when several ministers turned to gaze at the speaker with incredulity.

"Dainon, what are your thoughts on this matter?" The king regarded him thoughtfully.

But he already knows what I think. He knows what I will say. Slowly the light dawned. *And he wants me to say it.*

Dainon seized his courage with both hands. "I understand why the law was created in the first place. Procreation was of immense importance, if Kandor was to rebuild its population. But with an influx of new families, new blood, Kandor can be as great as it once was. True, it will be a very different Kandor than the one we have all known, but who is to say that would be a bad thing?" He fixed his gaze on the minister. "And contrary to what you believe, minister, people 'like that' are already here in Kandor. They hide their relationships, but they exist." He could not help adding, "They are all around you, every day and in all walks of life."

"Nonsense," the minister spluttered. "Who here can say they know of such people?"

Dainon wanted to smile when first one, then two, then three or more hands rose slowly into the air. The minister gaped at those around the table.

"Yes, minister, they do exist. The law has forced them underground, but change it and they can dwell once more in the light, free to love as they wish." Dainon had no idea from whence he had drawn such courage, but the words spilled out of him.

King Rohar smiled. "Then the law is changed. From this moment on, those who dwell in Kandor who wish to marry a person of the same sex should feel free to do so." Those closest to him nodded in agreement, a couple of them applauding him.

Twin gasps rang out. Dainon turned to see Garron staring at the king, mouth open, before he gazed across the chamber at Caro.

The king appeared stunned. "It would appear that such a wedding between two of my warriors is imminent, if what I see is to be believed."

Caro stared at Garron, who nodded. Caro grinned. "That it is, Your Majesty."

More gasps echoed around the table, but the smiles that began to appear filled Dainon's heart with joy.

Slowly the minister rose to his feet. "I feel the time has come to leave this council," he said stiffly, addressing the king. "I cannot remain silent while laws are passed which I know to be wrong."

"You must do as you see fit, of course," the king replied, staring at the document before him.

The minister stiffened, but then bowed his head and walked away from the table, head held high.

When the door closed behind him with a creak, King Rohar regarded Dainon with shining eyes. "You spoke well today. You spoke with Kandor's best interests in your heart, even though that meant addressing a difficult and delicate subject. Kandor has need of people like you, Dainon." There were nods from those around the table.

In that moment, Dainon knew what was coming. It was obvious. An empty chair on the council, the king's words....

Kei was mistaken. My destiny does not lie with him and Arrio, but in Kandor as a minister on the royal council.

He should have been soaring with pride, but instead his heart felt like lead. It had taken that thought to make him realize how much he had wanted to be wrong.

"Dainon, there is something I have kept from you, but now is the time to reveal it." The king rose to his feet. "King Tanish wrote of you in glowing terms. He praised your honesty, your integrity, and your sense of honor. He made a suggestion that I was loath to accept, but I see now that he is right." He smiled. "I am appointing you our Ambassador to Teruna, with immediate effect."

Ambassador—to Teruna?

CHAPTER
SEVENTEEN

DAINON STARED at his king in stunned silence. *But that would mean....* He hardly dared finish the thought for fear of somehow upsetting Fate.

"You seem perplexed," the king mused. "Am I to take it that you do not wish to accept this post?"

The king's question pushed Dainon into action. "Forgive me, Sire, but I had not expected such an honor." He breathed deeply in an attempt to clear his head. "What would my duties be?"

"You would return to Teruna with my responses to King Tanish's proposals. There, you would liaise between the two kingdoms, advising those who might wish to move here. I would expect you to organize the first and subsequent caravans that set out for Kandor. I understand this process might last a few years, but I would expect you to remain in Teruna as our representative. This new venture will forge great links between our two kingdoms, and you will be our voice there." There were murmurs of agreement from around the table.

One phrase repeated in Dainon's mind over and over again. "I would... remain in Teruna?"

The king smiled. "Apparently King Tanish and his consorts are eager for you to return. He writes that they will provide you with accommodation as befits your new rank." He tilted his head to one side. "That is, if you accept the position. You have not yet said as much. Do you wish for a little time to consider it?"

Dainon swallowed. "Sire, I—"

The king came around the table and approached him. "Dainon," he said in a low voice. "I do understand. I am asking you to leave your land and make your home in another. On reflection I was wrong to ask you to make such a decision so quickly. Take your time. King Tanish can wait a while longer to hear our reply." He patted Dainon on the shoulder. "I repeat, take your time."

Dainon bowed his head. "Thank you, Sire. May I take my leave?"

"Certainly." King Rohar stepped back, and Dainon bowed once more before walking out of the chamber.

Once in the corridor, the door shut behind him, his nerves got the better of him and his legs began to shake. He leaned against the wall and forced himself to take slow, deep breaths.

Ambassador to Teruna. It felt like a surreal dream.

The door opened again and Garron emerged. His eyes widened when he saw Dainon. "Man, you are as white as milk. Are you ill?"

Dainon was not about to show weakness, even if it was to a fellow warrior. He pulled himself upright and held his head high. "I am fine."

Garron shook his head. "Can you believe it? He changed the law, in the blink of an eye." He patted Dainon on the back. "And you…. You were amazing in there. I was so proud of you. Your words were uttered so fervently that I could almost have believed you spoke from personal experience. All those who have lived out their lives under the shadow of that law have reason to thank you this day. And that includes Caro and me." He hugged Dainon, his arms tight around him. "May the Maker bless you greatly, Dainon," he whispered.

Dainon closed his eyes. It seemed the Maker had designs for his life that he had never expected.

Garron released him and gave a brisk nod. "Would you join Caro and me tonight in my room? Some food, some wine, a lot of talking. We want to celebrate the news, and if you do accept this post, it may be the last chance we get to do this."

Dainon was about to refuse, but at the last moment, he stopped himself. *I can share in their happiness.* "Yes, I can do that."

Garron beamed. "Till tonight, then. But be prepared not to have much sleep. We have a lot to talk about—and a lot of wine to drink." He clapped Dainon on the back and strode down the corridor, whistling.

Dainon watched him go, his thoughts conflicted. *I need to go home, sit down, and think about my future.*

Someone, it seemed, wanted Dainon to go to Teruna.

Dainon sat on his couch, head in his hands. He had spent the last hour going to and fro in his mind, trying to see a way forward. The king wanted him to go to Teruna. King Tanish, Feyar, and Sorran apparently wanted Dainon to go to Teruna. And he already knew how Kei and Arrio felt on the matter.

Then why am I still sitting here, ruminating? What is holding me here?

"That is a very good question."

Dainon almost jumped out of his skin at the sound of that voice. His heart hammered. *It cannot be....*

Slowly he raised his head and looked into his wife's eyes.

Tarisa sat at the other end of the couch, wearing the floor-length, flame-colored dress he had bought for her on her last birthday. Her long auburn hair fell down her back, and those pale green eyes he had loved so much regarded him steadily.

"You... you cannot be here," he whispered.

"Of course I am not here. But you obviously need to talk to someone, and your brain has decided that it must be me." She smiled. "I am a figment of your imagination, Dainon. Accept that so we can talk about what ails you."

Dainon stared at her lovely face. "You look the same."

That smile again. "I look as you remember me. Now, tell me, why have you not accepted the king's offer?"

He arched his eyebrows. "I do not recall you being this blunt."

Tarisa sighed. "That is because you are talking to yourself, but for some reason, you would prefer to think you are talking to me." She smiled again. "Now answer the question."

Dainon sighed heavily. "I cannot go back there. To Teruna." He could not believe this was happening.

"Why not?"

"The way I left, without a word...."

"You were hurt. You withdrew. You have had time to process the hurt, to contemplate all that happened." She narrowed her gaze. "And yes, let us talk about what happened."

Dainon's heartbeat raced. "I do not know what you mean." *Then why is there suddenly a curling, writhing mass of snakes in my belly?*

"That moment when you first touched Arrio. And again with Kei." She hardened her gaze. "Are you going to deny what you felt?"

He was lost for words. He knew what it had meant for him and Tarisa, but it could not mean the same thing. It could not be....

"You are destined to be with them, Dainon."

He closed his eyes, but that did not stop her soft voice from entering his ears.

"How lucky are you among men, Dainon? You had a soul mate, but Fate took me from you. Now you have been given not one, but two men who want you, heart, body, and soul. Two men to love you, care for you. Two men for you to love as much as you loved me, if not more."

Dainon opened his eyes. "They do not love me. They love each other. Just as I loved you."

"Are you saying that because you loved me, you have no room left in your heart for them?"

For the second time that day, Dainon was stunned into silence. *Is that what I am saying?*

"Look into your heart. What do you want? And be truthful with me."

Dainon closed his eyes once more. Instantly he saw them, heard them, felt their lips upon his, the touch of their hands on him, and the thrill that coursed through him. "I want them," he whispered. "I want to love them, to be a part of their lives... to grow old with them by my side. If they will have me."

Silence fell, and he opened his eyes. Tarisa stood before him, her eyes glistening with tears.

"Then make it so, beloved."

"But... how?"

She smiled. "Let me go, Dainon."

His heart pounded. "I did. I let you go sixteen years ago."

She shook her head. "You have held on to your love, your grief, but it is time to let go of the past and embrace your future. Arrio and Kei are your future." Light radiated from her, a glow that began to fill his darkening room.

Dainon knew what the light signified. "Are you leaving me again?"

"Not this time. You are doing this, Dainon. You."

He sprang to his feet and reached out for her, but stopped his hand short of touching her.

Tarisa smiled. "Yes, my love. You know this is not me, but that is not why you stopped. You have finally released me, and you cannot touch what is no longer here." And with that she shimmered out of sight.

Dainon stared at the space where she had stood mere seconds before. *Did it happen? Was she really there?*

Then slowly it dawned on him that he felt... light.

"Thank you," he whispered. He had no idea whether Tarisa had really been there or if he had conjured her up in his own mind as she had said, but the result was the same. He had relinquished his hold on the past and was ready to move on.

I am going back to Teruna. Back to Arrio and Kei.

Then he realized there was something vital that needed to be done first.

He had to speak to his king.

"YOU ARE really going back to Teruna?" Garron asked for what had to be the fourth time that night.

"Yes, I am really going," Dainon replied patiently. "I have already given the king my answer. I leave tomorrow." He had lost count of how many glasses of wine he had drunk. What surprised him was how sober he felt. *Perhaps it is the thought that soon I will be with them.*

Then he changed his mind. That thought would make him dizzy with anticipation, with no need for wine.

"That is what I call a real step up," Caro said with a grin. "From a lowly warrior to an ambassador."

Garron snorted. "Dainon was never a lowly warrior." He raised his glass. "To Dainon, the finest warrior I have ever had the privilege to serve under."

Dainon laughed. "Now I know *you* are drunk." He leaned back on the thick cushions that Garron had spread all over the floor in front of the fireplace. There were so many that the coldness of the stone beneath was kept at bay. Dainon sighed. "This is really comfortable."

Caro hiccupped and then gave Garron a flash of a smile. "It is even better when you are the one being fucked on them—" He snapped his mouth shut, his cheeks flushed.

Garron roared with laughter. "I am sure Dainon has heard worse. And after today, you can shout it from the rooftops, my love." He shook his head, an awed expression creeping over his face. "Did you hear the proclamation, Dainon? This evening?"

Dainon had missed the royal messengers delivering news of the change in the law, but he had not been able to miss the noise that had broken out in the barracks after. "Just how many of the warriors like men?"

Caro whooped. "More than I would have believed before today." He raised his glass. "To His Majesty, King Rohar, who changed more than a law today—he changed my life." His gaze met Dainon's, and he gave him a warm smile. "And to Dainon, the man who helped him to change it."

"I'll drink to that." Garron brought his glass to meet Caro's, and after taking a long drink from it, he put it down and beckoned Caro with his finger. "Come here, you."

Caro put down his own glass and crawled across cushions to sit astride Garron's lap. "You want something?" He looped his arms around Garron's neck.

Garron gazed into his eyes. "The same thing I always want from you, but that can wait until our guest has gone." He cupped Caro's face. "You can stay here tonight, and tomorrow night, and every night for as long as you want."

"How about for the rest of my life?" Caro whispered and bent his head down to take Garron's mouth in a kiss.

Dainon watched, heat flooding his face when Garron reached under Caro's short tunic to grab his buttocks and squeeze them. Caro shifted, rocking against him, a low moan escaping him.

Dainon cleared his throat. "Who said something about waiting until the guest has gone?"

Caro coughed and climbed off Garron's lap. Garron's face was bright red.

"Sorry, but tonight was—"

"I understand, more than you realize." Dainon stopped and quickly took a drink of wine.

Garron stared at him. "Explain what you mean."

Dainon silently cursed the wine for loosening his tongue. Then it came to him that here was an opportunity not to be missed. "Can I ask you both something?"

"Tonight? You may ask anything you please," Garron said with a tipsy grin.

"When you and Caro are… together," he said, his nerves getting the better of him, "is it very different to being with a woman?"

Slowly two heads turned and two pairs of eyes focused on him, somewhat haphazardly.

"By the heavens," Garron whispered. "You've found yourself a man." He took a drink of wine.

"Not one," Dainon replied, "but two." His heartbeat raced.

Garron spluttered wine all over the cushions. "Man, when you leap, you *really* leap." He wiped his mouth on the back of his hand. "You dark horse. And there was me thinking nothing could surprise me at my age. You and our king set me straight on that in one day." He grimaced at the stains left by the wine, but then gave Dainon his attention. "To answer your question, Caro has never been with a woman, but I have, in my younger days, before I was ready to face the truth about myself. And no, it is not all that different, barring the one obvious distinction." He gave a drunken shrug. "You know where it goes—what else is there to know?" He waggled his eyebrows.

Caro sighed. "Men." He got up from the floor, walked over to the bed, and knelt beside it.

Garron frowned. "What did I say?"

Dainon was trying hard not to smirk.

Caro returned and handed a small flask to Dainon. "Yes, to quote my lover, you know where it goes, but when you put it there? Use this. Lots of it."

Dainon removed the stopper and tilted the flask carefully. He rubbed the viscous amber liquid between thumb and forefinger, and brought it to his nostrils to sniff cautiously. "It is an oil." A thick, pleasant-smelling oil. "But what am I to do with—" It was his turn to snap his mouth shut as the oil's purpose dawned on him. "Oh."

Caro nodded slowly and then indicated Garron with a flick of his head. "Easy to tell which of us two has never had a cock up his backside," he said bluntly, ignoring Garron's huff of indignation.

"You like being fucked!" Garron exclaimed.

Caro stared at him. "I do not dispute that, but as I am the one who takes that monster of yours on a twice-daily basis, allow me the opportunity to share the benefits of my wisdom." He gave Garron a sweet smile. "Believe me, if I tried to fuck *you* without this, you would soon know about it."

Garron mumbled under his breath, but Caro ignored him. He leaned over and kissed Garron on the mouth. "I promise, none of this will matter when you have me in your bed tonight, knowing I do not have to leave your room at daybreak."

That rendered Garron silent. He gazed at Caro, a huge smile on his face.

Caro returned it and then gave Dainon his full attention. "I was serious. Use lots of it." He tilted his head. "Your men, are they experienced?"

It was on the tip of his tongue to say yes, but for the first time since he had left Teruna, a doubt rose in his mind. "Perhaps," he said slowly. He had had time to think about that morning in the weeks since his departure. *The slightest noise on patrol and I am awake. Is it likely that they could have made love beside me and I did not hear them?* Unless he was not the light sleeper that he used to be. It was enough to give him pause, however.

Caro arched his eyebrows at that, but then tapped the flask with his forefinger. "Then yes, use lots. Especially if it turns out that they are as new to this as you are." He smiled. "And Dainon?"

"Yes?"

Caro grinned. "Enjoy it."

CHAPTER
EIGHTEEN

KEI AWOKE with a gasp, his chest covered in sweat, his breathing harsh and loud in the quiet of their chamber.

Arrio stroked a hand over him. "Was it a nightmare?" he asked, getting out of bed and bringing a towel to wipe away Kei's perspiration.

Kei closed his eyes, desperate to sink back into his wonderful dream. "No, far from it." He could still feel Dainon's hands on his body, caressing him, making him want so much more.

Then he realized the hands belonged to Arrio, and he turned his head into the pillow and sobbed.

Arrio cupped his cheek. "Please, do not weep. Tell me what troubles you. If it was not a bad dream, then why do you weep?"

"Because I wanted it to be real!" The words burst out of him.

Arrio stroked across his forehead, his fingers gentle. "Peace, Kei. Take a moment to calm yourself, and then tell me of it."

Kei let himself be lulled into a more tranquil state by those fingers that caressed his cheeks, forehead and neck. "That… feels good," he admitted. Arrio was propped up on his side, gazing at him, his features still discernible in the moonlight. Kei reached up to touch his face. "Thank you."

Arrio dropped back onto the bed beside him. "So, this dream…."

"I dreamed I was in the royal harem in Vancor," Kei began, staring at the ceiling. "I was watching three men making love, their bodies entwined under white sheets, their skin so dark against them."

Arrio chuckled. "I can see why that would be a good dream."

The sheet covering them twitched, and Kei craned his neck to see it tenting. He made no comment—his own cock was rising at the memory.

Kei lay back on the pillows. "But then it changed. All of a sudden, *I* lay between those sheets, you and Dainon on either side of me." He closed his eyes once more. "I cannot speak of this. It only makes me... want."

Arrio rolled onto his side and slowly pulled back the sheet to reveal Kei's hardening shaft.

"What... what are you doing?" Kei demanded.

Arrio reached across Kei's body, took hold of his right hand, and brought it to his length. "Speak of it. Close your eyes and go back there. Imagine it is Dainon's hand around you, and not your own."

Kei did as instructed, gently squeezing his cock, his other hand cupping his testicles. He shuddered.

"What is he doing?" Arrio's whisper pierced the quiet.

Kei gave himself up to his imagination. "His... his mouth is on my nipple while he slowly works my shaft," he said breathlessly. He could almost feel Dainon's hot tongue flicking the rigid nub. Kei rocked his hips up off the bed, pushing his cock through his fist.

"Now imagine my mouth is on your cock. My tongue laps the head every time Dainon pulls back to reveal it, the skin tight and shiny."

"Oh, yes." Kei rubbed the mound between his testicles and his hole before moving a finger lower. The skin was soft there, tightly puckered.

"Wet your finger," Arrio urged him. "Press the pad of your finger against your hole." The bed dipped and shook, and Kei did not need to look to know Arrio was seeking his own relief.

Trembling, Kei complied, letting out a soft moan when he rubbed over his entrance. His right hand pulled harder on his length, his hips moving faster. "Oh, how many times have I dreamed of this?" he groaned. "Your mouth on me, Dainon sliding a finger inside me, when all I want is for it to be his cock, yours, both of you taking me." He pushed his finger into the tight, hot channel and cried out with the sheer pleasure of it.

Arrio moaned. "I am close. One day I will spill inside you. We both shall."

A full-blown body shiver rippled through Kei at the thought. He gripped his shaft as it sent out an arc of warm seed that spattered his chest, reaching as high as his cheek and nose. He arched his back up off the bed and cried out, letting his climax have its way with him, until he dropped back onto the bed, shaking, body damp once more with perspiration and seed.

Arrio's hoarse cry rent the air, the bed shuddering.

Kei lay there, drawing in deep breaths until his heartbeat had returned to normal. He heard Arrio's breathing resume its previous pattern. When Kei opened his eyes, Arrio was gazing down at him, a towel in his hand.

"I like your dreams," he said with a grin. With care he wiped away all trace of Kei's climax and then his own before depositing the towel on the floor. Arrio pulled the sheet up over their bodies, leaned over, and kissed Kei's cheek. "Now go to sleep. If you have any more dreams, tell me about them in the morning."

"Hold me?" Kei could not fall asleep without the feel of Arrio's arms around him.

"Always." Arrio curled around him and placed his hand on Kei's chest. "I have you safe," he whispered into Kei's ear.

Kei let out a soft sigh and sank into a dreamless sleep.

"THERE, FIORE. Do you know where you are, boy?" Dainon patted the horse's neck. As if in reply, Fiore whinnied and tossed his mane. Dainon laughed. Before him lay the city of Teruna, its white walls glowing and sparkling in the late evening sun. The hill top city had never looked so welcome a sight.

Dainon leaned forward and stroked Fiore's soft neck once more. "We're home, boy." The journey would have been quicker, but for the second horse that had accompanied them. Both horses were weighed down with bags containing everything Dainon had wanted to bring to his new land.

He covered the ground between them and the city walls with a brisk trot, Fiore seemingly as eager as Dainon to reach the palace. When he arrived at the gate, he recognized the two guards on duty who grinned at him when they saw his heavy-laden companions.

"It seems as though you intend to stay awhile, Dainon."

Dainon returned their grin. "It looks that way, does it not?" He nodded to them as they pushed open the gates and stepped aside to let him pass.

The streets were quiet, all the traders packing up for the day. Dainon wound his way over the cobbles, drinking in the sights and smells. Delicious odors carried on the breeze, a reminder that it had been several hours since he had last eaten. Higher and higher he rode, the street rising up to where the palace sat atop the hill, long banners of bright colors hanging from its ramparts. The sight made his heart stutter and his pulse race.

I never dreamed I would be here once more, and certainly not as the Kandoran Ambassador. Such a strange twist of Fate, and yet, if Kei was to be believed, this moment had been planned.

The moment the thought flitted through his mind, Dainon berated himself.

If I am here to stay, then I must accept Kei's vision. I must believe him.

The prospect filled him with excitement and anticipation.

He rode up to the gateway that led to the stables, and the groom—*Oren?*—who bade him enter beamed at him.

"Dainon! You have returned!"

Dainon reached down and rubbed Oren's tousled hair. "And you are going to take good care of Fiore and Pellar for me, observant boy."

Oren groused good-naturedly and shied away from Dainon's hand.

Dainon brought the horses to a stop, climbed down, and stretched his back, feeling his spine pop.

"Hey there, Fiore," Oren said quietly as he took the reins and led the horses to the stalls. "Dainon, do you want to take the bags with you?"

"Better not." At that moment Dainon had no idea where he would be staying. That would be settled when he saw King Tanish. Then he remembered and followed Oren into the stall. He removed a scroll from his bag and tucked it under his belt.

"By the heavens, it is good to see you." Timur's deep voice rumbled as he approached Dainon at the stall door, hands held wide. Dainon accepted the firm hug. "I thought we had seen the last of you."

"It seems the Maker has other plans for me," Dainon said with a smile.

Timur flicked his head toward the palace. "Did you send ahead word that you were coming?" Dainon shook his head, and Timur grinned. "Oh, what I would give to be in there when a certain pair of princes see you."

"They are well?" His heart beat faster at the thought of seeing them.

Timur snorted. "Physically, yes." When Dainon gave him a questioning glance, Timur growled. "You should not have left like that. Those boys…. I have never seen Arrio so miserable, and I have known him all his life." He speared Dainon with an intense gaze. "Tell me all those bags mean you are planning to stay this time?"

Dainon knew he was being chastised, but he could not deny that he deserved it. That did not mean, however, that Timur got to know everything.

"I need to see the king," he said simply.

Timur raised his eyebrows but nodded. "You know the way." He clapped Dainon on the back. "Welcome back, Dainon."

Dainon nodded and strode out of the courtyard, heading for the path that led through the gardens, his heart pounding at the thought of finding Arrio or Kei there. The tranquil space was empty, save for birds, and he continued to the door that led into the palace. When he arrived at the royal audience chamber, his heartbeat still racing, he paused. The guards on either side of the door gave him a brief nod, but he hesitated.

Heavens help me, I am nervous. The realization made him want to laugh. A warrior, trained for battle, yet nervous at the thought of seeing the two men who were about to take his life in a new direction.

Then it is time to set foot upon my new path.

Dainon drew himself up to his full height. "I would speak with His Majesty."

"Wait here, please." One of the guards entered the chamber, and it seemed but seconds later that he returned. "His Majesty will see you now."

Dainon entered the chamber and walked toward the thrones where King Tanish sat, several men and women in black robes standing before him. All heads turned to watch him approach, and Dainon could not help noticing the king's knowing smile.

"Dainon, you are most welcome." King Tanish gestured to those before him. "This is my royal council. Your timing is, as ever, most opportune. We have finished our discussions for the day."

Dainon bowed his head to those present. What struck him was the average age of the ministers, who appeared much younger than their Kandoran counterparts, and the fact that there were women on the council. *Perhaps Teruna will bring more transformations to Kandor than King Rohar realizes.* The thought excited him. Kandor was about to change beyond all recognition.

Dainon removed the scroll from his belt as he approached the throne and knelt before the king. "I bring a message from King Rohar of Kandor." He bowed his head, the scroll held out.

King Tanish left the throne and descended the three marble steps of the dais to stand before Dainon. He placed his hand on Dainon's head. "Rise, my friend."

Dainon got to his feet and handed over the scroll. He waited while the king sat and broke the seal to unfurl the parchment. When King Tanish raised his head and beamed at him, Dainon felt a surge of relief flood through him.

The king addressed the guard who stood to one side. "Will you please bring Prince Sorran, Prince Feyar, Prince Arrio, and Prince Kei to me immediately?"

"Sire." The guard exited the room briskly.

King Tanish then addressed the council. "Please stay a while longer. I have an announcement to make." His remark had them murmuring to each other.

The king approached Dainon. "I am happy to see you, and even happier to read King Rohar's news," he said in a low voice. "When I have introduced you, the council will leave and we can talk."

Dainon bowed his head. "Your Majesty." He stiffened as the door to the chamber opened, but relaxed when Sorran and Feyar entered.

Sorran's smile was huge. "A most welcome surprise," he said, walking over to Dainon to give him a hug.

"A surprise, Your Highness?" Dainon remarked with a smirk. "You knew I would be back."

Sorran released him, his eyes twinkling. "There was always the possibility that King Rohar would reject our suggestion."

Dainon arched his eyebrows, not fooled for a minute.

Feyar clasped Dainon's hand in a firm grip. "We have not told them what awaits them," he murmured.

Dainon did not need to ask to whom he referred. Nor did he need to look up to know Arrio and Kei had entered the chamber. Two loud gasps announced their presence.

Dainon watched them approach the thrones, their gazes locked on him. The last thing he wanted was formality, but the situation dictated it. Arrio walked slowly, as if in a dream. Kei's lips were parted in an adorable expression of surprise.

"If I may have your attention?"

Dainon gave a start and snapped to attention before the king. Sorran and Feyar joined King Tanish on the dais, standing on either side of him.

"With regard to the Kandoran situation that we debated weeks ago, I am pleased to share Kandor's response to our proposals. They are agreed in full, and to this effect, I am proud to present to you the new Kandoran Ambassador to Teruna, Lord Dainon."

Applause broke out, but Dainon barely heard it. He stared at King Tanish, his mouth open. "*Lord* Dainon?"

King Tanish smiled. "The title goes with the post. Did King Rohar not mention this?"

"No, Sire, he neglected to mention that detail." Dainon's head was spinning.

"The title is also used to address members of Teruna's Great Houses, the oldest families in the kingdom, with the exception of the royal family," Sorran informed him. "As Ambassador, you would certainly be on an equal social footing with them." He grinned. "*Lord* Dainon appears to be in shock," he said to King Tanish, while Feyar was trying not to laugh.

Arrio walked up to him. "Allow me to congratulate you on your new post, Dainon." He kissed Dainon on the cheek and leaned close to whisper, "I am so very happy to see you again."

"As am I to be here, Your Highness."

Arrio stepped back and arched his eyebrows. "Are we to be formal once more? I thought that we had long passed that point."

Dainon smiled. "When I am standing in your fathers' audience chamber, surrounded by his ministers, I will be formal. I will not be so when we are alone." He awaited Arrio's response, his heart still rapid.

Arrio's eyes shone. "Then I will await such time with eagerness." He glanced over to his left and grinned. "Kei is also eager to greet you."

Dainon swallowed as Kei approached him, his dark eyes large and round. "It is good to see you, Dainon."

Dainon bowed his head. "I would speak with you and Arrio later. We have much to discuss, beginning with my apology for leaving so abruptly." He held his breath, aware of the roiling in his stomach when Kei's breathing hitched. Dainon had questions, but they would have to wait.

Kei nodded. "After dinner. We will talk then." He leaned up and kissed Dainon's cheek. "Welcome back," he whispered before withdrawing to stand at Arrio's side.

With a shock, Dainon realized that the council members had left. "They must think me ill-mannered," he said to Sorran.

Sorran shook his head. "You were deeply engaged in conversation with Arrio and Kei. There will be occasion to meet them another day. Now it is time for sharing a meal with our new ambassador."

"Who does not appear comfortable with his new title," Feyar added with a smile.

Dainon sighed. "Do you see everything, Your Highness?"

To his surprise Feyar clasped his shoulder with a firm hand. "Peace, Dainon. There is time to grow into your new role. Other gentler matters clamor for your attention." His gaze went to Arrio and Kei.

"Such matters can wait until we have fed Dainon, who must be both tired and hungry after his long journey," Sorran declared, giving Feyar a firm stare.

King Tanish laughed. "Dainon, are you sure you know what you are about to undertake? Your life will never be the same again."

Dainon was certain King Tanish's comments had nothing to do with becoming an ambassador. "Your Majesty, it has already changed irrevocably."

And is about to undergo yet another change.

Dainon awaited the prospect with both trepidation and exhilaration.

DAINON CLOSED the door to his chamber and breathed easier. The bath prior to dinner had removed all traces of his journey, and the food had served to renew his energy, but sitting at the table—Arrio at one side, Kei at the other—he had been aware of an undercurrent of... something. It was there every time Arrio or Kei addressed him, a feeling of anticipation that sent tingles down his spine, ice dripping down his back, and heat unfurling in his belly.

The three of them had to talk, if only to clear the air between them.

King Tanish had given Dainon his previous room until such time as arrangements could be made for his new accommodation. The vagueness of his replies as to when that might be led Dainon to think that perhaps his new role was not cut and dried.

When the soft knock at his door came, Dainon knew what to expect when he opened it.

Arrio and Kei stood in the corridor, their expressions guarded.

"Come in." He stepped aside to allow them entry.

Kei crossed the floor and walked out onto the balcony, with Arrio close behind him. Dainon followed them.

Arrio pointed to a balcony on the other side of the palace. "That is our room."

Dainon knew that only too well from—

"You share a room?" Cold gripped his heart to hear his fears confirmed. *They* are *together.*

"It was my idea," Kei said quietly. "I could not bear to sleep alone."

Dainon ached to ask him why, but the words stuck in his throat. Then it struck him. *We need to move forward, and something holds us back.* Dainon feared it was him. "We need to talk."

Kei turned slowly to face him. "We do. You mentioned an apology."

Dainon nodded. It was as good a point to begin with as any. "I was wrong to leave without saying good-bye, but the truth is, I was… hurting."

"You have spoken of this," Arrio said. "Of how we excluded you. Believe me, we did not mean to do so."

"That is not the hurt of which I speak."

Both of them gazed at him, their foreheads furrowed. "Then what?" Kei demanded. "What did we do that hurt you so much?" His breathing quickened.

Dainon took a slow, deep breath. "I thought you wanted me. Both of you. Then I saw how you connected with each other, and I felt… cast aside. And finally…." He bowed his head, eyes closed for a moment, searching for the words. When he found them, he regarded the princes, his chin high. "When I awoke that first morning by the river, it was obvious that the two of you had…." He could not bring himself to utter the words.

Kei stared at him. "You thought we had made love? Why would you think tha—?" His mouth fell open and his eyes widened. "Oh." He glanced across at Arrio. "My dream." To Dainon's amazement, he giggled.

Dainon frowned. "I do not understand."

Arrio sighed. "Kei dreamed of the three of us, making love. It was enough to make him spend. I had to help him clean away the evidence." His eyes widened too. "You could smell it when you woke up, and you thought…."

Dainon groaned. "No, I did not *think*—I reached a false conclusion. And to make matters worse, I did not provide you with the opportunity to tell me the truth."

Kei laid his hand on Dainon's arm. "I am at fault too. There are things I did not share with you. I should have spo—"

Dainon stopped his words with a finger to Kei's lips. "It is clear we have much to discuss, but we can talk of this tomorrow. The hour grows late." Slowly he withdrew his finger.

Arrio cleared his throat. "So your suggestion is that we should retire to our chambers and get a good night's sleep?"

Before Dainon could reply, Kei was in his arms, tugging him down into a kiss that stole his breath away.

Arrio chuckled. "I think we have something else in mind."

CHAPTER
NINETEEN

"LET ME breathe," Dainon gasped, breaking the kiss. The swift turn of events made his head spin even faster.

Kei did not move. Instead he pressed his body to Dainon's and slid his hands over Dainon's chest in a slow, sensual journey to his neck and face. "Breathing is good," he said, smiling.

Dainon grabbed hold of Kei's wrists and lowered them to his sides, Dainon's chest rising and falling rapidly. "Do you always pounce on a man like that?"

Kei's face flushed. "I cannot answer that. I have never 'pounced' before." His words gave Dainon pause, and he stared in confusion. Kei stood on his tiptoes and kissed him once on the mouth. "This is how I wanted my first time to be—the three of us together."

Arrio moved to stand at Dainon's side and put his arms around their waists. "We waited for you." He leaned forward until his lips brushed Dainon's neck, sending shivers coursing through him. "We are yours, Dainon, and you are ours."

"Yours." The whispered word was an affirmation. Dainon could no longer deny it. He closed his eyes as Arrio kissed him, soft as a whisper, his hand moving higher to stroke Dainon's back. Arrio's touch was light, his lips warm. Dainon let go of Kei's wrists, and instantly Kei was back in his arms, his hand easing under Dainon's robe.

"How I have dreamed of this moment," Kei murmured against Dainon's bared chest.

When he felt Kei's mouth on the other side of his neck, kissing and licking, Kei's hand moving in slow circles over his belly, Dainon gave up trying to think and surrendered to the two men whose sensual caresses were making him harder than he had thought possible.

"And now that you are here," Arrio whispered against his ear, "we are not going to let you go." His tongue flicked Dainon's earlobe. "We want you."

By all that is holy, I want them.

Kei broke from kissing him to unfasten the tie around Dainon's waist. Dainon opened his eyes and stared at Kei, who smiled. "Let us see you," he whispered.

Arrio too ceased kissing him to pull the robe from Dainon's shoulders, helping him out of it until he stood before them naked, his cock curving upward. Arrio drew in a sharp breath. "Our beautiful warrior." He grinned at Kei. "I think we need a closer look."

Dainon had no time to utter a word. Both Arrio and Kei sank to their knees before him.

Arrio gazed up at him, eyes shining. "I have always wondered how it would feel to take a man in my mouth," he said before licking his lips. Dainon caught his breath when Arrio rubbed his face along Dainon's length, inhaling deeply. "By the Maker, you smell good."

All Dainon wanted to do in that second was rub his cock over Arrio's cheeks and mouth, then part those warm lips with its head and push deep.

"My turn." Kei's beard was soft against Dainon's shaft. He nuzzled Dainon's testicles, his nose pressed up against them, and Dainon wanted to cry out when Kei took one in his mouth, so, so carefully. Dainon's legs trembled, and he placed his hands on their heads to steady himself.

His cry could not be contained any longer when two tongues licked the length of his cock and two mouths sucked at the hard flesh. "Oh heavens, yes!" It was not enough. "Touch me."

Arrio reached up Dainon's body to stroke his chest and belly, while Kei reached around to squeeze his buttock, the two of them moving in harmony, humming with pleasure.

Two mouths were definitely better than one. Four hands were certainly better than two.

Sanity returned when he realized where they were. "We… we can be observed here," he gasped, but still he kept his hands on their heads, unwilling to bring a halt to the exquisite worship of his shaft.

Kei gazed up at him, his lips shiny. "Then let us move this to the bed. There is room for all of us."

The bed. Heat surged through Dainon and his cock bobbed.

Arrio chuckled. "You like that idea." He was on his feet in seconds, Kei copying him, and they took Dainon by the hand and led him across the room. Dainon stared at the wide bed covered in soft sheets, and his heart pounded. It had been a long time since he had used a bed for anything other than sleep. He had imagined this moment during the journey back to Teruna, and now that he was on the point of realizing his fantasies, his body ached at the thought.

It is going to happen. A first for all three of them.

When they reached the bed, Arrio began to undress Kei, but Dainon stopped him. "Let me?"

Arrio shook his head. "Both of us."

Dainon smiled. "So be it." Between them, they parted Kei from his robe, who then helped Dainon disrobe Arrio. When they were naked, they pushed Dainon down onto the bed and lay on either side of him, caressing his belly and chest.

Kei trailed his hand slowly up Dainon's body until he cupped his face. Dark eyes locked on his. "I kissed you once. My first kiss."

"I remember." That moment in the garden was etched into Dainon's memory.

"Then kiss me now. Do not hold back."

To Dainon's ears, it was a plea—one he was not capable of ignoring. He pulled Kei down into a kiss, pushing his tongue between Kei's lips and exploring him, running his fingers through Kei's short hair. Kei responded with enthusiasm, his own tongue seeking entry.

Arrio let out a moan, and suddenly there were three mouths joined in a heated kiss, three tongues exploring. Dainon put his arms around both of them, loving the feel of their bodies on his, aware of two equally hard, hot shafts pressed against his belly. Arrio moved to take Kei's mouth in a fervent kiss, and Dainon groaned, watching him suckling on Kei's tongue, their soft moans feeding Dainon's desire. Arrio reached down to grasp Dainon's cock around its base and slowly slide his hand along its length. Dainon pushed up with his hips, wanting more.

"You take his cock—I shall take his mouth," Kei ordered, and Dainon moaned into Kei's kiss as his shaft was engulfed in wet heat. He lay there, hips rocking up while they sent him higher and higher, Arrio's tongue on the head of his cock, Kei's tongue in his mouth, until he wanted to cry out from the sheer sensual pleasure of it all. Then Kei broke their kiss and there were two mouths on his shaft once more, the pair of them taking it in turns to suck him, lick him, until he was shaking with need.

"If you continue thus, I will spend," he groaned.

"Not yet." Kei wrapped his hand around Dainon's length and held it steady, his gaze meeting Dainon's. "I want to feel you inside me." He moved as though to straddle Dainon.

"Wait!" Dainon pointed to the table when Kei halted. "Arrio, bring me that flask."

Arrio did as instructed. "What is this?" he asked, examining it.

Dainon cleared his throat. "The result of me asking for advice." When both princes stared at him, he let out a sigh. "I have no experience with men. I did not want to… hurt you."

Arrio was at his side instantly, his mouth fused with Dainon's in a lingering kiss. Kei bent to add his kiss to the heady mix. Dainon wrapped them in his arms, pulling them to him. When they parted, breathless, Kei slowly sat astride Dainon, his slender cock hot against Dainon's belly, leaving a wet trail as he slowly rocked back and forth. The friction as he moved, his testicles sliding over Dainon's shaft and sac, was delicious.

Kei nodded toward the flask. "Arrio, I know what this is. Pour a few drops onto your fingers." He looked down at Dainon. "Arrio will prepare me, so that you may take me."

"How do you know of this?" Dainon asked, stroking his fingers along Kei's shaft and watching a shiver ripple through him. Kei's words sent a frisson of anticipation up and down his spine. *I am going to take him.* When Arrio's hand gently caressed his hip, Dainon's heartbeat sped up. *By the heavens. I will take both of them.*

"I watched two men in the harem." Kei shuddered as Dainon wrapped his hand around Kei's length and gently pulled on it, the silken skin sliding over the rigid shaft. "Dainon." His name came out as a soft whine. "When you do that, my thoughts become disjointed, and I need to remember what I saw."

"Am I a distraction, then?" Dainon asked in an innocent tone, his hand not ceasing in its motion.

Kei growled at the back of his throat. "It is only now that we see your wicked side." He bent low to kiss his mouth, feeding him a soft cry of hunger. When he sat upright, Kei regarded Arrio, his breathing still rapid. "You must slide your fingers into my hole. Start with one." He caught Arrio's arm. "Slowly, *terushan*."

Arrio nodded. "I too will not hurt you." He kissed Kei softly and then knelt at his side.

"I will help, also." Dainon reached behind Kei and spread his cheeks, making Kei catch his breath. He locked gazes with him, watching for the moment Arrio penetrated him.

Kei's eyes went wide and his body stiffened, his breaths short and harsh. "Oh." The words shuddered out of Kei. "Oh. Oh, Arrio. Yes."

Arrio kissed his shoulder. "You are so hot, your body tight around my finger." He smiled, and Kei arched his back, mouth open. "All the way inside you now. Can you take another?"

"Do it." Kei bit his lip, raising himself up slightly on his knees, a low, strung-out moan escaping his lips. "Oh, by the heavens, yes. Go deeper, Arrio."

Dainon could not take his eyes off both of them—Kei writhing on Arrio's fingers, the sounds pouring out of him making Dainon hot, his shaft aching to be inside. "Does it feel good when Arrio fucks you with his fingers?"

Kei's eyes widened and Arrio's breathing hitched.

"Oh, yes." Kei began to move faster, rocking his body deeper onto Arrio's fingers. Arrio curled his fingers around Kei's length and Kei rocked between Arrio's hands, panting as Arrio sent him higher. "Oh, so deep now. More, I beg you." Arrio kissed his neck, and Kei tilted his head to give him greater access, his hips in constant motion, losing rhythm now and again.

"Can you feel them stretching you, getting you ready for my cock?" Saying the words sent a thrill through Dainon. It was a powerful sensation, like nothing he had ever experienced. Coarse talk among warriors was normal, but watching how the two men responded to such language made his pulse race.

"Speak more of this," Kei begged him. "You set my body alight with your words."

"What would you have me say, sweet prince? That I ache to slide my shaft inside you, until I am all you feel, all you know?"

Both Kei and Arrio moaned softly, igniting his desire further.

Dainon let go of Kei's cheeks and joined Arrio in stroking Kei's rigid shaft with his fingertips. Arrio's gaze met Dainon's, and he cupped Kei's testicles, rolling them through his fingers, both men working to pleasure their lover who shuddered at their touch. Dainon rubbed his thumb over the head to gather the glistening fluid from his slit and brought it to his lips. He tasted his soon-to-be lover for the first time, Kei's eyes fixed on him.

"How does it taste?" Arrio demanded.

Dainon licked his lips. "Perfect." He could not wait any longer. "Ready for me, Kei?"

"Yes, yes, now." Kei exhaled slowly as Arrio pulled free of his body and brought his slick fingers to wrap them around Dainon's cock.

Caro's words were suddenly there in his head. "Use more," Dainon told Arrio.

Arrio nodded and poured some of the oil into his palm. When he'd slicked the shaft, leaving it hard and glistening, Dainon pulled him over into a kiss. "Lie with me while Kei rides my cock."

"Oh yes." Arrio stretched out beside him, his hand on Kei's hip.

Kei raised himself up once more and shifted until the head of Dainon's cock was pressed against his virgin hole. The urge to enter him, to fill him completely, surged through Dainon in a rush of hot desire, but he pushed it aside. He reached out to stroke Kei's hip. "Slowly, my beautiful prince. Take your time. We will do this at your pace."

Kei nodded, lips parted, his breathing rapid. He kept his gaze focused on Dainon as he pushed slightly, a gasp escaping him when the tightly puckered muscle finally relaxed to allow the head to enter him. His eyes widened and he held out his hands. Dainon and Arrio grasped them and held on to him as he eased down onto Dainon's hard-as-steel shaft. He gripped their hands tightly and threw back his head in a sigh when at last Dainon's cock filled him to the hilt.

Dainon let out a groan at the sensation of Kei's hot channel snug around his shaft. "By the Maker, you feel good." The feeling of tightness was overwhelming, and he had to fight the urge to move. Everything in him was pushing him to take Kei, to slide in and out of that exquisite heat, but he tempered his desire.

"Is it how you dreamed it would be?" Arrio asked Kei, his gaze locked on his.

Kei looked down at him, his eyes bright. "It is better." He bent over, Dainon's shaft sliding out of him until he was only just inside him. Kei kissed Dainon on the lips and whispered against his mouth. "You are inside me, a part of me."

"There is no pain?" Dainon asked, tilting his hips to slowly push back inside, his hand on Kei's face.

"A little, but it is worth it to finally have you inside me." Kei's eyes were suddenly larger than ever, his pupils so full. "Again. Do that again." Dainon began to move in and out, keeping his movements measured. Each thrust into him made Kei cry out, his face alight with pleasure.

"There. Oh, there." He let go of Dainon and Arrio and leaned back, his hands on Dainon's thighs as he rocked back and forth, his cock bouncing up to slap against his belly.

Dainon pushed up to meet Kei, getting into a rhythm that sent tingles throughout his body.

Arrio moved swiftly to take Kei's shaft in his mouth, and Kei shuddered. "You will make me spend." Arrio's head bobbed faster, and Dainon felt Kei's body tighten around his cock. The sight before him was breathtaking: Kei riding him, eyes closed, short, harsh breaths and soft moans filling the air as he fucked himself on Dainon's shaft; Arrio's head moving as he sucked Kei's length, kneeling over Dainon, his firm buttocks within reach, his tight pink hole in sight.

Dainon wet his thumb and reached across to rub over Arrio's entrance, loving how he moaned around Kei's cock when Dainon slowly pushed the fat digit into his hole. He slid deeper, and when he encountered a small bump inside Arrio's channel, he watched as Arrio shivered, his moans intensifying.

"Arrio, I... I am going to...." It was as far as Kei got before he froze, his body taut, head back, his loud cry of ecstasy rebounding off the walls and ceiling of the chamber.

Arrio did not pull away, and Dainon's shaft throbbed inside Kei. *Not yet. I want to take them both before I spill inside one of them.* He had to inhale deeply to keep himself from going over the edge.

Kei grabbed Arrio's head and steadied himself, his body jolting as he pulsed into Arrio's mouth, his breath leaving him in short bursts. "So good," he sighed.

Arrio slowly licked Kei's cock clean, a low whine escaping his lips when Dainon pushed deep. He pulled away from Kei, gasping when Dainon pulled free of his body. Dainon groaned when Arrio straightened and kissed him, Kei's seed on his tongue, a burst of sharp flavor. When they parted, Arrio grinned. "He tastes good, does he not?"

Dainon had barely time to respond before Arrio whispered, "My turn."

Kei nodded and eased himself off Dainon's still-solid shaft. He grabbed the flask and added more oil, as Arrio threw his leg over Dainon and sat on his cock with a low cry.

"Less haste," Dainon begged.

Arrio stiffened, and Kei held him, kissing his chest and neck until Arrio was more relaxed, descending at a gentler pace until Dainon's cock was once more inside a tight body. Heat surrounded his shaft, and Arrio exhaled shakily. "I feel so full," he moaned.

"Maybe a little instruction was a good idea after all?" Kei said with a smile.

Arrio stared at him and then laughed.

Dainon groaned. "I feel that around my shaft." He placed his hands on Arrio's waist, resisting the urge to thrust up into him.

Arrio leaned forward, his hands flat on Dainon's chest, his gaze fixed on Kei. "He is hard inside me," he gasped, shuddering. "I do not think I will last long."

Kei's eyes gleamed. "Then it is my turn also." He bent over and took Arrio's long cock into his mouth, and Arrio shivered, his breathing quickening.

"More. Oh, by the heavens, more."

A low cry rumbled out of Dainon as Arrio's channel gripped his shaft. "Take him deep," he commanded Kei. He pulled out until he could feel the cool evening air on his cock before thrusting slowly into Arrio. Kei slid farther along Arrio's shaft, and Arrio pushed out a long moan of pleasure, hips rolling as he began to move, lowering his body to meet Dainon's thrusts.

Dainon slid his hands over Arrio's taut belly, loving how Arrio undulated on top of him, hips rolling in a fluid motion while his upper body remained almost still. "Look at you," he said with a sigh, transfixed as he gazed up at Arrio. "As beautiful as that day when you walked out of the sea, my bronzed prince."

Arrio's lips parted in a low moan, his blue eyes locked on Dainon's.

Dainon planted his feet on the bed and tilted his hips to slide faster into Arrio's hot hole. "Finally inside you. Is it how you thought it would be? Does my cock feel good inside you?"

Arrio bent over to kiss him, tongue plunging deep as he filled Dainon's mouth with a heartfelt groan. Dainon ran his fingers through Arrio's hair, grabbing on to the silken strands as an anchor while he thrust up into that tight body. He gave Arrio a heated kiss, and hissed when Arrio sat back on his shaft, impaling himself on Dainon's length again and again.

Dainon could not restrain his desire any longer. "On your hands and knees," he growled, pulling free of Arrio's body. "And spread your legs."

Kei freed Arrio's cock and helped him into position, his lean body stretched out in front of Dainon, legs wide, his loosened hole glistening with oil. Dainon placed the head of his cock against Arrio's entrance and sucked in a lungful of air.

Arrio glanced over his shoulder and nodded. "Now fuck me," he begged, breathing heavily.

Dainon's shaft throbbed and he slid home in one long, powerful thrust.

"Oh." The sound rolled out of Arrio like thunder and he shuddered. "Yes, oh yes. Again."

Dainon gripped Arrio's hips and began to fuck him with long, deep strokes, cries pouring out of Arrio, telling Dainon how good it was, begging him not to stop, to thrust harder. Tingles shot the length of Dainon's shaft, and he knew it would not be long.

"Kei, get on your back and lie beneath Arrio. Take his cock in your mouth again."

Kei scrambled to obey, hands reaching up to spread Arrio for Dainon while he took him deep, head bobbing. Dainon dug his fingers into firm flesh and buried his cock in Arrio's hot channel, moaning when Arrio began to tighten around him. He wanted to slam into Arrio, to crash into him with hard, deep plunges, but he held back. Joy flooded through him as he slid faster, lost in sheer pleasure.

This was meant to be. No doubt remained in Dainon's mind. There was a rightness to all of it, and he rejoiced in each sensation: the sight of Arrio and Kei riding him; their cries and moans; the smell of sex and seed all around them; the slickness of hard male bodies glistening with perspiration; the hot, tight channels that seared his cock and pulled him deeper....

It was as if those last thoughts unlocked something buried within him, and he had to give it voice.

"My soul mates," he cried out, grabbing Arrio's waist and bringing him down hard onto his shaft. Kei moaned around Arrio's length and reached up to cover Dainon's hand with his.

"Ours," Arrio said, his focus on Dainon.

When Arrio tensed, his thighs trembling, Dainon knew he could let go. He waited until Arrio jetted his seed into Kei's mouth, and then he gave himself up to his climax, shooting his essence deep inside Arrio's channel. His cock throbbed and pulsed, and Dainon curved his body over Arrio as he filled him with his seed, his shaft held tight as Arrio's orgasm rolled through him.

"I feel you," Arrio cried, his body shaking. Dainon stroked him and caressed him until the tremors ceased and his breathing became more even.

Kei took every drop until Arrio's shaft was limp. He extricated himself from under Arrio and knelt beside Dainon, his cock hard once more, rising against his belly. "I am not through with Arrio," he said, his chest rising and falling, hand slowly pumping his shaft.

Dainon eased his cock from Arrio's body, watching as Arrio rolled onto his back to stare at Kei, his eyes widening when he saw Kei's hard cock.

"Like this," he begged. "I want to watch you when you enter me."

Kei nodded, his eyes locked on Arrio. "I will not need oil when you are already wet with Dainon's seed."

Dainon lay beside Arrio and held his leg high to spread him for Kei, who knelt between his thighs to guide his shaft into position. Kei stroked Arrio's inner thigh with a gentle hand as he slowly pushed into him, both of them sighing with pleasure when Kei filled him. Kei lowered his body onto Arrio's, and Arrio wound his long legs around Kei's slim waist.

"Now, *terushan*." Arrio stared up at Kei, his eyes wide. "Take me now."

Kei nodded and began to move, Arrio rocking in harmony with him. Dainon kissed them in turn, the three of them connected as Kei's movements grew more erratic and his rhythm faltered. Kei lowered his head, and three mouths fused in a kiss, Arrio's soft cries filling the air as Kei pumped faster.

"Soon," Kei gasped. "Sliding into you is heaven."

"Harder," Arrio pleaded, and suddenly a loud cry burst from him. "There. Again. Again."

It was as if the two of them were carried along on a wave of pleasure, and Dainon was caught in its wake. He stroked them, caressed them, kissed them, his own excitement growing as he sensed the end of their coupling draw near. When Kei thrust deep and stilled, Dainon knew he had released again. Arrio clung to him, their mouths locked in a kiss while Dainon held them.

"My beautiful men." Dainon kissed them, rubbing Kei's back as he lay still on top of Arrio, his face buried in Arrio's neck. When Kei slid free of Arrio's body, Dainon pulled them to him, his arms around them as they kissed, feeding one another their sated sighs. He held them close, unwilling to break the bond of flesh that now existed between them.

Dainon lay there, lost in wonder and awe as Kei and Arrio curled around him, hands moving slowly over his body, murmuring softly to him, telling him that he was theirs, that he completed them, and that they were his.

My men. He knew the truth of it with every beat of his heart, and there was nothing that could part him from them.

CHAPTER
TWENTY

KEI WAS warm and comfortable, his head resting on a furry chest, two arms cradling him, and a hot, firm body curved around him. He opened his eyes and his heart soared. Dainon lay sleeping beside him, his arm around Kei.

It was not a dream. He came back to us.

Kei snuggled closer, moving slowly so as not to disturb him, beneath his hand the reassuring steady beat of Dainon's heart. Arrio stirred behind Kei, his arm tightening around his waist, his breath warm on Kei's neck.

Then we are truly three.

A quiet joy suffused Kei's whole body, bubbling up inside him until he wanted to shout it from the highest mountaintop. His body ached, but it was good. His mind was at peace for the first time in a long while. And the two men destined to love him held him protectively between them as though he were something precious.

His joy was there once more, just below the surface, ready to spill out into the silent bed chamber.

"Good morning."

Kei gave a start. Warm brown eyes regarded him.

"Good morning." Kei wanted to sigh with happiness when Dainon shifted to kiss his forehead.

"You stayed." Dainon's languid smile made his insides loosen and turn over, creating a fluttery feeling in his belly.

"That was an easy decision," Arrio said sleepily from behind him, his hand stroking slow circles over Kei's stomach. "Your chamber has the biggest bed." He chuckled against Kei's back, tickling him. "Good morning," he added, before kissing Kei's shoulder.

Dainon laughed quietly. "I see. And there was I believing you could not bear to be parted from me for even a few hours." He stretched out his hand to caress Arrio's hip, the three of them connected once more. Dainon craned his neck to peer toward the window. "The sun has not long risen." He sighed, the sound happy and content. "We do not have to get up yet."

"Good." Kei moved his leg to lie across Dainon, catching his breath when Dainon's sac and heavy cock rubbed against it. Arrio squeezed his buttock, and the movement pulled his cheeks apart so Arrio's shaft rubbed between them over his hole. It was a sensual onslaught, one that had Kei's cock filling.

"We were going to talk." Dainon's voice rumbled through his chest. "Now seems as good a time as any." He caressed Kei's thigh, moving languorously, seemingly with no other intention than to touch him.

"I would prefer to do… other things," Arrio said huskily, rocking gently so that his shaft slid through Kei's crease. "I would finish what we started that night by the river."

When Dainon stiffened, Kei knew that the talking took priority.

He held Dainon's face, meeting his gaze. "That night I awoke from a dream where the three of us were making love. Lust and urgent desire held me in their grip, and it would have been easy to let Arrio take me as he wanted, but everything in me knew it was wrong. The following night I told him the truth."

"When the two of you lay by the fire?" Dainon had not broken eye contact, his hand still on Kei's thigh.

Kei nodded. "I have other gifts that you know nothing of. One of them allows me to see into the thoughts of whomever I touch, specifically to know if they speak truth or not." He paused to take a breath.

"Go on," Dainon bade him, his voice calm. Arrio stroked up and down his arm, as if to reassure Kei of his presence.

Kei could not take his eyes off Dainon. "The reason I had never taken a lover was that I feared intimacy. I could never feel comfortable, knowing there was nothing about them that lay hidden from my gift."

"And yet last night…."

Kei smiled. "I told you I had seen in a vision that you were destined to be mine. But what affirmed that knowledge was the fact that with you and Arrio, my gift is useless. Your thoughts are hidden from me. From the moment when I first became aware of the gift of Truthspeak, there has never been anyone like you two." He sighed. "We were meant to be together."

"So when we joined last night?" Dainon returned his smile. "In your mind there was blissful silence?"

"Yes," Kei said, thankful that Dainon understood. "And there is one more thing. With everyone else, I see colors around them. These auras reveal much about a person—their moods, their state of health, their feelings...."

"You said with everyone else. Not with Arrio and me?"

Kei shook his head. "And for that reason, I had to tread so carefully."

"Ah." Dainon's face lit up. "You were uncertain as to what my reaction would be, and so you kept silent."

Kei nodded. "I had to trust in my visions that we were meant for one another. That was all that kept me from losing faith when... when you left."

Dainon closed his eyes and sighed. "What you must have gone through. What *I* put you through."

Kei leaned forward and kissed him on the mouth. "Peace, Dainon. You are here now, and that is all that matters."

Dainon opened his eyes. "And you?" He stared over Kei's shoulder at Arrio. "Is there more you have to tell me?"

"You already know about my gifts. But when I told you I was a virgin because no one had stirred my senses until you...."

"That was not the truth?"

"Yes and no." Arrio's sigh pierced the quiet chamber. "My senses bade me wait until the right time."

"And when was that?"

There was a pause. "When I could share my body with someone who meant something to me."

Dainon regarded them, his face impassive. "I am glad we spoke of these things. There should be nothing but truth between us." He inhaled slowly. "So I too must share with you. I do not have your gifts. I am only a warrior trained in the ways of battle and pursuit. There has been but one event in my life that comes close to your experiences—the day I met my wife, when I knew her for what she was, my soul mate."

"You loved her very much," Arrio said quietly.

"I did." Dainon's expression softened. "And because of that love, when that... lightning bolt happened again—not once, but twice—I told myself it could not have the same meaning. For it to be so felt like a betrayal of our love."

"Lightning bolt?" Kei stared at him, his breathing quickening.

Dainon nodded. "When I first touched Arrio, and then you. I know it now for what it was—*my* senses telling me that I had just met the two people who were destined to turn my world inside out and upside down. It was only when I let go of the past that I was ready to acknowledge the truth." He smiled. "Even if that truth meant I was going to discover what it was like to love a man."

Kei breathed freely for the first time since their conversation had begun. "Last night.... Was it as you had imagined?" he asked, rubbing Dainon's furred stomach and moving his hand lower to where he knew a thick cock awaited him.

"It was better. Nothing like anything I had experienced in the past, and certainly a night that made me hunger for more."

His words lit a fire in Kei's belly.

"I too hunger for more," Arrio whispered.

There was movement behind Kei, and before he could utter a word, slick fingers pressed into his hole. Kei groaned and tilted his bottom, offering it to Arrio. "Then take what you want," he said, his voice hoarse. He reached behind him, searching for Arrio's cock, and his hand encountered a long, hot shaft. "I want this." He stifled his moans as Arrio pushed deeper.

Dainon took hold of Kei's leg and held him firm. "I will hold you while Arrio takes you. I want to watch your face while our lover fucks you."

Kei twisted his upper body to take Arrio's mouth in a heated kiss, Arrio's fingers sliding in and out of him, nudging the spot inside that made him want to scream with pleasure.

Arrio kissed his neck, biting softly at the skin while he withdrew his fingers and replaced them with the head of his cock. He gave Kei a lingering kiss. "I have longed for this moment," he said, and Kei expelled a heady groan as Arrio slowly entered him, the motion pushing him against Dainon. "By the Maker. Your body pulls me in, and the heat inside you sears my shaft."

Dainon chuckled. "He feels good, does he not?" He took Kei's mouth in a tender kiss.

"He feels like heaven," Arrio said with a sigh, sliding faster, sinking deeper into Kei's body. With every thrust he pushed Kei into Dainon's arms. "Hold him tight."

Dainon gazed into Kei's face. "I have you," he whispered. "Does Arrio's cock feel good inside you?"

Kei groaned. "Your mouth. Your words inflame me, making me so hot inside."

"You should see his face," Dainon said. "The joy there when he thrusts into you. The way his body strains when he fucks you, his muscles tight."

Then Arrio slowed to a tortuous pace, rocking slowly into Kei's body, until Kei swore he could feel every inch of that thick shaft penetrating him. The gentle motion, the way Arrio's hips rolled, had him yearning to be taken, to feel Arrio plunging into his body, as Dainon had fucked Arrio the previous night.

"Arrio," he pleaded. "Harder, please." He pushed back, impaling himself on Arrio's cock.

Arrio slipped his arm around him, both he and Dainon holding Kei steady while Arrio snapped his hips, picking up a little speed as he pushed up into him.

"Arrio," Kei croaked. "Please."

Arrio's hot breath caressed his ear as he whispered, "Oh, sweet Kei, I—" He shivered, burying his shaft deep, and Kei felt the throb of his cock as Arrio spilled inside him. Arrio tightened his arms around him, his breath leaving him in short gasps.

Then Dainon's fingers were on Kei's shaft, and with one tug, two, three, he creamed Dainon's hand, crying out. Kei was pinned between them, his sac emptying its seed, his body shaking. Dainon kissed his cheeks, nose, and lips, while Arrio kissed the back of his neck, both men stroking him, caressing him so gently.

Kei could not deny that it felt good, but there was still a small voice in his mind.

What if I do not want them to be gentle?

Then all such thoughts were swept away on a tide of pleasure as he gave himself up to his men, loving how they held him and let him know without words that he was, indeed, precious to them.

If this is love, then more of it.

ARRIO AND Kei had pulled on their robes from the previous night, and Dainon had sent for fresh water to bathe. His belly gave out a rumble and he flushed. "I think I am hungry."

Arrio chuckled. "Does that surprise you, after all that energy you expended last night and this morning?" Then his eyes widened. "Oh. Now I understand." He shuddered.

"What is wrong?" Kei demanded. "What do you understand?"

Arrio gazed at him with a tortured expression. "Why some mornings my fathers seem hungrier than usual."

Dainon stared at him, and a rich laugh rolled out of him. "Is it so bad to realize that your fathers have a healthy sex life?"

Arrio gaped at him. "But they are my *fathers*."

"And one of them is *my brother*," Kei added with another shudder.

Dainon stilled. "And all of them are around my age. Is that what concerns you? You consider them too old to be fucking each other?"

"No," Kei insisted. "They can have as much sex as they like, but I do not have to know about it, do I?"

Dainon laughed again. "Come here." He held out his arms, and both men walked into them. Dainon held them close, surrounded by their scent, calmed by their presence.

Then it struck him.

Since my return, it is always thus when I am close to them. They calm my spirit, quieten my thoughts, bring me peace....

Yet more confirmation, if any were needed, that Kei's vision was true.

"We will join you for breakfast," Arrio said, "after we have returned to our room to bathe and put on clean robes." He wrinkled his nose. "We smell of—"

Kei silenced him with a hand across his mouth. "We know what we smell of, and to repeat your words, does that surprise you?" Slowly he withdrew his hand.

Arrio chuckled. "Perhaps not."

Dainon kissed them both. "Then go to your room. I will meet you for breakfast." He looked toward the window. "A pity to eat indoors. It is a glorious morning." The sky was a brilliant shade of blue, not a cloud to be seen, and already the temperature in the chamber had begun to climb.

"We shall eat in the garden," Arrio said with a smile. "I will make it so." He grabbed Kei's hand and tugged him from Dainon's arms. "Meet us there."

Dainon nodded. As they reached the door, he called out to them. "There is something important we must discuss later."

Kei turned to face him. "There is?"

Dainon nodded. "Sleeping arrangements. If I am to stay in the palace, I want you both in my bed."

Arrio beamed. "I will ask my fathers. It should not be a problem, especially as you are now one of the family." And with that he and Kei left the room.

Dainon stared after them. *One of the family.* Then a thought occurred to him. *He means to ask his fathers. Do King Tanish, Feyar and Sorran know what happened last night?*

Another thought hit him, this time with more force.

I will have four fathers-in-law, two of whom are kings.

Because whatever the future held for him, one thing was certain.

There was going to be a wedding.

Dainon bathed and dressed, unable to stop himself from smiling.

"THANK YOU. This is perfect," Arrio told the servants, who bowed and left the garden.

He gazed at the long table placed under the trees, laden with fruit, yogurt, bread, and other delicious morsels. Chairs had been placed around it, and the dappled shade gave respite from the day's heat.

"What a lovely way to start the day." Kei walked through the garden toward him, smiling.

Arrio took Kei in his arms and kissed his cheek. "A far lovelier way was what we were doing earlier," he whispered.

Kei giggled and nodded in agreement. They both looked up as Dainon entered the garden, striding over to them, also smiling. When he reached them, the three of them joined in a kiss, Dainon's arms around both of them.

"I could easily become addicted to such kisses," Arrio admitted.

"I would never have believed three mouths could join in a kiss until now," Dainon replied. "It has all the makings of a disaster, and yet—"

"And yet it's perfect," Kei interrupted with a sigh. "Again. Kiss me again."

Dainon laughed softly and met Arrio's gaze. "It seems you are not the only one who is addicted." He cupped Kei's face in his hand and kissed him slowly, pulling Arrio in to join them. Three mouths, three tongues, and yet one perfect kiss.

"That is a beautiful sight to see."

Arrio, Kei, and Dainon parted, and Arrio bowed his head. "Good morning," he said in greeting to his fathers.

His *papa* grinned. "You need not stop on our account."

"No, indeed," Sorran added. "I like to see three happy men."

"Three *very* happy men." Feyar too was grinning.

Arrio groaned. "Please, go no further, I beg you." He turned to Dainon and Kei. "Perhaps Dainon staying in the palace is not such a good idea. Maybe we should find a house, far from here." He glared at Sorran. "With no fathers nearby."

Tanish laughed loudly. "I would not like to think what the palace guards and servants thought of us, the first few nights we spent together." His eyes gleamed as he regarded Sorran. "One of us was incapable of keeping quiet."

Feyar snorted. "'Was'? Little has changed in twenty years."

Kei rolled his eyes heavenward. "I do not need to hear this," he said with a sigh.

Sorran approached Dainon. "I know we welcomed you as ambassador last night. We felt it unwise to say more until we knew for sure that all was well between you three." He smiled. "And all is well, is it not?"

Dainon nodded. "We have talked." His gaze alighted on Arrio and Kei, and Arrio caught his breath to see so much naked emotion in his eyes. "I am theirs, as they are mine."

Sorran clasped Dainon's hand in his. "Then now is the time to bid you welcome to the family." His face was alight with joy.

"Must Dainon commence his duties immediately?" Kei asked, his tone plaintive.

Tanish, Sorran, and Feyar regarded one another, and then Tanish smiled. "I think not. The process will begin with proclamations throughout the kingdom, informing our people of our intentions. This will take time."

Feyar nodded in agreement. "It will be several days before we will know more."

Sorran's eyes lit up. "I have an idea." He turned to Arrio. "Why not take Dainon and Kei to the lake? Three or four days to rest and relax, spend time with one another...."

"Perfect." Tanish gave a brisk nod. "You have all been under a strain these last few weeks. This seems a good opportunity to put it behind you." His gaze met Dainon. "Because when you return, there will be something important to discuss."

Dainon reached for Arrio's and Kei's hands and squeezed them tight. "Our future."

Arrio swallowed. It was like a dream. *It is really going to happen.*

Dainon's stomach rumbled like thunder, and he coughed. "First things first—breakfast."

Feyar chuckled. "Yes. Food provides energy, and you are going to need every bit of yours to keep up with these two."

Arrio bit back his smirk. *In* and *out of the bedchamber.* The prospect of spending almost a week alone with Kei and Dainon at the lake was a delicious one.

I cannot wait.

TWENTY-ONE

DAINON STARED at the landscape in amazement. "When I think I have seen all that is beautiful in Teruna, you bring me here." The lake reflected the sky, a solid mass of blue, and the varying shades of green that surrounded it were vivid and bright. At one end rose a rocky mass, over which water tumbled in a sheer curtain, crashing into the lake below. There were trees all around it, and Dainon caught the fragrance of pine and cedar.

"Was it worth riding for two days to see?" Arrio asked him, climbing down from his horse.

Dainon smiled. "Undoubtedly." The journey had had the added bonus of a night under the stars beside a fire, the three of them entwined in one another's arms. "And now I see why you wanted us to wait until we arrived before we... enjoyed each other." There was no one to be seen, unlike the previous night when a caravan of merchants had camped near them. "Is it always so quiet here?"

Arrio nodded. "My fathers told me they used to come here when they wanted to escape. They brought me here when I was small." He gazed out over the lake. "I loved to swim in the lake and play under the waterfall."

Dainon got down off Fiore and walked toward the water's edge, peering into its clear depths. "How deep is it?"

Arrio appeared at his side. "The center is the deepest part. Around the periphery it remains at neck height." He smirked. "Unless you are Kei."

"I heard that!" Kei yelled indignantly. "But there are advantages to being my stature."

Dainon could not resist. He strode over to where Kei stood beside his mare and picked him up in his arms. Instantly Kei wound his legs around Dainon's waist, his arms looped around his neck. "And this is one of them," Dainon said with a chuckle. It felt good to hold Kei like that, as if he held something very precious in his arms.

Kei nuzzled into his neck. "You smell good."

"What do I smell of?" Dainon asked, stifling a moan when Kei kissed his neck and nipped at his earlobe.

"Leather, horse, sun—last night," Kei added with a giggle. He tightened his hold around Dainon's neck and undulated his body against Dainon's. "I like it when you hold me like this. Later, will you…?" His cheeks flushed. "Will you take me standing up?" he whispered.

The image was right there in Dainon's mind, and his cock began to fill. "Why later?" he murmured. "Why should I not strip you down here and now, and sit you on my cock?" He slipped his hands under Kei's bare bottom and began to slowly raise him up and down, feeling Kei's shaft grow thicker against his belly. "Have I mentioned that I like you in this tunic?" he murmured into Kei's ear. "Everything is so much more… accessible." His fingers spread, seeking Kei's crease, and Kei's breathing changed. "Is that what you want? My fingers inside your tight hole?" Dainon knew how much he could inflame both his lovers with suggestive words and coarse language.

Kei clung to him, his breathing harsh in his ear, and soft, familiar moans told Dainon the idea was a welcome one.

When Arrio cleared his throat, Dainon stilled and both of them glanced at Arrio.

"We are going to be here for at least four days," he informed them. "Surely we can set up the tent and unpack the bags first? Especially as I made sure to bring Dainon's oil." He grinned. "It was the first thing I packed."

Reluctantly Dainon let Kei slide his legs to the ground, and he released him. Dainon took Kei's mouth in a fervent kiss, loving the sounds of sheer hunger and desire that Kei fed back to him. "Later," he whispered. He caught his breath when Kei reached down to palm Dainon's cock.

"Count on it," Kei said with a smile, giving his length a quick squeeze before darting out of reach.

Thirty minutes later the tent was erected and the ground within covered. Arrio put together a bed of layers of soft furs, big enough for all three. "Perfect," he said with satisfaction.

Dainon kissed his shoulder. "And this time we get to sleep curled around each other."

When Kei joined them, the moment seemed natural for the three to kiss, mouths and tongues meeting as arms slid around waists and backs, all three locked in a warm embrace.

Kei broke the kiss to peer at the lake. "Is the water very cold?"

Arrio's eyes gleamed. "I do not know. We could drop you into it and then we would know."

"Enough," Dainon said firmly. "We shall all swim, and then we will know." He kicked off his sandals and began to remove his clothing. The warm, late-afternoon sunlight felt good upon his bare body. He peered into the sky. "We have a few more hours of daylight. Let us make the most of them."

Before long all of them were plunging into the lake, laughing and splashing one another, their cries of joy loud and unrestrained. The water temperature was a little cool, but refreshing after their journey. Dainon swam out to the center of the lake, where the water was dark beneath him, the others joining him. A sense of peace stole over him, and he understood why King Tanish, Feyar, and Sorran had recommended this place.

"Swim toward the waterfall," Arrio called before heading in that direction.

Dainon and Kei followed, Kei easily keeping up with his long arm strokes. When they reached the rocks, Dainon was able to stand once more. Beyond the curtain of water was darkness.

Arrio walked slowly toward the tumbling waters. "Stand under it," he shouted to them. "It feels wonderful." He lifted his arms and turned his face skyward, eyes tight shut, the water cascading down his body.

Dainon was speechless before such beauty. Arrio's skin gleamed, the sunlight creating rainbows that danced over his body. He hastened to join him, and soon all three of them stood beneath the waterfall, the cascade pouring over and around them. Dainon put his arms around them and drew them to him, their mouths meeting in a kiss that grew more heated, while hands roamed over bodies, touching, caressing, tweaking, exploring.

"I want you both," he groaned. "Now."

Without a word, Arrio took their hands and led them through the water toward the lake's edge, where the grass was long and cool. Kei left them, sprinting toward their tent, and Dainon knew what he sought.

Arrio pulled Dainon down onto the grass, his lips parted. "Kiss me?"

Dainon could never refuse such a beautiful invitation.

KEI APPROACHED his lovers, flask in hand, and stood watching as they kissed, feeding soft moans of pleasure into each other's mouths while they stroked and caressed one another. What struck him was that he felt no pang of jealousy. It felt... right.

I love them both.

He listened as Arrio's moans grew more frequent, watched as Dainon bent to take Arrio's length in his mouth—and stared at the firm globes of Dainon's bottom. He grinned. A conversation with Feyar before they left for the lake had proved most... interesting.

And here is the perfect opportunity to put his advice into action.

Kei knelt behind Dainon, pulling his cheeks apart. Dainon stiffened and pulled free of Arrio's cock to glance over his shoulder.

Kei was still grinning. "Trust me," he said quietly. "You will like this."

Dainon stared as Kei kissed his cheeks, biting softly and licking where his teeth marked the skin. His pucker tightened and Kei kissed it, catching Dainon's brief gasp of surprise. Then Dainon dropped his head to the ground when Kei licked over his hole, taking his time. He felt the shudders that rippled along Dainon's spine, and Kei exulted in this new power.

"Where," Dainon asked with a shiver, "did you learn this particular skill? And do not stop, I beg you."

Arrio chuckled. "Let us say, we had a quick lesson before we left the palace." His gaze met Kei's and he grinned. "Well, Kei did."

Kei stifled a giggle. Arrio had been adamant that he could not sit there and listen to Feyar giving advice on how to pleasure Dainon. Kei pressed his face between Dainon's cheeks and rubbed his beard over Dainon's hole.

Dainon groaned. "By the Maker, Kei, you are clearly an excellent student."

Kei laughed. "Arrio, lie beneath Dainon to take his length in your mouth," he commanded.

Arrio shifted positions quickly, his hands reaching up to spread Dainon's cheeks. When Kei resumed his activity with a slow tongue from Dainon's hole down to his testicles, Dainon shuddered once more and thrust into Arrio's mouth.

Kei pushed at the tight puckered entrance with his tongue, little stabs at it, feeling it loosen until he could push inside. Dainon groaned and shoved back, as if to claim more of that soft invader. Kei set up a rhythm of licking and penetrating Dainon's hole, his heart soaring every time Dainon let escape his noises of pleasure and urgent need. Dainon's hips rocked as he thrust between Arrio's lips, and Kei came perilously close to spending at the sight of Arrio's lips tight around Dainon's thick shaft.

Arrio gasped. "Is he ready?"

Kei broke off from his worship of Dainon's entrance. "Almost." He opened the flask and held it aloft, letting some of its contents trickle down Dainon's crease. Kei slowly pushed his finger through the viscous fluid to penetrate Dainon's tight channel.

Dainon stiffened. "Oh, by all that is holy." Kei stilled inside him, but Dainon shook his head. "Do not stop, I beg you. More." As if to confirm his words, he pushed back with his whole body.

Kei slid in and out of him until he was sinking his finger deep inside Dainon's body, and Dainon was writhing, his cries frequent.

Arrio edged out from beneath Dainon and knelt in front of him, his hand wrapped around his own cock, slowly pumping it. "Do you want this inside you, *corishan?*" He stroked the head across Dainon's lips, moaning softly when Dainon flicked the ridge with his tongue. Arrio slowly pushed between Dainon's lips, and Kei sank another finger into his channel, hooking them to brush over the little knot that always took his breath away. Dainon groaned around Arrio's shaft, rocking back as if pleading for more.

"Does his mouth feel good?" Kei asked Arrio, gazing with longing at his lover's glistening cock sliding faster in and out of Dainon's mouth.

Arrio cupped Dainon's head and threw back his own with a low cry, hips snapping forward. "Too good." He gasped and pulled free, his gaze meeting Kei. "I need to take him before he makes me spend, and I want to spill inside him." He bent down to kiss Dainon, both of them moaning into it. "Do you wish that also? Do you want to feel me release inside you?"

Dainon caressed his cheek. "Yes, but please…."

Arrio stared into his eyes. "I will be gentle—to begin with."

Dainon shivered and Kei knew instinctively that fear was not the cause.

He wants this, to be taken thus.

Arrio shifted until he knelt behind Dainon, and Kei lay beneath him. "Kiss me," Kei demanded.

Dainon lowered his head, and their lips met in a lingering kiss. Kei knew the moment Arrio had entered him: Dainon's eyes widened and his breathing hitched. Kei stroked his face. "He is inside you?"

Dainon locked gazes with him. "He feels so big." Then he buried his face in Kei's neck. "By the Maker, he feels *huge*," he groaned.

Kei rubbed up and down his back, keeping his touch light. "Wait but a little while longer, and it will change. There comes a moment when the ache becomes a good ache, when you crave him deeper inside you, filling you."

Dainon raised his head to regard him, those brown eyes huge and dark, and Kei kissed his lips, exploring him with a leisurely tongue.

When Dainon began to move, rocking gently above him, low noises pouring from his lips, Kei smiled. "And there it is."

"Oh heavens above, you feel wonderful on my cock," Arrio said with a sigh, leaning over to kiss down Dainon's back.

"More," Dainon demanded. His lips parted in a breathless cry as Arrio grabbed his shoulders and slammed into him, his whole body jolting. Kei reached down to grasp Dainon's shaft and tugged, and Dainon arched his back. "Yes, oh, yes." Each thrust of Arrio's length sent Dainon's cock pushing through Kei's hand, and when Arrio picked up speed, violent shivers coursed through Dainon's body.

Kei took Dainon's mouth in a brutal kiss, claiming him. Dainon cried out as hot seed pulsed over Kei's hand, and Arrio's loud cry mingled with his as he buried his shaft inside Dainon's body. Kei watched with joy as his lovers climaxed, their connection renewed. He stroked and kissed them, his touch gentle.

When Dainon and Arrio had finished, they fell onto their backs in the cool grass, their arms around each other while they kissed and caressed. They gazed up at Kei and beckoned for him to join them, pulling him to lie between them. Kei put his arms about their necks and held on while both men spread his legs, hooking them over their own. He shuddered when both Dainon and Arrio slowly pushed a finger into him, moving together even as they took it in turns to kiss him and suck on his neck and nipples, sending him higher and higher until at last his cock erupted without a touch. They held him and kissed him through his orgasm, each of them whispering how beautiful he was, how he was theirs.

What broke him was when Dainon looked him in the eye and said quietly, "We love you."

What melted him was when Arrio kissed him and said in a low voice, "You bind us together, Kei, and we will never let you go."

Kei wept for joy, and his men held him until his tears subsided and were wiped away by gentle hands.

DAINON AWOKE early to find his arms full of Arrio, but Kei was missing. He stiffened until the sound of laughter came in through the open tent.

Arrio stirred. "Is that... Kei?"

Dainon kissed him on the forehead. "It is, though what he finds so amusing out here in the middle of nowhere is a mystery." He sat up, rubbing his hand through his dark hair and beard. Arrio watched him, and Dainon tilted his head. "The beard. Do I keep it?" He smiled. "Perhaps I might look younger without it."

Arrio straddled Dainon's body in an instant, glaring at him. "Do not even jest about such a thing. I love your beard, and you will not remove *one single hair* of it, do you hear me?"

Dainon chuckled. "I hear, Your Highness." Another burst of laughter greeted his ears, and he glanced in its direction. "What is he doing?"

Arrio climbed off him and held out his hand. "Let us find out." He helped Dainon to his feet, and they walked naked into the early morning sunshine.

Dainon took one look at the scene before him and his heart swelled with love.

Kei sat naked on the grass, his face alight with joy. Around him scampered little creatures, furry, big-eyed little things with fluffy round tails. One of them would have sat easily in the palm of Dainon's hand. The cute animals hopped over Kei's outstretched legs and pushed at his hands to be stroked and petted. Some nibbled at his toes, sending Kei into paroxysms of laughter. One stood up on its little hind legs, its tiny paws on Kei's arm, trying to claim his attention. Overall, there must have been at least twenty of the adorable creatures, scrambling over Kei and vying for his affection.

Dainon cleared his throat, and as one the animals froze, all heads turned toward Dainon and Arrio, their tiny hearts pumping visibly. Dainon held himself still, unwilling to break the fragile moment.

Kei murmured to the creatures, his tone coaxing, and slowly they relaxed. When Kei rose to his feet, they scampered away toward the trees, Kei watching them go with a smile. He turned to Dainon and Arrio, his eyes wide. "They were like the *temura* back in Vancor!"

Dainon shook his head, walked over to his lover, and pulled him into his arms to kiss him. "I will never tire of your gift for connecting with animals. Is there no creature who can resist you?"

Kei shrugged, his cheeks pink. "If there is, I have not found them yet." He reached behind Dainon and gently squeezed his buttock. "How are you this morning?" He bit his lip.

Dainon arched his eyebrows. "I am fine." Then he became aware of the ache where there had not been one the previous day. He sighed. "Although it may be a while before I let Arrio anywhere near my backside."

Arrio gasped in mock surprise. "What can you mean?" His lips twitched.

Dainon slid his hand down over Arrio's belly, taking his time, until he reached his shaft, already long and hard. "This should be classed as a weapon." Then he grinned. "Its heat is searing my hand. I think it needs to cool off." Swiftly he grabbed Arrio, threw him over his shoulder, and ran toward the lake, Kei running behind him, laughing.

"Dainon, no!" Arrio yelled, trying to wriggle free, his hands slapping Dainon's buttocks. "Dainon, put me down! Stop!"

Dainon didn't listen. Nor did he stop until he reached the lake and tossed Arrio into the water. Kei erupted into a peal of laughter that ended abruptly when Dainon grabbed him and threw him into the lake as well. Both princes gazed up at him, hair wet, spluttering, both vowing revenge, until he jumped in after them, splashing them.

"Well, you did want to bathe this morning, did you not?" Dainon asked with an innocent expression. He took one look at their faces and set off swimming away, both of them in pursuit.

Dainon had never felt so alive.

KEI GAZED into the fire and sighed. "I do not want this to end." He glanced at Dainon and Arrio, who sat beside him, Dainon's arm around Arrio's shoulders, his hand slowly stroking Kei's thigh. "Can we not stay longer? Would they miss us?"

Dainon laughed quietly. "If you remember, I have work to do? I cannot forget my new duties." His gaze met Kei's. "Though I too wish for more time here."

Kei had never been so happy. Four days of playing together, talking, laughing, swimming, making love whenever the mood took them.... Four days of heaven. Waking one morning to the sound of music, fragile notes that pierced his heart and brought tears to his eyes. Arrio sat by the lake, playing the *torishar* he brought with him, his fingers moving expertly over the strings. Both Kei and Dainon listened, enraptured, marveling at his skill, at the way he created such beautiful harmonies.

Mornings when Kei had awoken to kisses, caresses, and slow, sweet love as both his men took him, one after another, until he released his seed with a heartfelt cry. Nights when they lay together, arms entwined, Kei in the middle, rocking slowly between them, his shaft buried deep in Arrio's body while Dainon thrust slowly into Kei. Wonderful nights that somehow blurred into mornings.

"We have to return home."

Arrio's abrupt tone brought Kei sharply into focus.

"What is wrong?" Kei asked, his heartbeat racing.

Arrio sighed. "I do not know. But for the last few hours, I have felt apprehensive, anxious, and I know not why." He gazed at them. "There can only be one explanation. Something is wrong with my fathers."

"You do not know that for certain," Dainon said softly. When Arrio stared at him, Dainon held up his hands. "I do not say you are wrong, nor do I discount your feelings. But I beg you, do not let this tear you apart. We are two days from the palace. That we cannot change. Save your energy, because worrying will do nothing but sap you of it."

Arrio said nothing but regarded him steadily. Finally he nodded. "You speak wisely." Slowly he leaned forward and kissed Dainon on the mouth, his fingers wound through Dainon's hair.

Kei sighed. "I love to watch you kiss. That I can do this and feel nothing but love for you both only serves to prove how strong the bond is between us."

Arrio broke away from Dainon, his eyes wide. "Thank you!" He got up and went quickly to the tent.

Dainon met Kei's stare. "Did we miss something?"

Arrio walked across to them, smiling, a small leather pouch in his hand. "I had forgotten these. You two distracted me." He sat beside them and placed the pouch on the ground. "When I saw my friend Parina a few weeks ago, I gave her a task." He indicated the pouch with a nod. "This is the result. I wanted something for all of us, something special." He opened the pouch, took Dainon's hand, placed an object in it, and folded his fingers over it. "Do not look, not until Kei has his." Then he repeated the action. Arrio took a deep breath. "Now you may look."

Kei opened his hand and caught his breath. A gold amulet on a chain lay in his palm, a circle with three hands joined at the wrists. He knew it instantly. "This was the symbol of ancient Teruna," he said reverently.

"So beautiful," Dainon murmured, turning his over to examine it. The space around the hands had been cut away so they stood out, connected to the outer edge.

Kei jerked his head up. "Do you have one?" he asked Arrio, who nodded.

Arrio took Kei's amulet and placed it over his head, then did the same for Dainon. From the pouch, he removed a third and put it on. "From now on, all who see us will know of our bond," he said, his voice solemn.

Slowly Dainon drew them to him, until all three lay down by the fire. What began with slow, tender kisses morphed into gentle lovemaking and then into heat and passion, until their cries rang out into the night. Kei lost himself in the bliss of orgasm, dimly aware of Dainon carrying him to their tent afterward, where he fell into a deep, contented sleep.

CHAPTER
TWENTY-TWO

ARRIO WALKED swiftly to the royal audience chamber, Kei and Dainon close behind him. The knot of apprehension in his belly could not be ignored. He had awoken at dawn, anxious to undertake the final leg of the journey home. Dainon had not told him his fears were groundless, for which Arrio was grateful. Both he and Kei rode at Arrio's side, keeping pace with him, stopping only when absolutely necessary.

Something is wrong. The premonition was no more concrete than that, but it was enough to have Arrio's heart pounding and a cold sweat break out over all his body as he neared the chamber. The guards bowed their heads and opened the doors immediately.

A wave of relief washed over him when he saw his fathers standing by the dais, looking as healthy as when they had parted company several days previously.

They are well. They live. Thank the heavens, I was wrong.

"Oh, bless the Maker," Kei murmured. "I was so afraid." When Arrio fired him a glance, Kei flushed. "If I had told you that I too was concerned, it would only have added to your fears."

Tanish watched them approach, his expression guarded, his eyes troubled. When Feyar and Sorran turned to regard them, a similar look on their faces, that apprehension seized hold of Arrio's heart once more.

Something is *wrong.*

"Arrio, we are glad to see you." His *papa* gave him a tight smile.

Arrio came to a halt before him, his gaze flickering from Tanish to Feyar to Sorran. "What troubles you?" His heartbeat raced and his palms were clammy. From behind him he sensed his lovers draw closer: Kei's hand rested on his arm, Dainon's on his lower back.

Sorran sighed. "I should have known we could hide nothing from you."

Feyar stepped toward him. "Before we share our news, there is something I must say." He glanced at his husbands, who nodded. "That *we* must say," he corrected. He drew in a deep breath and locked gazes with Arrio. "*Nothing* has changed, do you hear me? We love you and we will continue to love you."

Fear clawed at Arrio's throat. "Tell me," he begged, his voice cracking.

Sorran placed his hands on Arrio's shoulders and looked him in the eye. "Two days after you left, a… visitor arrived at the palace, searching for you. When we heard his tale, we invited him to stay until your return."

"A visitor? Who is he?" Arrio could not escape the feeling that something was coming at him, faster than the bear's approach and with far sharper claws, ones that were about to deliver a cruel blow.

Sorran glanced at Tanish, who nodded once more. Sorran squeezed Arrio's shoulders. "He claims to be your father."

Shock ricocheted through Arrio's body. "My… my *father*? But… *you* are my fathers."

"Your birth father, then," Tanish said simply.

Arrio's stomach churned and a wave of nausea threatened to overcome him. Dainon's and Kei's arms were there instantly, supporting him. He could not speak, but he leaned into Dainon, his head spinning.

"Any man might wander in from the street and claim to be Arrio's father. How do you know he speaks the truth?" Dainon narrowed his gaze. "You believe him, clearly. Tell me why. What compelling evidence does he offer to make you believe his story?"

Feyar cleared his throat. "We do not say that we believe him, but there are things about him that give us pause. He knew of Arrio's birthmark, for example."

"So might anyone who has seen him in Teruna!" Kei burst out, his eyes wide. "That is not enough."

Sorran's gaze flickered to Tanish, who pushed out a heavy sigh. "There was something else. He had with him an image, a small painting he carries everywhere of… your mother."

"My mother? I never knew her, but…." Arrio gulped. "But you saw her. The day you found me." His heart hammered so loud, he was amazed they did not hear it. "Well? Was it her?"

Silence fell, as heavy as a stone, and in that silence, Arrio knew.

Tanish broke the silence. "He told us your mother had no family. It explained why no one came forward when we made inquiries about her. We had thought it odd when no one claimed knowledge of her."

"What was her name?" Arrio asked softly. "Did… did she have other children?"

"He says her name was Minea," Sorran said quietly, "and that you were her first child."

Kei laced his fingers through Arrio's. "Is it so bad that he comes seeking you out? Why do you react with such distress?"

Arrio turned to him, his heart aching. "Because my senses tell me there is more." He regarded Sorran. "Well? Tell me I am wrong. Tell me he is simply here to reveal his identity, and then he plans to leave."

"We have told him he is welcome to dwell here in the palace. He could have his own rooms and live out his days in comfort, but…." Tanish swallowed. "He plans to stay but a few days, perhaps a week, and then he will leave. He… he wants you to go with him."

Arrio gaped. "For what reason?"

"Does he have a name?" Dainon interjected.

"Lomar. His name is Lomar." Feyar's face bore an expression of sorrow. "And he says he wants to spend time with you, getting to know his son—just the two of you."

"How much time?" Arrio demanded. "Does this… Lomar say that? And what of my Dainon and Kei? What of them? Are they, too, to accompany us?"

"We spoke of this," Feyar said quickly. "We told him of Dainon and Kei, that Kei would ascend the throne of Vancor one day, and that you and Dainon would be his consorts until such time as you ascend the throne here, but…."

Arrio's heart sank to hear that last word. "But?"

"He was adamant that it would be the two of you. Not that this necessarily means he will get his own way."

"And we were just as adamant in our response," Tanish added. "We have strongly encouraged him to stay here in the palace."

Sorran shook his head. "And no matter what you think, you will speak to him with respect when you meet him."

Anger boiled inside Arrio. "He wants me to go with him, to put aside my own plans for my marriage, with no indication as to when I might return to them?" He wanted to scream at the heavens, to rail at the injustice of it all, the ill timing…. The feeling of being impotent in the face of this catastrophe thickened his throat and constricted his chest.

Then a small measure of calm seeped through him. *I am overreacting. This is not a catastrophe unless I allow it to be.* He took a couple of deep cleansing breaths.

"Must I meet him?"

"What excuse could we offer for not doing so?" Tanish asked, his eyebrows arched.

"It. Does. Not. Feel. Right." Arrio growled. "No matter what evidence he presents as to his identity, I am not convinced."

Sorran put his arms around him and held him. "Oh, Arrio, I know. I feel the same way. But I will ask you the question I put to myself: is it your senses that inform you thus? Or is it your own desires?"

Arrio could not answer that. He struggled free of Sorran's embrace, but Dainon caught him and held him close.

"You should meet with him, *terushan*," Dainon whispered into his ear. "Maybe your gifts will help to make sense of this once you see him and speak with him."

"Let *me* see him," Kei demanded. "You want to know the truth? Let me but touch him once and you will know all."

Arrio cupped Kei's nape and brought their foreheads together in a kiss of flesh. "I will consider it, *corishan*. It is certainly an idea, but only if the occasion presents itself." He gazed at Sorran. "What of his aura? Did you read anything there?"

"Nothing that made me doubt his word. If anything, his aura was oddly neutral. It told me nothing."

Kei exhaled slowly. "But you *do* doubt his word, in spite of his colors." He shook his head. "That does not alter anything." He gazed at the men around him, his jaw clenched. "None of us believe him."

"Come here," Dainon bade him. He drew Kei into the circle of his arms, both Arrio and Kei pressed up against his body. Arrio closed his eyes and breathed in their scent, their warmth, their love. "Peace, Kei," Dainon whispered, and Kei leaned against his chest.

"Based on what Lomar has told us, we have no reason to doubt his word," Feyar said, his tone grave. "Even if our senses—and our hearts— tell us otherwise."

Before Arrio could react, a guard approached them. "Your Majesty, your guest is outside. He wishes an audience with Prince Arrio."

Arrio's pulse raced. He gazed up at Dainon, his breathing rapid. "He knows I am here, then."

Dainon kissed his brow. "This seems as good a time as any to meet with him."

"Go into my private chamber," Tanish said. "I will send Lomar to you."

"Do you want us to be present?" Dainon asked him, stroking up and down his back. "You do not have to be alone with him."

It was a tempting thought. Then Arrio reconsidered. He straightened and met his lover's concerned gaze. "Perhaps it is best if I meet him alone. I have nothing to fear here, after all." He drew in several deep breaths before facing his fathers. "I will see him."

Sorran's eyes glowed with pride. "There speaks our son, Prince Arrio." When Arrio stared at him, Sorran smiled. "It is as Feyar stated. Nothing has changed." His face shone with love. "If this man is truly your father? You will always be our son, and I will always be proud of you." He kissed Arrio's cheek and then took a step back.

Dainon caressed his face. "We shall all be here should you have need of us." He kissed him, his lips pressed against Arrio's before brushing them over his ear. "I too am very proud of my beautiful prince." He released him and stood aside.

Arrio gazed at his family, his heart swelling with love. "It is time. Give me a moment to collect my thoughts?"

"Of course," Tanish said with a nod.

Arrio turned and walked toward the door that led to the private chamber, his head held high. Once inside, he sat quickly at the table, trying to regain his composure. He wanted to meet this man—his father— in a calm state. Arrio gripped the wooden arms of his chair, his knuckles white where the skin was stretched tight across them, his breathing rapid. He inhaled deeply, aware of the faintest aroma of perfume carried on the air, a reminder of the garden, his tranquil space.

It was enough to bring him some small measure of composure.

When the quick rap on the door pierced the silence, Arrio was ready. "Enter."

The door opened and a tall man entered. Arrio looked him up and down, trying to take in as much as he could. Lomar was taller than Arrio, with light brown hair and brown eyes. His arms and upper body appeared muscled, his hands large. He carried over his shoulder a soft leather bag, and he wore leather leggings and a long blue tunic.

I do not resemble him. The thought brought him a brief burst of hope that it was a mistake, until he remembered—he had two parents, and obviously he took after his mother.

Then he thought again. *If Lomar is to be believed, that is.*

"Oh, by the Maker." Lomar's voice was deep. "You have your mother's eyes." He smiled. "But my hair, alas." Arrio recognized his words as an attempt at humor to ease the palpable tension in the small chamber.

My mother's eyes.

A hunger burned in him. "Do you have her image for me to see?"

Lomar nodded, reaching into his bag and removing a small silver frame. "I painted this when we were first married. I think it captured her likeness accurately." He handed it to Arrio, who held it reverently, studying it.

She had been a beautiful woman, with long blonde hair and blue eyes. Her face was kind. While it was true that Arrio's eyes were similar, that was the extent of the resemblance.

"I do not strongly resemble either of you," he observed.

Lomar grinned. "Ah, but you are the image of your grandfather, Minea's father. A pity he did not live to see you." When Arrio did not smile, Lomar sighed. "I do understand how you must be feeling. This is a shock, after all these years."

Arrio gave a single nod. "Twenty years since my mother's death, and you come seeking me now?" Lomar stiffened and Arrio cursed silently. "Forgive me. That was blunt."

"But as I said, understandable. I should tell you why I have not found you before this." He gazed expectantly at the chair before him.

With a rush of shame, Arrio remembered his manners. "Please, sit." Lomar did as instructed, and Arrio placed the picture of his mother on the table, gazing at it. An impulse seized him, and he picked up the frame once more. He held it between his palms and focused his senses on it, shutting off his conscious thoughts. He closed his eyes and pictured her image in his head.

Let me feel... something? He sought any reaction to the painting, however small. There was a feeling deep inside him that he had been connected to her, but whether she had been his mother.... He opened his eyes and gazed upon hers, giving control to his senses.

They are my eyes.

And there it was, the connection he'd sought. "My mother," he said softly, tracing her hair with his fingertip.

"I should never have left her," Lomar said quietly.

Arrio jerked his head up. "What do you mean?"

Lomar sighed. "I was often away from home for long periods of time, leaving her alone, but she always said she liked it that way. Then when she became pregnant, I wanted to stay at home, but she insisted she could cope."

"Why were you away from home?"

Lomar regarded him keenly. "I was a gold prospector. I would look for new seams—not always successfully, I might add—and that was how we lived." His gaze flickered to her portrait. "She deserved so much more than I could give her."

His words spoke of love and caring, but there was an undercurrent that Arrio could not decipher. Then it occurred to him. *My gifts.*

He stared at Lomar, letting his awareness flow over the man. Those few seconds were enough to answer one vital question: Lomar was not *Seruan. Then my gift for divining comes not from him.*

"What was my mother's gift?" he asked suddenly.

"Her... gift?" Lomar blinked, then nodded. "She... she was a healer."

There was no reason why Arrio should have had the same gift as his mother, but to find Lomar was a prospector shook him. *Yet more evidence that reveals him to be my father.* Arrio knew no one would have spoken of his gift—the only people who knew were in the royal audience chamber—so if it were only a coincidence, it was a staggering one.

Arrio studied Lomar. "You said you should not have left her. What did you mean?"

Lomar gazed at the table. "We were living beyond the Narosan mountains at the time. She was due to give birth and I wanted to stay home, but our funds were low. She bade me go. I was away three weeks, but when I returned home, she was no longer there. Friends informed me they had not seen her since the week before my return. It seemed she had left me."

"But why would she do that? And why would she come here?" Arrio mused.

"I have asked myself the same questions during the last twenty or so years." Lomar's brow furrowed. "I have spent the intervening years working my way across many kingdoms, searching for her. If I found a rich seam, I would settle for a few years until I had exhausted it, and then I would move on. In every place, I asked after her. I showed her portrait and explained that she had been heavily pregnant, but no one knew of her." He looked Arrio in the eye. "I have never stopped looking, even when it seemed hopeless. I had to keep believing that she had delivered you safely, that you were both still alive somewhere. As the years went by and there was no news, I had to assume that she had died. It was only when I arrived in Teruna and began to ask my usual questions that I heard about a young woman found dying in some ruins, and that a baby had been with her."

"Which brought you here to the palace."

Lomar nodded. "I cannot deny, it hurt me to think of her sending me off to work, and all the while she was planning to leave me. I do not know what I had done to deserve that. But it no longer matters." He smiled. "I have found you at last, my son."

In spite of his initial misgivings, Arrio had to acknowledge there might be some truth to Lomar's claims. There were too many coincidences to be ignored.

Is he truly my father?

The thought only served to sadden him.

Arrio breathed deeply. "My—" He stiffened. He had been about to say *my fathers*, but the phrase seemed wrong in the circumstances. "King Tanish says you wish to leave soon."

Lomar nodded eagerly. "I want to take time away from my prospecting to get to know you. We can travel together, learn more about each other. What do you say?"

"Surely we can do that if you remain here?" Arrio suggested. "You could live in the palace."

"Yes, that suggestion was made to me earlier." To Arrio's surprise, Lomar's jaw was set. "I understand that you wish to stay close to these men, but you are not their son after all."

Arrio clenched his fists at his sides.

"It is my turn to beg your forgiveness," Lomar said swiftly. "It is obvious they raised you well, and that they love you very much. They are more of a father to you than I can ever be. I understand why you would not wish to be parted from them."

Arrio stared at Lomar. "No," he began slowly, fighting to keep calm, his heartbeat quickening, "but it is not just a matter of them. I have Prince Kei and Lord Dainon to think of. We have a wedding to prepare for."

"From what I have gleaned, you have only recently become betrothed. There is no hurry to marry, is there? You have many more years to be with them." He gazed earnestly at Arrio. "I am asking for such a small amount of your time, compared to the lifetime you will spend married to them."

"But you have not specified this 'small amount of time,'" Arrio said through gritted teeth. "Perhaps if you gave me an idea?" The more they discussed this, the more agitated he became, and he could not explain his reaction.

"Five, six months? A year? Enough time for us to travel beyond the mountains, where I can introduce you to your remaining family."

Arrio froze. "I have... family?"

Lomar nodded. "Would you like to meet your cousins, my siblings, my parents? They too have yearned to meet you, to find some news that you survived."

Arrio could not deny he liked the idea. Then logic took over. "And they will still be there after I am married. There is no hurry, is there? This journey can wait until after my marriage. But a year seems excessive. Perhaps a few months at most." He forced a smile. "I think my future husbands could survive that long without me."

Lomar regarded him steadily, his expression neutral. The silence that fell between them had the hairs on Arrio's arms standing to attention, and panic started to unfurl in his belly.

"I can see we will need to discuss this further," Lomar said finally. His expression relaxed into a smile. "But that can wait. We have some time before I must leave." He rose to his feet, their conversation clearly at an end. "Perhaps you would like to show me around the palace? I wanted to ask my hosts, but felt it wiser to wait until we had met."

Arrio stood slowly. "I can do that." He could not escape the feeling that Lomar was hiding something, but what that might be, he had no idea. "We have time before dinner. That is, if you allow me the opportunity to bathe and change first. We only returned to Teruna a short while ago."

Lomar gave him another relaxed smile, all trace of his previous tension vanished. "Of course." He gestured toward the door. "Shall we?"

Arrio bowed his head and walked toward it, Lomar behind him.

Why does he make me nervous?

CHAPTER
TWENTY-THREE

"WHY ARE you out here and not in our bed?"

Arrio turned at the sound of Dainon's voice. There was no moon in the night sky, but enough light from the city below enabled him to make out his lover's frown as he stood naked on the balcony.

"Because I cannot sleep," Arrio murmured, then sighed with pleasure when two strong arms encircled his body, one across his waist, the other across his chest. Dainon's mouth was warm on his neck. Heat pressed against Arrio's buttocks, and he rocked against it.

"Come back to bed and I will help you sleep," Dainon whispered. A hard, bare, hot cock slid between his cheeks. "I have all you need."

Arrio reached back to still Dainon with a hand to his hip. He leaned against him, his head resting on Dainon's shoulder. "My mind is troubled. Each time I close my eyes, my thoughts collide inside my head and sleep eludes me."

Dainon stroked his chest with gentle fingers. "Share your thoughts." When Arrio remained silent, Dainon kissed his temple. "Lomar."

One word, but it was enough to have him turning in Dainon's arms to seek out his face in the dim light. "I do not know why he plagues me so." When Dainon remained silent, Arrio scanned his features. "What do you think of him?"

Dainon frowned. "Not much. He has barely spoken a word to either myself or to Kei. In fact, he seems to have kept us at arms' length." Dainon gazed at him intently. "You have talked much with him these past days." He resumed his gentle stroking. "I watched you with him. You seemed uneasy. Has he asked you again to travel with him? Is that what troubles you?"

Arrio shook his head. "He has not mentioned it for a few days, but I know he has spoken of it with my—" His throat tightened and his chest ached.

Dainon held him against his broad, furry chest. "Arrio, Lomar's arrival does not change a thing. King Tanish, Feyar, and Sorran *are* your fathers. They raised you, loved you, cared for you, and nothing and *no one* will ever change that."

The words settled on him, as comfortable as a warm blanket. *Yes.* This was Truth.

Arrio buried his face in Dainon's chest, the hair tickling his nose. "I do not want to go with him," he mumbled.

Dainon lifted his chin and looked into his eyes. "What did you say?"

Arrio held his head high. "I do not want to go with Lomar." His voice emerged firm and sure. "I have thought about this constantly since he mentioned it, and it does not sit well with me. But as to what I should do now…." There was still something about Lomar's insistent desire to travel that pebbled Arrio's skin each time he considered it.

Dainon smiled. "You tell him so. I understand that he wants to build a relationship with you, but this is not the way. There will be time, when we are not thinking about vast numbers of Terunans migrating to Kandor, or organizing caravans of supplies to go there, or visiting Vancor to ask for Kei's hand in marriage, or—"

Arrio laughed softly and stopped Dainon's word with his hand across his lips. "Enough. You paint a clear picture." He withdrew his hand and slid it around the back of Dainon's neck to stroke his hair. "Kiss me?"

Dainon pushed out a low moan and pulled Arrio tight against his firm body, their mouths fusing in a kiss that held the promise of hours of lovemaking. Arrio's shaft was hard against Dainon's belly, and he could feel the push of Dainon's length against his hip. Arrio's tongue sought Dainon's, his fingers moving restlessly through Dainon's hair.

Dainon broke the kiss long enough to murmur, "Bed. Now."

"I have a remedy to help you sleep." Kei's quiet voice crept out of the semidarkness of their chamber.

"And what is that?" Arrio asked as Dainon guided him back inside, his arm around Arrio's waist.

Kei had lit candles, and their soft light played over his body as he knelt in the middle of the bed, his hand slowly pumping his shaft. He grinned and waved his length at them. "Two cocks, taken in quick succession, until there is not one drop of seed in you and you fall asleep sated in our arms."

Arrio gasped as Dainon lifted him into his arms and carried him toward the bed, cradling him. "I concur. We will fuck every thought from your head until you are too tired to think." The words rumbled through Dainon's chest.

Arrio buried his face in Dainon's neck, relishing his strength. "I too concur." When Dainon lowered him gently onto the bed, Arrio lay on his back and spread his legs wide, gazing at his lovers, heat growing in his belly. "Take me, both of you."

He sighed with pleasure when two mouths descended to worship his cock.

Lomar can wait.

ARRIO SAT beneath the spreading tree in the garden, his eyes closed, letting the tranquility roll over and through him. Birds filled the air with their sweet music, and the trickling of the fountain added to their harmony. Peace pervaded the air, and he drank it in greedily.

I need this. The garden was always his haven, his escape when he wanted to concentrate his mind or to slow down his thoughts.

Lomar's voice broke through his meditation. "I can see why you spend so much time here."

Arrio opened his eyes, pushing down on the first flare of anxiety that threatened to disrupt the garden's serenity. "Good morning, Lomar." He could not bring himself to call him father. He supposed that time might come in the future, but it was too soon.

"Good morning. I do not wish to disturb you. I only came to bid you farewell."

Arrio caught his breath and stared. "Farewell?" He rose to his feet. "I thought you meant to stay longer with us." Shame flushed through him at his instant relief, but he could not help it.

Lomar shrugged. "That was my plan, until I remembered I had arranged to meet with a fellow prospector. It had slipped my mind. I intend to return, however, when my business is concluded. I should not be gone for more than two days, three at the most." He tilted his head to one side. "But I think when I do leave here eventually, you will not accompany me. Am I correct in that assumption?" He seemed calm, at ease with the idea.

It was enough to bring Arrio to his decision. "You are," he said with a bow of his head. "I am sorry, Lomar, but I will stay here. Perhaps in the future we will spend more time together, but at this moment, there are too many things that demand my attention for me to leave Teruna."

Lomar held up his hands. "I understand." He lowered his gaze until it came to rest on the amulet that lay against Arrio's chest. "Your mind is occupied with your wedding and your new life with your husbands-to-be. Perhaps, as you say, there will be time in the future. I know I can never be as much a father to you as the king and his consorts, and I can certainly never hope to provide for you as they have done, but—"

Arrio shook his hand. "What they provide for me here is of no consequence. I have never thought of myself as Prince Arrio. I am Arrio, a man like any other." He smiled. "And when you know me better, you will see that." He extended his hand. "I wish you a safe journey. We will speak more of this when you return." He knew he would not change his mind, however.

Lomar nodded. "I will be back to see you married, at any rate. I would not miss that." He released Arrio's hand and bowed his head. "Till we meet again."

Arrio bowed also, and Lomar exited the garden. Lightness suffused Arrio's being, and he wanted to laugh out loud with joy.

It was the right decision.

He could not wait to share it with his lovers.

KEI COULD not account for the feeling that had been with him all day, but it showed no sign of abating. He had not shared his anxiety with Arrio and Dainon, but he knew his troubled state had not gone unnoticed. There had been frequent searching glances and more embraces from them than usual, if that were possible. Kei had done his best to alleviate their fears, but as night neared, it was growing more difficult to hide his agitation.

Finally he hit on a solution, one he knew they would agree to.

"Go to bed," he told his lovers. "I will take a ride to clear my head, then I will join you."

"Shall I accompany you?" Dainon asked, stroking his cheek. "A ride down to the beach, perhaps?" He grinned. "A night swim would relax us."

Kei laughed heartily. "You are not thinking of a night swim, and you know it." He slid his hand down Dainon's belly to where his cock tented his robe. "And *this* proves it." Dainon chuckled, and Kei reached up to cup his face. "I will return all the sooner if I know this awaits me." He returned Dainon's grin. "So make sure it is ready for me."

Arrio glanced around before pushing aside his robe to reveal his thick shaft, already poking up toward his navel. "Both of us will be ready for you." He covered himself once more. "No more. You will have to wait until you return."

Kei shook his head. "You are a wicked man, and I think none of us will get much sleep tonight." He kissed them both and left the room.

In the stables, he found Timur taking a last look around before retiring. He shook his head when he saw Kei. "Another late-night ride, Your Highness? Surely those men of yours can do something to help you sleep." He waggled his eyebrows.

Kei stifled his giggle. It seemed the three of them had already gained a reputation. Not that Kei was surprised: they were not quiet when they made love.

I do not care who hears me. I love them.

The thought warmed him inside.

"Take Dainon's horse, Fiore," Timur said. "Yours needs shoeing. The grooms will take care of him when you return."

Impulsively Kei gave him a brief hug. Timur was a sweet man beneath his gruff exterior, and it was apparent in everything he said and did that he loved Arrio like a son. "I will not be too late. The ride will clear my thoughts."

"Do you wish a guard to ride with you?" Timur asked.

Kei shook his head. "There is no need." His late-night rides were beginning to be a regular occurrence. No dangers awaited him.

Timur patted his back. "Then do not go too far. I am away to my bed." He grinned once more. "I have a husband waiting with food and… other things." He left Kei in the stables with a last wave of his hand.

Kei saddled up Fiore and trotted out of the stables. The beach was too far a destination, but a trip to the ruins would provide a decent ride. He patted Fiore's neck and bent over to whisper in his ear. "Just an hour, boy, then you can sleep."

He rode through the quiet streets, the cobbles lit by lights from windows and doorways. An air of peace had settled over the city. Kei loved to ride at night. No one to disturb him, empty streets, no hustle or noise…. It was not long before he had passed through the manned city gates and was riding through the open countryside. Occasionally the silence was broken by the screech of a night bird or the babbling of a nearby stream, and Kei drank it all in.

As he neared the ruined temple, Kei sniffed the air. *Wood smoke.* Somewhere a fire was burning. He slowed Fiore down to a trot and approached the ruins. When he got closer, he was able to pick out a shape. It was a carriage, drawn by two white horses. The carriage had seen better days: it was old and in need of fresh paint. Windows were set into it, but no light shone through them. Several feet away from the carriage a fire burned. He glanced around, but there was no one in sight. His curiosity spiked, Kei brought Fiore to a halt and climbed down to investigate.

The canopy of trees was black against the sky, but the stone ruins glowed in the light of the fire.

"Is anyone here?" Kei called out.

"How fortuitous."

Kei froze at the sound of the familiar voice. He peered into the darkness at the figure who stepped out from behind the carriage. "Lomar?" It could not be him. Lomar had left early that morning and was doubtless many miles from Teruna. "Is that you?"

"Good evening, Your Highness. I repeat, how fortuitous a meeting." As the figure drew closer, the dying light of the fire revealed more. It was indeed Lomar.

"What are you doing here?" Kei's heartbeat raced and he caught his breath.

"I was about to ask you the same question, but it does not matter. You have saved me a journey."

The hairs on Kei's arms and neck lifted and his hands became clammy. "What do you mean?"

"I have been watching you all day since I left the palace, waiting for an appropriate moment. I had no luck today and was about to rest for the night and try again tomorrow." He beamed. "And then you appear. What good fortune."

"You were watching... me? Why?" In spite of Lomar's cheerful countenance, Kei's legs began to tremble. *Is* that *what I was feeling? That there were eyes on me?*

"I was waiting for the right moment to grab you, Your *Highness.*"

The insolent voice cut through him, and the abrupt change in tone made Kei shiver.

He did not need to hear another word. He turned and ran toward his horse, but all the breath left his lungs when a hard body slammed into his back, sending him crashing to the hard ground. Kei put out his arms to keep his face from smashing into the stone flags, but then rough hands grabbed them and tugged them behind his back, pinning them at the wrists where they were bound.

"Oh no, my fine prince. You will not escape me. I have need of you." Lomar pulled him to his feet and spun him around, giving Kei a mocking smile. "We are going on a journey, you and I." He began to drag Kei toward the carriage. "Do not think to call for help. There is no one to hear your cries. We are too far from the city for that." All trace of the pleasant man Kei had encountered in the palace was gone, and in his place was someone who made Kei's blood run cold.

He struggled against Lomar's strong hands, but when a wave of nausea overcame him, he staggered.

Lomar caught him. "Careful now, Your Highness. I need you alive and well."

That touch of Lomar's hand to his arm sent a spark of awareness slamming into his consciousness. Kei was seized by a sudden inability to speak, his new knowledge sending spikes of adrenaline flooding through his body. He stared in horror at Lomar, his eyes wide, mouth open.

"Have you gone mad?" Lomar demanded. "Is that it? Have you lost your wits?"

From somewhere deep inside, Kei found his voice. "You," he croaked. "You are not… Arrio's father."

Lomar froze. "Now how do you know that?" He drew back, eyes narrowed. "*Seruan*," he hissed. His lips twisted cruelly. "And what else do your mystic powers tell you?" His hands gripped Kei's upper arms, digging into the flesh.

One word burned in Kei's brain, and he had to bite back his scream.

Lomar's eyes were like slits. "You know, do you not?" He drew back his arm, and Kei knew what was coming.

Before the blow landed, pain ripped through Kei's chest and he cried out the terrible truth. "Murderer."

Then his head rocked back, the world grayed out, and he knew no more.

TWENTY-FOUR

"IT HAS been two hours," Dainon growled, pacing the floor of the bed chamber. "You told me not to worry an hour ago—*now* may I begin worrying?" He came to a halt in front of Arrio, scraping his fingers through his hair. "I am sorry, Arrio. My mind is in turmoil. Something tells me all is not right." He turned his face to their balcony. "Where is he?"

"You need not apologize." Arrio put his arms around Dainon's waist. "Your instincts are good."

Dainon lifted Arrio's chin with his fingertips. "And what of your instincts? Is there aught I should know?" He scanned Arrio's face for any sign that his lover was hiding something from him. "You would tell me if you… felt anything?"

He knew as soon as the words left his lips that he had hurt Arrio. The wounded expression in his eyes said it all.

"How can you think that I would keep that from you?"

Dainon clasped Arrio tightly to him. "Please, forgive me. I am more overwrought than I should be, given the circumstances."

Arrio buried his face in Dainon's neck. "We have waited long enough. Let us do something."

Dainon nodded. "I will saddle up Fiore and go out into the city. There might be some sign of him." He released Arrio and then pulled on his tunic.

The knock at the door had both of them hurrying toward it, to be confronted by a guard, red-faced and breathless.

Dainon's chest tightened, but his training took over. "Report, warrior."

"I have come… from the western gate, sir. Your horse… was found there." The guard drew in a deep breath. "The guards say Prince Kei passed through there an hour and a half ago, riding Fiore. They grew concerned when the horse appeared, but with no sign of the prince."

Arrio caught Dainon's arm. "He might have ridden to the ruins." His face was pale. "Perhaps he has fallen and is injured."

Dainon nodded. "The first place I intend to check." He kissed Arrio's cheek. "Wake your fathers. We may have need of a search party if he is not there."

"I pray you find him," Arrio called out after him as he exited their chamber.

Dainon hurried through the dark corridors, the guard at his side, heading for the stables.

When he arrived there, Timur stood by the stalls in conversation with four or five of the royal guards. He glanced at Dainon, his brow furrowed, his eyes tired. "And before you say a word, my husband roused me from sleep and told me to come here. He had a dream about Prince Kei."

"What was in the dream?" Dainon's pulse raced.

Timur held up his hands. "Nothing more than a feeling that all was not well. Erinor woke up in a cold sweat, apparently, and that was when he decided I too had had enough sleep." He scowled. "If anything has happened to that boy...."

"Ready?" a voice barked out. Deron, the captain of the guard, strode through the courtyards.

"We are ready, sir." The guards stood in attention.

Deron gave a brisk nod. "One of you will ride with Lord Dainon to the western gate. The others will split up and search every street, every square, every corner of Teruna, including beyond the city walls. Miss nothing, do you hear me?"

"We hear, sir."

Dainon nodded. "Mount up, men." The guards moved quickly to mount their horses. Dainon glanced at Deron. "If we do not find him, have your men ready for a full-scale search when dawn breaks."

"They will be ready. Now go find him."

Timur indicated a saddled black stallion. "Dainon, take Porento. He's the fastest horse here. And I pray to the Maker that you find your man."

Dainon nodded and swung himself into the saddle with the swiftness and ease of many years. "That is my prayer also."

"Open the gates!" Timur yelled.

Dainon led the five riders through the stone gateway and headed for the western gates.

Please be there, sweet Kei.

ARRIO PACED the floor of the throne room, pausing at every noise to gaze at the door before resuming his pacing.

"Arrio, please. You can do nothing until Dainon returns."

Arrio stared at Feyar. "How can you be so calm?" His stomach was in knots.

"Because to be otherwise would not help you." Feyar gestured to a chair. "Sit. There are men out looking for him. We will learn something soon, I am sure." When Arrio continued his pacing unabated, Feyar stopped him, grasping his upper arms. "Believe me," he said in a low voice, "I am not calm. You do not see what lies beneath." A shiver ran through him. "I did not think that I would have to live through this a second time."

"Peace, *corishan*." Arrio heard the strain in Tanish's voice. "We do not know what has happened."

Feyar's eyes blazed. "Tell me you are not thinking the same thing. *Tell* me you are not thinking about our *dorishan*'s abduction all those years ago. One would have to be blind not to see the similarities."

It took a second or two for his meaning to sink in. Then Arrio recollected the tale of how a Vancoran warrior had taken Sorran, and how his *papa* had ridden out to find him.

Tanish flushed. He crossed the room and grabbed Feyar in a tight embrace. "This is different. Teruna faces no threats. There is no one who would harm Kei." He kissed Feyar on the mouth, and Feyar clung to him. "We have to think positively."

Feyar gazed at him, swallowing hard. Then he nodded. "You are right, of course." Tanish caressed his cheek before Feyar approached Arrio, his arms outstretched. "I am sorry for my outburst, my son."

Arrio gazed into his *papi*'s eyes. "Forgive me. I had forgotten. This has brought bad memories to the surface."

Feyar kissed him on the forehead and released him.

Tanish walked over to the window where Sorran gazed down into the still darkened city. "No visions?"

"Nothing." Sorran leaned against him. "Why can I not see him?"

"How can that be?" Arrio's fingernails cut into his palms. "Keep trying."

Sorran faced him, his expression weary. "My visions do not come to me on command, Arrio. That is not how they function." Under his breath he muttered, "Much as I would like otherwise."

All of them turned toward the door as noise filtered through from the hallway beyond. When the door creaked open and Dainon walked in alone, Arrio's heart sank.

"He was not there." He swallowed.

Dainon shook his head. "We found signs that a fire had been lit there, and tracks made by wheels, but nothing of Kei." He addressed Tanish. "In a few hours, it will be dawn. A patrol will be ready to ride out and conduct a more thorough search during daylight. As of now, there is nothing more we can do." His face was drawn.

Arrio stared at him, open-mouthed. "You cannot leave this. Kei is out there somewhere. He could be hurt. He—" He sank into the nearby chair, his head in his hands.

"Dainon speaks wisely." Tanish spoke in a low voice laced with fatigue. "We can do nothing but await the dawn."

Strong yet gentle hands alighted on Arrio's shoulders. "I know how you feel, *corishan*. My mind is in turmoil and my body is weary. I need to lie down for an hour or so. I do not think sleep will come, but I can try to rest until it is time to ride out once more." Dainon crouched before him, his brown eyes pained. "Lie with me?" Their foreheads touched. "I need you, Arrio," he whispered.

"I need you too." Arrio closed his eyes. *Kei, where are you?* The irony of his situation had not escaped him. The one time when he yearned for a sign, anything to bring him hope, and yet all that greeted him was silence and darkness. He knew in his heart that Dainon was right, but the idea of doing nothing lay heavy on him, as if they were abandoning Kei.

"We too shall rest." Sorran sighed. "Although my thoughts are as Dainon's: sleep will not come."

Dainon helped Arrio to his feet. "Come with me." He put his arm around Arrio and guided him to the door. Arrio leaned into him, drawing strength from his presence. His fathers walked behind them, their steps slow.

Sorran paused at the door and kissed Arrio's cheek. "Try to sleep. You need to be rested if you are to help find him."

Arrio nodded. "If you... see anything...."

Sorran nodded. "I will tell you." He glanced at Dainon. "Both of you, rest."

Arrio's sigh echoed Sorran's. *How can I sleep, not knowing what has happened to him?*

KEI OPENED his eyes, his head aching. Wherever he was, there was little light. The air was cool and damp, and it took a moment for him to realize the constant tapping was the sound of water dripping onto a surface. He gave an experimental wriggle. His arms were bound behind his back, his ankles tied too. Kei struggled up onto his knees and tried to shuffle across the hard ground, but only got so far before all forward motion ceased.

Something anchors me. He pulled hard, but there was no give.

Kei slumped to the ground, his body aching along with his head. He closed his eyes and pulled his memories to the forefront of his mind. His jaw stung from the blow, and around his face clung traces of something sweet yet heady. *A drug?* Kei had no recollection of anything after Lomar had knocked him out. *Lomar.* Kei's heart ached at his betrayal, and the pain to come when Arrio learned of it.

Arrio. Dainon. I am alive. For now. He knew why he lived, of course. He had seen it all inside Lomar's head, seen Lomar's plan. *He brings Arrio.* Kei's heart pounded at the thought, his blood running cold when he realized there could be only two possible outcomes.

Kei attempted to focus, to send out a message to whomever had skill enough to hear him. *But do I have the skill to send it?* He prayed to the Maker that it would be so.

A snuffle. Another. More sounds filtered through from where daylight pierced the gloom of his surroundings. Kei concentrated on them, letting his senses take control. There was a familiarity to the sensations he was experiencing, a memory, something that….

The hairs on his neck lifted. *Praise the Maker. I know where I am.*

Kei began to speak, his tone soothing, his voice low, all the while praying silently and furiously that his words would be understood.

DAINON WAS weary to the bone. Two nights with little or no sleep, his days spent searching—to no avail. No visions. No dreams. Nothing to give any indication where Kei was.

"Why has no one seen him?" he muttered. "Surely there is one *Seruan* in Teruna who has seen something."

Arrio got up from his chair at the breakfast table to walk behind Dainon. He bent over to rest his chin on Dainon's shoulder, his arms around him. "I share the same thoughts, *terushan.*"

Dainon closed his eyes, his hands resting on Arrio's. "In all my time here, I have never heard the city so quiet." It had been thus since the news had got out. The streets were silent, the trading stalls deserted. People gathered at the palace gates, their faces lined as they waited for news.

"They share my *papa-turo*'s anguish," Arrio said. "And ours."

It had brought home to Dainon how much the Terunans loved their royal family. When he rode through the streets with the search party, cries and blessings followed his steps.

"Where is Sorran?"

Arrio's sigh caressed his ear. "In the garden, meditating. *Papa* sits with him." Abruptly Arrio stood and moved toward the window. "It is strange. I cannot think of them as anything other than my fathers." He gazed down into the city, a faraway look in his eyes.

"Not strange at all." Dainon joined him, slipping his arms around Arrio's waist. Arrio leaned against him, and Dainon breathed in the scent of his hair, his skin, conscious of the missing aroma that was pure Kei. The thought sent a pang through him.

Part of us is missing.

Arrio turned in his arms, clinging to him. "I want him here, with us. I want him in our arms, in our bed."

"I know." Dainon kissed his forehead. Sleeping without Kei had been impossible. They had lain awake all night, neither of them speaking. As if Dainon needed to hear the words. He felt Arrio's pain as surely as if it were his own.

"I do not understand what could have happened. If he had been hurt, someone would have taken him in or brought him to the palace. No one in Teruna would harm him." Arrio's expression was grave. "There can be only one explanation. He is no longer in Teruna."

Dainon had reached the same conclusion. "Then he has been taken. But for what purpose? A ransom? And who would take him? Teruna has no enemies." None of it made sense.

"Your Highness."

Both Arrio and Dainon gave a start at the guard's voice.

Arrio straightened, his breathing quickening. "What is it? Is there news?"

The guard's face fell. "Would that I could be the one to bring you such news. You have a visitor." He paused. "The man who was here three days ago. Lomar."

Arrio stared at him as though the words made no sense.

"He said he would return, did he not?" Dainon reminded him gently.

"I am in no mood to see him." Arrio set his jaw.

The guard waited, his head bowed.

Dainon's thoughts were in collision.

"What are you thinking?"

Dainon did not respond but addressed the guard. "Wait by the door, please." The guard bowed and withdrew. Dainon locked gazes with Arrio. "I am thinking about coincidences."

Arrio widened his eyes. "Go on."

"Lomar leaves, and the same day, Kei disappears."

"You think Lomar is connected to Kei's disappearance?"

Dainon shrugged. "We know so little about him. I am only a wa—"

"Only a warrior, you have said this, but I trust your warrior training, your instincts."

Dainon sighed. "And I trust your senses. You have already told me that Lomar unsettles you. Perhaps it is he who took Kei."

"But for what purpose? And why return here, if that was the case? Surely if he had abducted Kei, this would be the last place he would visit." Arrio scowled. "This makes no sense. What can we do about our suspicions? Confront him? If we are wrong, we will offend him greatly."

"And if we are right?" Dainon rubbed a hand over his face. "This is all supposition. It may be that Lomar has no idea what has come to pass since he left. And seeing him will provide some distraction from the thoughts that torment you, if only for a short while."

"I do not need distraction—I need Kei!" The cry burst from Arrio, and Dainon stiffened. Instantly Arrio was before him, his hands cupping Dainon's face. "I am sorry."

Dainon rubbed across Arrio's back. "We both need him. But Lomar does not need to see our fears, so we will hide our pain from him, just as we will hide our suspicions. I will be here with you." His face grew grim. "And I will be watching him."

Arrio turned his head and kissed Dainon softly. Dainon loved that he did not mind their embrace being witnessed.

"Are you ready?" he murmured.

"Yes. You speak wisely." Arrio nodded to the guard. "Bid him enter, please."

The guard bowed and withdrew. Minutes later, he reappeared, Lomar following him, his brow furrowed.

"I trust your meeting went well?" Arrio asked him politely.

"My meeting? Yes, yes, it was good." Lomar appeared confused. "What has happened? The city is so silent. Has someone died?"

Arrio winced.

Dainon bade Lomar sit and then quickly explained the situation. Lomar's eyes widened.

"But this is horrible. When did he disappear?" He appeared genuinely appalled by the news.

"Three days ago. You left early, and that night, he went for a ride and did not return." He watched Lomar carefully.

Lomar stared at them. "Have you conducted searches?" When Arrio returned his stare, he flushed. "My apologies. Of course you have. You are clearly overwrought." He rose to his feet. "I should leave."

Arrio sighed. "Forgive me. It is true that I am not myself, but that is no excuse for bad manners. Stay with us awhile."

"If you are sure," Lomar ventured with some hesitation.

"You are welcome here," Arrio assured him. "I will have a room prepared for you."

"No," Lomar replied quickly. "There is no need. I will have to take my leave of you tonight." He gave them a strained smile. "I have yet more business that awaits me in the west. But it will be good to spend a little time with you. My prayers are with you and your family." He flushed. "I hope one day to be as close to you as they are." Lomar bowed. "Thank you for the offer of hospitality. Now if you will excuse me, I will go into the city. There are several people I need to meet."

"Join us for dinner this evening." Dainon offered.

Lomar smiled. "That is very kind. Thank you." He bowed once more and withdrew.

Arrio expelled a long breath. "And still he makes me nervous." He regarded Dainon. "What did you think of his reaction?"

Dainon's forehead was furrowed. "On the one hand, he made no demands of you and he plans to leave, giving us no reason to be nervous." "And on the other?"

Dainon stared at the doorway. "I trust my instincts." He could not account for the way Lomar made his skin creep.

He hides something from us. I am sure of it. But why would he take Kei?

He could see no motive, and that was enough to have doubts creep into his mind.

Perhaps we misjudge him.

Perhaps.

ARRIO WALKED slowly around the garden, taking in the sound of running water, the heady perfume of the night-blooming flowers, the soft burr of crickets. He had left Dainon in their chamber while he came to seek the peace he usually found in the tranquil spot, but his mind would not be still.

"You are worried about Prince Kei."

Lomar's softly uttered words made Arrio jump. "I did not think anyone else was here."

"My apologies if I startled you. I tried to be quiet so as not to disturb you." Lomar approached him, hands clasped in front of him. "I am here to help."

Arrio stared at him. "In what way?"

"I can help you find him."

Cold spread out from Arrio's core. "How? You have knowledge of him? Share it with me. Why have you not spoken before this?" In his mind he blessed Dainon's warrior training. His senses were every bit as powerful as those of a *Seruan*.

Lomar held up his hands. "Patience, Arrio, patience. Meet me in an hour at the southern gate." He smiled.

Masking his suspicions and playing the polite host all night had already frayed Arrio's nerves. "You speak of patience? Tell me now or I will call the guards, because my father or not, if you have information that will help us find Kei, by the Maker you *will* share it." He turned to head into the palace.

"Take one more step and you will never see your lover again." Lomar's voice was like ice.

Arrio halted, turning slowly. "Where is he?"

Lomar wagged a finger at him. "Not here, and not now. One hour's time, at the southern gate. Come on foot and cloaked, so that none who see you will recognize you. And do not tell anyone of this. If anything happens to me, you will never see him again."

The thought tore through Arrio's being. "Why would you do this to me? My own father?"

Lomar's eyes were cool. "You waste precious time, Arrio. One hour. I will be waiting. Make sure the guards do not see you. And do not be late." He turned and exited the garden, his footsteps swift and sure.

Arrio sank onto the bench, his stomach tight, heart hammering as he replayed Lomar's words in his head. When realization swept over him, he wanted to weep, but his throat had seized up.

Kei is in danger. And it was up to Arrio to save him.

CHAPTER
TWENTY-FIVE

"ARE YOU going to tell me where you are going?"

Arrio froze. When he glanced at the bed, Dainon was sitting up, appearing more alert than he had done five minutes previously when Arrio had looked at him. "You were asleep."

Dainon arched his eyebrows. "How many times do I have to tell you? I sleep lightly." He swung his legs out of bed and stood, his gaze fixed on Arrio. "And you have not answered my question." He walked over to Arrio and ran a finger over the red robe that he held. "Nor why you have need of a *Seruan* cloak on such a warm night." He examined it closely. "This is beautiful. Is it yours? I have not seen it before."

Arrio stroked the soft fabric. "It was my mother's. *Papa-turo* kept it, and when I was old enough to learn of my history, he gave it to me." His heart pounded. Dainon awake created problems. "Go back to sleep, *terushan*. I am going to take the air." He waited for his lover to return to their bed, silently willing him not to be difficult. He had not been surprised when Dainon had fallen asleep so quickly. *Neither of us have slept much in recent days.*

Dainon folded his arms across his broad chest. "You will also recall that although I may not have your *Seruani* gifts, I do have abilities of my own." He narrowed his eyes. "I thought there was to be nothing but truth between us?"

Arrio had never been so torn.

"I… I cannot share with you. Please, I beg you, do not ask this of me." All he could think of was Kei in danger, and Lomar holding Kei's future in the palm of his big hand.

Dainon had his arms around Arrio in an instant, holding him against his body so that Arrio could feel the thump of Dainon's heart beating against his own. "Now you worry me," he murmured. "Please, *corishan*. You must tell me."

Arrio lifted his head to look Dainon in the eye. "Even if to do so might endanger Kei?"

Dainon froze. "Words cannot harm him. Unless you fear my reaction to what you tell me...." Arrio swallowed and he nodded. "Then I give you my word. Share what you know, and I swear I will do nothing—until you tell me otherwise." When Arrio bit his lip, Dainon cupped his face gently. "You must trust me, Arrio. If you love me, trust me now."

"You know I love you." The words tumbled from Arrio's lips in a groan.

Dainon gazed at him in silence for a moment. Then he nodded and led him to the bed, where they sat, his hand clasped in Dainon's. "What has happened? And is Lomar a part of it as we suspected?"

A shudder ran through Arrio and he nodded. Quickly he shared the conversation from the garden.

Dainon's face grew grim. "He means to take you somewhere. Why else would he choose to meet at the gate?" He peered intently at Arrio. "You have no clue as to what he intends?"

Arrio shook his head. "And now you see, there is nothing you can do with this knowledge. If you go with me, or if he senses someone watching, then Kei is lost to us." He shivered. "Who knows what Lomar has already done to him?"

A bell tolled quietly in the distance, and Dainon frowned. "We have thirty minutes before you meet with him. Time enough to set events in motion."

Arrio was on his feet in a heartbeat. "And if he is watching? What then?" Cold sweat popped out on his brow. "You can do nothing until I meet with him."

Dainon pulled on his robe. "And how does Lomar think you will pass through the city gates unnoticed by the guards?"

"I will think of... something to tell him."

Dainon grasped Arrio's shoulders. "Listen to me. You will meet with Lomar as planned, but just before midnight, the guards will change their duties. The two replacement guards who watch over the southern gate will have instructions to note everything they can about Lomar's transportation and the direction you take. We will give him a head start, long enough that he does not suspect. If we follow too soon, he may pick up on it. No, we will let him think all goes well with his plan."

"And then?"

"Then I will do what I do best." Dainon gave a smile. "I will track you. And I will bring others with me."

Arrio nodded. "Once I learn what Lomar intends, I will play along. And I will pray you reach us before anything happens."

Dainon gave him a sharp glance. "Such as what?"

Arrio could not put into words the feeling that plagued him, but when he tried to focus his senses, it was as if a shadow crawled over them, blocking his sight. "Something lies hidden from me, something that fills me with a cold dread." He prayed to the Maker to protect Kei.

Dainon cupped Arrio's face with both hands and stared into his eyes. "I will find you, Arrio. Both of you. It cannot be otherwise." He kissed him slowly on the lips. "Fate would not be so cruel, to bring us together only to part us."

Arrio said nothing. He did not trust himself to speak, for fear of the consequences. He felt as though he trod a very fine line, and that one step in the wrong direction would change their future.

Dainon unfurled the cloak and draped it around Arrio's shoulders. "Let me speak with Deron before you leave. The guards will have instructions not to challenge you when you pass through the gates, although you might need to explain that to Lomar. He is bound to be suspicious." He scowled. "I wish I knew why he is doing this."

Arrio shuddered. "We will know all, soon enough." He stood, and Dainon held him once more. Arrio breathed him in, letting Dainon's scent pervade his consciousness.

Dainon kissed his forehead. "Time to go," he whispered, releasing him and stepping back.

Arrio nodded. His heart pounded and his skin was slick with perspiration. It was time to meet with his father—*if* that was who Lomar truly was.

KEI'S BELLY ached, but he knew he could survive without food. He lay on the cold, hard ground, no energy left in him. His throat was parched, his mouth dry, and that was the far greater problem.

How long has it been since I drank? He had slipped in and out of consciousness until he had lost what little hold he had on reality. *How long have I been here?* The *drip drip drip* of water never ceased, and he feared it would drive him mad.

Water.... Desperation brought a burst of lucidity.

Kei rolled onto his side and inched his way, slowly and laboriously, like a worm crossing hot stone in search of cool earth, in the direction of the water. When he dropped onto his back and felt the first cold, single drop splash upon his face, he wanted to yell in triumph, but he had neither the energy nor the voice. Instead, he moved until that pinprick of moisture burst upon his tongue once. Again. Again.

It was not much, barely enough to keep a bird alive, but it would do.

It was better than nothing.

The soft snuffle from beyond his prison's boundaries and the scratch of claws against wood gave him hope. *I am not alone.*

Kei closed his eyes and used what little strength he had to focus his senses. *Find me. Please, find me.*

ARRIO APPROACHED the carriage under the trees, his pulse racing, the lights from the city showing the way. Lomar stood in the shadows by the horses, his gaze trained on Arrio, his forehead creased in a frown.

"Did the guards question you?"

Arrio shook his head, most of his face obscured by his hood. "They did not see me," he lied.

Lomar blinked. "How could they miss you?" Then he sneered. "Unless one of your skills is the ability to make yourself invisible."

Arrio removed his hood and gave Lomar a cool stare. "You know nothing about my skills, nor what I am capable of. You would do well to remember that." His heartbeat quickened.

Lomar appeared taken aback by Arrio's response. Then he recovered and swaggered toward him. "On the contrary, I am intimately acquainted with one of your skills. If it were not so, we would not be having this conversation." He jerked his head toward the carriage. "Get in the back. None shall see you there."

Arrio knew better than to argue. "We are taking a journey, then?" he asked, walking up to the carriage. Lomar opened the door and helped him up the two steps into it. Once inside, his eyes quickly became accustomed to the dark interior. There was a blanket and pillow on the floor on one side, but on the other were boxes and crates, rope looped around them to fasten them to the sides of the carriage. He peered inside and saw rock picks, axes, coils of rope, pans….

"So you really are a prospector." Arrio had seen such equipment before when he had visited a gold mine. He stiffened when Lomar roughly pulled his arms behind his back and tied his wrists together. "Do you need to do that? Why would I try to get away? You are taking me to Kei—are you not?"

Lomar shoved him onto the floor of the carriage. "Sit there. And I am taking no chances."

"How far do we travel?" Arrio asked.

"Far enough." Lomar busied himself on the opposite side of the carriage, his hands hidden from view.

"Kei is well?" The question burst out of him.

Lomar glanced over his shoulder and gave him a grim smile. "He was when last I saw him, but that was three days ago. It would be better, Your Highness, if we did not delay. I would hate for us to reach him and find it was too late."

Icy fingers clutched Arrio's heart. "If you have hurt him…."

"You will do what?" Lomar glared at him. "Do not think to threaten me, Arrio."

"Are you truly my father?" Arrio hoped with all his heart that it was not so. He could not bear to think that Lomar and he shared the same blood.

Lomar scowled. "I grow weary of your voice. And as we have a fair distance to cover before we reach our destination, I shall do something about that now." He lunged forward.

Before Arrio had time to react, Lomar shoved a rag under his nose and over his mouth. A sweet, cloying fragrance infiltrated Arrio's nostrils and the world began to spin. He slipped further and further from consciousness, the carriage fading from his sight, his ears barely registering Lomar's words.

"Sleep well."

DAINON STRODE into the courtyard and headed for Timur and Deron. "Is all in readiness?" The lamps were lit, as the dawn was still a few hours away. "We have waited long enough." The last three hours had been a sore test of his nerves and patience.

Timur handed him the reins. "I know the temptation will be to ride until you are exhausted, but the horses will tire long before you do. Try to stop for rest, food, and water along the way."

Dainon clapped him on the back. "I will not push them beyond endurance."

"Good man."

"The warriors are armed and ready," Deron said.

Twenty men were already on horseback, swords sheathed.

"As am I."

Dainon turned at the sound of Sorran's voice. The prince wore a leather tunic, a sword in his hand. Tanish and Feyar were with him, their expressions tight. The warriors straightened instantly in their saddles and bowed their heads.

"Are you sure about this?" Dainon asked.

Sorran's face was grim. "I will not sit in the palace while my brother and my son face uncertain danger. I know you are more than capable of finding them, Dainon, but I want to accompany you." He glanced at his husbands. "And I will not be dissuaded."

Dainon had to smile. "Now I see how alike you and Kei are." He embraced Sorran in a brief hug. "I would not dream of telling you not to go."

"Very wise," King Tanish muttered under his breath.

"And there is something I must share with you," Sorran continued. "Last night I—"

A clatter of hooves from beyond the courtyard had all heads turning.

"Open the gate!" Timur yelled. When it swung open and a red-cloaked figure galloped into view, he froze. "What are you doing here?"

The horse and rider came to a halt before the men. Erinor threw back his hood, his eyes bright. "I had a vision," he burst out.

Dainon was at his side in a heartbeat. "What did you see?"

"Only an image of gold, shimmering in the sunlight." Erinor breathed deeply. "I did not think it important, until it kept returning again and again."

"It makes sense," Sorran suggested. "Lomar is a prospector. And I too had a vision, but it was nothing I did not already know."

"What was it?" Dainon demanded.

Sorran smiled. "A bear." He gazed at Dainon. "That is you, is it not? Kei's bear of a warrior?" His smile grew sorrowful. "I only wish it had been of more use."

"We are losing riding time," Deron advised.

"So we are." Dainon swung himself up onto Fiore. "We ride, men." His sword was sheathed and fastened to Fiore's flank.

"I ride with you." Erinor sat up straight in his saddle. When Timur let out a growl, Erinor gazed at him, eyes pleading. "I need to do this."

Timur hesitated, his forehead creased in a frown. Then he waved his hand. "Like I can refuse you anything when you look at me like that."

Erinor bent low and kissed his husband on the mouth. "I will return, my love, when we have them," he said in a low voice.

Timur said nothing but caressed Erinor's face before straightening. "May the Maker be with you all," he cried out.

A chorus of raised voices acknowledged his words, and with Dainon leading them, the group rode out of the courtyard and down through the city streets, heading for the southern gate.

Dainon knew what signs to look for. The guards had described Lomar's carriage and two horses, and had made note of their direction. As long as there were tracks to follow, Dainon would stick to their trail.

I am coming for you. I will find you.

He told himself that Kei and Arrio would soon be back in his arms, sharing his love.

His plans for Lomar were far darker.

THE MIDDAY sun's rays hit the mountain peaks, making them sparkle as quartz reflected its beams. Arrio's heart sped up when he saw where they were headed. It was difficult to believe that only weeks before the three of them had been here. The sight of the mountains merely confirmed his suspicions.

This is about gold. And somehow, Lomar knows of my gift. But how?

"Walk faster," Lomar growled, and seconds later Arrio felt the point of Lomar's knife against his back. He quickened his pace.

They had abandoned the carriage when the path grew too narrow and were traveling on foot. Arrio carried a soft pouch containing water around his neck, and Lomar wore a belt weighed down with tools, the long knife always in his hand. Arrio had expected them to take the horses, but when Lomar had left them tethered to the trees, Arrio's heart had sunk. Another suspicion was growing in his mind, and he did not like its implications.

Talking was useless: Lomar ignored him.

They had walked for about an hour and Arrio had begun to despair of ever reaching Kei, when Lomar stopped them in their tracks near a disused mine, the one he had pointed out to Kei and Dainon. Lomar pointed with the knife to the stony ground. "Sit."

Arrio complied, his breathing rapid.

Lomar crouched down in front of him. "So, Your Highness. Here we are at last, at the end of our journey."

A sense of foreboding laced his words, and Arrio shivered.

"Now for your role." Lomar gestured to the mountains behind them. "You are going to find something for me. A nice, fat seam of gold, one that will provide for me for the rest of my days."

Arrio's heart sank. *All this for the sake of greed.* But permeating that thought was the knowledge that Lomar needed him.

Knowledge is power.

"If you think I will raise one finger to find you so much as a particle of gold, think again." Arrio stared Lomar in the face. "Not until I know Kei is alive and well."

Lomar stared back at him for several seconds before shrugging carelessly. "It is no more than I expected." He rose and left Arrio to walk toward the abandoned mine, its entrance covered with boards.

Arrio watched with bated breath as Lomar pulled aside three of the boards and crept into the mine. When he emerged, staggering, with Kei slung over his shoulder, his wrists and ankles bound, Arrio wanted to cry out with relief. Until Lomar dropped him to the ground and Kei did not move.

Arrio's chest tightened and panic clawed at his throat. "You let him die. You left him there like that for *three days.* You left him to die." Pain tore into him, so acute that he felt as if his heart was ripped from his body.

When I get free of these bonds, you are a dead man, Lomar.

CHAPTER
TWENTY-SIX

LOMAR SNORTED. "Dead? No, he lives. A man can survive without food for many days. He needs water, that is all." He came to where Arrio sat and grabbed the water pouch from around his neck before returning to where Kei lay.

Arrio scanned Kei's body, searching for signs of life, anything to prove his lover lived. Kei's chest rose and fell feebly, its rhythm erratic, but it was enough.

He lives. Praise the Maker.

Lomar eased Kei into an upright position, his back to Lomar's chest, and began to trickle the water into his mouth.

"Slowly!" Arrio shouted. "Start him with drops, until he can take more." He watched, his heart aching, as Lomar did as instructed. Within a short space of time, Kei's breathing grew more even, and he attempted to lift his hands to clutch at the pouch while he drank greedily.

Lomar pulled it from his lips and secured it. "That's enough for now."

Kei closed his eyes and slumped to the ground. Lomar lifted him up and brought him over to Arrio, leaving him on the ground in front of him.

"There's your precious prince."

"Untie my hands," Arrio begged. "Let me tend to him."

Lomar barked out a laugh. "You must think me stupid. And he needs no tending." Lomar pointed at Kei's face. "See? The color is returning already."

Arrio waited, watching anxiously as Kei's signs improved. When his lover's eyelids fluttered open and Arrio saw those beloved dark eyes, tears pricked the corners of his own eyes.

"Arrio," Kei croaked, blinking as he focused on him. "I knew you were coming."

Arrio ached to stroke that sweet face. "Easy, *corishan*. Do not exert yourself."

Kei swallowed. "Lomar…. He is not your father."

Arrio was weak with relief to hear his own thoughts confirmed. "It is as I suspected."

Kei shook his head, and a look of such sorrow washed over his face that Arrio's heart gave a lurch. "You do not understand," he whispered.

"Be silent," Lomar hissed, his knife once more drawn from his belt.

Kei slowly turned his head. "Arrio will hear the truth, either from my lips or yours. Which shall it be?" He narrowed his gaze. "I know everything, Lomar. Your thoughts were as transparent to me as glass." His voice was weak, but the look he aimed at Lomar was not.

"Save your strength," Arrio begged him. "Lomar shall tell me, starting with how he knew of my gift when no one except my fathers, you, and Dainon know of it."

Lomar laughed. "I learned of it from your own lips, Prince Arrio." When Arrio gazed blankly at him, Lomar cackled. "That day you came here with your lovers? I watched you, heard every word. I watched you find a new seam of gold." His eyes burned with greed. "How unfortunate that I could not use the knowledge. It was obvious miners would come once they knew of its existence." His smile grew avaricious. "But you… you found that new lode in a matter of minutes, as if the gold sang out to you and you were the only one to hear it. That was when I began to make plans."

"He followed us back to Teruna," Kei said quietly, his face miserable. "Now we know why Dainon felt we were being watched."

"How could I not follow?" Lomar retorted. "Especially when I learned your name was Arrio." Before Arrio could question this remark, Lomar plowed on. "It had been many years since I had last spent time in Teruna, but I estimated it to be long enough that no one would recognize me. I followed you as far as the palace." He scowled. "That shook me at first. I envisioned spending endless days, watching and waiting for a chance to get you alone. But while I waited, I began to notice how much Teruna had changed. I watched how the people interacted with the *Seruani*. There appeared to have been a major shift in perception."

"He started asking questions about the *Seruani* and how their status seemed to have changed," Kei said, his voice barely audible. "One question led to another, and to another, until he had the whole story: Tanish, Feyar, and Sorran, the baby in the ruins, adopting him as their son…."

Lomar shook his head, still smiling cheerfully. "The coincidences were stacking up."

"What do you mean?" As soon as Arrio asked the question, he caught the hitch in Kei's breathing, and his scalp prickled.

"The king naming the baby Arrio, for one thing. The Arrio I saw here who clearly had a gift, for another."

"But… coincidences?" Arrio was lost.

Lomar gave him a cool stare. "I worked with a partner for many years. That man could locate a mother lode in a heartbeat. He had all the talent while I had all the business acumen." He snorted once more. "I certainly had no talent whatsoever. But Arrio…. He had a real gift, just like you."

"Arrio?" His head was spinning.

Lomar nodded. "My business partner, whose name was Arrio— your father."

"My… father?" Cold fingers spread over Arrio's skin.

Lomar nodded, his eyes never leaving Arrio. "We worked well together, up until the year when Minea became pregnant."

"Then that part was true," Arrio said with a heavy sigh. "What changed?"

Lomar scowled. "She was sickly all through the pregnancy, always asking him to stay home with her, sending for him. We had just located a wonderful rich lode of silver when yet another message arrived from her. Arrio had been fretting all the time we had been away because she was close to her delivery. When he saw this, he wanted to pack up and return home."

"Except Lomar would not let him go," Kei said in a low voice.

"Be silent." Lomar glared at Kei, who ignored him.

"They fought about it, and Lomar hit your father, rendering him unconscious."

"I said silence." Lomar's eyes were dark slits.

Kei gave Lomar one long glance and then met Arrio's gaze. "He dealt him such a blow that he never regained consciousness."

Arrio's heart stuttered. "You… you killed my father."

"It was an accident!" Cords stood out on Lomar's neck, his face red.

"But you leaving him alone there to die was no accident, was it?" Kei did not break eye contact with Lomar. "You left him, took his possessions, everything he had used his talent to find for you, and you

K.C. WELLS

fled. You sent no word to his wife, who would never know what had happened to her husband."

"I think you have said enough, *Seruan*," Lomar hissed, pulling his arm back.

Kei flinched, but he did not look away.

"And you have done enough to him. Strike him and I will never help you." Arrio forced all the authority he could muster into his voice.

Lomar slowly lowered his arm, his face like thunder. He stood next to Kei, towering above him, hands clenched into fists. "You will not speak again unless I give you permission, is that understood?" When Kei nodded, Lomar turned to Arrio. "We have wasted enough time. Do not think I did not notice how you tarried once we left the carriage. Merciful heavens, you walked slower than an infirm old man near death's door."

Arrio said nothing. He had done his best to slow the two of them down. Anything to help Dainon catch them up.

"So now you and I will go on a journey together. You are going to find me a lode, and once I am satisfied that it will meet my needs, I will let both of you go."

"We will be free?" Arrio focused on Lomar, using every sense he possessed.

"Yes. Did I not just say this?" Lomar growled.

Arrio was not stupid. Even without the knowledge that screamed at him, he knew Lomar would never free them. *He never intended to free us. He knows I would return with warriors once I had shown him where to search. As if he would wait around to be captured.* No, Lomar had two options—either he would keep Kei alive to ensure Arrio did his will, the two of them his prisoners, or he would wait until Arrio had found him enough to satisfy his greed, and then he would kill them both. With cool logic Arrio assessed the situation. *I know which option I would choose in his place.* In that moment, he saw Lomar's intent. *He means to kill me.*

Arrio took hold of his courage.

Then I must kill him first.

The thought filled Arrio with cold horror, but he had to face reality. There was no other option open to him. He observed Lomar, taking in the muscled physique gained from years of prospecting. *He is stronger than I. Can I overpower him?*

Then reality sank in once more.

What choice do I have? Even if Arrio died in the struggle, Kei would be safe. *Dainon will find him.* There was always the chance that Dainon would arrive before Arrio had to act, but he could not rely on that. Dainon might be only hours from them, but Arrio had no way of knowing exactly when their rescuers would burst upon them.

He took a deep breath and came to a decision.

If the opportunity arises, I will have to seize it. His heart quaked at the thought.

"Before we leave, there is some business I must take care of." Lomar bent down, scooped Kei up, and tossed him over his shoulder as though he weighed nothing. Lomar moved toward the disused mine.

"Wait! Will you not give Kei something to eat first?" Arrio's heart pounded.

"He has lasted this long without food—he can last a little longer. He will eat when I return," Lomar called back. He halted and glanced at Arrio. "I meant, when *we* return. Think of it as incentive for you to work fast." Lomar reached the boards and placed Kei on the ground.

His initial choice of pronoun had not been lost on Arrio.

"Then let me say good-bye to him before we leave." *Especially as this may be the last chance I get.* He stared at Lomar, his breathing rapid.

Lomar turned and sneered. "What—you cannot bear to be parted from him for an hour or so?"

Arrio schooled his features. It would not do to let Lomar see his plans had been discovered. "It is not a great thing that I ask of you." He kept his voice low and even, so as not to aggravate Lomar further.

Lomar studied him in silence, until Arrio squirmed beneath his scrutiny. Finally he nodded and indicated Kei with a flick of his head. "Get over here, then, and get your farewells done with."

Arrio shifted up onto his feet and stumbled across the ground to where Kei lay at the entrance to the mine. He dropped to his knees, aware that Lomar stood over them. Arrio lifted his head and stared at him until Lomar muttered under his breath and withdrew to stand a few feet away.

Arrio bent low until his face was inches from Kei's, his breath soft against Arrio's lips.

Kei fixed his dark eyes on Arrio. "You know what you must do," he said in a hushed voice.

Ice spread its spiky tendrils around Arrio's heart. *He too has seen what must be.* "I know, *terushan.*" He swallowed. "I will do what I must to keep you safe."

Kei stared up at him. "I will pray to the Maker that you return to me, unharmed. With all my heart, Arrio." His eyes glistened. "I love you," he whispered.

"As I love you," Arrio replied before bringing their mouths together in a sweet, tender kiss that he felt with his whole body. When they parted, Arrio smiled. "Look after our warrior."

Kei set his jaw. "We will *both* look after Dainon, until all three of us are old and gray. It shall be so."

Arrio smiled at him. "You have seen this?" When Kei's breath caught, Arrio shook his head. "Keep believing it, *corishan.* May your hopes make it so." His gaze alighted on Kei's amulet. "Have faith in our bond."

"Always," Kei murmured.

"Enough of the touching farewell scene." Lomar pulled roughly on Arrio's bonds and heaved him to his feet. He lifted Kei once more and disappeared into the dark mouth of the mine. When he returned a minute or so later, Lomar replaced the boards and then regarded Arrio. "Time to go." The knife was in his hand once more. "Move."

Arrio walked from the mine to stand several feet away, gazing up at the mountain. He had no intention of helping Lomar. His sole purpose was to delay him until such time as Dainon and the warriors arrived.

"Which way do we go?" Lomar demanded. "What do your senses tell you?"

Arrio recalled what he knew about the terrain, assessing where best to make a move to secure their freedom. When the thought came to him, he repressed his shiver.

One false step and both of them would end up broken on the rocks. *I will have to go carefully.*

He peered off to the left where a wide path wound its way up the side of the mountain. "That way," he said, pushing as much confidence as possible into his tone. He sought for a way to convince Lomar, and took an uncertain step. "My hands are already starting to itch."

"So like your father," Lomar murmured. He gestured with the knife. "Move. You go first."

Arrio heaved an internal sigh of relief and set out up the path, his wrists still bound, the point of Lomar's knife still jabbing into his back at intervals.

I need to get that away from him.

"THEY MUST have continued on foot," Deron said, studying the abandoned carriage. "But why?"

Dainon scanned their surroundings. "I have been here before," he murmured.

The group had stopped when the tracks ended with the empty carriage and the two white horses, tethered to a tree, eating long blades of grass in its shade. Dainon had ordered a brief rest period while the horses were watered and fed. The sun was nearing its highest point in the sky, and the trees provided a welcome cool canopy. Warriors sat or lay on the grass, drinking from their water pouches and eating.

A day of hard riding had left Dainon tired and aching, but his own bodily needs would have to wait. With every passing hour, he tried to narrow the gap that separated him from Arrio. There had been few stops along the way, and now the horses were weary and in need of rest.

Sorran joined Dainon. "This way leads to the mountains. The path is too narrow for carriages, but they could have taken the horses. Why they chose not to is a mystery."

"But a mile or so ahead the path divides into many," Erinor said. "They could have taken any one of four or five routes. How will we know which one? Do we split up and search them all?"

"Of course." Dainon groaned. "Now I recognize this place. I was here with Arrio and Kei." Something tugged at his thoughts, and he closed his eyes for a moment to focus. Suddenly he snapped them open and stared at Erinor. "Your vision. You saw gold?"

Erinor nodded. His lips parted and his eyes shone. "That tells you something?"

It was Dainon's turn to nod. He could not repress his grin. "Yes. It tells me where they are going." He swiveled his head to look at Sorran. "I know where they are. Better yet, they are close."

"Praise the Maker." Sorran was vibrating with excitement. "Enough rest, men. We know where Lomar has taken Prince Arrio."

In an instant the warriors were on their feet and heading to their horses. "Who needs rest?" Deron said with a grin. "We can rest when we have them safe."

Dainon climbed into the saddle and bent to pat Fiore's neck. "Come on, boy. One last run before you can rest. Give me all you have, for Arrio and Kei." He led the others onto the path, his heart full of thanks for Erinor's vision. He focused on the ground, looking for signs that his instincts were correct, and when he spotted the tracks, he rejoiced. "We are indeed on their trail, men." He kept his voice low.

Hushed noises of jubilation followed his words as the riders picked up speed.

Ten minutes later he spied the place where he, Arrio, and Kei had stopped. There was no one in sight and the air was still.

Dainon surveyed the landscape, his body tensed. *Where are you?* His stomach was tight, his nerves raw. *This is the place. I know it.*

"You are sure this is the spot?" Sorran asked quietly from behind him. "There is no sign that anyone has been here."

Dainon nodded as he got down from Fiore and pulled his sword free of its sheath. As silently as possible, the warriors, Erinor, and Sorran dismounted, weapons drawn. Dainon gestured for the warriors to be quiet and gathered them around him. "We must go carefully," he told them. "There is a bear with cubs nearby, and while we lived to tell the tale when she went on the attack to protect her children, we survived only because of Prince Kei's rapport with animals. I have no wish to disturb her again."

"A big bear?" one of the warriors whispered.

His companions grinned and dug him in the ribs with their elbows. "No bear will eat you—your meat is too tough," one of them whispered back. The others laughed quietly.

"Be quiet," Sorran growled, and the warriors fell silent.

Dainon gave Sorran a grateful glance and, holding his sword aloft, he crept forward. The only sounds were the harsh cries of the birds that circled in the air above their heads. There was no evidence of human activity.

Kei. Send me a sign. Anything.

"Look at that," a warrior said, pointing toward the disused mine Arrio had shown them.

"It is boarded up to prevent accidents," Dainon said. The he looked closer at the boards that covered the mine's entrance. There were deep gashes in the wood.

"Your bear has been here," Erinor murmured. "And she has sharp claws." He shivered.

The bear.... An idea began to form in his mind. *Kei and the bear. Kei's connection with animals. Can it be?*

"Sorran," Dainon whispered urgently, beckoning the prince to join him.

Sorran crept forward to stand at his side, his gaze falling on the claw marks. "She is still nearby, then."

Dainon shook his head. "Your vision. You spoke truly. I am Kei's bear of a warrior." He nodded toward the mine. "But your mistake? You were thinking of the wrong bear." He edged forward, his heart hammering as he knelt at the entrance, his palms flat against its scarred boards. "Kei?" Nothing. He raised his voice louder. "Kei!" *Please, let me be right.*

A cough, very faint but unmistakable, came from behind the boards, and Dainon's heart soared.

He lurched forward and tore at the wooden planks, ripping them from their housing to reveal the dark, yawning entrance. He plunged himself into the gloomy interior, and when he saw the body lying on the ground, bound, he wanted to weep for joy. "Kei! He is here!" He cut through Kei's bonds with his sword before sliding his arms under Kei's knees and back to lift him gently into his arms.

Kei's head rolled to one side, and for one awful moment, Dainon feared he was too late. Then Kei tried to lift his head, and two dark eyes fixed on Dainon's. The slow smile that spread across Kei's face sent his heart soaring. "You found me," he said, his voice cracking. A gentle hand caressed Dainon's cheek.

Dainon cradled Kei against his chest. "And I will never let you out of my sight again." He kissed his head, forehead, cheeks, nose, and mouth, as though he feared any second he would awake and find it had all been a dream.

Kei rested his head against Dainon's chest, still smiling. "Now I know I am not dreaming. I would know this heartbeat, this body, from among thousands."

Dainon carried his precious cargo out into the light, where Sorran stood, his body trembling. Gently he laid Kei on the ground, he and Sorran kneeling beside him.

Sorran lifted a water pouch to his lips. "Drink, brother, but slowly."

Kei took several swallows before he pushed the pouch aside. "Dainon," he said urgently, his voice still harsh. "You must leave me and go after them."

"Lomar and Arrio?"

Kei nodded. "Arrio… is in grave danger. He led Lomar up the path into the mountains." His eyes locked on Dainon's. "You must find them before Lomar kills him."

Dainon suppressed the urge to howl his rage to the skies. "Lomar will not survive this day."

"Go," Sorran urged him. "Take Deron and a few warriors. I will take care of Kei."

Dainon nodded. He bent down and kissed Kei on the lips. "I love you," he whispered.

Kei met his gaze. "I love you too. Now find our Arrio." He lifted his hand and touched Dainon's amulet. "Make us whole again."

"I swear it." One more kiss and Dainon was on his feet, shouting for Deron, his sword in his hand as he went for Fiore.

"Dainon!" Sorran called after him. "You must go on foot. As the path climbs higher, it narrows. At best two men could walk abreast, but there is nowhere for a horse to turn. And take care. It can be treacherous up there."

"Thank you." Dainon headed up the path, Deron and two warriors behind him.

Arrio, be strong. I am coming.

CHAPTER
TWENTY-SEVEN

THE PATH had become steeper and with it Arrio's steps became slower. He had stopped several times in the last thirty minutes, under the pretense of checking a possible lode. His senses told him there was no gold that high up, and he thanked the Maker for Lomar's greed. Each time Arrio halted, Lomar's reaction was the same. His breathing quickened and he began to perspire, only to growl in disappointment when Arrio announced that "the signals were confusing him."

I will need to be careful not to push him too far. Arrio had no idea which would prove the stronger emotion—Lomar's greed or his impatience. Arrio kept his eyes on the path, noting how it had started to narrow.

If I am to do anything, it will need to be soon. And there was still the matter of Lomar's knife.

"May I ask a question?" he asked.

Behind him, Lomar groaned. "Must you talk? Save your energies for finding gold."

"I simply wanted to know about how you came to be in Teruna." Anything to put off the moment when Arrio would be forced to act. "Where have you been since—" It was on the tip of his tongue to say *since you murdered my father*, but he dared not utter the words. "Since my father died?"

Lomar sighed. "I moved about from place to place, living on what we had amassed. But after seventeen years, the money ran out. The last few years have been miserable, while I tried to get by on very little. When I grew tired of merely existing, I decided to try my hand at prospecting. After all, your father had done it, so why shouldn't I?"

Arrio said nothing. He was not about to offer sympathy for Lomar's poverty, not when he had taken everything Arrio's father had ever worked for. And not when he had left him to die. "So you came back here."

Lomar snorted. "I have been everywhere, and with nothing to show for it. I had been scouring these mountains for months, cursing my own ineptitude. Your father made it look so easy, and yet I could not find one nugget of gold. I had started to think that the mountains had already given up all their treasure when I happened upon the three of you. It was simply good timing that I saw you that day."

Good timing were not the words Arrio would have chosen.

"Once I got to Teruna and realized who you were," Lomar continued, "I knew what I had to do. I knew your parents well enough to be able to convince the king and his consorts that I was your father."

Arrio snorted internally. *My fathers are not so easily fooled.* "And the painting of my mother? Was it truly your work?"

"Ha. As if I have the ability to produce such a thing. No, that was yet another of your father's talents. Painting, playing musical instruments, those magic fingers of his…."

There was an edge to Lomar's voice that told Arrio if he were able to see Lomar's aura in that moment, the color would have been pure green. Arrio wanted to know more about how his father died, but something in him stilled his tongue.

Why cause myself more pain? At least he knew the truth. From what Lomar said, Arrio's father had been a wonderful man who loved his wife, and whose life had been cut short by greed.

And my father's killer has me in his sights. Me and Kei.

If Arrio was going to survive this, he needed an opportunity to turn the tables on Lomar. Just one.

He scanned the path ahead of them, his heart pounding. To the right were sheer walls of rock, but to the left of the narrow path was the edge of a ravine. The chasm was about twenty feet across, and on the other side was nothing but the rock face. Arrio glanced into it, trying to assess its depth. One slip of the feet on the path would be fatal.

Here. Now. It has to be now.

His heart hammering, Arrio gave a visible shudder. Instantly he felt the point of Lomar's knife at his spine.

"What is it now?" Lomar muttered.

Arrio shivered again, this time more violently. "I… feel something."

"What?" Lomar's whisper was hoarse. "What do you feel?" The air around them was almost crackling with energy.

"I am not sure. It could not possibly be a lode—it is too large to be that."

"Large?" Lomar's breathing hitched. "How large?"

The seed was sown.

Praying silently for all he was worth, Arrio turned to face Lomar. "I need my hands," he said urgently.

Lomar's gaze narrowed. "Why?"

"I have to place them on the surface of the rock, to check for a possible lode." He fell silent, holding his breath.

Lomar observed him for a moment and then shook his head. "Just like your father. The number of times I watched him do that, like his fingers could see into the rock." He grabbed Arrio's upper arms and spun him roughly until his face and body were pressed up against the rock.

Thank the Maker. Arrio waited, his legs shaking, his belly in knots. When he felt the cool blade ease between his bound wrists, he fought the urge to shout in triumph. Seconds later his hands were free, and he faced Lomar, doing his best not to tremble.

"There. Do what you have to." A jab of the knife at his belly made Arrio jump, and he stared into wild eyes. "But do not try anything."

Arrio pressed his palms to the rock and proceeded to edge his way farther along the path. "Oh, by the heavens," he whispered, doing his best to appear awed.

Lomar was in front of him, his back to the path, gaze locked on Arrio. "Tell me." He licked his lips, his eyes glazing over.

"So much," Arrio murmured. "Never before have I felt such a mass." He smoothed his hands over the rock, his arms spread wide.

His motions apparently lit a fire in Lomar. "That much?" His voice cracked.

Arrio nodded. "But what is strange is the depth."

"What do you mean?"

Arrio waited until they were at the highest point of the path, only two feet between the rock wall and the path's edge. He stood still, his hands on the cool rock. "I cannot tell how deep the lode runs. There seems to be no end to it, as though it goes back so far as to be the heart of the mountain."

"Truly?" Lomar took his focus off Arrio and gazed up at the rock face, eyes wide. "How far below the surface?"

"That is another strange thing." Arrio laid the last piece of his trap before Lomar. "It feels as though it is just below the surface, so close that you could graze the rock with a pick and the gold would shine through from beneath."

From the corner of his eye, Arrio watched as Lomar laid his knife on the ground and pulled a rock pick from his belt. "Let me see. I must see," Lomar whispered, his voice thick with lust.

Now. Now.

Arrio slammed hard into Lomar's side with his shoulder, sending the pick tumbling from Lomar's hand and Lomar tumbling to the ground. With a howl Lomar went for the knife, but Arrio kicked it out of his reach, sending it skittering down the path.

Lomar looked up at him, eyes gleaming with hate. "You will pay for that." He started to rise.

He must not get up!

Arrio kicked Lomar's legs from under him, and once he was down, arms flailing as he tried to get up, Arrio kicked him again. There was no room on the ledge for Lomar to grapple with him, and already overbalanced, it took one last powerful kick to send him hurtling over the edge.

Lomar's screams rebounded off the rock, cut off by the dull thud as his body hit the walls of the ravine below.

Arrio lay on his belly, fingers clutching at the rocky edge of the path, panting. When all was silent once more, he struggled to his knees, his body shaking, the realization of what he had done burning into him.

I killed him.

Hot bile rose in his throat, and he bent over, his guts heaving as he emptied them over the edge, spasms racking his body. *I am no better than Lomar.* Arrio bowed his head, shivers coursing through him as he begged forgiveness of the Maker.

He had no idea how long he knelt there, his mind attempting to process it all. When he heard footsteps approaching, Arrio froze, but his fears melted when a beloved voice called his name.

"Dainon!" He raised his head to see his lover with Deron and two warriors.

Dainon hurried to his side and sank to his knees on the hard rock, his arms encircling Arrio and tightening around him. Arrio clung to him, breathing in Dainon's familiar scent, taking comfort from those strong arms about him. Deron and the warriors remained a short distance from them.

"I have you, *terushan*," Dainon whispered. "Thank the Maker you are safe." He kissed Arrio's head, his hands gentle on his arms and back. "Where is Lomar?"

Arrio looked toward the ravine, his chest tight.

Dainon lifted Arrio's chin. "He fell?"

"With some help." Arrio swallowed. He buried his face in Dainon's broad chest. "I killed him," he whispered.

Seconds passed. Dainon did not move, his breathing slow and even. Finally he lifted Arrio's chin once more. "Would Lomar have let you live? Be truthful with me. Look within yourself and answer that with your senses." Those warm brown eyes locked onto his.

Arrio held himself still, his focus inward. "No," he said at last. "He meant to kill both of us, I am certain of it."

"Then you did what you had to do to save Kei and yourself," Dainon told him quietly. "I know how it feels, Arrio. It is not something easily forgotten, and I pray you never have to take another life, but there was no other way." Slowly he kissed Arrio on the lips, a gentle pressure, nothing more. Then he pulled back. "And at the foot of this path, our prince awaits us, desperate to know if you live."

Arrio straightened. "He is safe?"

Dainon helped him to his feet, rising also. "Sorran is with him."

"My *papa-turo* is here?" Arrio's heart swelled with love for his father.

Dainon laughed. "Not even Tanish and Feyar could dissuade him." He peered at their feet. "Now, we shall have to be careful. There is little room for maneuver. Follow Deron and the others, and I shall be behind you."

Impulsively Arrio wrapped his arms around Dainon and held him close. "It is over." His legs felt shaky, but his heartbeat had returned to its normal pattern. *Will I ever forget this day?* He would banish the fear and dread from his mind, but perhaps some things needed to be remembered.

"How do you feel?"

Kei smiled at his brother. "Not as dizzy as I was. At least I can sit up now without falling over." He did not share the fact that the dizziness had not left him. *He will only fuss over me.* Kei did not want fussing. He wanted his lovers.

He nibbled at the fruit one of the warriors had placed in his lap. "This tastes so good." The sharp tang burst upon his tongue, and juice flooded his mouth. *Did food* ever *taste this good?* A few bites was all he could manage before he felt nauseous, but it was better than nothing.

"When we return to the palace, I will send for the physician and you will be spending time in bed." Kei groaned, but Sorran stared at him. "Three days with no water? Have you any idea what that will do to your body?" He shook his head. "I am amazed that you are not in a worse condition."

Kei thought of the precious drops of water that had dripped from the roof of the mine. "I was fortunate."

"In more ways than one," Sorran informed him. "You had an ally out here who alerted us to your presence."

Kei gaped. "The bear? Then I did not dream it? She was really here?" There had been moments during those dark, confusing hours when he had been less than certain. "I tried to connect with her, but...."

"Evidently it worked." Sorran glanced up, his gaze going to the path Dainon had taken.

Kei knew the reason for his glance when he heard voices, and his heart beat faster. "They return." His heartbeat raced when he caught sight of Deron and the warriors, and behind them, Dainon's arm around his waist, was Arrio. When they saw him, their faces lit up and they hastened forward.

Kei wanted to weep for joy. *Both of them, alive.* Seconds later he was in their arms, and everything became a blur of kisses, embraces, tears, and murmured declarations. He cared not for the opinion of the warriors. All that mattered to him were the two men on their knees beside him, whose lips met his in one kiss after another.

When they grew calmer, Sorran cleared his throat. "That was truly beautiful to behold." His eyes glistened and he wiped at them. "And now I would hold my son."

Kei watched his lover and his brother embrace. When Arrio murmured, "I love you, *Papa-turo*," tears pricked Kei's eyelids once more and his heart overflowed with thankfulness.

My family is whole again.

Sorran released Arrio and addressed Dainon. "I would suggest returning to Teruna as quickly as possible, but I feel some rest is required. We have pushed the horses hard, not to mention ourselves." He rubbed his eyes. "I need to sleep."

Dainon nodded. "The river where we camped is not far. We could spend the night there. There will be water and food—once someone catches some fish."

Kei giggled and nuzzled Dainon's neck. "I notice you do not say you will be the one who will be fishing." Arrio snorted, and Kei glanced around him and shivered. "Yes, let us get away from here."

"Arrio can ride with me," Sorran informed them.

Dainon tightened his arms around Kei. "And you shall ride with me," he said softly.

Kei said nothing, but nodded against Dainon's chest. He could not think of a more perfect way to travel.

"THE STARS are so beautiful." Kei's voice was full of wonder. His head lay on Dainon's arm as he gazed up into the night sky. "And so many of them, like dust, strewn across the heavens."

Arrio was not looking. He lay at Dainon's other side, his ear pressed to Dainon's chest. "I will never tire of this sound," he murmured, trailing his fingers over Dainon's chest hair. He chuckled, and Dainon felt it reverberate through him. "Deron was funny."

Dainon tried not to laugh. The captain of the royal guard was several feet away, but Dainon did not want to take the chance of being overheard. "At least he caught a fish, which was better than I managed to do."

"Yes, but think how wet he got in the process," Kei added. "Erinor was amazing."

Dainon had to agree. Timur's husband proved to be a handy fisherman, and there had been plenty to eat, cooked over the fire. Dainon had been concerned by Kei's lack of appetite, but he said nothing. Kei had been through enough, and doubtless his appetite would improve when he was rested and hydrated. Both Dainon and Sorran had made it their task to ensure Kei kept drinking all afternoon and evening—not huge volumes of liquid, but a constant flow of water in small amounts. Kei was no longer disorientated, but he was obviously weak.

Arrio had been quiet since they had returned to the river. Dainon knew from experience that Lomar's death would be preying on his mind, but there was little he could do. Time would do more healing than words could.

"Why are we the only ones with blankets?" Kei asked.

Dainon laughed. "Because the only blankets they had were the ones from Lomar's carriage, and because they all claim to be big, tough warriors who do not need covers and are more than capable of sleeping on hard ground." What he found amusing—and also touching—was how the warriors had given the three of them space. A small fire burned close by, with a larger one at a distance where everyone else slept, including Sorran and Erinor.

Kei sighed. "I am glad my brother is over there."

"Why?" Dainon stroked his arm.

"Because I want you both to touch me, and the last thing I want is for Sorran to be within sight and sound of us."

Arrio chuckled. "There will be no touching, at least not the kind that will lead to… anything. You need your rest."

Kei's soft whine of disappointment brought a smile to Dainon's lips. He shifted under their blanket until Kei lay in the middle. "But we *will* hold you all night long. And when the palace physician declares that you are fit, then there will be as much touching as any of us desire."

"You promise?" Kei's voice had taken on a husky tone.

"We promise," Arrio whispered, edging closer to Kei and putting his arm across Kei's chest.

Dainon's arm lay across his waist. He lay there listening to the crackle of the fire, the low hum of chatter from the warriors, and his lovers' breathing growing more regular.

Thank the Maker they are both safe.

Lomar was gone, Arrio and Kei were alive, and once Dainon had them safely back in Teruna, *then* he would relax, but not until then.

The future loomed before him, its paths hidden from sight, but for the moment, Dainon could afford to put it from his mind and concentrate on what mattered: having his men back where they belonged, in his arms.

CHAPTER
TWENTY-EIGHT

KEI SCRAPED his fingers through his short hair and groaned. "It does not matter how we look at this, it will not work." He rolled his eyes heavenward. "And now Sorran informs me my parents will be here in two days' time. Two days!"

Dainon had to admit Kei made a good point. It had begun as a simple conversation about the wedding, but had quickly evolved into a major issue once reality had sunk in. "Let us be calm about this," he urged. "There must be a way." He glanced at Arrio, standing on the balcony, who had appeared distracted for much of the conversation. "Have you any ideas?"

Arrio brought back his attention from the city below and sighed. "I keep coming back to the same points, again and again. Kei will rule in Vancor. I will rule in Teruna. Two kingdoms, two days apart. Whichever way we view it, this marriage is bound for failure." He gazed at Dainon. "And then there is you. What will *you* do—travel back and forth between the two lands, spending time with one husband, then the other?" Arrio scowled. "This is not the recipe for a happy union."

"I cannot believe we were so blind as to not see this coming," Kei grumbled.

Dainon gave a half smile. That part was easy to understand. "Love blinds us to many things." They had spent weeks in a bubble of joy, pierced only by Lomar's arrival. But the imminent arrival of Kei's parents had forced them to face reality, and it had affected everything, including their nights. In the two days since their return to the palace, there had been an uneasy feeling in the pit of Dainon's stomach. All was not as it should be between them, and he was determined to root out the cause.

I cannot lose them. Not after all we have endured.

Arrio straightened abruptly. "I need to speak with my fathers," he announced, and without another word, he exited their chamber.

Kei stared after him, mouth twisted unhappily.

Dainon rose from his chair and came to stand behind him. He bent down and kissed his head. "Let us pray they are able to help him." Dainon had tried to engage Arrio in conversation, to discover what lay at the root of his depression, but Arrio had not been forthcoming. Dainon had his own ideas, but he was loath to bring up the subject of Lomar once more.

If that is what ails him, I pray his fathers have wisdom enough to reach him.

All he knew was that Arrio was hurting, and watching him brought Dainon pain too.

ARRIO SAT at the table in his *papa*'s private audience chamber and shared all their concerns about the wedding. Across from him, his *papa* listened, nodding now and again. When Arrio had finished, he sagged into his chair. "I do not see a way forward."

To his surprise, Tanish smiled. "My son, I would be a poor ruler indeed if I had not already foreseen this issue."

Arrio stared at him. "Truly?"

Tanish nodded. "And while I appreciate this is a cause for concern for the three of you, I would ask you to be patient. Plans are being drawn up as we speak." He smiled once more. "Did you think the king and queen of Vancor would travel here simply to check on their son?"

"You... invited them?"

"Of course. This is something that requires discussion and cooperation. If all goes well, then we can proceed with the wedding plans." He spoke so calmly and with such confidence that Arrio's fears quelled. Tanish tilted his head and regarded him steadily. "And now perhaps we can talk about what really troubles your mind."

Arrio swallowed and straightened in his seat. "There is nothing that troubles me."

The king got up from his chair, came around the table to sit next to Arrio, and took Arrio's hand in his. "Open your heart to me, son. I do not have your gifts, but I can feel your pain."

Arrio looked into his father's eyes and his breathing hitched. "*Papa*, I… I killed a man." His chest tightened. "And it matters not what anyone says to me. I cannot put it from my mind."

His father nodded slowly. "You regret killing him?"

Arrio gave a slow bob of his head.

"Regret is good, my son. If you did not feel thus, I would be concerned. No man should take the life of another and step away from the act as though it is nothing." Tanish placed his hand on Arrio's shoulder. "One day you will be king, and as such, you will need to rule wisely. Remember how you feel this day. There may come a time when such feelings prove useful. I know that does not alleviate the burden you carry now, but time *will* heal the ache in your heart."

"That is what Dainon said," Arrio murmured.

Tanish nodded. "And as a warrior, he understands what you are going through better than I ever could. Listen to your fine warrior, and trust him." He withdrew his hands.

Arrio knew his father spoke wisely, and it pleased him that Dainon was held in such high regard. "Thank you, *Papa*."

"One more thing. The physician reports that Kei is well and recovered from his ordeal. This is good news. May I suggest that you spend the time before his parents' arrival with your future husbands? Because if what your fathers, the council, and I have in mind comes to pass, there will be a wedding, and soon. We see no reason to delay it."

"Then there are things to be discussed," Arrio said, rising to his feet. "With your permission, I shall take my leave of you."

His father bowed his head. When Arrio reached the door, Tanish stopped him. "Arrio, your fathers and I love you very much, and we are very, very proud of you."

It was Arrio's turn to bow his head. "I pray I may never do anything to change that love." He left the chamber and walked slowly along the corridor to the door that led to the garden.

I need some quiet time to think.

DAINON WAITED until they were in bed, making sure Arrio lay between him and Kei. The air was softly perfumed and the far-off cries of night birds pierced the silence. Kei lay on his side, his head on Arrio's chest.

When he lifted his chin in a silent demand for a kiss, Arrio did not hesitate but pressed his lips to Kei's. Satisfied, Kei resumed his position.

Dainon could not wait any longer. "You need to talk to us, Arrio," he said in a low voice, his hand on Arrio's belly, rubbing in a slow circle.

Arrio's breathing caught, but Dainon kept up the slow rubbing until the tension bled from his body. "You already know what troubles me," he said with a sigh. "The fact that I took Lomar's life. I keep asking myself if there was anything else I could have done. And even though I tell myself there was not, it does not help when I look at my reflection in the mirror and a murderer stares back at me." He swallowed hard.

Kei stared at him. "You forget. I saw Lomar's thoughts. I may not be able to read yours, but you are no murderer, Arrio." He stroked his hand across Arrio's chest and brought it to rest over his heart. "Here beats the heart of a good man."

Arrio sighed. "By all accounts my father was a good man. How, then, could he have worked with Lomar all those years?"

Kei's voice was as gentle as his hand. "Perhaps Lomar was not always the man we saw. We know greed ruled his life at the end, blinding him to all else. Who knows what happened to him in the years since your father's death? Or indeed, how he dealt with the fact that he'd left your father to die? His soul might have been in torment, for all we know." Kei shivered. "But that does not alter the fact that I saw his true intent. You had no choice, *terushan*."

Before Arrio could speak, Dainon rolled on top of him, propped himself up on his elbows, and gazed into Arrio's troubled blue eyes. "There is something else you need to consider." He took a deep breath— even the thought caused him pain. "If you had not killed Lomar, tonight Kei and I would be lying in this bed, grieving for you. We would be contemplating a life without you, though I do not think it would have been a long one. The thought of living without you would have been more than I could have borne."

"Do not say that," Arrio gasped, reaching up to cup Dainon's cheek.

"Why not? It is the truth." Dainon locked gazes with him. "I never thought I would love again. I never believed I could love anyone as much as I loved my Tarisa, and yet here you both are, and here I lie, so in love, I would not have thought it possible." He bent low and kissed him on the lips. "You have given me so much. You make me dream that one day I may hold in my arms our child."

Arrio's eyes widened. "You... you would like us to have children?"

Dainon nodded, unable to break eye contact. "I do not know how such a thing could come to pass, but yes, I want to be a father again, to have the joy that was taken from me, to share that joy with you two." Another kiss. "But I would not have that dream if you had not acted to save Kei. And do not think I have not realized how selflessly you acted. You went against Lomar, knowing you might have been killed in the attempt, but still you acted to save Kei."

Arrio's face flushed. "I love you both. I could not let Lomar destroy that love." He shook his head. "But children? Perhaps... we might adopt." Then he bit his lip. "Because I do not think even Kei's powers are capable of rendering him able to bear a child."

Beside him, Kei stiffened slightly, and Dainon leaned over to kiss him, loving how he melted into the tender embrace. He gazed at them, his heart swelling. "I love you both." On impulse, he reached for the flask of oil that was always beside their bed. With slick fingers, he eased into Arrio's tightness, his own breathing speeding up when Arrio nodded, eyes locked on him. "Kei, kiss our prince. Let him know how much we love him."

With a sigh Kei covered Arrio's lips with his own, and both of them moaned softly.

Dainon lifted Arrio's legs until his ankles rested upon Dainon's shoulders, and then slowly he pushed into him. Arrio did not remain passive for long. His arms slipped around Kei while they kissed, and he wrapped his legs around Dainon's waist, pulling him deeper into his body, moving with him, pushing up with his hips to meet Dainon's slow, measured thrusts.

Dainon was in no hurry. He stroked his cock in and out of Arrio's hole, murmuring how much he loved them, how much he loved making love with them. He listened to the sounds pouring from both Arrio and Kei's lips as they neared orgasm, watching how Kei wrapped his hands around both their shafts, bringing them closer, edging toward their mutual climax.

When they released together, not with loud cries but with whispered words of love, Dainon felt as though his heart would burst.

DAINON WAS stunned into silence by the magnitude of the proposals. What amazed him more was that all those gathered in the audience chamber were in complete agreement. The ministers, Kei's parents, Arrio's fathers—no one had voiced any concerns. Indeed, the faces of all those around the table were alight with smiles.

"So we are all agreed?" King Tanish asked. Nods and murmurs of assent greeted his words. He turned to his chief minister. "Please, read out to us the proposal in its entirety."

She bowed her head. "Yes, Your Majesty. 'King Tanish and King Beron hereby agree that after the marriage of Prince Kei to Prince Arrio and Lord Dainon, all three will live in Vancor, until such time as Prince Kei becomes ruler. Prince Arrio will remain heir to the throne of Teruna, and Lord Dainon shall continue in his post as the Kandoran Ambassador to Teruna. Upon their marriage, both kingdoms will employ their finest architects to design and build a city, with construction to begin immediately. It shall be built on the border between the two lands, equidistant from both capital cities. Upon the death or abdication of King Tanish, Prince Arrio shall become ruler of Teruna and both kings shall reign over both kingdoms from the new city. Regents are to be appointed in each kingdom to see to the day-to-day needs of their people. It is hoped that this will deepen the alliance between the two kingdoms, and that both shall flourish.'" She lowered the parchment. "If Your Majesties are content to sign?"

King Tanish smiled and picked up his pen. "With pleasure." He signed it, and the document was passed to King Beron, who sat facing him. When the task was completed, King Tanish sat back with a satisfied sigh. "It shall be announced to the people by proclamation in a few days' time." He glanced at his royal visitors and smiled. "Perhaps there will be other news to be relayed at the same time?"

"Perhaps," King Beron murmured, with a glance to his wife. "But there are protocols to be followed before such an announcement can be made." His gaze met Dainon's. "Are there not, Lord Dainon?" He smiled.

Arrio coughed, and Dainon resisted the urge to glare at him. Then Arrio leaned closer. "That was your cue," he whispered, not hiding his grin.

Sorran was doing his best not to smirk.

Dainon was not worried. He knew the proposals would not have been agreed upon had King Beron not wished for the marriage to take place. What was required of Dainon was a formal request, and he had expected nothing less.

"If the council members could withdraw, there are matters to be discussed with King Beron and Queen Vasha," King Tanish requested respectfully. "Thank you for your views and invaluable help in this."

The robed ministers got to their feet, and after bowing to the king and his visitors, they left the chamber.

Dainon cleared his throat. "Your Majesties, I formally ask for the hand of Prince Kei in marriage." Arrio's hand slipped into his, and he amended his request. "That is to say, *we* ask for his hand."

King Beron opened his mouth to speak, but his wife got there first.

"I know we have spoken with both of you during our visit here," she began, her cheeks a delicate shade of pink. "And while we are pleased with Kei's choice of husbands, we feel we must make certain… facts clear to you."

Judging by King Beron's expression, he was neither comfortable nor happy with his wife's impending statement. Sorran regarded his parents with a similar expression. King Tanish and Feyar became still.

Dainon's heartbeat picked up a little speed. *What can she mean to say?*

Next to Dainon, Kei shifted on his chair.

Dainon reached across and laid his hand over Kei's on his thigh. "What causes you concern?" Dainon asked, his tone polite.

The queen regarded Kei with adoration. "Kei has known so little of the world, prior to this visit. And after learning what befell him recently, we feel he is ill-prepared for the day he will take on the role of king. After all, he is barely twenty, still a child in many respects."

Dainon stared at her, aware that this was impolite, but he could not believe what he heard, nor the condescending tone in which it was delivered.

Kei's hand clenched into a fist.

The queen was not finished. "We are pleased with your age and experience, Lord Dainon, and it is our hope that when he becomes king, you will guide Kei and advise him. He needs a mature husband who will shield him, protect him, and encourage him to make mature decisions."

Kei bowed his head, and Dainon's heart went out to him. Arrio's face fell, and he stared at Kei's parents in frank dismay.

King Beron coughed. "I am delighted to welcome you and Prince Arrio into our family, Lord Dainon, as Kei's husbands and our sons-in-law." His gaze flickered briefly in his wife's direction. "I see no reason to delay this wedding, and King Tanish assures me that it can take place within a week. Therefore we will remain here in Teruna until that time." He rose and bowed to King Tanish. "With Your Majesty's permission, the queen and I shall withdraw from this meeting. We thank you for your considerable efforts to find a solution, and commend you on what has been agreed this day."

Beside him, the queen stood, and with her hand on his arm, King Beron led her from the chamber.

As soon as the door closed, King Tanish glanced at his husbands, his expression disquieted. Before he could speak, Kei got up.

"If you will all excuse me, I will take my leave." Stiffly, and without waiting for Dainon and Arrio, he strode from the chamber.

Dainon stared after him, his stomach churning. When he turned to regard the others, he was met with several unhappy faces.

"This should be a time for rejoicing," Sorran murmured, his gaze fixed on the door.

Feyar put his arm around Sorran's shoulders. "I know, *dorishan*. Your mother has… changed since we first met her." He gazed unhappily at King Tanish. "I had to bite my tongue and remember this was my mother-in-law who spoke."

"Your father was doing the same, I think," King Tanish said to Sorran.

"*I* think we need to tend to our prince," Arrio said quietly.

Dainon nodded in agreement. He did not need Arrio's powers to know their lover was hurting.

"Go to him," Sorran urged. "And join us this evening for a celebration. It shall be the six of us, perhaps with the addition of Timur and Erinor." His smile was kind. "We will share our joy at your impending marriage."

Dainon bowed to them. "Until then." He and Arrio left the chamber, Dainon's heartbeat racing.

Where are you, Kei?

TWENTY-NINE

KEI STOOD on the balcony, his hands clenched so tightly, his nails dug into his palms. He yearned to hurl his rage at the sky, to storm into his parents' chamber and vent his anger, but he knew he would do none of those things. A royal prince did not behave in such a manner.

And yet a queen may shame her son before others, and none sought to contradict her.

When he heard footsteps from the corridor, he stiffened. He did not trust himself to speak calmly. *But if I had wanted to avoid a confrontation, I would have chosen some other place as my sanctuary, rather than our bedchamber.* Kei was not prepared to hide his feelings. He pulled himself upright and turned to face his lovers.

The door closed, and Dainon was the first to reach him. "Thank the Maker you chose to remain in the palace. I had feared you might have taken a horse and left us to take a ride."

Arrio appeared at Dainon's side. "We understand why you fled. My fathers were unhappy also at your mother's words."

Kei arched his eyebrows. "A pity, then, that they did not think to rebuke her." He stared at them. "And you. You did not think to say something?" His stomach roiled. "You stood there, both of you, and let her speak of me in such a way?"

Dainon's face fell and his lips parted, but no words came forth.

Arrio recovered more quickly. "And what would you have had him say, exactly? Would you rather that he spoke his mind to a *queen*, who is to be his mother-in-law? Even my fathers knew better than to insult a guest—a royal guest at that. And if you had stayed, you would have heard what they truly thought."

Kei closed his eyes briefly, drawing in deep breaths to steady himself. When he opened his eyes, he regarded them both. "Am I a man?"

Dainon's eyebrows lifted high, and Arrio's mouth fell open.

Kei unclenched his fists. "I shall repeat my question. Am I a man?"

"Of course you are a man," Dainon said at last. "No one has suggested otherwise."

Kei snorted. "You were present in that chamber. You heard the way my mother referred to me. Clearly I am not a man to her, but some little boy who needs protecting—a boy who has not the wisdom to be king, but instead requires guidance to make simple decisions."

"Your mother was wrong," Dainon said softly. "You are one of the strongest men I know."

"Dainon thinks as I do," Arrio added.

Kei glared at him. "Really. And yet when you jest about one of us becoming pregnant, I was the first name on your lips. Why me, Arrio? Why not yourself?" He tilted his head. "Is it perhaps because I am smaller in stature than you two? Less of a man?" His heart pounded.

Dainon approached him slowly. "*Corishan*, what is at the heart of this? You know how we think of you. You are our equal, in every way."

Arrio nodded in agreement, his eyes unhappy.

Kei swallowed. "And yet...." He paused, seeking the way forward. He gestured toward their bed with a flick of his hand. "When we are together, I notice the differences."

Arrio was at his side in an instant. "What do you mean?"

Dainon put his arm around Kei's back. "Please, share with us. Have we three not promised to have nothing but truth between us?"

Kei gazed up at him. "Do not misunderstand me. I love it when you lift me in your arms and carry me to the bed. I love how it feels, as though you hold something precious and fragile."

Dainon remained silent, his gaze fixed on Kei.

"But I am *not* fragile. I will not break." Kei stuck out his chin.

Arrio seemed bewildered. "Have we ever suggested that?"

"In words, no, but...." Kei regarded their bed. "With each other, you are rough. You let go of yourselves, you are passionate, urgent, relentless—yet with me? You are tender, gentle...." He clenched his fists.

Dainon let out a long, drawn-out sigh. "There are times when you do not wish us to be gentle."

Kei wanted to sigh with relief. "Yes."

"Why did you not say something?" Arrio asked.

"But I did!" Kei ran his fingers through his hair. "What, exactly, do you hear when I yell 'harder' and 'fuck me'?" He bit his lip, ashamed of his outburst.

They stared at him, and then both burst out laughing.

Dainon grabbed him, lifting him into his arms. "I love you, my feisty prince."

Kei wrapped his legs around Dainon's waist and locked his hands behind Dainon's neck. When the kiss came, it was not tender but harsh, a clash of teeth and tongues, and its effect was instantaneous. Heat surged through Kei's body and his shaft began to fill against Dainon's belly.

Dainon's eyes flashed. "I feel you," he whispered. He lowered Kei and pulled at his robe, baring Kei's body to his sight. "Arrio," he called out. "Naked. Now." Kei's robe became a crumpled pile of fabric at his feet.

Kei shivered at the hoarse quality to his voice. He watched as Dainon hastily removed his own robe, licking his lips at the sight of Dainon's broad, furred chest, his nipples standing proud, his abs that begged to have Kei's tongue trace every contour and line, and his thick, heavy cock. Kei's own shaft rose up and his hole tightened at the thought of what was about to pass.

The feel of bare flesh suddenly pressed to his back gave Kei a start. Arrio kissed his shoulder, then bit gently into it. Kei shuddered as Arrio rocked against him, feeling the heat and hardness of him sliding between Kei's buttocks. A soft gasp escaped his lips when Arrio reached around to grasp his length and tug it.

"He wants us, Dainon," Arrio murmured before kissing down Kei's neck and sending shivers coursing through him while Arrio continued with that slow rocking.

Dainon grabbed Kei's head and looked him in the eyes. "No gentle lovemaking tonight, *corishan*. Tonight we shall take you, again and again." He grinned. "Put your arms around my neck."

Kei did as instructed, and his heartbeat sped up when Dainon lifted him into the air, hooking Kei's legs over his arms until he was almost bent in two. Dainon held him securely, his gaze focused on Kei's face.

"Arrio, you have the oil?"

Arrio chuckled. "My fingers are already slick with it."

Then Kei moaned when Arrio penetrated him, pushing two into his body, filling him, stretching him. Kei leaned against Arrio, his head on Arrio's shoulder while Arrio fucked him, fingers gliding into him, gaining momentum. "Yes, yes," he breathed, bucking on Arrio's fingers, gasping when two became three and his channel was stretched even further.

"Enough," Dainon ordered. "Grab his legs behind the knees."

Kei sighed when Arrio pulled free of him, leaving his hole loosened and aching. Arrio moved closer, pinning Kei between the two of them, Arrio's hands under his knees. Dainon let go with one hand and guided his cock into position, Kei reaching down to help him, his body burning with need. Dainon slowly thrust up into him, and Kei groaned at the sensation.

"You said you wanted me to fuck you like this," Dainon purred. He and Arrio moved in harmony, allowing Kei to bounce on Dainon's shaft while he clung to Dainon, who rocked into him. Arrio shifted to support Kei's buttocks in his hands, Dainon leaning forward to claim Kei's mouth in a heated kiss.

Kei groaned into the kiss, lost in the feeling of two hot, firm bodies surrounding him, caging him, while Dainon's thick cock plunged in deep as he buried himself in Kei's body. His own shaft rubbed against Dainon's belly, the friction driving him wild, sending white-hot surges of desire shooting up his spine.

"Too much," Kei moaned. "I shall spend if you continue thus." He wanted it to last. He yearned for the image Dainon's words had painted in his mind—the pair of them taking him all night long.

"Oh no, my fine prince. We cannot have that." Dainon grabbed hold of his buttocks, his cock freeing itself. "Arrio, clear the table." Arrio moved away from Kei's back, followed by the sound of parchment softly hitting the stone-flagged floor.

Kei had no time to ponder on Dainon's instruction as he was carried swiftly to the table, where Dainon released him and let him stand once more, turning him roughly to face away from him.

"Bend over the table," Dainon commanded him, "and spread your legs wide. Grab the far edge of it and hold on."

Kei acted swiftly, the wooden table top smooth and cool against his chest. He spread his legs, the air cool against his slick hole. His fingers gripped the edge. Dainon moved to stand behind him, his slippery shaft sliding between Kei's cheeks. Kei tensed, waiting for the glorious sensation, that wonderful moment when Dainon entered him.

Dainon stilled, and Kei wanted to groan aloud in frustration. "Arrio, kneel under Kei and take his cock in your mouth."

Kei gasped when Arrio's hot mouth took him deep, and then all the breath was punched from his lungs when Dainon drove hard into his channel, burying his shaft to the hilt. He clung to the table while Dainon fucked him, long, deep strokes where his body slammed into Kei's, pushing him into that waiting mouth.

Kei cried out with sheer joy as his men took him, Dainon hammering into him, Arrio sucking him hard, neither of them the tender, gentle lovers who had taken his virginity, but two men who were enjoying his body every bit as much as he enjoyed their rough fucking. He was buffeted between them, moaning as Arrio pulled his cheeks apart, allowing Dainon to slide in even deeper. "Oh, by the heavens, yes!" His orgasm approached, his body sending out messengers to warn him. Kei closed his eyes and fought it, desperate for more, unwilling to let the ecstasy come to an end.

When Arrio pulled free of his cock, Kei sent up a silent prayer of thanks.

"Dainon, take him to the bed and let him ride your shaft," Arrio said breathlessly.

"You heard him." Dainon's deep voice rang with authority. He slipped free of Kei's body, and Kei shivered at the loss. He allowed himself to be led toward the bed, where Dainon lay back, holding his long, hard cock around its base while he applied more oil. "You like a good ride, do you not, my prince?" Dainon was grinning. "Then ride this."

Kei straddled him, impaling himself in one long glide down that thick shaft until Dainon was as deep inside him as it was possible to be. He leaned forward to kiss his lover, each moaning into the other's mouth while their tongues danced their erotic duet. He sighed into Dainon's parted lips when Arrio pressed up behind him, leaning over to add himself to the kiss.

Arrio's lips brushed Kei's ear. "Remember your lesson with my *papi, terushan?*" he whispered. "Remember his other… suggestion? The one that made us both hot and cold inside simply by thinking about it?"

Kei froze. *He is not going to…. By all that is holy.* "Arrio," he whispered back urgently. Oil trickled down his crease, and Arrio gently but firmly pushed him until Kei's chest met Dainon's. Kei's heart raced, his breathing quickening.

Dainon stared up at Arrio over Kei's shoulder. "What are you…?" His eyes widened when Arrio slid a finger into Kei's channel alongside Dainon's cock. Dainon gasped. "Oh. Oh, how that feels." His hands were on Kei's back, softly stroking up and down.

Kei groaned at the increased pressure, and Arrio became still. His breath tickled Kei's ear. "Do you want me to stop?"

"No." Kei shivered. He held his breath when one finger became two and suddenly everything was tighter. Arrio slid deeper, and he groaned again. "So full." When Feyar had spoken of this, Kei had not believed it possible, yet a part of him had yearned for it to be so.

Dainon stared up at him. "You know what Arrio has in mind?"

Kei nodded, closing his eyes briefly when Arrio slowly moved in and out of him. He tried to relax, but the idea had set him alight, and he squirmed in anticipation.

"Dainon, put your legs together and be still for a moment," Arrio instructed, kneeling behind Kei. He leaned in and kissed down Kei's back, but then Kei felt it, the heat from Arrio's shaft between his cheeks, poised above Dainon's cock, ready….

He shuddered, and Dainon kissed him, Kei feeding his sharp breaths into his mouth.

"Breathe, *corishan*. Let me in," Arrio coaxed. "Take us both, feel us inside you, claiming you."

Kei took a deep breath and let himself go limp in Dainon's arms, just as Arrio pushed his cock into Kei's already stretched hole, easing it in above Dainon's.

Oh, merciful heavens. Kei was full, his entrance stretched tight around their shafts, his own cock twitching, jerking up toward his belly and leaking steadily down its length. *Have I ever been this hard?* His world had narrowed down to one single point, one simple event—two men were inside him, their heat and girth filling him until all he could feel was the gentle push-and-pull as Arrio moved in and out of him, sliding against Dainon's cock. Dainon held him still, his arms around Kei's back.

Kei dropped his head and buried his face in Dainon's neck, unable to repress the shivers that were multiplying, spreading through him in a wave of unexpected pleasure.

"Kei." Dainon's voice was gentle. "Do you want him to stop?"

"No!" Kei let out a soft moan. "I want you both to release inside me. Please, do not stop." His cock rubbed against Dainon's muscles, the friction bringing him closer and closer to his climax. He lifted his head and sought Dainon's mouth. "Kiss me."

Dainon's lips met his, and Kei closed his eyes and let himself go, swept along by the sensations, soaring higher and higher, lost in the feel of their shafts inside him, their bodies surrounding him, the feel of silky skin and soft hair, the sound of their breathing, the moans and cries of pleasure from his lovers—

And he was there, his cock erupting as never before, pulsing out of him as though it would never stop.

Dainon groaned into Kei's kiss, his body stiffening beneath him, his cock swelling inside Kei's stretched channel. "Arrio, now," he urged. "Fill him with your seed." He reached out for both of them, pulling them together, and Kei was pinned between his lovers, his ears filled with their cries of ecstasy as Arrio too released inside him. His heart sang when both of them kissed and caressed him, both told him they loved him, that he was *theirs*, their man, their lover, that he completed them.

"I love you both," Kei cried out, unable to keep the words inside him. "You are my life."

Lightning speared into Kei's consciousness, sending a flood of adrenaline surging through him and taking his breath away. His body felt as though it were on fire, the flames dancing over his skin, an explosion of white light in his head.

"Kei. *Kei!*" Dainon clutched Kei's upper arms, a note of panic in his voice.

He fears I am hurt. He thinks he has done this, they have done this. He—

Kei froze, open-mouthed.

Arrio stilled inside him. *He berates himself for thinking of this. He wishes he had spent more time in preparation, before—*

"By the Maker." Kei closed his eyes, and the tears came spilling down his cheeks. "Thank You. Bless You."

Dainon and Arrio eased out of him, and suddenly he was on his back between them, both of them regarding him with concern, fear radiating from them.

Kei shook his head, joy filling his heart. "I hear you, my *terushani*," he whispered. When they stared at him, their brows furrowed, Kei smiled.

"I hear your thoughts." It had taken this unexpected occurrence to make him realize how much he wanted that deeper, more intimate connection. To hear the thoughts of the two men who loved him was more than he could have hoped for.

Arrio's breathing hitched, and Dainon's face broke into a beautiful smile. Kei pulled them to him in a kiss, the three of them joined, mind and body.

Our souls too. Kei believed that with all his heart.

He lay in their arms as they kissed and caressed one another, the momentary elation of their union giving way to a far more permanent joy.

This is meant to be. Of that, Kei had no doubt.

One week later.

"Look at you." Sorran's voice cracked as he regarded Arrio in his wedding robe—long, flowing blue silk that matched his eyes. "Your *papa* looks well in this color also." He smiled. You are a handsome man, my son." They embraced, their foreheads touching.

Kei cleared his throat. "And how do I look?"

Sorran disengaged himself from Arrio and came over to where Kei stood before the silvered mirror. They stared at Kei's reflection, Sorran's hands on Kei's shoulders. "Ivory works well against your skin. It was the same for me on my wedding day." His face glowed. "My little brother has grown into a beautiful man." Sorran smirked. "But you might have considered removing the beard, today of all days."

"The beard stays," both Dainon and Arrio yelled simultaneously, and Kei laughed.

"You heard them," he said with a shrug. "They like it." He was not about to share *why* they liked it so. *Will I ever become comfortable with the idea of discussing sex with my brother?* He thought about it for a moment. *Perhaps when he reaches eighty and no longer feels the inclination.* Then he reconsidered. *Knowing my brother? Perhaps not even then.*

He glanced at Dainon and did not bother to hold back his sigh of pleasure. Dainon wore a long robe of bronze silk, his amulet bright against it. Kei reached up to touch his own, something he did frequently.

"I did not come here simply to pay compliments to the bridegrooms," Sorran said. "Tanish, Feyar, and I were in discussion with the council, and there is something you must consider."

Kei stilled. "That sounds serious."

Sorran nodded. "Dainon needs to resign his position as ambassador."

Dainon sighed. "I had reached the same conclusion, but I was going to wait until after the wedding."

"Why do you need to resign?" Kei demanded, and Arrio joined him.

Dainon grasped Kei's hands. "Where shall we be living?"

"In Vancor."

Dainon nodded. "How can I be eligible to be the Ambassador to Teruna if I am living in Vancor? And once we take up residence in the new city, the kingdoms will merge." He smiled. "And as consort to both you and Arrio, I shall have my hands full. I do not imagine a royal consort sits around all day doing nothing. What do you say, Sorran?"

Sorran laughed. "I say you have a good grasp of the situation. Have you sent word to King Rohar about your marriage?"

Dainon nodded once more. "By now he will know what happens today. Doubtless he will reach the same conclusion, and I am certain to receive a message from him soon."

"Your life has changed beyond all recognition, has it not?" Sorran observed. "From warrior, to ambassador, to royal consort."

"You missed out an important stage," Dainon informed him. "From a man who never thought he could love another man, to one who is deeply in love with two." He put his arms around Kei and Arrio, pulling them closer. "My men," he said quietly before their mouths fused in a kiss.

Kei loved these kisses. The three of them, made one. When they parted, Kei sighed. "Do you know what brings me great joy?" he asked quietly. "That I can read your thoughts and know you are both as happy this day as I am."

Arrio took Kei's hand and placed it over his own heart. "My heart beats with joy. Can you feel it?"

Kei nodded. "Your heartbeat mirrors mine."

Dainon took his free hand and slipped it inside his robe, covering it with his own. "And mine also." Kei closed his eyes and concentrated on the rhythm of his lovers' hearts, their warmth, their vitality, the feeling of Dainon's firm chest with its thick layer of hair, and smelling Arrio's spicy scent. These simple things brought him great happiness, but greater still were the thoughts that echoed in his head, *their* thoughts no longer hidden from him. He could feel their love, their joy.

When he opened his eyes, Sorran was watching them, his eyes glistening. "I never tire of seeing you share your love. And *my* heart is full of joy that you found one another."

A servant appeared and addressed Sorran. "Queen Vasha asks if she may enter, Your Highness."

Kei stiffened. During the last week, he had spoken little with her, although there had been frequent conversations with his father. They had talked of his coming abdication, the wedding, and the new city. His father had been excited by the prospect, and the two of them had discussed the plans already being drawn up. Kei's chest had swelled with pride when he saw how his father valued his opinion.

His mother was another story. *And this is as good a time as any to speak out.*

Sorran looked to Kei. "Would you like us to leave?"

Kei shook his head. He addressed the servant. "Let her enter, please." He gazed at the others. "I will speak with her, but I need you here."

Dainon and Arrio had not moved from his side. "You have us, *terushan*," Dainon whispered.

Queen Vasha blinked as she entered the chamber. "Oh. I had thought to share some time with Kei before the wedding." She gave a half smile. "I wished to impart some advice for a happy marriage."

Kei regarded her levelly. "If your advice is similar to that which you gave Dainon, then thank you, but I have no need of it." He took Dainon and Arrio's hands and held them aloft. "Everything I need for a happy marriage is here, in my hands. My future husbands believe in me. They trust me as an equal, and we will face all that is to come as equals. They will stand *beside* me, not in front to shield or protect me. They give me strength, just as I give them strength."

She stared at him, her cheeks pinking. "To hear you speak, one would think you have no need of a mother."

Kei released their hands and took a step toward her, his heart racing. "You raised me to be the man I am, Mother. The man they fell in love with." He observed her closely. "When you married my father, you left your parents and made him your life. Today, I do the same." He glanced at Dainon and Arrio with love. "These two men are my life."